Praise for

THE COPERNICUS LEGACY
SERIES

"I had to keep reminding myself *The Copernicus Legacy* was intended for a young audience. Full of mystery and intrigue, this book had me completely transfixed."

—Ridley Pearson, *New York Times* bestselling author of the Kingdom Keepers series

"*The Copernicus Legacy* takes you on a fantastical journey that is as eye-opening as it is page-turning. With mysteries hiding behind secrets coded in riddle, this book is like a Dan Brown thriller for young readers. The further you get, the more you must read!"

—Angie Sage, *New York Times* bestselling author of the Septimus Heap series

"*The Copernicus Legacy* has it all: a secret code, priceless relics, murderous knights, a five-hundred-year-old mystery, and a story full of friendship, family, humor, and intelligence."

—Wendy Mass, *New York Times* bestselling author of *The Candymakers* and *Every Soul a Star*

"With engaging characters, a globe-trotting plot, and dangerous villains, it is hard to find something not to like. Equal parts edge-of-your-seat suspense and heartfelt coming-of-age."

—*Kirkus Reviews* (starred review)

"Fast-paced and clever, the novel reads like a mash-up of the National Treasure films and *The Da Vinci Code*."

—*Publishers Weekly*

TONY ABBOTT

★BOOK 3★

THE GOLDEN VENDETTA

ILLUSTRATIONS BY BILL PERKINS

KATHERINE TEGEN BOOKS
An Imprint of HarperCollins Publishers

Katherine Tegen Books is an imprint of HarperCollins Publishers.

The Copernicus Legacy: The Golden Vendetta
Text copyright © 2015 by HarperCollins Publishers
Illustrations copyright © 2015 by Bill Perkins
All rights reserved. Printed in the United States of America.
No part of this book may be used or reproduced in any manner whatsoever
without written permission except in the case of brief quotations embodied
in critical articles and reviews. For information address HarperCollins
Children's Books, a division of HarperCollins Publishers, 195 Broadway,
New York, NY 10007.
www.harpercollinschildrens.com

Library of Congress Control Number: 2015935759
ISBN 978-0-06-219449-7 (trade bdg.) — ISBN 978-0-06-237821-7 (int.)

Typography by Michelle Gengaro-Kokmen
15 16 17 18 19   CG/RRDH   10 9 8 7 6 5 4 3 2 1
❖
First Edition

To those who travel the world with every book they read

★BOOK 3★

THE
GOLDEN
VENDETTA

CHAPTER ONE

London, England
April 2
9:42 a.m.

Wade Kaplan squinted toward the end of the long hallway.

His lungs ached. The air was chilly down there. Almost refrigerated. He counted the cold fluorescent bulbs ranged along the low ceiling. Twelve. They cast a pale white light on the inside walls, on his family—his stepbrother, Darrell; his father, Roald; his stepmother, Sara—and on the tall man in the navy-blue suit who stood facing them.

"Behind me is the steel-reinforced titanium entry

door to the vaults," the navy-blue man said. "Each portal is equipped with multilayer encryption combinations that are refreshed at random. We are, in a word, unbreachable. Follow me, please. Bring your item."

The man, whose name Wade hadn't heard clearly, was head of vault security at the British Museum in London. He spun around neatly on his heels and walked down the corridor.

"This is it," Darrell whispered. "The official end of the London episode."

"I hope so," Wade said. They paused at the end of the hall.

After the man entered a key card, a thumbprint scan, and a voice command—"Five, seven, nine, four, two, eight"—Wade heard a series of electronic bolts releasing, followed by a whoosh as the heavy door opened. They passed through to the other side, where two armed security officers stood guard. Once inside, they heard a similar series of reboltings as the door closed, and they were among the warren of underground vaults.

"The vault level of the British Museum is among the most secure in Britain," the man explained. "In the world, actually. Your box will be safe here."

The box Wade's stepmother now held, an unassuming steel container the size of a large hardcover, housed

Crux, a mechanical cross crafted of amber, inside of which was some manner of mysterious, and heavy, internal mechanism. Crux was one of twelve relics that powered the time machine of Nicolaus Copernicus.

"We're nearly there," Darrell said in his ear. "You can start breathing now."

"Not yet."

"You really should. In, out, in, out. It helps with the whole being-alive thing. I find it useful to begin breathing almost as soon as I wake up in the morning. The day turns out so much better. There have been studies."

"I'll bet there have," said Wade.

"Boys," said Sara. They continued to the end of another blank corridor, which, the navy-suited man told them, "parallels Great Russell Street, running some twenty feet above us." He helpfully pointed up.

It seemed to Wade that he'd been holding his breath for the last week. Or, actually, the last three weeks, for it was in early March that they'd first learned of the twelve mysterious parts of Copernicus's time-traveling astrolabe and gotten swept into the global search for them.

They had battled the deadly agents of the infamous Teutonic Order of Ancient Prussia—and their leader, Galina Krause—and had rather amazingly discovered two of the relics so far. The first was a heavy blue stone called Vela, currently stored at the Morgan Library and Museum in New York. Crux, the second, would be temporarily housed here, in Subvault 17 of the British Museum.

"Too many things aren't right," Wade whispered as they entered the final room through yet another thick steel door. The room was empty except for a metal table and a chair, and a safe, built into the rear wall.

"This here is right," said Darrell.

"Yeah, but not Becca."

Becca Moore was currently recovering at Great Ormond Street Hospital—if, Wade thought, you could ever quite recover from what had happened to her. Becca had traveled through time.

Sort of.

The previous week Becca had had episodes, like visions, that shot her back in time—in her mind, if not her body—to the sixteenth century. It was her weird coiling paths back and forth in time that had allowed them to find Crux and thwart their dark pursuer, Markus Wolff, Galina's assassin. But it had cost her. Not only had Becca learned a terrible truth—that traveling in time opened the door to horrible catastrophes— but through the whole adventure she had suffered blinding headaches and nosebleeds. She was finally too exhausted to see Crux to its new home.

"Yeah, and not Lily, either," Darrell admitted.

Lily Kaplan, Wade's cousin, was supposed to have met her father at Heathrow last week. He was going to bring her home. They had all expected him. Then, at the last minute, he'd canceled his flight. Lily's parents were "going through a rough patch," as Wade's stepmother put it. Very rough, it turned out. And it wasn't a "patch" so much as a plain old ugly divorce. Lily had become depressed and quiet (so unlike her) and was at that moment at Great Ormond Street, keeping Becca company in her hospital room. The past week had been an ordeal for everyone, but especially for the two girls.

The navy-blue man positioned himself in front of an alphanumeric keypad on the wall next to the safe door, where he input a long series of numbers and letters. Then he pressed his thumb to the scanner and entered a metal key.

Wade, Darrell, and their parents had examined Crux extensively but hadn't found any clues to the next relic. Each relic was known to hint at where the next one might be found, but technically they had located Crux out of order.

It was *Serpens*, the relic Galina Krause had stolen

from them in Russia, that would show where the very next relic lay hidden. Even so, they'd taken dozens of photographs and X-rays of the amber cross. They'd study them until Crux, too, gave up its secret.

The safe door opened slowly. "Any last words?" asked the navy-blue man. He beamed a distant but confident smile.

Wade's father glanced at them all, then shook his head. "It will be good knowing it's housed here."

Sara placed the box into the safe. The man carefully turned the key, which had remained in the lock. The safe door clicked closed. Another few seconds of inputting into the keypad, rescanning his thumb, and removing the key, and the relic was secure. Wade breathed. In. Out.

"Well, then. There you are," said the navy-blue man. "There is twenty-four-hour camera surveillance, and there are temperature scanners on every inch of the vault level, including each room." He pointed vaguely to several lenses and grilles recessed into the ceiling. "Thirty guards patrol the vault system at all times. You are fortunate to have the influence of the Ackroyd Foundation, a major benefactor of the museum."

Terence Ackroyd and his son, Julian, had become their close friends and essential team members in the relic hunt. After the Kaplans and the Moores boarded their flight back to the States that evening, they would enter a kind of private witness-protection program designed to keep the Order from finding them.

They would, Terence told them, effectively vanish from sight. Until, that is, they had to begin searching for the next relic. As the man in the navy-blue suit led them away from Subvault 17, Wade hoped Crux would be safe there.

But something told him that nothing was really safe.

Not anymore.

CHAPTER TWO

Olsztyn, Poland
April 3
11:43 p.m.

The sky was a black shroud prickled with a smattering of stars, a slow-rising crescent moon, and a clearness that seemed to spread to the far reaches of the universe.

Galina Krause, the dark-haired, nineteen-year-old leader of the Teutonic Order, looked up to the heavens, and the valves in her heart fluttered.

"A hole in the sky," she said.

Ten feet behind her, shivering in his thin coat, the pasty, bent astrophysicist Ebner von Braun raised his face from his phone.

"Yes, Galina? You said?"

"Magister Copernicus uses those words just prior to the astrolabe's first entry into the flow of time. He writes of witnessing *a hole in the sky.*" Pain trembled from her throat to her chest, her arms. "What shall we make of it, Ebner?"

"Five servers at the Copernicus Room in Madrid are specifically dedicated to his riddles, this one in particular. Better now, perhaps, to focus on the business at hand. The plane will appear over the castle in seven minutes."

Despite the streetlights and spotlights surrounding it, Olsztyn Castle rose up, a medieval darkness against the greater dark of the sky. Galina walked up a steep path toward its walls. Construction on the castle had been begun by the Teutonic Knights in 1347. Of greater interest to Galina was that at various times from 1516 to 1521, Nicolaus Copernicus lived and worked inside its walls. This was a matter of historical record. There was, moreover, a fresco of his astronomical research still visible in his rooms along the northeast wall of the castle.

What was not generally known, however, was that precisely during the years of his residence there, the astronomer began dispersing not only the relics of his time-traveling astrolabe, but the machine's larger framework. From these Galina hoped to gather clues about the remaining relics. Her goal: to attach them to Kronos III, the most successful of the Order's own time machines.

According to a cryptic fragment in a recently located letter, one major section of Copernicus's Eternity Machine was buried beneath Olsztyn Castle's walls.

And so, naturally, they required a plane.

Ebner scurried up to her. "It is approaching." He took from his overcoat a box and drew out its long antenna. "Delectable that something so compact can fly a sixteen-hundred-kilogram airplane with a twitch of a lever. The pilot will certainly be surprised when all instrument control is lost. Interestingly, besides being an expendable junior operative of ours, the pilot is—"

"Do not tell me," Galina said.

He swallowed. "No. Of course. No."

Footsteps sounded. She turned. It was Markus Wolff, just arrived from London. He approached the castle like a pilgrim to a shrine, and yet he was not so much a pilgrim as a spy waiting to be debriefed.

"Tell me about Crux," she said. There was never small talk between them.

"A mechanical cross encrusted in amber. The Kaplans located it in a church crypt. It was transferred yesterday to a vault in the British Museum. Herr von Braun claims to have a man on the inside—"

"I do indeed!" said Ebner. "Do not doubt it."

"We shall see," said Galina.

"As it happens," Wolff continued, "in 1517, Copernicus passed Crux to the martyr Thomas More. On his death, the relic went to his daughter and finally to his daughter's friend, or 'sister' as she was called. You will want this back."

From the inside pocket of his leather overcoat, he produced a small golden locket. Taking it from his gloved hand, Galina felt her palm go cold. Inside was a portrait of the sister, Joan Aleyn: mesmerizing, sorrowful.

Galina closed the miniature and pocketed it. "Her crypt . . . ?"

"Was a terminus of time change. The girl, Rebecca Moore, was deeply involved. There is a problem with removing the children just yet. I saw this."

He drew out his phone, swiped the screen.

The image was hazy, taken from a distance at night, showing a church tower, a shattered window, a blur caught in haste. Still, what Galina spied in the glimmer of crisscrossing flashlights and spotlights was unmistakable: a bronze disc inlaid with colored glass in a flower pattern. It hung from the belt of one of the children inside the tower, one whose face was in shadow. She had seen the item before.

"The rose window . . . ?"

"Of Westminster Abbey," Wolff said. "A trinket from their gift shop. It is one of four purchased for the children by your former captive, Sara Kaplan."

"Which of the children is this?" asked Ebner, hovering over the phone.

"It was dark," Wolff said. "One of the boys."

"One of the boys." Galina turned away from both men. The sky was blacker still. "So he or one of the others will lose the trinket in the ruins of Albrecht's castle at Königsberg."

Wolff tilted his head slightly. "Perhaps he—or she—already has. The past is such a curious creature. Has Serpens given up *its* clue?"

A sudden pain spiked in her neck. What began inside her as a tiny ripple in the middle of a vast ocean gained strength second by second and became a wave. She tilted her head, breathed the pain away.

"The legendary curse of the serpent has proved all too true," she said.

As with every relic, this one was said to indicate the location of the next one, so when Serpens had pointed south, Galina had traveled south to Damascus. Once there, however, the relic had pointed west. She'd flown west to Tripoli. There it had pointed north to Eastern Europe. Then east. Then south again, circling the Mediterranean in a teasing, spiteful round.

"Serpens is unwilling to give up its secret. That is why we are forced to rely on secondary methods to find the relics," she said. "Best keep the Kaplans alive for now. In the meantime, we will continue our search for the astrolabe's fragments. Also, we must obtain the Voytsdorf Ledger."

"Which is?" asked Wolff.

"A coded document said to enumerate the various parts of the astronomer's original astrolabe. This will provide hints to the location of the remainder of the relics. Ebner, send the bookseller to find it—"

"The plane!" said Ebner.

A pair of blinking lights moved slowly toward them out of the northern sky. Ebner gently touched the control levers on the remote, and she saw the plane's wing lights wobble. Another touch, and the plane dipped. Ebner gave a final flick to the altitude lever, and the little plane dived. It slammed into the castle's northeastern face. Galina stepped back. The blaze was horrifyingly sudden.

"One astonished pilot," Ebner said, shielding his face from the fire. Minutes later several emergency vehicles accelerated up the road: EMS, fire, police, and others that could only be described as excavation equipment.

"If we are correct, the armature of the Eternity Machine lies buried beneath the crash site," Ebner whispered. "This accident will screen our search for it. We'll soon see if our intelligence is valid. Move in," he barked into his phone. "Remove the pilot's body. Find the astrolabe's frame!"

Galina shivered in the heat, stepped toward the blaze, then felt the trembling in her legs and knew. The air seemed suddenly airless. Clutching the miniature in her palm, she let it cut into her skin to stave off the wave of unconsciousness.

Ebner rushed to her. She barely felt his presence. In the midst of wailing sirens and grinding engines, the flames swept up the castle wall and into her mind. She saw them burning away the earth beneath the castle wall. And there it was, intact five centuries later: a vast ring, ten feet in diameter and crafted of iron, steel, bronze, and heavy gold.

"Ebner," she said, her voice already distant, "discover

the other pieces. Send the bookseller to Paris. The Voytsdorf Ledger . . ." Before she could finish, she spun away and away into the dark, fluttering like an empty shroud.

As the flames began to recede under the assault of the fire hoses, and the excavators advanced, Ebner held her, held her close. He fixed on her eyes—one silver iris, one diamond blue—and saw them glint and flash at him before her eyelids closed and she sank away.

"Medic!" he cried out. "Medic!"

CHAPTER THREE

He was known as "the bookseller."

Of compact stature, Oskar Gerrenhausen was a gray-whiskered cat of a man, somewhere between sixty and seventy-five, who had been forced by threats to do an evil young woman's unscrupulous acquisition work.

Forced? *Yes*, he mused. But his long history in antiquities, as well as a stint in the anticommunist Czech underground in the eighties, had given him a deep love of pursuing the forbidden, uncovering the unknown, possessing, even for a short time, objects of inestimable value.

Having left the busier boulevards of the Left Bank to the evening tourist crush, Gerrenhausen wove from awning to awning along Rue Jacob. He cowered, shoulders bowed against the warm rain, stepping lightly along the sidewalk until he arrived at Rue Bonaparte. There he turned right, toward the river.

He walked fifteen paces, and stopped.

Librairie Fortier. Gold lettering on its windows read: *Spécialiste des documents, lettres, gravures, et livres de voyages anciens du 15ème et du 16ème siècle.*

Specialist indeed. Henri Fortier had, unknowingly, just taken possession of the so-called Voytsdorf Ledger, a rather boring document about sheep, cattle, acreage, and currency reform penned by Nicolaus Copernicus in 1519. Boring, that is, if you didn't know that the ledger contained a hidden list of the components of a machine that obsessed Galina Krause. His next acquisition was to take place at a private auction in two months' time. June 5.

Gerrenhausen stepped beneath the awning and gently tried the shop door—it was locked. He slid a small bag of tools from the leather messenger bag he wore under his coat, selected one, pried the door lock, and slipped inside the store. No alarm. Was someone still here? He spied a thin stream of light from the back room of the store.

So. Instead of a simple theft, there could be a murder, too. He gripped the gun in the pocket of his coat, slid back the safety. He tiptoed toward the light, peeked in through the door's slender crack, and saw Henri Fortier bowed over a bundle of old papers. Oskar's senses tingled.

But wait. Fortier did not raise his head, and his slow, rhythmic movement suggested he was sleeping. Gerrenhausen smiled. *And under the cover of dreams, what mischief may happen!* He relaxed his grip on his gun and approached the desk nimbly. Reaching in front of Fortier, his fingers and movements as sensitive as delicate seismic instruments, Oskar slid the document out from under the sleeping man's magnifying glass. The top page had a silvery sheen to it; Fortier had apparently become mesmerized by its strange glow. So the auction in June was more important than ever.

Oskar Gerrenhausen rolled the ledger into a tubular container, which he then placed in his messenger bag. He silently left the back room and exited the shop. He relocked the front door, reset the safety on his handgun, repocketed it, and gave it a pat. "Not tonight, my friend. Soon, perhaps, but not tonight."

Smiling to himself, the bookseller disappeared down the sidewalk, huddled against the rain, and made deliberately toward the river.

CHAPTER FOUR

Motel Nowhere, Marble Falls, Texas
June 2
6:48 p.m.

Darrell sat back in the only chair in room 113, looked longingly at his old passport, and sighed. "There should be a death date on these things. I've been dead exactly two months today."

Wade looked up from the bed where he was reading. "You know you're supposed to keep that old passport hidden. Put it away before Dad catches you."

"My old *real* passport, you mean. You realize that, right? Two months have passed since we boarded that jet in London, and I died."

"I do know how to read a calendar. Two months is right. But the 'died' part isn't so much."

Darrell stood. Sunlight bounced up from the cars through the louvered window of their junky motel outside Austin. He had had this same conversation with his stepbrother almost every day for the last eight weeks. Only the dates changed. Yesterday it had been "tomorrow will be exactly two months."

"You didn't die," he said to Wade. "But I did. Two months ago. The same day the relic hunt ended. Just ended. Like it . . . *ended*."

"You kinda like her, don't you?"

Darrell shot a look at Wade, who was grinning. "Who? Lily?"

"No, lover boy. Galina Krause. You can't wait to see her again."

"Galina?" Darrell growled. "I can't wait to *not* see *you* again."

"Too late. I'm right here."

After London, the whole bunch of them had gone into Terence Ackroyd's private witness-protection thing. Because Lily's parents' divorce had become so angry and messy, Lily had asked to stay with Becca and *her* parents "somewhere" (Terence wouldn't tell them for security reasons—"radio silence," he called it). Darrell, his mother, his stepfather, and Wade were currently residing at Motel Nowhere, the brothers being tutored by grad students from the university, while their parents settled their business there before taking a dual leave of absence. Terence had cleverly arranged for false identification documents, licenses, and passports.

Ever since landing in the States, the Kaplans were the Parker family: Sara was Cynthia; Roald was Gary; Wade was Michael. And Darrell?

Darrell was Dana.

It was Dana who had killed him. Exactly two months ago.

Dana was a girl's name. With Becca and Lily and now Dana, people looking at their names would think there were three girls in the group. His real passport, with a real picture of his real self, only made the whole thing intolerable.

Still, the Galina Krause situation was probably worse. She had simply disappeared. Vanished. Evaporated.

If Darrell had returned from London alive to every possibility of where the hunt might take them next, what he *hadn't* expected was for the hunt to take them nowhere at all.

According to the investigator Paul Ferrere in France, Chief Inspector Simon Yazinsky in Russia, Isabella

Mercanti in Italy, and Terence's friends in the British intelligence services, Galina had dropped off the face of the earth.

Her absence was totally bewildering.

More than bewildering, it was worrying. If no one had heard a word about her for two whole months, she must be planning something amazingly huge.

Something unutterably evil.

But day after day there was no word. Nothing.

It *could* have been a welcome break for them. After all, the Order's lousy agents didn't seem to know where the "Parkers" were. But Darrell couldn't relax. He was a person who did things, a person who moved, a person who couldn't sit still. He was, as his real passport so completely spelled out, Darrell Surawaluk Evans Kaplan!

His first last name came from his father, who was Thai. When his parents had divorced, he'd taken back his mother's name. When his mom had married Wade's father, he'd added Kaplan to the bunch. It was a mouthful. But it was kind of cool. It made him seem international, which, of course, he was. A good background for a relic Guardian, which, of course, he also was. But Dana Parker?

No.

As he zipped his passport back into the hidden pocket

in his jeans—his mother had sewn such secret pockets in all of their clothes—his stepfather came into the bedroom from the shared bathroom, wiggling a toothbrush in his mouth.

"I'm going to campus in about five minutes. Your mother's just finishing up there. We'll come back here together. Terence says he has a new place for us to go, a hotel not so—"

"Nowhere-y?" said Darrell.

Brrng. Brrng.

The room phone that never rang—rang.

Wade tossed down his book. "No one knows we're here. Only Terence and Julian. And they'd use our cells."

Brrng. Brrng.

"It wouldn't be Sara," Roald said.

Brrng. Brrng.

"It could be Lily. I'm answering it." Darrell snatched the phone from its cradle. "Hello—"

"Is fazzer?"

"Lily? Wait, who is this?"

"I speak wiz fazzer. Hurry!"

Darrell gave the phone to his stepfather, who put it on speaker.

"Hello, can I help you?"

24

"I call from Petrescu," the voice said.

"Petrescu?" said Roald. "Where is that? Who is this, please?"

There was a pause, then the voice continued as if it were reading. "Seven, eight . . . ten, three . . ."

"Wade!" Darrell whispered. "Get this down!"

Wade grabbed his notebook from the nightstand, flipping past the pages covered with the clues, riddles, and number codes they'd solved in the past.

". . . eleven, two . . . thirteen, eight . . . sixteen, one . . ."

"Excuse me," Roald started.

"*B-T-Z!*" said the voice. "English edition. Issue fifteen thousand nine hundred forty-seven. Not online. Real paper."

The line went dead. Roald replaced the phone in its cradle.

Darrell leaned over Wade's notebook. "It's a code. We have a new code. Look, the first number in each pair is higher than the first number in the pair before it. Did I solve it?"

"Oh my gosh, Darrell!" Wade said, with a grin. "No, you didn't. Dad, what do you think *BTZ* means?"

"They're letters," said Darrell, giving him his own grin back.

"*BTZ* could be a newspaper," his stepfather said. "A foreign one, if we're supposed to read the English edition. 'Petrescu' sounds Romanian. A city, maybe."

"Either way, we're doing it," said Darrell, slinging his jacket on. "Mom's still on campus. She can scour the newspapers at the library while we head over there." He peeked outside the door and looked both ways. "Clear. Let's go."

Because his father was driving and Darrell was bouncing too much at the thought of a new code, Wade made the call to his stepmother, only to find that Sara was already on her way back to the motel but would call a library colleague to know to expect them. Then she called back a few minutes later.

"You were right," she said. "*B-T-Z* is indeed a newspaper, a German daily named *Berliner Tageszeitung*. Be careful. See you back at Motel One Chair."

The Perry-Castañeda Library, or PCL, at the University of Texas maintained paper holdings of international newspapers for several months before digitizing them. Wade hoped that this issue of the *BTZ* hadn't already been scanned. They were in luck. When they arrived, the on-duty librarian walked them directly to the hard-copy stacks of the *Tageszeitung*. The papers were in good shape and clearly labeled. It took Wade less than ten minutes to locate a copy of issue number 15,947.

When he pulled it from the shelf, his heart thumped.

"Dad, look. It's from March eleventh, two days after Uncle Henry died."

"A sign that maybe it *is* a Guardian message," his father said.

"Oh, it is. I've already decided," said Darrell.

Uncle Henry was not Wade's actual uncle, but Dr. Heinrich Vogel, his father's college teacher and a long-time friend of the family. When Wade was seven, Uncle Henry had given him a sixteenth-century star chart. It was that chart that had helped them solve the first clue relating to the Copernicus Legacy.

Find the twelve relics.

That clue had led them to Berlin, where Uncle Henry had been murdered by agents of the Teutonic Order under the command of Galina Krause. After the old man's violent death, they'd taken up his cause to locate and protect the twelve relics.

"You start on this," his father said, laying out the newspaper on a broad study table. "I'll see if I can find out what Petrescu is. I'll be over there." He pointed to a nearby bank of computers. "Yell if you find anything."

Darrell nodded. "Except it's a library, so we'll whisper."

The two boys searched the issue page by page, through articles on politics, economics, concerts, books. Wade tested the number sequence against page numbers, then column numbers, and finally against any numbers—even sports scores, stock market and weather reports, and picture captions.

"Nothing is obvious," he said. "Maybe we need a third clue to figure it out."

Then Darrell turned to the obituaries on page 31.

It contained the following notice.

Heinrich Vogel, Physicist, Scholar, Dies

BERLIN—MARCH 11. Dr. Heinrich Rudolf Vogel, esteemed professor of astronomy and nuclear physics at Humboldt University from 1971 to 2006, was found dead near his apartment on the Unter den Linden. He was 83. A police spokesman reported the cause of death as a heart attack. Vogel possessed eight advanced degrees from several universities, including the Max Planck Institute (Munich).

In later days, Vogel was a frequent consultant

at CERN and authored many articles and monographs researching critical subatomic particles and dark matter. He made no secret of his belief that his greatest professional achievement was attending the founding meeting of the International Atomic Energy Agency (IAEA) in 1957. His papers have been bequeathed to the Harry Ransom Center at the University of Texas (Austin). Services were held yesterday morning, March 10, at Alter St.-Matthäus-Kirchhof.

"We were at those memorial services," Darrell said.

Wade breathed heavily through his nose. "It's where we first saw the Teutonic Order and realized we were being followed."

"And the hunt began," said Darrell. "What's CERN?"

"The international research lab for nuclear stuff. They have the Large Hadron Collider. It's famous. All the best nuclear scientists work there. I told you about it like a thousand times. You don't listen."

"Wait. What? Sorry, I wasn't listening. Who are you? And why do you have that look on your face?"

"You don't think . . ."

"Yes I do. What?"

"That the numbers the man said on the phone go with the obituary?" said Wade. "I mean, it would be the way a Guardian contacts us. Becca told us about a number code that works with books."

"I remember. The book code," said Darrell. "It gives you three numbers and tells pages and lines and words. Well, the numbers are in pairs here, so maybe we're supposed to assume that it's Uncle Henry's obituary and use just the line and the word. Try it."

Wade took out his notebook and turned to the page with the numbers the phone caller told them. "The first pair is seven, eight. So the seventh line, eighth word." He counted down. "Hmm. The word is *of*."

"To throw you off," Darrell said, pushing his way in. "You have to try it without the title. The seventh line, eighth word is . . . Ha, told you. It's *eight*. The message begins with the word *eight*. I *did* solve it!"

"The next pair of numbers is ten and three," said Wade, "which means tenth line, third word. *Days*. Darrell, *I* solved it. The message starts *eight days*!"

Eleven and two was *CERN*.

Thirteen and eight was *secret*.

Sixteen and one was *meeting*.

The entire message read:

Eight days CERN secret meeting

"We got it!" Darrell said, not whispering.

His stepfather trotted back from the computer with a notecard in his hand.

"Dad," said Wade, "we figured it out—"

"Mostly I did."

"The message is 'eight days CERN secret meeting.' There's going to be an important meeting at CERN in Switzerland in eight days."

"We got the clue today," said Darrell, "so we're talking eight days from today, which is Tuesday, June tenth. Whoever sent the message probably wants you—and definitely us—to be there."

His father studied the obituary and the code side by side. "This explains Petrescu."

"What does it mean?" Wade asked.

"Dr. Marin Petrescu is the new director of CERN. He worked for years at the IAEA. He may have known Uncle Henry from there."

"Maybe he's a Guardian, too," Darrell whispered. "Even if he isn't, this is about the Legacy. I knew it had to be. Why else would he send a message using Uncle Henry's obituary?"

"Dad, if the director of the world's most famous nuclear research laboratory wants to see you, something big is going on. How can Darrell and I and you, of course, not go?"

"I'm not sure a message sent to me means that we all have to go," Wade's father said with a small smile. "But come on. We need to talk. Let's get home."

"Motel Nowhere is not home," said Darrell. "I'm just saying."

When they arrived back at the motel, Sara was on the secure computer, speaking with Paul Ferrere, the French private detective who had helped rescue her in Russia.

"Paul," Sara said, "will you please repeat what you just told me?"

"Certainly," he said, as the others gathered around the screen. "One of our agents snapped a photograph of Ebner von Braun speaking with a man outside the Paris Opera two months ago. It was the day *after* the fatal plane crash in Olsztyn, Poland, and hours before a well-respected book dealer on the Left Bank here was robbed of a sixteenth-century document of Polish origin."

"Aha!" said Darrell. "Go on."

"We have formally identified the other man as Oskar

Gerrenhausen, a reputed antiquarian bookseller whom we now suspect to be the thief. Like Ebner and Galina, he has not been seen since. Until now. Tonight he purchased a ticket for tomorrow evening's Paris-to-Rome train, leaving from the Gare de Lyon. I advise you to be here as soon as you can, or the man may slip through our fingers."

Roald took a breath. "Paul, are you saying the Order is active again, after two months of virtually no activity?"

"It most certainly is."

Wade felt his blood shoot through his veins like electricity through a wire.

"We need to tell the girls," he said. "Mom, Dad, where do you think they are?"

"Doesn't matter," said Darrell, leaping to the dresser with his open backpack. "Just get them. Get them and tell them the relic hunt is back on!"

CHAPTER FIVE

Tampa, Florida
June 2
11:24 p.m.

Becca thought "radio silence" was a miserable idea. Safe and secure, maybe. Smart, definitely. But miserable all the same.

Two months without a single word about Galina's whereabouts or the Order's nasty business had been torture. For all Becca knew, the relic hunt was completely dead. Or the boys were doing it without them.

"Are you going to want to read the diary again?" Lily asked.

Becca shook her head. "It's so late. My eyes are tired."

"All of me is tired, but what else is there to do?"

The two friends were sitting cross-legged on Becca's bed in the bedroom they shared in their two conjoined "suites" in a so-so motel on the outskirts of Tampa. The Copernicus diary, Becca's red notebook, and Lily's secure tablet were spread out between them. Becca's parents were sleeping in one of the second suite's two bedrooms, her sister Maggie in the other.

This was the latest hiding place Terence Ackroyd had moved them into because of the Order's threats against their families. The truth was, however, that there hadn't been a direct threat against the Benson family (which was who they were now). His witness-protection program was working well. Maybe too well.

Terence called it Code Red whenever they had to pack up and move. Each time they did, Becca hoped it would be because the relic hunt had started again. Each time, she was disappointed. She'd waited for something to tell them that Galina Krause was blazing across the world searching for the next relic. But the creepily young and kind-of-beautiful murderer had simply vanished.

There'd been no Code Red in the weeks since they'd

35

come to Tampa. Becca felt she was hanging in midair, waiting for something. What she'd learned in London from Copernicus himself—that time travel caused unimaginably horrible events to happen—seemed more and more like an old memory.

Still, the worst part of the last two months was the Lily situation.

Her parents had totally broken apart, and her family was angry and silent and in shreds. It tore Becca's heart to see her friend so hurt. Lily was damaged much more, of course, but she wouldn't show it. Lily was Lily, bright and perfect, and that's all she wanted people to see. Becca would have been crying all the time.

You'd actually never have expected them to be able to stand each other. They were as different as lobster and peanut butter. Becca was overly booky; Lily was way too electronically connected. Becca was moody and quiet; Lily was totally out there and quick and talky and funny. At least before her parents started throwing things.

The breakup of Lily's parents—after fifteen years—was inconceivable to everybody. Becca didn't know what to say or do for her friend except to be with her as much as she could. And that was the best part of the Lily situation.

To keep both their minds off the breakup and the slump in the hunt for the relics, Becca had delved deeper and harder into Copernicus's secret diary, trying to decipher several coded passages dated directly after Nicolaus left Serpens with Maxim Grek in Russia.

Lily, meanwhile, had created a database of all the tragedies that had happened around the world since the beginning of March, when the relic hunt began.

Because she and the others frequently had to discard their phones, they'd all begun storing critical data remotely on one of the secure Ackroyd computers in New York. This newest database contained data on several strange incidents of suspected time travel in Florida and Spain, the destruction of an office building in Rio, the murder of a Swedish diplomat, the sinking of a tanker in the eastern Mediterranean, and no fewer than three midnight thefts from famous art museums in Europe and Asia.

"All right," Becca whispered. "Eyes refreshed. Let's get back to it. Maybe this time, we'll discover something real."

Grateful for any distraction from the divorce, Lily dragged her tablet over, swiped it on, and wiggled her fingers, ready to enter search terms. If she didn't have what it took to keep her family together, at least she was good at this.

Trying to sound as eager as possible, she said, "Go."

"Okay, so. Remember I said that the diary pages right after the last Serpens entry were written in English? Well, I passed over it before because it's way too odd if you read it straight, but now I think there's a code here. Just listen."

While packing I watch Hans bundling up the books and maps of Russia that I no longer need. "Hans, go in the downstairs cupboard to find the map of Italy, if you please. And on your way collect my red shaving bowl. My poor beard's too long."

"Will we ship the bowl, too?"

"Perhaps later. In one short hour we meet with those who battle for the rights of the poor. We have our orders, Hans. We must be fleet to make it there."

"It goes on for another page like that," Becca said.

For a secret diary, it wasn't what Lily expected to hear. "It's so not relicky."

"Is that a word?"

"I'm a groundbreaker. What's that mark?" Lily

pointed to a tiny blot of ink positioned under the last word of the last line of the passage.

Becca reached for a second pair of reading glasses— the girl had, like, a dozen of them, all bought since she experienced those weird blackouts in London—and slid them on over the first pair.

"Not a look, by the way," said Lily.

"Thanks for the warning. I don't know what this thing is, but I'm thinking it's just an ink blot or defect on the page."

"It could be more," said Lily. "We live in Code World, after all."

"I'd need a magnifying glass to make sure."

"Really?" said Lily. "Or you could just snap a picture of it on your phone and enlarge it."

"Oh, right."

"Gosh, you people need me!" Lily took a photo and enlarged it. The "ink blot" turned out to be nothing of the sort. It was a triangle, with numbers inside it.

"Five-five-five," said Becca. "Better than six-six-six, the devil's number."

"Is it the cipher?" asked Lily. "If I'm using the word right."

"You are. What do you mean?"

"Well, maybe the number's a key to the passage above it. Maybe Nicolaus isn't writing about packing junk for a trip at all."

"How is it a key?"

Lily sighed. "I don't know! What are five and five and five? Fifteen. So maybe the fifteenth word means something. I'll do it." She scanned the passage. "The fifteenth word is *I*. I did it!"

"Girls!" Mrs. Moore hissed through the open door from the other suite. "It's midnight. Go to sleep!"

"Sorry, Mrs. Benson," Lily said, then whispered, "I did solve it, didn't I?"

"You didn't," whispered Becca. "But maybe you have something. Maybe it's not every fifteenth word, but it could be the fifth, then the tenth, and then the fifteenth, like that. Or maybe every fifth word, just repeating five, five, five all the way."

"If that turns out to be right, I still solved it," said Lily.

Becca underlined every fifth word in the passage as written in her notebook.

> While packing, I watch <u>Hans</u> bundling up those books <u>and</u> maps of Russia that <u>I</u> no longer need. "Hans, <u>go</u> in the downstairs cupboard <u>to</u> find the map of <u>Italy</u>, if you please. And <u>on</u> your way collect my <u>red</u> shaving bowl. My poor <u>beard's</u> too long."
> "Will we <u>ship</u> the bowl, too?"
> "Perhaps <u>later</u>. In one short hour <u>we</u> meet with those who <u>battle</u> for the rights of <u>the</u> poor. We have our <u>orders</u>, Hans. We must be <u>fleet</u> to make it there."

Every fifth word yielded something quite different than a story of books and bowls and maps. The text appeared to break into two distinct sentences.

> Hans and I go to Italy on red beard's ship. Later we battle the orders fleet.

"Whoa!" Lily said. "Bec, this could break the hunt wide open."

On the surface, the next passage appeared to be about a set of horseshoes for Hans Novak's new horse.

Put together, the underlined fifth words told a very different story.

> *I visit my old friend in his workshop and we talk.*
>
> *"The sun does not move?" he says. "Hmm. I learn something every day."*
>
> *I beg him to be the silver relic's Guardian.*
>
> *"I am far too old," he says. "But I'll craft a beautiful place to hide it!"*

"Becca, we are getting so close!" Lily whispered. "Who's this old workshop guy? Hurry up, decode the next passage!"

"That's just it," Becca said. "The next several pages are scribbled over with some kind of silver stuff—ink or paint or something. There are no words at all, just lines going in every direction. Except that the pages are worn and smudged, as if someone read them over and over, but you can't see any words."

Lily leaned over the diary. The page shimmered under the nightstand lamp. "Whoa. I feel a little dizzy just looking at it."

"I know. Me too."

"So maybe there are words written in invisible ink—"

There was a sudden screeching of tires in the parking lot below.

Then the sound of several doors squealing open at the same time and the thump of quick footsteps across the lot.

"Lily!" Becca whispered. "It's Code Red! I can't believe it—it's Code Red!"

CHAPTER SIX

L ily slid all the books and papers from the bed into
Becca's new super-tough go-bag, then snatched up
her own while Becca flew into the other room to wake
her sister.

"Mags, we're moving again."

Maggie slid out of bed half-asleep and pulled on the
clothes that Becca had gathered for her. "Has Galina
Sauerkraut come back?"

"We don't know," Becca said. "We just have to go."

It was frightening to move in the middle of the
night, and although Lily and Becca had signed on for it,
the others hadn't. Lily switched off the nightstand light
and peeked out the shades. A large black Escalade was

parked sideways in the hotel lot. *Terence?* She waited by the hall door for the signal. A minute went by, another half minute . . . Then it came, a persistent tapping on the door.

Five knocks, two knocks, four knocks. A pause. Then again.

The sequence—five, two, four—meant the fifth month, twenty-fourth day: May 24, the day Copernicus died. Becca had wanted to add the year—one, five, four, three, for 1543—but Lily had argued that by the time someone got all those knocks out, the bad guys would be all over them. So they'd settled for five, two, four. Lily answered with five slow taps, one for each of the occupants in the suite.

"Mr. and Mrs. Benson," she hissed, "time to move again—"

"Please let Terence in," Becca's mother answered.

Lily pulled open the hall door. A familiar middle-aged man stood there, rumpled but alert and friendly. Terence Ackroyd had dark hair that was graying at the temples and a pair of bright green eyes blinking behind glasses.

"You've been tracked down," he said softly. "And there's something else."

Becca came out of Maggie's room, slinging her sister's

45

extra bag over her shoulder.

"We'll be okay," Lily said to Maggie. "We're pros at this, and I am seriously ready to move on. The AC here is not what *I* call AC."

"Terence?" said Mrs. Moore, carrying a large satchel. "Is it—"

"Serious? Yes," he said, lending a hand with the bags. "I've just received a message from Roald. The Kaplans, excuse me, the Parkers, are on the move to France. Down the stairs quickly."

"Are they all right?" asked Becca.

"Tell us they're all right," Lily added.

"They will be," Terence said under his breath to the two of them, "once you two get there."

Just the way those words sounded made Lily want to burst into a shout, or a scream, or a sob, or *something* to show how eager she was to get away from her own life, no matter how serious or dangerous it might be.

Terence trotted down the outside stairs two at a time, tucking his shirt in as he went. The night was warm and breezy, and the air sweeping in reminded Lily of Uncle Roald's house in Austin. It was where Wade and Darrell and she and Becca had put together the first clues about the Copernicus Legacy.

Crouching low between the cars, they ran across the

parking lot to the Escalade. An armed man popped out of the front and opened the doors and closed them as soon as the family was inside.

They were soon passing through streets of houses that reminded Lily of her old neighborhood, where she and Becca lived before the Teutonic Order started harassing them. Lily tried not to look, but she caught sight of a house that looked like hers. She cringed to see it. It was dark and appeared empty, like hers was now. Was that because of the Order? Sure. But it would have been empty anyway.

Twenty minutes later, Becca watched the van pull into the parking lot of the John F. Germany Public Library. The dark bulk of the building, lifeless in the middle of the night, would have been intimidating, frightening, even, but in the few weeks the "Bensons" had been in Tampa, Becca had come to know nearly every room in the library, from the book repair on the bottom floor to the most isolated study carrel on the top. She had already spent many hours in it and had come to love it as her second home, like her favorite, the Faulk Central Library in Austin.

There was a faint glimmer of light coming from one of the windows on the ground floor.

"What's going on?" Becca's father asked. "Terence, we have a right to know."

Terence turned off the engine of the Cadillac. "You do. I wish I could tell you. But I don't know much myself. It looks like Galina is on the move again." He motioned to the light coming from a ground-floor window of the library. "A woman, a very old woman, has crossed half the world to get to you."

"To us?" said Becca's mother.

Terence shook his head. "To the girls."

"Who is she?" asked Lily. "What does she want?"

"I don't know, and she wouldn't say or can't say. Not to me, anyway. As near as I can determine, she made her way here without any sort of legal identification. How she did that, I can't tell you. How she knew you were here, I can't tell you either. She was ambushed in Tampa by agents of the Order. My men intervened and brought her here on the way to a hospital. We think she might be a Guardian, but there's no proof. All she said was 'Becca. Lily. Becca. Lily.' So I fetched you. I pray she's still alive."

They piled out of the SUV, and Terence sent a text from his phone. A few seconds later, the rear library doors buzzed and clicked. He pulled them open, and everyone entered a yellow-lit hallway.

In the repair room at the end of the hall, a woman

dressed in a swirl of black robes, the lower half of which were wrinkled and smeared with blood, lay supine on a worktable. A hood obscured most of her face, but Becca could see that the woman was pale, thin-lipped, and very old, more than eighty, possibly more than ninety. She had a bandage taped hastily across one side of her face. Her hands and skin were as white as snow, except for a lot of blood smeared on her fingers. Blood, and what looked like silver paint . . . or ink.

Attending her was a young man in scrubs. Terence introduced him as a friend whose name they didn't need to know. He wore a stethoscope around his neck. He looked at them all, then shook his head. "Not much I can do here but keep her stable. She needs to get to the hospital, stat."

"Five minutes," said Terence. "Girls."

They moved to the table and bent down to the woman.

"Hello?" said Lily. "We're here. Lily and Becca. It's us."

The old woman opened her wrinkled eyelids. Her lips trembled. She mumbled something softly. Both girls bent down closer. "Carlo told me . . . you are here."

"Carlo?" said Lily. "You know Carlo Nuovenuto?"

It was Carlo who had given the Copernicus diary to

the children. He was one of the very first Guardians they had ever met, though his whereabouts right now were a mystery.

"I . . . Guardian," she said. "Mother . . ."

"Mother?" said Becca. "Are you Carlo's mother?"

"No! Mother!" the woman croaked. "We stay, we always stay!" It didn't make sense, but Becca vowed to remember every word, every syllable. The woman shook, then held the girls by their wrists, lifted her head up, and through her convulsive coughing shouted as loudly as she could:

"La harrrr! Ghh . . . harr!"

As soon as the sounds left her lips, she fell limp to the table, and her hands loosened their grip. Her eyes lost their fire and flickered closed. The doctor leaned over, pressed his stethoscope to the woman's sunken breast, and pulled out his phone. "We need to go. Now."

Terence nodded to the armed man who'd ridden with them. "Please help her into the doctor's car."

Becca let out a long breath, felt her chest heave. Maggie was whimpering in the corner, cowering with her parents.

"What did she mean?" Lily asked softly. "She's a mother and 'la har'?"

Becca had learned—from Copernicus himself in

London—that the hiding of the relics for hundreds of years had depended on a complex, and sometimes seemingly random, collection of codes and riddles and hints. Most Guardians had to be kept in the dark, for the greater security of the Legacy.

"That's a mystery for later," Terence said. "Look, the Teutonic Order is closing in. I have a plan to throw them off, but it requires that you split up—"

"No!" said Maggie, lunging at Becca, wrapping her arms around her. "No."

"Maggie, I'm sorry," Terence said. "The girls are suddenly needed, and our escape will work only if we send you off in different directions. Not for long—"

"No, not again," said Becca's mother. "We won't allow it."

Becca wanted to feel the same way, but she honestly felt she couldn't afford to. As much as she loved her family, if Copernicus had taught her anything in London, it was that nothing was more important than finding the relics of his Eternity Machine. If only to keep them from Galina Krause.

"Lily and I are getting these clues for a reason," Becca said to her parents.

"I know, dear," said her father, "but you're not leaving us again. You can't. It's too dangerous."

"It's very dangerous, I agree," said Terence. "And I know it's difficult to hear, but I'm afraid we don't have a choice." He gave the girls a grim glance. "An hour ago, Paul Ferrere called me. Apparently, the theft of an old Polish manuscript two months ago may be directly related to a fatal plane crash in Poland at the same time, both of which are connected to the search for the relics. The Order is hatching something very big. The Copernicus diary is vital to stopping them, and Becca and Lily are vital, too. I will personally accompany them both to Paris. You'll all meet up in a matter of days, I assure you. Becca and Lily are necessary to the success of this project. They are, in a word, *needed*."

Becca was so thrilled, she nearly screamed. *We're needed! Yes, we are!*

As Terence handed the Moores a travel waiver, giving him permission to take both Becca and Lily—because they were acting as Lily's temporary guardians—out of the country, the door opened. Terence's son, Julian, entered the repair room. He hugged the girls. "We need to move. The Order's slumber is over. They're after us. All of us. Mr. and Mrs. Moore, Maggie, I'm Julian, by the way. You'll need to come with me."

"Lily, do you want me to call your parents?" Terence asked.

"They don't care."

Becca's mother practically launched herself at Lily. "They *do* care, dear; they do!" She pulled her into a tight embrace. "It's very difficult for them right now. You know they love you. You've always known."

Lily hugged Mrs. Moore as tightly, then wiped her cheeks. "I know. But it's better for them if I'm out of the picture for a while. Besides, the Legacy."

There was the sound of more than one car approaching the library.

"Maggie, I'm sorry," said Becca.

"It's okay," Maggie said, trying impossibly to dry her face. "You'll have more stories to tell me. You better keep safe."

Becca wrapped her arms around Maggie. "I will. I will."

"Come along now, please." Terence slid his hand into his jacket and tugged out airline boarding passes to Paris made in the girls' aliases.

There came a shout from outside the building. It was followed by the racing of an engine and more squealing tires . . . and Maggie's stifled scream.

"Out, everyone, out!" Terence said as he and Julian spirited the girls and Becca's family off in different directions.

CHAPTER SEVEN

Côte d'Azur, France
June 4
7:27 a.m.

"It's finally coming together."

"Not me and sleep. They're not coming together. Not while you're awake."

The clacking of iron wheels on the rails beneath his compartment on the train had kept Darrell awake for the last two hours, and it seemed that Wade should be awake, too. Why? Because it was finally coming together.

"So you're *not* sleeping."

"Yes, Dana. I'm not."

"Don't call me Dana."

"I wouldn't have to if I were asleep. Dana."

Lily and Becca had arrived in Paris the afternoon before. That night, they and Terence had met up inside one of the less chaotic corners of the vast Gare de Lyon train terminal in south Paris. There was two months' worth of reunion in three minutes—all awkward hugs and looks and sweaty palms.

Then, at precisely 10:14 p.m., Oskar Gerrenhausen, suspected of stealing a Polish document for Galina, appeared at the station. He presented his ticket for the Paris-Rome sleeper train and boarded. They did the same.

Now, the morning after, the girls were still asleep in the compartment they shared with Darrell's mother, while Roald was in the dining car assembling breakfast to bring back to them. The thief was in the compartment next door to the boys. Darrell, Wade, and his stepfather had listened in stages all night, but Gerrenhausen hadn't emerged from his cabin since the train had left Paris.

Darrell stood and stretched, though there was hardly room for either. As soon as the girls had arrived the day before, Becca had told them about the old woman at midnight and her incomprehensible words, "Har-har," or something like that, before she fell unconscious, which was strange enough. But then Becca related how, after reading and rereading the diary pages on the plane halfway across the Atlantic, she and Lily had found something else, and it was big.

"Look," Becca had said, and she'd read out a bit about Copernicus meeting an old man in his workshop. "Together Lily and I found another passage about that meeting. There Copernicus says, 'A good man lost something saving Hans once, but you, my Mechanicysta Mediolanu, have restored it to him again.'"

"Of course, I instantly found out that 'Mechanicysta Mediolanu' means 'the Mechanist of Milan,'" Lily had added. "Which refers to a particular person, who I will now show you . . ." She'd flipped open her tablet to a picture and grinned.

Wade had frowned. "That's Leonardo da Vinci. You aren't saying—"

"We are!" Becca jumped. "Leonardo da Vinci! Can you believe it? Leonardo da Vinci and Nicolaus met, and he actually *made* something for Copernicus!"

Wade had nearly turned himself inside out. "Da Vinci is the greatest genius of all time! He invented the helicopter; he painted the *Mona Lisa* and the *Last Supper*; he made all kinds of weapons. He invented everything!"

"Except whispering," Paul Ferrere had said. "There. Look."

And that was when they'd seen the little bookseller head toward the train.

Now Darrell raised the window shade. Leonardo and Nicolaus. Everyone was still stunned by that. Or not *everyone*. After the excitement of last night in Paris, Lily seemed to have crashed. Her parents' divorce was draining her: of her perkiness, her usual sparkle, her bounce, if that was a thing.

Darrell had been through a divorce. If only he weren't so tongue-tied, he might have come up with something helpful to her. He joked around, as usual, thinking a dose of Darrell was good for anything, but the spell wasn't working. He'd try harder.

A sign flashed by: Nice 32km. The train was now on what he'd read was the Côte d'Azur—the blue coast—France's southern shore that bordered the Mediterranean Sea. Dawn came on strong, with bold rays of sunlight glimmering over the fields and little towns visible from that side of the train. He was thinking how beautiful and peaceful it all was, when something crashed against the wall to his left.

Wade sprang up. "What was—"

"Shh!" whispered Darrell.

A muffled voice shouted from the far side. It was garbled. Then came a second, high-pitched shout, which was cut short. This was followed by a deep, dull thump, then silence.

Darrell's mouth dropped open. "Dude, that was a gunshot!"

CHAPTER EIGHT

Still staring at Darrell, Wade jumped to his feet, suddenly wide awake. His veins turned to ice. *Gunshot. Murder. The Teutonic Order. Galina's active again.*

There was a sudden, heart-wrenching groan from the compartment.

"I'm texting Dad," he whispered, switching his phone on and tapping in a text. As they went out into the hall, he saw his father running down the corridor to them. Darrell nodded toward the bookseller's door and made the universal hand signal for shooting a gun.

Urging the boys aside, Wade's father tapped the door. "Hello? Is everything all right in there?"

A small voice said, "Yes, yes. Come in."

Sharing a quick look with them, Wade's father entered the compartment first, while they stood half in, half out. On the floor, amid a scattering of clothes and papers spilling out of a small roller suitcase, was the body of a large man. His arms were splayed across the space between the bunks, his suit was twisted around him, and his white shirt was stained with a growing island of deep red.

Wade cupped his hand over his mouth.

"No, no," said the small voice. "It's quite all right. He's dead."

That much was obvious, and it didn't help.

The bookseller, quite a bit older and smaller than the man on the floor, was huddled in the corner, quivering like a leaf in a storm. He had wispy white hair and thick spectacles, and in one hand he held an automatic weapon, its barrel lengthened by a three-inch noise suppressor. In the other he had a cell phone, which he slid into a pocket the moment the boys and their father entered.

The sharp smell of gunpowder hovered in the air. The scene inside the cabin was in complete contrast to the sunny day dawning outside the window.

"I shot him," the little man said, in a squeaky voice tinged with an Eastern European accent. "And he died.

Just like that." The little man's shirttails were untucked. He wore only one slipper; the other foot was bare. It appeared that he'd been sleeping when the man entered his cabin.

"We'll call the conductor," Wade's father said.

Wade found a small red button near the door. He picked out a word or two of French and guessed that pressing the button would contact the nearest conductor.

Darrell stood quietly. "In the meantime, why don't you put the gun down?"

"Of course. Of course." The little man stared at the gun in his hand but made no effort to put it down. "He tried to rob me. I had no choice but to kill him."

To kill him.

Wade's father removed a handkerchief from his jacket and used it to slip the gun carefully out of the man's hand.

"I am a bookseller," the man said. Wade knew he was. Would he say he worked for Galina Krause? "Mostly a bookseller, that is. I locate other things upon occasion. He would have killed me, you see. I had no choice in the matter. He came at me. It is warm in here. But perhaps it is only me. . . ."

He's in shock, Wade thought. *Trauma does that to you.*

61

The bookseller had just killed a man, the man on the floor covered with blood.

Wade stifled a second impulse to be sick.

"Boys," said his father, "why not go and find the conductor?"

"Okay." Wade didn't move.

Even in the circumstances—a dead man, a gun, a crime—there was something Wade couldn't put his finger on, and he didn't want to leave before it came to him. The relic hunt had made him like that. An observer. But what bothered him?

The compartment was as small as theirs, and beyond the single piece of upset luggage, there were only the five of them in there—the dead giant, Darrell, himself, his father, and the old man. Somewhere in the compartment might be the Polish document he had stolen in Paris. But where? There was a leather messenger bag hanging in the closet. Then it came to him.

What was bothering him was the gun.

"Did you use this other man's gun?" he asked.

Gerrenhausen studied the pistol lying on the bunk next to Wade's father. "The Beretta? No. This is mine. Often I travel with valuable items, so . . ."

"So you had a silencer?" Darrell asked.

And that was it. Darrell had asked the question. *You*

only have a silencer if you're a killer. Maybe this man really is a bookseller, but he's also an agent of the Order. Wade liked that he—and Darrell—had noticed the details.

"The conductor's taking his time," Darrell whispered. "The button's not working. I'll get him." He slipped past Wade and his father into the corridor.

Because the man on the floor was clearly dead, Wade didn't want to look at him, but he noticed something anyway. A small tattoo on the upper side of the man's left wrist. It was nearly obscured by the cuff of his shirt. It resembled a circle with four small bars crossing into it, but not meeting in the center.

Odd for such a big man to have such a small tattoo, he thought.

Darrell arrived a few minutes later with the conductor and two railroad security officials, who questioned them. Some minutes after that, Sara came down the corridor and took them aside.

"We need to stick close to this man," she whispered. "We all remember what Becca learned in London. The horror that Copernicus saw, the horror of letting Galina do what she wants. We have to follow this bookseller."

Wade's father nodded slowly. "They'll take him off the train at Nice. Terence has a flat there where we can stay. It's simple enough to fly from Nice to my meeting in Switzerland. Agreed?"

Agreed.

Oskar Gerrenhausen was handcuffed in nylon zip cuffs by one of the security officers and taken into custody. His cabin, now a crime scene, was sealed and guarded, and the train rolled on under the rising sun toward the city of Nice.

CHAPTER NINE

Katha, Upper Myanmar
June 4
Afternoon

A hole in the sky.
A hole in her life.

After becoming aware of when and where she was, Galina realized that her collapse and eight weeks in a coma had put her maddeningly and agonizingly far behind schedule. Yet her two months of oblivion were not without one victory. Her mind had continued to work, to dream, to create. Her coma had in fact left her mind free to wander. And wander it had. A long-buried memory had surfaced with a scorching vengeance.

And her plan had birthed itself, fully formed, like Venus emerging from the sea's foam.

With only one hundred and eleven days left, the looming deadline rose like a great black poisonous cloud that enveloped everything in its path. She couldn't risk losing any more time. She would move with terrifying speed, a scythe, hewing every obstacle, leaving nothing in her path.

She would pursue a vendetta against the world.

A golden one.

Everything would come together in a single global operation.

She spoke its name in her mind. *Aurora.*

Aurora. Its first two letters the symbol for gold. Light. Dawn. The golden sun.

She opened her eyes to see her slender-fingered, tawny-skinned doctor leaning back from the gurney she lay on. He smiled a lifeless smile. "Fully awake, then, are you? I must say, when your man Ebner brought you here in April, I had little hope."

"Did you?" she said, sitting up. "And now?"

His hazel eyes scanned her face with no more emotion than if he were reading an EKG. "Miss Krause, the tissues at the site of your surgery are deeply inflamed. You have been on a regimen of Carbora thirty-one, high doses, but you are now beyond Carbora's help altogether. The body can only endure so much abuse, and you have treated yours poorly. I cannot help you. In fact, I dare say your cancer has developed beyond *anyone's* skill or capacity to—"

"Wrong answer." Galina slid the tubes off herself and took up her phone from the bedside table. She tapped out a message and sent it. An instant later there was a quiet *bing* from outside the door. The doctor swung on his heels and stared at the door as pair of jumpsuited militiamen pushed through it into the hospital room.

"What is the meaning—" the doctor said.

The men took hold of the doctor and pinned him roughly against the nearest wall. A third man, dressed in high-level military trappings, entered. He was short, powerful, a brick of a man in a uniform. He bowed slightly to Galina.

"Colonel, meet the doctor," Galina said. "Doctor, meet the colonel."

"What?" The doctor was wild-eyed. "Colonel? Help me!"

The colonel's face was cold. It bore the emotion of a corpse. He drew a small object from a pouch at his belt. It was a syringe. He raised it, pressed its plunger.

Galina shook her head. "Wait a moment."

"You wish to spare him?" the colonel asked, glancing from the doctor to the needle in his hand. He tapped it again; a spout of clear liquid shot into the air.

Galina walked up to the doctor, looked into his eyes. Such fear there. "No. Merely to do it myself. After two months in a coma, I am out of practice."

The doctor shuddered, screaming, "No!"

Galina slid the syringe from the colonel's hand and injected the doctor's arm. He struggled for a few moments, then slumped to the floor. She heard the rain start up again, a light pattering.

The two militiamen removed the body as efficiently as movers hauling a refrigerator. Operatives of Galina's Burmese militia, a crack mercenary unit numbering six thousand, were headquartered delightfully nearby.

"Colonel, shut down the lab, then go to Station Two in Berlin. A package is awaiting transport. I will notify you soon of its destination."

The man bowed silently. Galina donned a blue robe hanging on a rack by the door, swept a gold scarf around her face, and left the clinic. Outside, the world swept around her in a noisy mess. The air was a heavy fog dragging itself painfully up from the earth.

Breathing was like chewing wads of cotton soaked in hot water.

Katha was not large, a city bordered by the Irrawaddy River and haunted by the foothills that ranged across the country to the north. She made her way to the river, alley by alley, through narrow streets of tumble-down shacks and shops and houses where stray dogs scrounged for food.

She was a stray, too, wasn't she?

Strays always found a way to live.

Reaching the river, she turned north, when the insistent chiming of her cell phone tore her from her thoughts. She swiped away the lock screen.

A message from Ebner, forwarding a text from Oskar Gerrenhausen.

Killed man to protect ledger. I will be arrested in Nice. Auction tomorrow. Thief's wrist wore this mark. Please advise.

Galina's pulse sped up at the sign. Who was this? Another player in the relic hunt? She did not know the symbol. She replied to the bookseller's message.

Our man in Nice will arrange your release. Proceed to Monte Carlo. Do not fail to acquire the item.

She sent another text to Ebner—*What is this symbol?*—then studied the tattoo for a moment. It was the calling card, no doubt, of a new entrant in the relic hunt.

"So the Kaplans are not the only ones interested in the relics? Fine. Let us play this game to the end."

She slid a hand beneath her flowing robe, reached for her Beretta Storm, patted it twice, and kept her palm on its grip as she pushed through the winding alleys along the Irrawaddy River and the rain-soaked bazaar.

A dozen or so minutes northeast of Galina's position, under the awning of a shop selling tin objects for home and office, the sunken-chested nuclear physicist Ebner von Braun studied a transaction between an old woman and a goat.

He was trying to predict which of them would win the contest, when his phone buzzed. It was the Copernicus Room in Madrid, responding to the text he'd sent after receiving Galina's.

Q

Company logo of Ugo Drangheta, industrialist. Known to require his inner circle to wear this tattoo. Amassed his fortune in real estate, airlines, steel factories, shipping after breakup of Yugoslavia. Chief residences include Helsinki, Shanghai, Hanoi, Moscow, Casablanca. Born Sarajevo October 1974, unmarried, parents deceased, one sibling—Uliana Biszku, pilot, joined Order 2013—deceased.

Ebner shuddered as he read those last words. He knew the name Uliana Biszku, though he knew for certain Galina did not. How could this have happened? The pilot had volunteered for the assignment. Had *anyone* known she had a brother? *How will I tell Galina?*

Just then, proving her uncanny ability to be everywhere at once, Galina approached him, a dervish of robes and scarves, hovering above the rubbish of the street. His heart pounded like the quick rapping of a lover on a door.

And then, as she removed a scarf, a shock. Galina's face. Her face was the color of ash; her eyes were hollow; she was but a ghost of herself. So the treatment had not worked after all. Did the girl know how she looked? He was aghast, dizzy, his heart fluttering, but he would say nothing.

"The doctor talked," she said softly.

"As in he talked *too much*?"

"Not anymore."

Ebner was well aware of Galina's habit of cleaning up the space around her. "You'll run out of them one day, you know. Doctors."

She shot him a look. "Not if you keep finding them for me."

"Of course, Galina. It is what I do."

"Walk with me, Ebner. And tell me, what news?"

He swallowed slowly. "The would-be assassin on the train was an employee of Ugo Drangheta. Drangheta is . . . the brother of a woman named Uliana Biszku."

"Who is . . . ?"

"Who *was* the pilot of the plane that crashed into Olsztyn Castle in April," he said. "A mistake was made in our lower ranks, although I must say that the pilot volunteered for the assignment."

"Not for her death," said Galina, who displayed less emotion than he had anticipated.

"No," said Ebner. "But this sudden appearance of a hitman on the train suggests that our pilot's bereaved brother seeks retribution."

"By attacking Gerrenhausen and inserting himself into the hunt for the relics?"

"Rather, I think, to force a confrontation with you," he said.

After several interminable minutes in which the crush of individuals streaming through the streets threatened to overwhelm them, Galina said, "The search for the astrolabe fragments."

He blew out a breath. Good, another topic. "We have not been idle. Over two hundred pieces of the astrolabe's main framing mechanism, both large and small, have been excavated. The majority of them are gathered at Station Two in Berlin. Others in Kraków, Prague, Salzburg, elsewhere. Together they make, naturally, no more than a pile of bones, if I may say so. An unassembled skeleton lacking sinews, flesh, organs, blood. We have gained *some* knowledge of the remaining relics. One, for example, appears to be forged of ancient iron and bears the shape of a wolf. Our investigation is ongoing."

"I had a vision in my long sleep, Ebner," she said. "Operation Aurora."

"Aurora. What is it?"

"It will proceed at full throttle simultaneous to the hunting down of the relics. I'm texting you a location. Arrange with the colonel to retrieve all the fragments and deliver them there at one p.m. Central European Time on Tuesday, the tenth, six days from today."

Ebner checked his phone uneasily. Appearing on the screen were the coordinates 42°27′14.4″N, 13°34′33.6″E. He copied them into his GPS app and watched as it pinpointed the location on a map. His uneasiness deepened.

"My dear Galina, I know this location. Of course I do. But is this wise—"

"The world is against me, my health demands quick action . . . And so, a vendetta against them all."

"Vendetta? Galina, perhaps you are not ready to reveal the full scope of Operation Aurora to me—that is fine—but would a more careful consideration—"

"There is no time." She shot him another text. "Make these things happen on the same timetable. Aurora rises in the next six days. See that you rise with it."

She looked not at him but through him, beyond an open temple door to the darkness within. "What of the Kaplans?"

He swallowed, glancing at the new text. "Information has surfaced that they are on the Continent, posing as a family called the Parkers. We are zeroing in on them as we speak. The family enjoys the help of a wealthy man of considerable resources and contacts worldwide. Beyond this, the Kaplans have grown very smart very quickly. Apparently, one cannot pursue, kidnap, torture, or harass them without their rising to the occasion."

She refocused. "Good. Until we know which ones are expendable, we need them all. I will deal with them. You have your orders."

Galina drifted away on a cloud of midnight blue and gold and flashes of silver.

Ebner followed her movement until he could no longer see her.

His orders, then. According to that last text, all manner of things must be made to happen across the globe simultaneously. In the Kara Sea in the Russian Arctic. In Pyongyang, North Korea. In the waters north of Cyprus. All part of Galina's brand-new vendetta against the world. Aurora. The goddess of the golden dawn.

He opened his phone, reversed the camera lens, and gazed at himself. His fingers went unconsciously to his face, smoothing the eyebrows, shaping the unshapable wisps of sweat-soaked hair that lay matted across his scalp. A revolting blemish on his left cheek, a weak chin, four eyes. A specimen.

And yet . . . who in this present world is as close, hour after hour, to the brilliant and ghostly Galina Krause? I held her in my arms once for countless seconds, after all. Who is as close to her?

No one is.

Only Ebner von Braun.

Only me.

CHAPTER TEN

Nice, France
June 4
8:11 a.m.

Lily looked out the corridor window as their train slowed to a clattering crawl toward the Gare de Nice-Ville. She was outside the boys' compartment and had just overheard Darrell and Wade whispering.

"Lily's in a mood."

"She'll be okay, Dana. I hope."

"We both hope. And don't call me Dana."

The world outside was gorgeous, a postcard of palm trees and blue and green houses and red tile roofs and café umbrellas and golden light and infinite sky.

It twisted her stomach to have people thinking things about her, and she had to get them to stop. It would mean doing the opposite of what she felt like doing. It had been tough to be awesome after she first saw her parents actually screaming at each other. Sometimes she simply failed. But she'd try harder. Be bubbly. Extra bright.

That she couldn't let anyone into her grief was either just plain weird or deep or whatever, but her crumbling family was her business.

So I'll be perky and sparkly.

Until I can't anymore.

"So beautiful," she announced brightly, turning as the boys entered the corridor. "Isn't it? France plus sunshine plus palm trees? Wow."

Becca was now at the window with her. "I can't wait to get out in it."

"We'll have to wait for the transfer," Wade said. "The actors."

Earlier, Roald—who was with Sara now in the dining car—had called Terence to tell him of their change of plans. To throw off any agents of the Order who might be waiting in Nice, the best Terence could do on such short notice was to arrange for a group of local actors, including two boys and two girls roughly their ages, to impersonate the Parkers and the Benson girls continuing on to Rome, while the real them slipped off the train at Nice. The impersonation plan reminded Lily of her own stratagem to escape a killer back in London. Terence said the actors in Nice had worked with him before, so they didn't find the request strange, and they understood its possible danger. Finally, during the transition, the actors would pass over a brand-new set of passports to them.

"I hope my name will be Erik, with a *k*," Darrell said. "It's how I see myself."

Lily tried to come up with a snappy comeback, but couldn't. Instead she smiled. Brightly.

The station ceiling slid slowly overhead as the train rolled toward the platform.

She kind of liked the open-closed ceilings of large European railroad terminals, arching over them like a giant pair of iron-and-glass tunnels. And here, beyond the smell of diesel exhaust and scorched rubber were the lush, lemony-green scents of summer from the town and the Mediterranean a half mile away.

Maybe it wouldn't be so hard to be excited after all.

Darrell popped back into the room and restuffed as many changes of clothes as he could into his backpack. They would leave some luggage for the actors.

"Do you really think this will work?" Wade said, doing the same as his stepbrother. "I mean, will the Order be fooled?"

"If the kid playing me is as handsome as me, sure."

"Seriously."

"Then no," said Darrell. "Galina will know within a couple of hours that we've gotten off here." He nodded out at the station. "We're in Order territory. We're always in it, and we're never out of it, but we're in it again, which is where we always are anyway."

As Darrellish as that was, Lily felt pretty much the same. The compartment she'd shared with Sara and Becca had seemed a safe little haven, even with the shooting so close, but that part of the journey was over. They'd be out on the streets soon, prey to the spying eyes of the Order.

Darrell heaved his overnight bag onto the luggage rack, then whispered to her, "You're thinking the same thing I am, aren't you?"

She stepped back. "Before I answer, tell me what you're thinking."

"You're thinking that if the bookseller is working for Galina, and he shot Tattoo Man, then who's Tattoo Man?"

"I wasn't thinking that," Lily said, "but I could."

"That's our first mystery," Wade said, and tried to sling Becca's go-bag over his shoulder, but she took it back with a mock-annoyed look. "If someone new is after the relics, we need to know."

Darrell pointed toward the platform. "There's one cool kid and a dorky stepbrother type on our platform, so they must be me and you, in that order."

"I'm laughing," Wade said, straight-faced. "Really. I am."

Even amid the usual flurry of activity that accompanied a train pulling into the station, it was easy to spot the singular odd factor—a half-dozen waiting policemen, some in uniform, some not. A contingent of medical personnel appeared, pushing a wheeled gurney through the crowd toward their compartment.

Sara and Roald met the kids in the corridor outside the room. "I'm texting the actors," she said. "Keep your heads down, everyone. We'll make the switch in the first rush of passengers. With hope the Order won't catch on."

"Unless it's already too late," said Darrell. "Take a look at them."

Lily shot a glance into the crowd at a young man bouncing a child in his arms. Both the man and the infant wore pink shirts and green shorts. "That's a fashion statement, not the Teutonic Order—"

"Not them. *Them.*" Darrell moved her head in his hands three inches to the left. Who'd told him he could just do that, she had no idea. "The two goons at the luggage rack," he said. "They're pretending to load baggage on the rack, but all the stuff they throw on, they take right back off. Dead giveaway."

It was true. The porters appeared to be working, but as they moved the luggage on and off the rack, they were really scanning the crowd under the brims of their caps. Lily felt the familiar combination of thrill and nausea in her stomach. "Uncle Roald—"

"I see them," he said. "Good eyes, Darrell."

"Oh, I know," he said. "I've been practicing two months for this."

The train finally stopped with a soft hush, followed by a sigh of exhaust and the slight squealing of brakes. Then, as if a director had shouted, "Action!" everything moved. A swarm of people rushed up to the train cars, while Gerrenhausen was now out on the platform, being drawn away on the edge of the crowd by two policemen. Two other officers helped the medical crew remove the body.

"The luggage guys. Look," said Becca.

No sooner had the police disappeared into the station

with the bookseller than one of the two porters left the luggage cart and swiftly wove through the crowd after them. The other one got on his cell phone and turned toward the train.

"He's looking for us," said Wade. "Avert your faces."

In the chaos of incoming and outgoing passengers, Terence's actors positioned themselves in front of the six of them. The Kaplans descended and pretended to have just exited the train to stretch their legs, while the "mother" of the group handed Sara their new passports. Lily saw the second "railroad porter" hop on the train after the actors. Good. One less agent to deal with.

Roald guided them into the background, and they slipped inside the terminal, where Sara quickly distributed the new IDs.

"The Parkers are now the McKay family," she said. "I'm Theresa."

Darrell whipped his passport open. "Are you kidding me?"

Wade peeked over his shoulder. "Robin? Wow, bro, I'm sorry. I'm Ross. Robin and Ross. I kinda like Ross better."

Darrell hid the passport in his jeans. "We shall never speak of this again."

"Kids, be alert," Sara said.

Roald cautiously gathered them, and they hurried through the terminal and out onto the streets. Amid the bright glow and warmth of the blue coast, a kind of darkness seemed to pursue them like a cold, pale shadow.

CHAPTER ELEVEN

Novaya Zemlya, Kara Sea, Russia
June 4
Late morning

Konradin Ivanov hoisted his binoculars, looked out across the frozen sea, and wondered if he was alive. But how would he know? Being stationed in Novaya Zemlya froze the body and deadened the soul. He could have died weeks ago and not noticed.

Novaya Zemlya. The southernmost tip of the narrow crescent of earth was four hundred and fifty kilometers north of the Arctic Circle. Add another five hundred kilometers to get to where Konradin was now, and you were in a place that was useless, mindless, pathetically isolated, and stupid.

The Kara Sea surrounding it lay unthawed. It had been a bitterly cold spring, so even in June the sea around it was still a continent of ice. And yet he had received the sudden command: *Do it now.*

Annoying. But profitable. He and his men stood to make hundreds of thousands of rubles each for finding what the Order wanted. Luckily, he and Vitaly had anticipated something of the sort and arranged for an old ice drill to be delivered from Murmansk last week. It stood behind him now, groaning like a dying monster, waiting to chew up the frozen sea.

Wearing a thick polar anorak with a fur-lined hood, Konradin braced himself out of the wind, against a hut made of corrugated steel panels. Through his large pair of binoculars he scanned and scanned.

"Anything?" It was Vitaly Dershenko, like him a good soldier, also huddling pathetically from the cold, also dreaming of a big payday.

"Soon, Vitaly." Konradin spat, and the mucus froze on its way down and shattered into crystals—*clink*—on the ground at his feet. Just like in the tales of the Gulag. Not much had changed in seventy-five years.

"When we find it, are you going out to it?" Vitaly asked.

"I have to. The little German, von Braun, sent the order to me personally."

"Poor Konradin."

"And poor Vitaly. You're coming with me."

It was Vitaly's turn to spit. *Clink.*

The whole thing made him ill. Poison lurked beneath that frozen sea out there. The great Soviet nuclear test site that had become the great Soviet nuclear dumping ground.

"There?" said Vitaly, pointing his padded leather mitten due east.

Konradin adjusted the distance meter on his binoculars, and now, yes, he could see it. A faint vertical rod protruding from the ice a kilometer or so from shore.

"You always had good eyes, Vitaly."

Konradin turned and waved his hand. The monstrous engine behind him sent out a cough of smoke. Hiking up to the drill's cabin, he showed the driver where to go, gave him coordinates. Vitaly joined him in the cabin. The ground shook as the drill crawled like an enormous insect down to the shore, a half-dozen men with hand picks following on snowmobiles. The caravan moved slowly over the frozen sea to the spot and stopped. Konradin climbed down from the cabin with Vitaly, pointed to the ice, and waved to the driver. The drill lowered its head. The great shaft of steel met the surface of the ice and began to grind into it.

One hour later, the drill had struck steel. As the drill withdrew, Konradin sent a video camera down the shaft on a long wire. He turned the wire slowly, then pulled it back up. He replayed the video, pausing it fourteen seconds in.

The camera's screen bore the designation he had been told to look for.

K-27

Konradin Ivanov nudged his comrade. "Think about how you'll spend your money, Vitaly. Think about your family. Your children. Your new car."

CHAPTER TWELVE

Nice, France
June 4
Morning

Moments after the Kaplans left the rail terminal and entered the city streets of Nice, Wade heard his father's phone ring. He hoped it was Terence. He didn't want to spend any more time not knowing where he was going.

It was Terence.

"Dad, put it on speaker," he said.

"Hello, all," said Terence. "I heard about the fancy footwork at the station. Good job. Go directly to number five Rue de la Préfecture. It overlooks the Place du

Palais. I have two floors there; you'll be on the top one. The bookseller's been charged on suspicion of murder, which may eventually be reduced to manslaughter or self-defense. He's been taken to the Palais de Justice, the police headquarters in Nice's old quarter, which is conveniently across the square from the apartment. I like it because I frequently need to talk with the police for my novels. Your cover stands right now, although, as always, that will change."

Wade's father gave them each a look. "We'll be careful."

"It's in our blood," Darrell added as they crossed a busy avenue and into a shady street that wandered south to the water.

"What about the document the bookseller stole in Paris?" Becca asked.

"Confiscated, most likely," Terence replied. "Paul Ferrere found out it's called the Voytsdorf Ledger. Why Galina wants it, we don't know yet. My man inside the police will look into it. Listen, I'll arrive later. I'm following up with Paul, but you need to know that he and his investigators are hearing about several accidents that took place around the same time as the plane crash in Poland. Galina's up to something."

"Besides the relics?" asked Roald.

"It seems so. I'll be there tomorrow afternoon to give you a full briefing. Julian is coming in from the States. Don't know his flight time. Until then." He signed off.

"I knew it," said Darrell as they wove toward the Place du Palais. "Galina is planning a massive operation. We're here just in time. In time for what, we don't have a clue, but we will. This won't end until it ends, and even then it won't end because there will be the next time and the—"

"Darrell, shh," said Lily. "My ears are tired. The rest of me is tired, too. There, Rue de la Préfecture, not a minute too soon. I need to decompress."

"Just don't decompose," Darrell said.

She looked at him. "What?"

"Nothing."

Terence's housekeeper, a severe woman in her sixties named Madame Cousteau, met them outside the apartment. Wade glanced at his watch. It had been, all told, a thirty-minute evasive walk from the station. Good to know. Using gestures and a few English words, supplemented by a conversation with Becca, the woman showed them into an open elevator with a wrought-iron gate across the front.

"Elegant," said Sara.

"Old," said the housekeeper.

Wade still wanted to grab Becca's bag from her and swing it up over his shoulder. He would never forget the horrifying moment Becca was wounded by Galina in the cave where they found their first relic. He couldn't see the scar, but Becca kept her bag tight against her side and wouldn't let it go.

"So the arm's getting better?" he asked.

"I've been on antibiotics off and on since they discovered toxin in the wound. I took my last dose in Paris last night." She shook the orange bottle soundlessly.

It seemed to Wade a really personal detail, though he wasn't sure why.

The Ackroyd safe flat in Nice was indeed large.

Besides taking up most of the top floor of the building, which gave it window views on three sides, it had a narrow balcony overlooking the bustling square. The *place* below was a short walk to the seaside promenade and a major boulevard, but far enough from both to be out of the crush of tourist throngs.

Madame Cousteau told them that the *quartier* also boasted restaurants and cafés on nearly every corner.

"I can't wait to try them," said Sara.

"But for you, only one."

"One?" said Roald. "But the food in Nice—"

The housekeeper shook her head. "Ground floor. Secure. No exceptions."

Wade shared a look with the others. "Well, food is food, right?"

"Not really," said Becca.

"I found my room," Lily said. She had walked into a small windowless room that resembled a well-stocked computer store. It was obviously Terence's office when he was there. There were lots of computers of all different sizes networked to a black box that could have been a steel-plated safe designed to withstand a direct bomb blast. It was a server.

"We can bring in a bed for you," Sara said with a laugh.

"You got that right," she said.

"No bed," said Madame Cousteau, wagging her finger at them. "Is Mr. Terence's office."

Knowing that the bookseller had been arrested and was in jail nearby, and after their jet lag and the impossible-to-sleep-in sleeper compartments on the train, not to mention a huge lunch prepared by Madame Cousteau, everyone eventually sank into their beds to take naps. Wade's turned into a deep, overnight sleep.

It was the next afternoon when he and everyone else finally felt alert enough to get to work.

While his father and stepmother were busy on several phones with Terence and Paul Ferrere, Wade spent two hours spread out at the dining room table with Becca, scouring the Leonardo parts of the diary.

Together, they found something new.

Facing the first "silver" page was one that appeared black, but seemed to have marks on the other side of it that were different from any writing on the previous page. "Becca," he said, "could this be another one of those double pages, like the cipher we discovered in San Francisco? A hidden page folds out and . . ."

Becca slid her fingernail in the gutter of the book as before, and an unseen page became visible. Drawn on it was a triangular grid of symbols. "Whoa!"

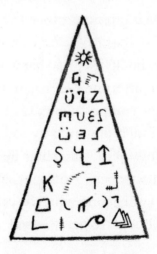

"Those aren't letters," said Wade. "At least not all of them are."

It reminded him a little of the Holbein puzzle they'd discovered in London. That code had been made of symbols describing alchemical processes.

"The column running down the left side looks kind of like letters," Becca said. "Under the sun there's a *G*, then a *U* with two dots—an umlaut—over it. The other characters could be some language I don't know."

"Let's take out the letters we can recognize," said Wade. Following the letters down the left-hand column, he wrote them down in his notebook.

G Ü M Ü Ş K O L

Becca frowned. "The umlauts could mean it's German, but the accent on the *S* isn't. Either way, I don't know what it means."

"Lily?" said Wade, looking around. But she was still in her room. "We could use a translator. Maybe Terence's office."

They found a laptop and started it up. After finding a translator site, Becca entered the letters. "Huh. The Detect Language button on the program says it's Turkish."

Darrell walked in, biting the end off a croissant.

"Turkish? From Turkey? Did Copernicus know Turkish?" He stuffed the rest of the croissant in his mouth.

"In Turkish it's two words," Wade said. "*GÜMÜŞ* and *KOL*. And *gümüş kol* means 'silver arm.'" He stared at Becca.

"'Silver arm'?" she whispered. "Is that what Leonardo made for Nicolaus in his workshop? The old woman in Tampa had silvery fingers. Everything's silver!"

"But does 'silver arm' *mean* anything?" said Darrell, leaning over the computer. "I mean, besides that I really want one?"

Wade keyed the words into the laptop's search engine. A few seconds later, the reference came back. He scanned it, felt his heart quicken.

"Okay. We have something here. There was a *pirate* nicknamed Silver Arm. A Barbary pirate from North Africa. He had a silver arm because he lost his real one in a battle. His name was Baba Aruj, and he was one of two pirate brothers called Barbarossa, because they had . . . Becca, they had red beards! Red beards!"

Becca screamed as she flipped back several pages in the diary. "The first passage that Lily and I read! So this pirate Barbarossa friend of Nicolaus's had a silver arm . . ."

"I don't want one if I have to lose my real one," said Darrell.

Wade stood up from the desk. "So Copernicus asks Leonardo da Vinci to be a Guardian. Leo says, 'No, I'm too old.' But he agrees to make a thing to hide the relic in. What he makes is an arm—out of silver—for a pirate who saved Hans's life during a battle. And this is where Copernicus puts the relic, whatever it actually is. The relic is inside the arm."

He turned to Becca and Darrell. "Is this right?"

Becca began to nod slowly. "I think so. But you know what else? I'm thinking that because this story appears in the diary right after the Serpens story, whatever relic is in the silver arm is the one that Serpens points to."

Wade sat down in front of the laptop again. "Yes. Which could mean that Galina has a head start on it. But she doesn't have the diary to tell her some important details, so we could be even with her."

Darrell loved it, the way that things connected one to another and another. Even if they didn't know yet what the relic actually was, they were assembling the mystery. He had to tell Lily. Her room door was closed, but he went over to it and was ready to knock when he heard her voice through the door.

She was on the phone, talking quietly. To her parents? He voice was very soft. And . . . choked. Was she

97

crying? Lily never cried. He pulled away and went back to the dining room, where Wade and Becca were still at it, sewing up their discovery into a package that worked. They were good at that. He wasn't so much. Was Lily actually crying? He paced the dining room, then found himself walking all over the apartment, peeking in all the rooms, his brain methodically determining escape routes and memorizing the position of all the doors and windows. When he finally came back to the dining room, Lily was there. Her eyes were normal, not red. Maybe he was wrong. Maybe he didn't know anything.

"Guess what," he said, glancing at her, but not too long. "There's another elevator, a private one, in the back of the apartment. I think it takes you all the way down to the street and lets you out on the back side of the building—"

"You not take it," said the housekeeper, suddenly appearing from nowhere.

"I didn't!" Darrell said. "I won't. You can just tell from the buttons where it goes." Afraid of the woman's dark stare, he escaped out onto the balcony.

The sky was a giant royal-blue dome, marbled here and there with a light scrim of clouds. The quaint orange- and red-tiled rooftops spread out around the square in varying heights on all sides. Beyond them was the great inviting expanse of the sea.

"So . . ." It was Lily, stepping out next to him but looking away, out over the water. He couldn't see her eyes.

"Everything okay?" he asked, being sensitive.

"Sure. What are we looking at out here?"

"France," he said. "Strange you don't know that."

"Ha. Ha. Did you hear what Wade and Becca found? It's big." She brushed her cheeks.

"I know," he said. "You're sure you're okay?"

"I'm good," she said in a way that ended that line of conversation. "So, this is France, huh?"

"The French Mediterranean," said Becca, coming out onto the terrace with Wade behind her. Both of them were glowing about the discovery of Copernicus and Leonardo and the silver-armed pirate.

"All the way to the right is the rest of the French Riviera, then Spain," Becca went on. "On the left is more France, then Italy. Straight ahead on the other side of the water is, if you can believe it, Africa. *Africa!* Where the Barbarossa brothers lived their pirate life."

"Barb One and Barb Two," said Lily.

"Exactly," Becca said. "Of course, every bit of this was Roman Empire at one time. There are Roman ruins and a famous amphitheater not far from here—"

"Bringggg!" said Lily. "History class is over. I actually like what Darrell said better. This is France. And you know what? We should eat French food at a French restaurant. It's practically dinnertime. Somebody ate the absolute last croissant, there's nothing left in the fridge except cheese, and I'm hungry for more than cheese. I've never been so hungry. Madame Cousteau didn't shop today, and all I can think of is the food they give you on the train, which is not actually food but a kind of recycled wood chips with gravy, and of course you eat it because you don't want to starve to death in your compartment, but then later—like exactly later enough to be the farthest away from any kind of bathroom—you realize that wasn't food, but it's already way too late. Right, Bec? I mean, I'm right, right? You didn't like your wood chips, either, right?"

Becca stared at her. "I did not."

Maybe the phone call was all right after all, thought Darrell. Lily's up, happy, maybe a little over the top, but that's so much better than not having her here at all. Holy cow, what would *that* be like?

Sara insisted that they go to the downstairs restaurant and bring the *charming* housekeeper with them. "We'll be down a little later, as soon as Roald finishes this last phone call. The café is open in front," she said, "so you can see the square, but it has a back room where you can eat privately."

"As long as they have French food," said Lily.

"They do," said Roald, cupping his hand over his phone. "Look, the Teutonic Order will know by now that we didn't continue to Rome. You know what to do."

They did. It was a way of life now. The kids took the public elevator with the housekeeper, who seemed to be liking them less with each passing hour.

The Place du Palais de Justice, which the apartment overlooked, was a public square free of cars. On three sides were restaurants, on the fourth an imposing classical building that could have been anything from a library to a bank but turned out to be the Palais de Justice.

The café in the building was exactly as Sara had described it. The back room was secure, but it had a full view of the square outside through a wall of mirrored glass. Madame Cousteau stood guard at the doorway like a statue.

"This is the life," Becca said, relaxing into a chair next to the two-way mirror. "I can't believe we're actually here. Two days ago, Lily and I were in a motel in Florida. Look at us now, about to order French food in France."

A waiter in a long white apron slid between the tables to them. *"Oui, messieurs, mademoiselles. Que voudriez-vous commander aujourd'hui?"*

They ordered two grilled ham-and-cheese sandwiches of the kind called *croque-monsieur*, two authentic *salades niçoises*, and four Orangina soft drinks. The cold drinks arrived first, the food after ten or so minutes. Lily proclaimed that food had never tasted so good, "or so real!"

While they ate, the sun slowly lowered in the sky, and a cooler breeze swept across the square and into the café. Here and there lights came on, windows twinkled, and soon the open part of the café was blue with late-afternoon shadow. The waiters began to light candles on the tables. Wade realized that his father and stepmother hadn't joined them. He got out his phone.

"Don't spoil it," said Becca. He didn't make the call.

"Excusez-moi," said Lily, and she went off down a corridor to find the restrooms. Becca went, too. Madame Cousteau followed them.

"She's like a ghost, that lady, shadowing us everywhere," said Wade. "I kind of like it. I wouldn't like to be the bad guy that meets her."

"However, as usual, grown-ups don't like us much."

Wade nodded. "Well, you."

Darrell scanned the menu again. "I completely admit that. My question now is, what's a *profiterole*? Second question: Should I be getting one? It sounds French and gooey. Is it? Well, it's probably French. But is it gooey? I feel like something gooey."

"You look like something goo—" Wade's phone buzzed. He swiped it on. "It's from Dad." On the screen was a series of numbers. "Coordinates. Why doesn't he just tell me?" He plugged the numbers into his GPS app.

The screen showed a map. He zeroed in on it. It was an image of that very square, the plaza outside their café. The coordinates identified a table under an umbrella at a bistro on the far side of the square.

"What is it . . . ?"

"That's what I'm asking," said Darrell. "Is a *profiterole* a kind of *roll*?"

Wade stood up from the table and stared through the mirrored window across the square to the exact spot the coordinates pointed to. Suddenly, the skin on the back of his neck began to prickle. His blood pounded in his ears.

"No . . . no . . . no . . ."

"No, what?" said Darrell. "It's not how you pronounce it?"

"No . . ." was all that Wade could manage to say.

"Yeah, you see, that kind of answer doesn't help—"

"Robin, stand up and look!"

Staring straight across the Place du Palais, Wade had spotted a face he'd hoped he would never see again.

CHAPTER THIRTEEN

D arrell grumbled. Wade was doing it again: not saying the thing, but just pointing his face at it. Still, in the interest of stepbrotherhood he paused on his quest for dessert and followed Wade's weird stare across the Place du Palais.

Fifteen or twenty small round tables were scattered under a café awning. Looking beyond them, he spied the table Wade's eyes were fixed on. Two men sat at it. One had his head down, reading the menu like Darrell had wanted to do.

The other . . . the other wore wraparound sunglasses.

"I can't believe it!"

"No kidding."

The man in sunglasses—this particular man in sunglasses, code-named Sunglasses—had tried to kill them about a hundred times. Worse, he had nearly incinerated Lily and Wade. Worse than worse, he had kidnapped Darrell's mother in Bolivia, then flown her to Europe and finally to Russia.

In a coffin.

After Markus Wolff, Sunglasses was the scariest person they'd ever met. And the person Darrell most wanted to . . . to . . . never mind. But it was grim.

"Mom must be freaking out," he whispered.

"Is he here because of us?" said Wade. "Does he know we followed the bookseller? He's good, but we've been so careful."

When Lily and Becca returned with the frowning housekeeper, Darrell told them. "Look over there, but don't look like you're looking."

"No one can see us," said Becca. "Mirrored walls."

Lily seemed to shiver from her head to her feet. "Oh my gosh, I hate that creep. Let me go over there and pour hot café au lait over his head."

The man sitting next to Sunglasses lifted his face. It was the taller of the two fake porters from the train station yesterday. Instead of a jumpsuit and work cap he wore dark pants, a green polo shirt, and a narrow-brimmed straw tourist hat.

"This is no coincidence," Darrell said. "Sunglasses is after us again."

Sara entered the café from a side door. She now wore a green sundress and matching sun hat. The moment she actually laid eyes on the man who had kidnapped her, she turned red in the face. But she kept her rage down. "We spotted him from the balcony upstairs and sent the coordinates. Terence was delayed. He should be in Nice soon. He told us his police friend said to expect something we wouldn't like."

"What won't we like more than we don't like Sunglasses?" asked Lily.

"That."

Sara nodded toward the staircase outside the entrance of the Palais. Two policemen emerged from the building and hurried down the broad stairs to the plaza, holding a small man by the arms.

"Oskar Gerrenhausen," said Darrell.

"Do you think they're going to take him to prison?" asked Lily.

Becca shook her head. "That's not how they do it, is it? Not out the front door and right in the street like this. Don't tell me they're going to—"

"They're letting him go," Darrell said. "He's not even

wearing zip cuffs. You can't go killing people, even in self-defense, and then just get set free so soon."

"Not without help," said Lily.

"And we all know who helped him," said Wade. "And who sent Sunglasses to be his bodyguard."

The two police officers paused at the bottom of the stairs, spoke with the bookseller for two or three minutes, handed him his messenger bag, then stepped back. They nodded in unison and hustled back up the stairs without him.

Gerrenhausen rubbed his wrists and loosened his shirt collar.

Darrell blew out a quick angry breath. "Galina has agents inside the French police. No more zip cuffs for this guy."

"Zip cuffs. Zip cuffs," said Lily. "What even are they?"

"Look 'em up," said Darrell.

"You bet I will."

Gerrenhausen adjusted his spectacles and scanned the tables at the café to his left. The railroad porter raised his hand. Soon the three men were sitting together, their backs to the Kaplans, drinking from tiny cups.

"I wish we had a bug at that table," said Becca.

The three men spoke closely to one another for a

while, then rose to their feet.

"They're leaving," said Wade. "Sara, can we see where they go?"

"From a long distance," she said. "With all of you behind me."

They hovered inside the café until the three men left their table. Gerrenhausen passed over his messenger bag to the porter, who mounted a motorbike that was parked nearby and took off in one direction, while he and Sunglasses left the square together and walked the opposite way, south toward the beach.

"Becca, come with me," said Sara. "The rest of you meet us back at the flat."

"Mom, I don't know," said Darrell. "I think we should tag along."

"All right, but keep far out of sight," she said sternly.

"But why me?" Becca asked.

"The bookseller didn't see you on the train, at least not face-to-face," Sara said, pulling her hat low. "And in case we get near enough to hear something, you can translate. Maybe we can find out where they're going."

"Not into Galina's secret lair, I hope," said Becca.

The two followed Sunglasses and the bookseller for several blocks to Promenade des Anglais, the wide, bustling avenue that ran by the beach. They walked on the inland side of the street for a little while, when Sunglasses tugged a set of keys from his pocket and pressed an alarm release. A sleek silver Mercedes nearby gave out a subtle *beep-beep*, and its doors automatically lifted from the body of the car, slowly, like a pair of wings.

The men spoke for a while before getting in.

Becca snapped several pictures of the car, including the license plate, then had an idea. "Sara, without a ride, we're going to lose them. We need to get closer."

"Becca, don't you dare—"

But she slipped away and moved quickly out of whisper range. It was an odd thing to do. She was the least adventurous of them all and hated to disobey Sara. On the other hand, she'd gone five centuries into the past and returned to talk about it, so she could obviously handle herself. She ducked past several pedestrians, moving as close as she dared, but could hear nothing of their conversation. The street noise was too loud.

Then another idea. Hoping the computer setup in Terence's apartment was really as hard-core as it looked, she switched on her phone's recorder and while they weren't looking lobbed the phone into a nearby trash barrel, hoping it wouldn't fall into something wet.

The men spoke—in what sounded like German—for

another minute or so, then slid into their seats, and the doors folded back down into the car. With a great roar, the Mercedes squealed away from the curb.

By the time Becca rushed over and picked the phone out of the barrel—it was dry—the car was lost in traffic.

"Oh, Becca," Sara said. "That was just so—"

"I know. Super dumb."

"Yes, but brilliant!"

CHAPTER FOURTEEN

Geneva, Switzerland
June 5
Six hours earlier

A squat, middle-aged, balding gentleman in a light-weight gray suit, blue shirt, and red tie walked out of his apartment at 7 Rue Sismondi in Geneva and met a squat, middle-aged, balding gentleman in a light-weight gray suit, blue shirt, and red tie.

The first man was the physicist Dr. Marin Petrescu, who had recently been named director-general of CERN, the European Organization for Nuclear Research. He stared at the second man. "Who the devil are you?"

The second man, whose name was Johann, or

perhaps Esteban, was an employee of the Teutonic Order and said nothing. His chief qualification for this encounter were his height, weight, and facial construction.

"This is ridiculous!" Dr. Petrescu protested, trying to step away from the second man. "I have a meeting to attend. My car is waiting. Let me pass."

Petrescu then performed a neat twirl on his heels and pushed past the other man, making for the corner around which his private car and driver, François, usually waited. Before he got to the corner, however, he was pulled off the pavement by two large men in ski masks; then he was bound and gagged and dragged into a black van that drove up at that moment. At the same time, his impersonator entered the director-general's private car, his head bowed. In a reasonable imitation of Dr. Petrescu's voice he said, "Drive around the lake, François. To Montreux."

His driver flicked his eyes to the rearview mirror just as the divider rolled up. "Sir, that is two hours, round-trip. You'll miss your meeting, Dr. Petrescu."

"It will wait," his passenger said.

"But . . . two hours?"

"To Montreux, François."

* * *

Galina Krause stared at the bewildered man in the back of the van. Her agents were moving across the globe to effect Operation Aurora. One aim of the operation—a major one—was dependent upon the cooperation of Dr. Petrescu.

The van motored slowly away from Rue Sismondi and took a left at Rue de Berne, which after several name changes finally became the Route de Meyrin.

She loosened the gag and let him spout his outrage.

"What is this? Who are you? Are you kidnapping me? No one will pay a ransom. I have no family, and no one will pay. My organization is instructed to ignore the demands of terrorists. You will not receive a single euro from killing me. You are committing a serious crime. Let me out at once! I repeat—"

Dr. Petrescu was indeed a man without a family. He was a man without a life, which made him fearless regarding his own safety. A man without fear must be convinced in other ways.

"You do not recognize me, do you, Doctor?"

His response was swift and dismissive. "I do not memorize the faces of terrorists."

"Doctor, this van will soon arrive at the CERN laboratories. I have two demands. First—"

"Never!" he interrupted her. "Whatever it is—never!"

"First, I will attend the meeting you have scheduled at CERN headquarters in five days' time."

"Meeting? What meeting? There is no meeting. And if there were, I would certainly not—"

"I understand that you are planning to inform the attendees at your secret meeting about certain temporal disturbances your instruments have discovered. That you have chosen your attendees for their expertise in atomic physics. That you can prove the existence of a rogue group undertaking experiments in time travel."

"How can you possibly know . . ." Dr. Petrescu paused. He scanned her face like a painter preparing to render a portrait. "Those eyes . . . that scar . . . I have seen you before. . . ."

"Three years ago. I was sixteen. I asked you then for access to your laboratories, to Project ICARUS, to the Obelisk Papers. You dismissed me with a wave of your hand."

"You are she! Galina Krause. Your organization of thugs and hoodlums—"

"You will not dismiss me now, Doctor. For my second request, I require complete and unrestricted access to your facilities and equipment in Meyrin and at your partner laboratories. I will need your data on every project, including DarkSide-Fifty, OPERA, the others, as well as your access to the intelligence services of world governments—"

"I cannot be blackmailed!" He laughed a hollow, frightened laugh. "Murder me, go ahead. I will never give you such access. You don't belong in a laboratory. You belong in an asylum! You are mad, little girl. Mad!"

Galina smiled as she pulled her phone from her pocket. "Let us see how mad I am, shall we, Doctor? Do you know what this is?"

She opened her phone to an image taken inside a Soviet submarine long buried in the arctic ice.

K-27

His eyes grew wide. "How did you . . . You are toying with nuclear disaster!"

"This warhead is one of several I am gathering," she said. "Tell a soul, a single soul, and I will detonate it and flood countless coastal cities. Believe me, Dr. Petrescu. It is not my wish. I will be present at your meeting in

Geneva. I will speak with your guests at the conference. I will have access to your research."

"No! No! I demand to be let go! I demand—"

Galina slid the gag roughly over his twisting mouth. As she had expected, this was not the visit that would change his mind. This was merely to prime him for the next time they spoke. Dr. Petrescu would soon discover how quickly his estimation of her changed from "mad" to "she who would change his world forever."

She turned to the driver.

"Drop the good doctor back home. Then drive me south to the Côte d'Azur."

One thousand thirty kilometers northeast of Geneva, if anyone were paying attention, he might have seen Marius Linzmaier, the driver of a gray, oversize, and somewhat beat-up delivery truck, depart Schwarzsee, Galina Krause's lakeside estate in the forests northeast of Berlin, and travel south.

The truck was loosely accompanied by three large old vans, one in front and two following, but all hundreds of yards apart. It barely looked as if there was any connection among them. There was.

All four trucks carried what Marius could only call "strange cargo" and were attended by thirty-five knights of the Teutonic Order, not including Marius's odd front-seat passenger. In addition, the convoy was on a strict timetable. They were to arrive at their destination at one p.m. Central European time on Tuesday the tenth, five days from today. Their first stop was Vestec, south of Prague in the Czech Republic, to pick up more strange cargo.

In the truck's passenger seat, with his eyes trained coldly on the gray road ahead, sat a cold brick of a man in the uniform of a colonel from some indistinct Southeast Asian paramilitary group.

He said nothing as the truck gained speed.

CHAPTER FIFTEEN

B y the time Wade and the others met up with Sara
and Becca, then ran together back to the apartment on the Place du Palais, his father was deep in the
middle of a private conversation on the phone—Wade
didn't know who with. However, Terence had finally
arrived and was firing up the computers in his study.
After hearing about the photos and the recording, he
took Becca's phone and attached a USB cord to it.

"Bad news, I'm afraid," he said. "The results of our
investigation into Olsztyn Castle reveal that the plane
crash there was one of at least seven similar accidents through Poland, Germany, and Slovenia at the
beginning of April. All the sites are associated with

Copernicus's life in one way or another."

Sara frowned. "Not relics? Galina hasn't found more relics?"

He shook his head. "We don't believe so. But here's the thing that's worrying. Excavation equipment was present at all seven sites."

"Galina is digging for something," said Becca.

Sara nodded, keeping an eye on Wade's father in the other room. "She's started on some big operation. We'll need to find out what it is."

Wade loved that his stepmother was so completely into the hunt for the relics. He shared a look with Darrell and found the same sense of awe on his face.

"Oh, man," Lily murmured when Becca's photos of the sleek silver Mercedes flashed on Terence's monitor. "Evil guys get the best cars."

Terence tapped the mouse and an array of audio controls appeared.

"Do you think you can get anything from Becca's recording?" Darrell asked.

"I'm certainly going to try," he said, donning a pair of headphones. "Applying a series of filters should isolate ambient sounds, leaving only voices. Julian built this software. He'll be here later today, by the way, with a report about your folks, Becca. And yours, Lily."

"Really?" she said. "Thanks."

"Julian will be great, and we can use the help," said Wade, peeking in the other room, where his father was listening intently to someone on the other end of the phone.

"All right," said Terence, "tell me if this makes any sense to you." He unplugged the headphones and turned up the speakers.

Becca's recording was a babel of odd noises, clunks, traffic, and garbled voices. They heard the whoosh and pop of wind, what could have been seagulls, the roar of buses. After several final adjustments, Terence canceled most of the conflicting sounds. "If this actually works, it's going into my next novel."

There it was at last—a dull rumble of background noise, then four words—three from Gerrenhausen, one from Sunglasses.

"Brille . . . Silber tinte . . ."

"Carlo . . ."

"Gerrenhausen is speaking in German," said Becca. "Can we play it again?"

They played the recording several times, just to be sure they had heard everything. They had. No other intelligible words came from the recording.

"*Spectacles, silver ink,* and *Carlo,*" said Becca.

"They can't be talking about the ink used in the diary," said Sara, "because they don't have the diary. So there must be silver ink somewhere else."

"On the ledger that Gerrenhausen stole, maybe?" said Wade.

"Or the silver arm?" said Lily. "No, you don't read arms."

"Unless they're tattooed," said Darrell.

"Helpful. Really."

"Well, what about Carlo?" Darrell said. "Do we think it's *our* Carlo? You said the old woman in Tampa said his name, too."

"*And* she had silver ink on her fingers," said Becca. "We know that Carlo and the diary are connected, but 'spectacles'? We can't read the silver pages. Maybe there are special glasses to read them . . . I don't know. Lily?"

"Yeah, X-ray glasses," she said. "They'd be good."

Terence stood from the computer. "Allow me to suggest a simpler explanation for 'Carlo.' In this part of the world, it may simply mean Monte Carlo, a city twenty kilometers east of us."

"Right. The playground of the super wealthy," said Sara. "I've heard stories." She turned to Darrell. "It's a bit of a spy capital, too."

He grinned. "I'm ready."

"So . . ." Wade stood now. His father was still on the phone in the other room. *What is it about? He'll tell us.* "So . . . Oskar Gerrenhausen steals something called the Voytsdorf Ledger from a dealer in Paris. A guy on the train tries to steal it from him, but Gerrenhausen kills him. Now we hear that there might be—*might* be—glasses that help with the ledger. And the bookseller and Sunglasses are going to Monte Carlo for them. Is that right?"

Sara listened. Pressing her lips together, she nodded. "We may as well make the leap. Let's assume that the silver ink the bookseller is talking about is the same silver ink used in the diary. And both of them have to do with the old woman's silver fingers, the pirate's silver arm, and the relic we think is inside it."

"Then we should go to Monte Carlo to see what we find," Wade said, looking at the others, then at his father, still on the phone. "Does everybody think so? It's not like we have a lot of other leads."

He heard the click of the phone. When his father entered the computer room, his face was grim.

"Who were you talking to?" Sara asked.

"Partly talking, mostly listening to a message over and over, a very puzzling and encrypted message," he said, rattling a paper. "I finally worked it out."

"From who?" Darrell asked.

"Dr. Petrescu. He's changing everything about the secret meeting. It's not going to be in five days. Instead, he wants me and several other physicists to come immediately. But not to CERN headquarters in Geneva. He's asked me go to Gran Sasso, their partner laboratory in Italy. Petrescu is afraid, and he knows something about what we've been up to. He's taking all kinds of precautions."

"Roald, maybe you shouldn't go at all," said Sara. "It could be a trap."

He stood on the balcony, looking out, then turned back. "I don't think it's a trap. I mean, not one that he's setting. I don't know. But I think it's even more urgent that I attend. I don't know exactly what it's all about, but given the Uncle Henry connection, we know it concerns Galina and the Order. Whatever Petrescu knows, it's big enough to take these extra steps. I have to go."

Terence paced the living room, rubbing his forehead. "I rather agree with Sara here. Something's fishy about this change of time and place. Geneva is very public; Gran Sasso is quite the opposite. Roald, I'd like to go with you, if you don't mind. Just to make sure of security. Forewarned is forearmed, as they say. Maybe ask

Paul Ferrere to come along as backup. *And* we absolutely should go now, to case it out as much as we possibly can before we go into the laboratory. Sara, what do you say I send Julian to Monte Carlo as soon as he gets in from the airport? He'll contact you there. I'll go with you, Roald."

Wade's heart thudded. He didn't like having his father going off somewhere away from the rest of them. He felt he had to watch over his father as much as he knew his father watched over them. He watched his stepmother's eyes narrow to pinpoints. She wouldn't stop his father from going, not really, if Galina was involved, but she was processing what it might mean.

She went up to his father and, in front of all of them, kissed him. They held each other for a long time. But it wasn't uncomfortable—for Wade or, he realized, for anyone else. They were all bound in a strong way, as a family, and as Guardians.

"Take care of yourselves," she said finally. "And you, sir, better call me every ten minutes."

His father smiled at her. "Maybe every half hour."

She brushed tears from her eyes. "Okay, then. All right."

All right? Maybe. But a key team member was being ripped out of the lineup. Wade didn't like it and said so.

"I know," his father replied. "It's not good. It's not the best. But this is the way we live now." He paused, as if choosing whether to say what he was thinking. He did anyway.

"I hate what's happening to us. Sara does, too. It's not normal for people as young as you to live this way. Fearing and distrusting so many people. But then, our lives aren't normal. Not since Uncle Henry died."

"Was murdered," said Darrell.

Wade's father's face went dark, distant. "Yes, was murdered."

But we're still kids. Wade wanted his father to know that. They hadn't been ruined by the weird life they were leading, not yet. They were still hopeful, if that was the right word. They had gotten closer to one another in a way that was hard to define, maybe, but it was a good thing. Sure, the world was dangerous; at least *their* world was. And it was just common sense to be on the alert. It didn't have to mean that you lost hope. If anything, you celebrated good people and things more when you *did* find them. That was what he wanted to say.

What he came up with was simpler.

"We'll be okay, Dad. You have to be, too."

His father hugged him and Darrell and Sara tightly

after that. A long minute or two. No words. And that was it. Their new style of reunions and good-byes. Back to business. Find the next relic.

"I'll ring for the car," said Terence.

CHAPTER SIXTEEN

The airport nearest to the Gran Sasso laboratory in Italy was Fiumicino in Rome, also known as Leonardo da Vinci airport—which, Darrell concluded, "totally means we're on the right track."

Wade wasn't sure of anything just yet, but he'd long ago given up on the idea of coincidence. Everything meant something.

Just after a cab came to take Roald and Terence a few miles west to the Nice airport, a pristine and roomy 1972 four-door Citroën DS Super 5 appeared in front of the apartment. The car was black, shiny, long, and low, with huge windows and bug-eye headlights. A driver hopped out, leaving his door open.

"For Mrs. Sara to drive," he said. "To Monte Carlo—"

"Shotgun!" said Darrell, settling in next to his mother as she slid behind the wheel, with Wade, Lily, and Becca piling into the roomy backseat. After accustoming herself to the dashboard, Sara pushed the car into gear, and they set off for Monte Carlo.

It was going on six p.m., and the traffic in the thick of Nice lessened slightly when they took the main road to the east. It curved up from the outskirts of the city's waterfront and climbed away into the foothills. Wade could see the wandering coast, lit up against the dark water.

"It's been a while since we saw the Mercedes," said Becca. "It could be anywhere at this point. We might have lost it forever."

"Or we could be incredibly lucky," said Darrell. "I vote for lucky."

Sara sped along as quickly as speed limits would allow. More than once, she was forced to stop short as vehicles lumbered carelessly onto the road from driveways hidden on the right. One tiny car popped out from a villa, nearly hurling them off the road into a mess of jagged rock and pine trees.

"Geez, French people, get a license!" Lily shouted out the window.

"Can you imagine a car chase on this road?" said Wade.

"And now you did it!" Darrell groaned. "You pretty much just *asked* to be in a high-speed car chase on the skinniest road known to man. Nice job, Wade."

"That's soooo . . ." Wade started, but stopped. "Actually, it'd be fun."

"Not with me driving, thank you," said Sara.

Darrell grinned. "It would be fun! Like I said, nice job."

"There's a faster road," Becca said, scanning a road map on her phone. "The left after the next one will take us up onto a freeway. We'll make better time."

"Good call." Sara smoothly exited the slow coast road, and they were soon motoring far more quickly on the highway.

After a while, Lily, who had been quietly tapping away on her tablet, cleared her throat. "I've been searching on all kinds of image and language sites, and I think I found something about the tattoo, if your sketch is right, Wade."

"It is," he said. "Of course, I'm no da Vinci."

"I should have traced it," said Darrell. He never let anyone forget that he traced very well. "But I don't trace tattoos. Too icky."

Lily shot him a look. "Anyway, the symbol you saw—an *O* with lines coming into it—seems to be very close to a letter from an old runic Hungarian alphabet. I can't find any secret society that uses it as a symbol, but it's a corporate logo belonging to a company called Drangheta Enterprises, a shipping company run by a rich guy named Ugo Drangheta. They do lots of stuff, but mainly shipping."

"Ugo Drangheta," said Darrell. "By 'rich' let's assume he's super rich, and has armies of tattooed assassins doing his dirty work, which means this quest just went up a notch on the danger scale."

Wade turned to him. "Armies? No one said 'armies.' And 'danger scale'?"

"I just invented it."

Becca cleared her throat. "Lil, the triangle with the fives in it is a gift that keeps on giving. I just found another passage. I really thought I'd found them all, but listen to this."

In the workshop of the Milanese master we sit by candlelight. He first presents me with a pair of cryptologic lenses, then fashions the silver arm.

Appropriately, the relic, a three-sided mirror, a prism of silvery light, is to be the arm's internal engine. He uses

leather gloves to keep the starry prism from burning his
fingers. He crafts the arm so that the prism powers it.

"I know what a prism is," said Darrell. "I can't picture a three-sided mirror."

"Unless it's like the kind you see in a dressing room
where you can see behind you and on the sides at the
same time," said Lily. "Maybe?"

"Cryptologic lenses could be a way of describing
spectacles," said Sara.

"Yes, good." Wade pulled out from his backpack
the leather binder he kept his antique star chart in. He
removed the chart. It glistened with gold and silver ink.

"Copernicus says it's 'appropriately' three-sided,"
he said. "There's a constellation called Triangulum.
It's formed by the narrow triangle of its three brightest
stars. It's between Andromeda and Aries in the northern sky."

"Leonardo was fascinated by mirrors late in life,"
said Sara, downshifting in heavier traffic. "In his villa
at Clos Lucé he was supposed to have had a whole workshop devoted to his study of mirrors and their qualities.
And their powers."

"That could be it," said Wade. "There have been a lot
of triangles in the clues so far. I wonder if the relic is

simply Triangulum. . . ."

"Mom, take the next exit," said Darrell.

They headed south toward the coast again. The narrow walled roadway was bordered by terraced hillsides, sprinkled with red tile roofs and marble steps on one side and daggerlike pines on the other. At last, the road wound down through the hills, past a handful of small villages, to the glittering coast of Monte Carlo, another magnificent jewel on the Mediterranean.

Magnificent, sure.

But Wade couldn't forget that they'd followed a pair of killers there.

CHAPTER SEVENTEEN

Monte Carlo was tiny, and Lily found the evening streets crushingly jammed.

There was an irritating backup at every intersection. Pedestrians swarmed across the road whenever they wanted. And not only did it appear that somebody had just polished every surface in the town, but the gull-wing Mercedes she'd thought so distinctive was one of about a billion high-end sports cars cruising the pinchingly narrow streets.

So they had no lead at all, other than a hope that five sets of eyes scouring every single street would spot something.

"Let's drive around a bit," Sara said.

"And look for silver cars," Becca added.

"Silver Mercedeses," said Darrell.

Unlike Nice, with its broad, elegant seaside, the Principality of Monaco—of which Monte Carlo was the main part—was compact, built all the way up a surrounding ridge of hillsides, at the base of which stood a U-shaped harbor overflowing with mega-yachts.

"If you can believe it, they race cars on these skinny streets," said Darrell.

"And now *you* did it," said Wade. "We'll be racing around in no time."

Darrell wiggled his eyebrows. "You're welcome."

They cruised the streets slowly for the next half hour or so, until Sara pulled the car over. "This is pointless," she said. "For all we know, they're driving around, too. We could be a street ahead of or behind Sunglasses and the bookseller, but we'll never catch up to them. I don't know what to do."

Then Julian called.

Darrell snapped up his mother's phone and put it on speaker.

"Guys, I think I know why Gerrenhausen's in Monte Carlo. Meet me up at Casino Square, and hurry. It starts in an hour." He clicked off.

Hearing his voice, a kind of whispered excitement,

Lily's senses jangled. Normally, they were being watched, pursued, hounded by the Order's agents. But since they'd shadowed Sunglasses and Gerrenhausen in Nice, something new was taking shape. They were going on the offensive. They were tailing one of the most dangerous agents in the Order and a little murderous bookseller. The Order hadn't spotted them yet, and they had to keep it that way.

"Casino Square," she said. "I saw a sign. It's up the hill past the harbor."

Sara motored up a long curving road from the harbor and into what Julian had called Casino Square, a collection of grand stucco buildings at least a hundred and fifty years old, nestled around an ornamental public garden. Julian waved them down from an open parking space on the street in front of the baroque wedding cake itself, the Casino de Monte-Carlo.

Julian really looked like his father, Lily thought, which made her wonder what his mother was like. She had died when he was little and living in Myanmar. Obviously, she must have been pretty. *What? Never mind. I'm tired.*

"Julian, man, good to see you," said Darrell, slipping out and doing a boy handshake with him. Wade did the same. Julian's small vintage Fiat sports car—Darrell identified it as a 1962 Spyder—was parked between a Maserati and a Maserati. There sure was a lot of money in the South of France, she thought.

Julian flicked his finger at another wedding cake, sitting perpendicular to the casino. "The Hôtel de Paris is hosting an auction of fifteenth- and sixteenth-century books, manuscripts, and artifacts. I'm willing to bet that Gerrenhausen is here in his official capacity as an antiquarian to purchase something for Galina."

"Something we probably also want," said Becca.

"No doubt," said Julian. "I've been here for about thirty minutes. I took a stroll inside the hotel, helped pad the desk clerk's wallet. Neither Gerrenhausen nor Cassa has appeared yet, but I'm hoping they will."

"Cassa?" said Sara. "You mean Sunglasses?"

"Sorry. His name's Bartolo Cassa. He's Spanish. Been with the Order for the last three years. Galina recruited him in South America. Which is why he was assigned to . . . you."

Sara darkened. "It doesn't help, knowing his name."

"He'll pay someday," said Darrell. "He will."

"Look!" Lily gasped. "The Mercedes. Ha! I am such a homing device."

The silver Mercedes rolled to a stop in front of the hotel. The passenger door swung up. The bookseller got out, and the door lowered behind him. Sunglasses—Cassa—tore away from the curb around the back of the building.

Oskar Gerrenhausen stood on the sidewalk, checking the time on his wristwatch. Then he spun on his heels and walked nimbly up into the lobby.

"Okay, everybody listen." Sara collected them behind a large tree. "We have to assume that both Sunglasses—Bartolo Cassa—and the bookseller either know we're here or will soon. It's only a matter of time. We have to stay out of sight, no exceptions. Even you, Julian. So let's be smart. Come on."

"Wait a second," said Julian. "Cassa didn't use the hotel's valet parking, but he surely won't leave the bookseller here alone. To me, this means he's parking the car himself and may come back this way on foot. We can't have him stumbling on you from behind. Maybe I should wait here and text you if I see him return, stall him if I can."

"Good idea," said Sara.

"Don't do anything brave," said Becca. "He's a creep."

"I heard."

Sara looked around and spotted a loose group of tourists crossing the square. "We go with them. Pretend

like you're with them, but don't draw attention to yo
selves. Come on."

Three minutes later, they had crossed the darkening
square and were inside the Hôtel de Paris.

CHAPTER EIGHTEEN

Wade breathed in a soft gasp when they entered the lobby. "Whoa . . ."

"Uh, yeah," said Darrell.

The room flashed with the brilliance of a million chandeliers. Massive columns held up a very high ceiling that was painted blue and gold with hundreds of chubby baby angels flying from corner to corner. The slick marble floors reminded Wade of a museum's, except for the constant rumbling noise and movement of people crisscrossing the floor like at a railway station.

With so many rolling suitcases, the pattering of flip-flops, the tootling of bellhops' whistles, the smell of coffee and sea air, and piano music floating across the lobby from a woman surrounded by a jungle of blooming pink and blue flowers, it was hard to focus on any one thing.

Becca did. "There he is," she whispered.

The bookseller was speaking to a middle-aged man in a light-colored suit. The man wore a name tag on the lapel of his jacket. He gestured up the grand staircase toward a room with double doors. A small easel stood outside the room, and two security guards were stationed, one on either side.

"The auction," said Darrell, checking his watch. "In forty-five minutes."

Gerrenhausen glanced at his watch, too, for the hundredth time, turned from the man in the light suit, and hurried straight to the elevator.

"I'll ask at the front desk if we can get in," said Sara.

Wade went with her. The young man behind the marble counter smiled stiffly when they approached. *"Oui, madame?"*

When Sara asked about the auction, his smile faded.

"I am very sorry, madame. It is an auction by invitation only. You must have proper credentials, yes?"

"Where do we get those?" asked Wade.

The man glared at him. "One does not *get* credentials. One *has* credentials! Now if you will excuse me, I

141

have guests to deal with"—there were none waiting at the counter—"and I em *completed* wis you!"

"Thank you," said Becca as she pulled them away from the desk. "Julian texted. Sunglasses is coming up the street."

Sara hissed under her breath. "Everyone behind the palm trees. Hurry."

Wade hated how his stepmother had gotten sucked into the relic hunt—kidnapped, shuttled halfway across the world in a coffin, trapped like a prisoner by Galina Krause in Kronos, the Order's creepy time machine. But he totally admired how she had accepted the whole espionage deal they'd had to adopt—and were still refining. Staying under the radar, keeping safe, being bold when you had to, hiding otherwise. Sara was good at it.

He didn't like that his dad wasn't there, but if his father had to be away for a little while on Guardian business, Sara was proving a good leader.

Moments later Bartolo Cassa pushed into the lobby, took three or four long steps, then opened his phone. He read a message, then texted a reply. He waited for an answer. When it came a few seconds later, he read it, pocketed the phone, and headed directly to the elevator.

"I think my names for people are better than their actual names," said Lily. "It helps keep them not real people but units. Lousy murdering units."

"Okay, Lily," said Sara. "Look, I'll call the university in Austin and talk to my director. I'm sure I can get into the auction because of my archive work."

"Smart, Mom," said Darrell. "Using your connections. We need to know what Gerrenhausen is after."

"Which is what Galina's after," said Lily. "Which is what we want."

Becca grinned at her. "You sound like Darrell now."

"It's idol worship," Darrell said. "I get that. Wade does it, too. . . ."

Wade stopped listening. A broad-chested man in a jet-black suit swept in from the street, speaking over his shoulder in a language Wade had never heard before. Behind him floated a slender but sturdy woman in a flowing black dress with a black headscarf fastened under her chin and framing her face. Not stopping at the desk, they went directly to an open elevator, and the doors closed behind them.

Becca admired the way Sara's position as archivist at the University of Texas gave her quick last-minute entry to the auction. Her director even agreed to give her authorization under her latest fake name: Dr. Theresa McKay.

But there were two minor hitches. They needed a

certified check—a problem Julian easily solved even at night because of his father's extensive bank contacts—and only two people per party were allowed into the salon. Obviously, Sara had to be one of them.

"I think Becca should be the other one," Wade said, and Becca wondered how that would go over. "It makes the most sense," he went on. "Becca's the translator. She knows the most about Copernicus, really. They're practically personal friends. Becca is my choice."

Which was way too odd to respond to, but she didn't have to, because Julian said, "Even in a blond wig?"

"A blond wig? Who said anything about a wig?" said Becca.

"With bangs," said Lily. "And glasses. You, too, Sara."

"And shades," added Darrell. "Not like you-know-who, but nice ones. Stylish. But not too stylish, or you'll attract attention. And a hat so low you have to peek under it to see anything, but no one will see you. It's either that or body armor."

It was settled. Sara and Becca would go undercover while the others stayed outside. Not so secretly, Becca was overjoyed. She *was* the right choice. But there was also the danger of being discovered no matter how blond-wigged she was.

One of the Ackroyds' "acquaintances" in the Nice

underworld, a gentleman known as Maurice Maurice, was able on short notice to provide a wire—both audio and visual—for one of the chosen people to wear, so that the others could see and hear what happened at the auction. Maurice Maurice claimed it was waterproof, too.

"In case you must go swimming," he said. "Or are thrown into a fountain!"

It was decided that Becca would wear Mr. Maurice's wire. The others would watch the auction on Lily's tablet from the restaurant located just off the lobby.

Evening fell over the sparkling city, and Julian, Wade, Darrell, and Lily set up shop in the restaurant. Lily's tablet was hooked up to Becca's camera, her earpiece, and her microphone.

After they made sure the connection worked, Becca and Sara entered the gilded salon.

CHAPTER NINETEEN

"Z is way, pliss," said the pert young woman sitting at a table inside the doors. Her jet-black hair was cut in a sharp angle across her forehead, and she drew the papers from Sara with the barest tips of her fingers, as if the papers were covered with slime.

She then nodded toward a stack of green cardboard paddles. "For you, Dr. Mack-eye from Owstin, Tax-eze." The top paddle was marked 23 in large white numerals on both sides of the card. "Ze catalog," she gargled, and pointed at a stack of them. She finally directed them, without even making eye contact, to a line of people waiting to examine the items. "Next in line, pliss?"

"Never mind the brat," Darrell said in Becca's ear. "Show us stuff."

Becca did a casual turn around the room, knowing that the camera lens attached to her collar would catch most of the action. The auction hall was neither jammed nor empty, but the excitement in the room bristled.

"See the security guys?" she whispered into her microphone. At least a dozen beefy men with no obvious interest in the sixteenth century lined the walls. Four of them were speaking softly into walkie-talkies.

"Becca, look here." Sara stood at a long bank of display cases.

Most of them had old books and maps, but in one of them, labeled Lot 14, was an old—and very odd—pair of handcrafted silver spectacles.

A label read:

> *Ocularia arcanum. Purpose unknown. 16th-century French (?)*

"Oh," Becca breathed.

The glasses were completely silver, from their rims to the tips of the arms curling gently to fit behind the ears. The lenses were mirrored, triangular, and prismatic, and each one contained three surfaces, at slightly different angles on slightly different planes, that were geared to be movable.

A series of tiny numbered dials on the outer sides seemed to be the mechanism for adjusting the three lenses into a particular combination.

Extending out from the sides of the lenses to hold the glasses to the face were a pair of delicate, looping rods.

A curved nose brace, cushioned with velvet, sat between the lenses.

All in all, the glasses appeared like something from a science-fiction movie or—as Darrell whispered in her ear when he saw the picture through the camera— "total sci-fi futuristically backward steampunk!"

"This is it. Wade, everyone, do you see this? These glasses are why the bookseller is here," Becca whispered. "The cryptologic lenses that Leonardo made for Copernicus. It's how Nicolaus wrote the silver pages in the diary, and how Guardians can read them. We can't let Galina get hold of them."

Becca wanted to break open the display case and run off with the glasses.

"Do not touch!" said the young woman with the angled hair, who had been eyeing her. Becca pulled away, lowered her hat over her face, and drifted to the back of the room.

"If Triangulum *is* the next relic," Wade said into her earpiece, "and Galina needs these glasses to discover it, it means that Serpens isn't telling her where the next relic is. She needs the glasses to read the map. We're not behind. We're neck and neck."

Becca felt her heart skip a beat or two. "This is big."

Sara whispered into Becca's collar to the others. "I need everyone to start thinking of a way to get these things without getting killed."

"Who else is in the room?" Julian asked Becca through her earpiece. "Cassa?"

Becca turned slowly. "Not yet—"

"Stop moving," said Wade. "That guy in the dark suit. The fireplug guy at the back of the room. I saw him in the lobby before. He looks like trouble."

Becca kept the camera on him. The man in the suit stood like a powerful black stone planted between the two visible exits.

"Until we know his name," said Lily, "we'll call him Darksuit. And maybe even after that. He looks suspicious enough to be involved in this."

"But why does Galina need two bidders?" asked Darrell. "Wouldn't just one be more efficient? And cheaper? Because don't two bidders work against each other to raise the price? Or maybe I don't understand auctions."

"I think you're right," said Becca. "We'll keep an eye on him."

"Is the woman there?" asked Wade. "A woman in a headscarf was with him."

Becca scanned the room. A woman all in black from her hood to her shoes came in and stood next to Darksuit, who was now on the phone.

"She's here, too. They're all here."

"She looks like a gymnast," said Lily.

"Why do you think that?" asked Darrell.

"Because I used to be one. I know the muscles you need, and she has them."

Becca felt her brain speeding up, her thoughts flying. *What if I can actually read the silver pages in the diary with these weird glasses? We would zoom ahead of Galina, find the next relic, leave her in the dust. How can we get them?*

"Attention, please," said an older woman at the podium at the front of the room. "We will begin the auction in three minutes. Please take your seats."

She gave a nod to the security guards. "Gentlemen, secure the doors."

The inspection period had formally ended, and the doors closed quietly.

The auction had begun.

CHAPTER TWENTY

Not ten minutes from the Hôtel de Paris, Galina Krause's yacht was motoring toward Monte Carlo's harbor. Soon the city would be in sight.

She didn't care right now. She stared instead at the radar monitor in the communications room, studying the slow progress of the green blip on the screen. The caravan from Berlin was now leaving Prague. Another portion of the astrolabe's fragments had been collected.

"Keep me informed of any deviation from the plan," she said to the operator.

"Of course, Miss Krause."

She took the stairs up one level and entered her private room, where she stood alone for a minute, two minutes, and felt the floor sway. Would she be sick again?

No—she suppressed the urge. The harbor was visible now, glistening through the portholes. It would not be long. On a table in the center of the room sat the Voytsdorf Ledger, whose secret text was readable only by the *ocularia arcanum* that Oskar Gerrenhausen would soon bring her.

Using the strange spectacles crafted by da Vinci, she would finally understand the clever construction of the astrolabe's pieces, the devilishly precise method that Copernicus had revealed to his assistant Rheticus on his deathbed.

Her golden vendetta would begin its unstoppable progress.

And yet the location of the next relic stymied her.

The latest report from the Order's computer servers in Madrid was baffling.

By connecting infinitesimally small shreds of data, the Copernicus Room's analysts had ferreted out a mysterious series of events:

1. In April 1519 Copernicus embarks on a secret journey.

2. In April 1519 Leonardo da Vinci embarks on a secret journey.

3. In April 1519 Heyreddin Barbarossa embarks on a secret journey.

4. In May 1519 Leonardo da Vinci dies at Clos Lucé in France.

5. In April 1543 Heyreddin and Copernicus, both nearing their deaths, embark on a second journey together.

Were the first three the same journey? To date, all of the relics were given to Guardians in a single year, 1517. What occurred two years later to require the three men to undertake secret journeys? Her mind rolled the information over and over and over. And why had Copernicus dragged himself from his deathbed to make a second journey with the younger Barbarossa?

What had Markus Wolff said? *The past is a curious creature.* It was indeed.

Suddenly, Ebner von Braun stormed into the cabin, perspiring like a wrestler. "Drangheta!" he gasped. "Ugo Drangheta has appeared at the auction! The man is surely out of his mind!"

Her heart stopped. She felt the blood draining from

her head. She clutched the table. "Drangheta seeks the Leonardo glasses. Send for the Crows. Have them meet us at the hotel. Ten men. More. Arm yourself, Ebner. There will be gunfire tonight."

CHAPTER TWENTY-ONE

Darrell grumbled under his breath. As much as he wanted to see and hear everything going on inside the auction salon, he hated staring at a screen. Listening through earphones. Eavesdropping, lurking, *following*.

Operatives didn't follow. Guardians certainly didn't. They moved. They acted. They operated. They led. And yet, so far, following was all they'd been doing. It was wrong. He was Darrell Surawaluk Evans Kaplan, after all!

"Calm down, Robin."

Darrell flashed Wade a look. "Have your fun. You're still not Batman."

All the spy books he'd ever read always talked about

leaving your emotions out of it. You needed to be calm to be smart, a hard thing for him to do. The calm part. He'd been wired from birth, a jittery kid, usually on edge, and since Greywolf and his mother's captivity, Darrell's edge was closer. Right now he felt close to falling right off.

"Seriously, Darrell," Wade said. "Our mom is on it. We're good."

"Except we're not good," said Darrell. "I want to case the room for myself. See where the exits are, who's packing a gun. I want to *control* Becca like a character in a video game. Move left. Back up. Move right. Zoom in on that guy. Spin around."

"She would so not go for that," said Lily.

"No, I would not," Becca said through her microphone.

Darrell grumbled again.

In the salon, Becca eyed the bookseller like a hawk. Behind her blond bangs she studied his moves, his little twitches, the way he lifted his eyeglasses and rested them on his forehead, the way he tapped texts into his phone, with his nose practically on the screen. Bad eyesight, probably, from all the reading a bookseller has to do. Still, the small man managed to be both a thief and a killer.

"Are you guys getting all this?" she asked quietly.

"We are," said Lily. "You're a good cinematographer."

A rapid tap from the podium signaled that the auction had begun.

Becca tensed up. The first items were paintings and drawings. Some were by names she knew, others not. Neither Gerrenhausen nor Darksuit bid for them.

Soon enough the glasses came up.

"Lot fourteen," the auctioneer said, "is a one-of-a-kind pair of mirror-lensed glasses, dubbed *ocularia arcanum*, dating from the early sixteenth century. They are crafted of silver, of silver thread of very high quality, and of mirrored glass. Although undocumented, they are believed to have originated at a French workshop."

Becca's heart beat double time. "They're documented in one place," she whispered. "I wonder if anyone besides us—and Gerrenhausen and Galina—knows that da Vinci made them for Copernicus."

"To hide Triangulum," Sara added.

"Bidding will open at three hundred thousand euros, and rise by increments of one hundred thousand thereafter. This is a one-of-a-kind example of very fine craftsmanship from a European workshop."

There was momentary silence in the hall. Becca kept her eyes and camera trained on the bookseller in the second row. He seemed to draw in a breath, and he started to raise his bidding paddle, when the auctioneer made an announcement.

"Three hundred thousand is the opening bid from the gentleman in the back."

Gerrenhausen practically exploded in his seat. He swung around, his forehead wet with perspiration. His placard went up, and his phone appeared in his hand.

"Darksuit was the first bid," Becca whispered. "You were right, Wade. He wants it."

"Four hundred, thank you. Do I hear five hundred? Yes, five hundred thousand euros bid from the gentleman in the last row. Six hundred?"

Gerrenhausen raised his paddle, then Darksuit. It was a quick round of up-bidding from the two men. Becca was amazed at how swiftly the price rose.

Every once in a while, someone else would enter a bid, but would be quickly overtaken by the two men at opposite ends of the salon. The bidding held at seven million euros for a very long minute.

Finally, Darksuit threw his placard on his seat and spat out words in a language Becca didn't know. He stormed from the salon before the bidding for the next lot began. Gerrenhausen had won the item.

The woman in the headscarf lingered in her seat until the little bookseller entered a private room for the financial transaction; then she slipped out, too.

CHAPTER TWENTY-TWO

Becca and Sara left the salon and met the others in the lobby restaurant.

"Look who's back," said Darrell, nodding with his chin. No sooner had Gerrenhausen left the auction hall than Sunglasses appeared with the agent they'd first seen dressed as a railroad porter. They took the elevator together and were gone.

Darrell tapped Wade's shoulder. "We should go up the stairs. Follow them—"

"Hold on." Sara snagged the boys before they went anywhere. Three armed guards pushed a rolling cart across the lobby and into the elevator. The doors closed behind them, and it went up.

Becca grumbled. "This is happening too fast. They're taking the glasses to Gerrenhausen's room. Galina will get them. We can't just let her do that."

"Mom, I know it's dangerous, but we have to be up there," said Darrell.

It had long ago been decided that if they ever *had* to split up, one of the two parents would always be present, unless it was completely impossible. With Roald in Italy, Julian was the most likely replacement.

"Look, I'll totally go up there," Julian said. "Alone or with a team."

Sara nodded. "A team. Lily, Darrell, you stay here with me. We need to have eyes in both places. Becca, please keep your wire on."

"Will do."

Julian led the way up the staircase, Becca and Wade following quickly behind, while Sara, Lily, and Darrell staked out a dim corner just off the main lobby. It had a full view of the front and one of the side exits.

Darrell paced between the tables, keeping one eye on the lobby.

"Something's going to happen," Lily whispered. "I feel it in my bones."

"Me, too," said Sara. "Darksuit was very angry. He wants those glasses—who knows why—and he's not just going to let them go. He'll try something."

Darrell was more impressed with his mother's recovery every day. Kidnapped, then strapped into a deadly device. He wouldn't have been able to deal with it so well. She was good.

Suddenly, the elevator doors flashed open, and Darksuit emerged, his face a somber mask. A hotel porter followed him, pushing a dolly filled with luggage.

"Your car has just pulled up, Mr. Drangheta," the desk attendant said.

"Drangheta!" Lily whispered. "It was his guy who Gerrenhausen killed on the train. He really wants those glasses!"

The gymnast wasn't with him, although a garment bag of dresses on the dolly was obviously a woman's. A half-dozen beefy bodyguards formed the rear of the little caravan.

"Where's his companion?" Sara said under her breath. Her eyes flashed across the lobby, searching. "Is she staying behind?"

Darrell shook his head. "Her stuff is here. Drangheta's bodyguards are here, too, so he's checking out. Maybe he's just giving up."

"Or maybe she's waiting for him, and we don't have to worry about them," said Lily. "Let's make sure."

All three of them slipped out of the lobby and down the front steps to the street, keeping near the bank of potted plants on the side. The whole casino square was glittering with lights. A black SUV and a driverless cream-colored Bentley convertible idled out front. Darrell watched the porter load the luggage piece by piece into the SUV's rear compartment. Drangheta spoke to his bodyguards. Neither he nor his people paid any attention to Darrell or the others. Maybe because they were being so invisible. Still, the hairs on the back of Darrell's neck prickled. Something wasn't right. He brushed the hairs down and felt cold.

One of the hotel's valets trotted down the stairs. It looked for a second as if there was going to be a fight about who was going to open the door of the Bentley, the valet or one of the bodyguards. The valet got there first.

"Mr. Drangheta, we hope you enjoyed your stay at the Hôtel de—"

"I did not."

"I'm very sorry, sir. Perhaps next time—"

Drangheta brushed the man away and slid behind the wheel. He snapped his fingers, and his bodyguards funneled back into the hotel.

"What's going on?" Darrell whispered. "He's leaving

without his bouncers, and the woman? She's his wife, isn't she?"

"Or girlfriend," said Lily. "But still."

Darrell's mind wandered for a second but was back when Drangheta revved the Bentley. Before putting the car in gear, he slowly glanced up the facade of the hotel. He scanned the sky for a fraction of a second, then released the hand brake. The Bentley screeched away. The SUV stayed out front.

"What did he just do? Look at the stars?" Darrell slid out from behind the row of potted palm plants and stared up.

There she was.

The woman in black.

She was climbing like a spider up the side of the building and onto a balcony on the top floor.

CHAPTER TWENTY-THREE

L ily couldn't believe how fast everything went.

Seconds after Darksuit drove away, Galina Krause pulled up to the hotel and bounded up the lobby stairs like a black storm cloud, her eyes flashing.

Ebner von Braun skulked behind her—of course—doing his best impression of an evil assistant, rubbing his hands and whispering in her ear as they crossed the lobby. They were followed only seconds later by at least ten men in bulky black sweatshirts and jeans and earphones. One trotted over to what might have been a service door, while the rest entered the elevator with Galina and Ebner.

Lily tapped the microphone on her tablet. "Becca, listen . . ."

Upstairs, Wade and Julian were poised around the corner from Gerrenhausen's room on the fifth floor, waiting for something to happen, when Becca jumped.

"Lily, *what*?" She pressed her earpiece in. "Are you serious? Everybody, the woman is climbing up to the balcony *from outside*! And Galina's just arrived—"

They heard a soft *whump*, and a cloud of smoke poured into the hall from under the bookseller's door. Seconds later, the little man staggered out of his room, gasping, coughing, retching. He waved his way frantically across the hall, swiped a key card at another guest-room door, and fell inside.

"The thief is in Gerrenhausen's room!" said Julian.

The elevator door at the far end of the hall flashed open, and Galina strode out like a tornado, fuming, a pistol in each hand. Ebner jammed the elevator Stop button and followed her. The alarm began to ring. The kids and Julian ducked back behind the corner. A bunch of giant men with nasty handguns charged down the hall.

"Everyone stay down," whispered Wade.

At the same time—*wham*—the door to the stairway swept open behind them, and six of Drangheta's goons in matching gray suits pushed past them.

The smoke hadn't yet cleared when the hallway thundered with gunfire, shots flying from both ends, with the bookseller's room in between. Wade and Becca were flat on their faces, Julian behind them. Plaster flew off the walls over their heads. One of Drangheta's men thudded to the floor. There was a low cry from the far end of the hall. Two Knights fell in a heap. The Order's men pulled back, shielding Galina, while Drangheta's men pushed forward, past the bookseller's room. Galina disappeared down the hall to the left. Drangheta's thugs followed.

Suddenly the lights went out, plunging the entire floor into darkness. Stupidly, the gunfire started up again in the dark. Then two shots resounded from the bookseller's room. The railway porter staggered out of the room, holding his stomach. He crashed into the wall across the hallway carpet, pivoted, then collapsed through the opposite door, groaning but alive. Gerrenhausen dragged him inside and slammed the door behind him.

They waited.

"We need those glasses!" Becca whispered.

"But Cassa could still be in there," said Julian.

Darrell burst out of the staircase behind him, followed

by Sara and Lily. "Security's coming," he hissed.

"They'll take the glasses, if the thief doesn't have them already," said Becca.

"But she's got to come out that door. Maybe we have her trapped," said Lily.

"She's smarter than that," said Wade. "She'll go back down the side—"

"Stay here." Suddenly, Julian was on the move. He crawled on his hands and knees down the hall.

"No chance," Becca said. "We need those *ocularia*."

She slipped away from Wade and darted ahead, crouching. The smoke had nearly dissipated by now, and she moved down the hall toward the door of the suite. Julian slowly pulled down the handle of number 517. The door opened a crack. He slipped inside with Becca. Wade next. The others followed.

It was as black as night inside the room, too. The only light came from the open doors of the balcony, a deep purple western sky, a glittering sprinkle of lights from the casino opposite. Night noises splashed up from the street. From what Wade could make out, the suite was large—double size, maybe, with a door connecting two adjoining sets of rooms.

Then, over the distant gun battle, a sound.

A quiet footfall from another room.

Wade felt a touch on his arm. He turned. It wasn't Julian, who stood flat against the opposite wall with Darrell and Lily, Sara next to them. Becca had tapped him, her finger carefully laid across her lips. She pointed. *Look.*

Beyond him, through the doors to the other suite, Sunglasses lay motionless on the floor, a gash of red across his cheek, his arms twisted behind his back

Is he . . . ? Wade wondered. But no. The guy twitched slightly.

The thief was searching the second set of rooms for the antique glasses. Wade moved with Becca along the inside wall to the connecting door. She edged around him and looked through the space between the door and the hinges. He peeked over her shoulder. The thief broke open the room safe.

There was a click. A box lid opened. The room shone silver in the darkness. She closed the box, shutting down the light, and popped it into a small backpack on her shoulders. She drew her gun and made for the other room.

Thinking fast, or not at all, Wade reached awkwardly close to Becca. The sound would alert the others. He slammed the door between the two suites. A shot whizzed past his face and tore plaster from the wall. A splash of something hot hit his cheeks. A vase exploded on a nearby table, spilling water.

An instant later, the balcony door crashed closed, and the light from the street vanished. Then nothing. Wade burst out the balcony doors. Something clattered over his head. He looked up. The woman was sprinting across the slate rooftop. He heard the squealing of an iron door, then nothing. The elevator bell kept dinging in the hall. Then came a rush of footsteps toward the room and shouting in French. Hotel security.

Too late. The thief had disappeared. The gunfire had ended. Drangheta's goons were gone. Galina and her men were nowhere at all.

CHAPTER TWENTY-FOUR

In a flash the hotel was in crisis mode. Darrell's heart thumped like a drum as he pushed his way through the security and firefighting teams jamming the halls.

"Come on! They'll lock down the hotel. Come *on*!"

They were able to slip out in the general evacuation and were on the street in time to see Drangheta, in his Bentley convertible, shrieking away with the thief next to him.

"She's got the glasses!" said Becca. "Sara! Julian!"

"I'm up for the chase," he said, zapping his Fiat open. "If you are . . ."

Sara didn't hesitate. "Go. We'll follow in the Citroën!"

Wade dived into the passenger seat of Julian's tiny

Fiat, while Darrell had to squish into the puppy-size backseat. Wade wished he could grab the wheel and take control of the car. But Julian tore away from the curb, fishtailing into night traffic like a stunt driver. Then, out of nowhere, the silver Mercedes appeared with Galina herself behind the wheel. She raced quickly down the serpentine streets after the Bentley.

"I knew she'd be back!" said Darrell.

"Drangheta will head for the airport in Nice," Julian said as they skidded through a snaky hairpin then down into a long tunnel that led to the harbor. "That's the fastest way out of here. I'd go that way if I had a stolen object."

"And here's the race Darrell wanted," said Wade. "Go, Julian, go!"

The next few seconds were a blur of speed for all four cars. Drangheta's Bentley tore first out of the tunnel and roared toward the harbor, then spun completely around, accelerating toward Galina's Mercedes. Julian downshifted the Fiat, then hit the gas. Though Sara's Citroën was vastly underpowered, it held the road well and was only a few yards behind them. Galina braked suddenly, and Julian reacted quickly, but not quickly enough. He struck the rear end of Galina's Mercedes, sending it careening toward the outside harbor wall.

The Bentley was racing toward them now, and the thief began firing at Galina. Shots thumped into the Mercedes and then into Julian's Fiat. Galina braked close to the guardrail. Julian swerved right, slammed the clutch and brake at the same time, and bounced onto the sidewalk, nearly crashing into a jewelry store.

The silver Mercedes shunted the Bentley as it passed, Galina shooting back at the thief in the passenger seat. Ducking, the thief kept firing. The Mercedes's rear tires blew out. Galina lost control. The car catapulted off the roadway and crashed through the harbor wall, coming down flat onto the surface of the water with an explosion of spray.

The Bentley shrieked its brakes once, twice, then roared away into the night. It vanished into traffic before they could follow it. Julian backed his Fiat away from the storefront and tore down to the harbor. The Citroën pulled up right behind.

They rushed to the wall, crammed together, searching the water.

The silver Mercedes was sinking quickly, both gull-wing doors shut.

"Holy cow," Becca whispered. "Galina's in there. She could drown."

Multiple sirens keened from either end of the street.

"We'd better get out of here," said Sara. "Everyone, back to Nice. Now."

The Fiat and Citroën were just able to slither up the streets and away as fire trucks, police cars, and emergency medical vehicles jammed the harbor side.

CHAPTER TWENTY-FIVE

The devil will pay. The devil will pay. *The devil will pay!*

The words pounded in Galina's ears over and over as she struggled to kick open the door of the sinking Mercedes. The window cracked. Water filled the cabin; such an odd sight, water inside the windows, sloshing over the dashboard. Hair floated around her face like black tendrils; blood seeped across her eyes; rage battled despair fighting confusion.

Ugo Drangheta will die. His thief will die! I will have the ocularia!

Stars erupted in her eyes, knife blades in her forehead. She was screaming—*Not like this! Not like this!*—when the wrenching and ripping of steel focused her.

After slicing through the harness and snapping the steering post, three divers pulled her out. She would not die like this. She would not die today.

A half hour later Galina was aboard her speeding yacht, motoring away from the Monaco harbor at full speed. The police motor launch had been sent away, its occupants each a thousand euros richer.

"To the airport," she said, barely controlling her rage. Her heart was thrumming like a turbine. The scar on her neck burned with white-hot pain.

"To the airport and wherever Ugo Drangheta has taken my *ocularia*!"

CHAPTER TWENTY-SIX

After dropping the damaged Fiat at an Ackroyd-friendly garage, Julian joined the others in the Citroën. On the screaming drive to the Côte d'Azur airport, Darrell found himself pounding things—his car seat, the side panels, the ceiling over his head, his legs, Wade.

"Cut it out," Wade snapped. "I can punch myself if I want to. And no, I don't want to."

"We have to up our game."

"We know, Darrell, we know," Lily groaned. "No sports metaphors."

They had emerged from near-death chaos with nothing, thought Darrell. Nothing! They were empty-handed.

They should have done better.

"We need to go on the offensive," he continued. "Which is maybe a sports thing, but it's also a military thing, which is what we need to be now. Soldiers."

"You will be," said Julian. Sara parked in a short-term lot and they made their way into the noisy terminal together. "Listen," he went on, "according to my dad, Ugo Drangheta is a ruthless character. A businessman, but as arrogant as he is wealthy. His place in Morocco is his closest villa, and I'm willing to bet that's where he's flying right now. The place is a fortress, guarded by a private police force. And by that I mean a small army."

"We hope it's small," said Lily.

"Granted, yes, we don't know troop strength for absolute sure," said Julian. "But speaking of soldiers, my dad knows people in Morocco. Ex–special forces. Very private. Very good. They'll be able to help." He headed toward the Royal Air Maroc ticket counter. "This way."

"Africa?" said Becca. "We're going to Africa?"

"Morocco's a short trip by plane," Julian said. He tugged out his wallet. "No need for visas, or shots, if you're staying in the north." They got into line.

"Besides being ruthless, this guy Drangheta is reckless," said Wade. "He was so public about stealing the *ocularia*. He's taunting Galina. He wants her to go after him. And she will. She absolutely will."

"I just hope he doesn't do something like destroy the spectacles," said Becca. "What happens if a relic never gets discovered? If Drangheta is mad at Galina, he might do something disastrous."

"I don't think he will," said Darrell. "Not until she gets there."

Sara breathed in and out slowly. "We'll find out. We're going after him. Julian, we're ready to go. Are you?"

"Unfortunately"—Julian looked from one to another of them, a half grin on his face—"I won't be able to share in the fun."

"You're not going?" Lily asked.

"I . . . can't. There was a little . . . incident. Last February. Technically, Dad and I are not friends of the Moroccan state, so they put us on the no-fly list. We'd be arrested. So they tell me."

"What did you do?" asked Wade.

Julian ran his fingers through his long hair. "I sort of accidentally on purpose helped a human rights activist out of the country. He seemed like a nice guy, so I couldn't let him go to jail. He *is* a nice guy. But he had a price on his head. Dad didn't know I was doing it and was crazy mad at me, but come on, he would have done the same thing. He shared the rap, and they gave us both the boot. Don't worry, though; someone will meet you at the airport. I'm not sure who just yet, but he'll be first-rate and up to speed and have a bunch of well-armed friends. I'll give him a code to identify himself with—"

"Have him say, 'The red condor has landed,'" Darrell said. "That's a good one. And we'll answer, 'Barracudas like spaghetti—'"

"No, tortellini," Wade amended. "Less obvious."

Julian looked at them both. "Something like that."

He and Sara stepped up to the Royal Air Maroc ticket agents and booked five seats for the next flight to Casablanca, under the names of Theresa McKay, her two sons, and two wards.

After they were done, Becca turned to Sara. "I don't know that we have much choice, but I guess we'd better tell Uncle Roald what we're doing."

"I was waiting to tell him where we were going." Sara made the call, and told Roald to put them on speaker. "Where are you now?" she asked.

"Central Italy," he said, "not far from Gran Sasso. We were hoping to wait for Paul Ferrere to join us before we go in, but I received another urgent call from Dr. Petrescu, so we may not be able to wait."

"Roald and I will still arrive before most of the others," Terence piped in. "Which will give us a chance to case the place before we go under the mountain."

"It sounds a little too *Lord of the Rings* to me," said Sara. "Be careful."

"You, too," said Roald. "What's happening there?"

"We're off on the road to Morocco," she sang.

"What?"

"Well, on the jet to Morocco, actually."

"You're kidding."

They explained briefly what had happened that evening. He listened patiently. "Oh, man. Okay, I get it, but kids, listen. Promise me that you will *not* be doing anything dumb or dangerous that will make Sara freak."

"We won't," said Wade. "Promise."

"And Sara, I know you know this, but I have to hear myself say it."

"Go."

"It's just that I remember my mother saying that she always felt slightly crazy worrying about my brother and me. She told me that if she didn't feel crazy, an alarm would go off in her head."

"I have the same alarm," Sara said. "And I promise to be crazy at all times."

"Then good luck. I love you all. Call me every ten minutes."

"Half hour," said Wade. "Good luck, Dad."

The call ended, Julian waved, and they moved together into the security line. An hour and a half later they were in the air.

CHAPTER TWENTY-SEVEN

Casablanca, Morocco
June 6
1:23 a.m.

The sleek cream-colored Bentley convertible, an exact twin to the one sitting outside a private hangar in Nice, powered swiftly under the stars away from the Mohammed V airport in Casablanca.

It was headed east.

Ugo Drangheta's beautiful driving companion, named simply Mistral, sat in the passenger seat, clutching a seven-million-euro pair of glasses that she did not own. Removing her scarf, she let the wind sweep through her hair.

"Do you ever intend to use these glasses, Ugo? Or did I climb up the side of the Hôtel de Paris merely as bait to lure that woman here? Your contacts in Monte Carlo reported her yacht leaving the harbor, which it would not have done unless she was onboard. She survived her crash. She has nine lives. Nine times nine."

Drangheta laughed. It was a deep, angry sound, and unpleasant. He seldom laughed in his life, and when he did, it was an aggressive noise, even to his own ears. He didn't bother to hit his directional signal as he took a sharp right up a sweeping driveway.

He turned his face to her. "Galina Krause will regret every moment of her short life when she sets foot on this property. The murder of my sister, my gentle sister, was unforgiveable. It took my investigators over two months to prove it was not an accident, so well had she covered her tracks. Now that I know, I will end Galina Krause."

The road to the main property on Drangheta's estate was long, an S-shaped mile of crushed shell, lined the entire way with cypress trees jutting like rockets at the sky. What one couldn't see, unless he knew to look, were cameras and remotely controlled guns stationed every few feet along the road.

Drangheta slowed the Bentley in the wide forecourt

and stopped. His vast Moorish villa sprawled over several acres. It featured marble floors, indoor fountains, high, tiled walls, and an ostentatious gold dome from whose observatory one could view not only the sky but also the dazzling purple Atlas Mountains zigzagging north to the sea.

He walked Mistral into the entry hall. "Place the *ocularia* in the vault," he said. "If the night is quiet, I'll inspect them in the morning."

"The night will not be quiet," she said, tossing her black headscarf onto a sofa. "The woman will not be able to resist."

"I do hope you're right. It would be much more delightful to study the glasses knowing that Galina Krause has died at my hands."

Drangheta felt rage edge up his throat as he snapped his stubby fingers. *Do not anger a powerful man,* he thought. *You just might die from it.* Four men in riot gear emerged from a hallway obscured behind a barrier of columns.

"Sir Ugo?" said one.

"The villa will be attacked tonight. Put all necessary precautions in place immediately."

"Sir," the soldier responded. The men disappeared silently behind the columns. Soon the sound of the villa's fortifications engaging began. Gates slid over every window and door. Inch by inch, the walled-in gardens grew tall iron spikes that rose up to various heights. What had been a stone walk receded into its retaining wall, revealing a deep artificial moat around the villa. Searchlights blinked along the entire perimeter. Miles of fencing hummed with electrification. The gate across the driveway was reinforced with a titanium barrier. Finally, seven military transports in the stables roared to life, each carrying a dozen heavily armed mercenaries. They began their patrol of the perimeter roads.

"If she tries tonight," he said, "she will be killed."

"There are others who may want the *ocularia*, too," said Mistral. "Let's not discount them, my dear. What about the others in the hotel suite? The American family. They have an interest in Galina's plans."

Drangheta's lips grew into a tight smile as he ascended the wide stairs toward the second floor, then paused on the landing. On the wall hung a portrait of his brilliant sister, Uliana, eight years his junior, an excellent pilot, killed before she'd had a chance to live. *I will squeeze Galina Krause until there is nothing left.*

"This is war, Mistral. The Americans will be mere collateral damage."

He paused on the landing and found he could not move from it. Staring into the eyes of his sister, he felt his chest shudder.

"I love . . . *loved* . . . my sister beyond all life."

Mistral joined him on the landing. "What if you could bring her back?"

Not taking his eyes from the portrait, he half turned. "What?"

"A time machine. This is what your investigators said Galina Krause may be assembling. Many deaths have been attributed to it. Many more. For a machine? Think about it, Ugo."

He faced her now. "Do not mock me with a fantasy."

"Galina Krause is not a fool. If she believes in this machine and murdered your sister for it, is there not reason to believe in it? Should we find out more, Ugo?"

Tears began to flood his eyes, spill onto his cheeks. "Perhaps. For now, please take the glasses to the vault. I will be in the dome, awaiting the battle to come."

He turned from the landing and walked up the dark stairs, deep in thought.

CHAPTER TWENTY-EIGHT

Airports were airports were airports.

But after sleeping on the short flight over, when Lily set foot in Casablanca's Mohammed V International Airport, she felt different. Beyond the speedy passport control—it was in the wee hours and the lines were thin—the arrivals terminal was airy and open and light, and it blossomed with sound and color that despite the heaviness in her made her seem to float. Even at 2:14 in the morning.

Yeah, she thought, *it's weird. But I'll take it.*

"Which one of you is Darrell?" a voice said.

They turned to see a dark-haired man of around forty. He had a rough face, tanned to a deep brown. He was dressed in sport clothes and running shoes.

"Why are you asking?" said Sara, stepping in front of Darrell.

"Because we don't have condors in Morocco, and they're not red anyway. We have other birds, but not condors."

Wade narrowed his eyes at the man. "Wait. Is this the code?"

"It might be," said the man. "We have Egyptian vultures. You could have had me say 'the Egyptian vulture has landed.' That would have worked. People would think I know what I'm doing, at least." He looked at Darrell from his dark eyes. That lasted a long time before he added, "And your response is . . . ?"

Becca laughed as Darrell said, "Barracudas like spaghetti. No, tortellini."

The man nodded slowly. "They don't, but let it pass. My name is Silva. Just Silva. I've known Terence and Julian for a long time. Come on, then."

He spun around on his heels and led them outside and along a row of spotlights to a large Land Rover in the short-term parking area. Over his shoulder he said, "My men are watching Drangheta's compound. It's in hill country, so the house has a bird's-eye view of the surrounding miles, except for a ring of foothills to the southwest. That's where we're going now. If things are still quiet, they won't be for long. Your friend Galina may already be in Morocco, so we need to get a move on."

"Do you have a plan for getting the, uh, object back?" asked Becca.

"The da Vinci glasses?" he said. "Julian trusts me. And yes, I do. I'll explain on the way."

As soon as they piled into the Rover and motored away from the airport, Lily knew they were entering a world unlike anything she'd seen before. Blue buildings. Gold domes. Arches. People crowding the streets so long after midnight.

Africa! What did she know about Africa?

"Listen," Silva said, "you need to know exactly what we're up against tonight. Ugo Drangheta is a brute, a nasty businessman with a trail of corporate corpses in his wake. Besides that, he's waiting for trouble tonight, which will make his villa a tough nut to crack. The place is a high-security fortress. He has a battalion of private soldiers, vehicles, arms. An arsenal that rivals that of a small country."

"Do you think he's on our side?" asked Wade. "I mean, I kind of hope that he is, but also that he's not. His men at the hotel were as bloody as the Order's.

Guardians would never do that. I hope."

"No, Guardians wouldn't," said Sara.

"Consider him a violent enemy, a real piece of work," Silva said. "If he's anything else, you'll be pleasantly surprised. I doubt he has a beef with you, but the moment you reach for the glasses, you're a target. Bear in mind that Drangheta has friends in the government and a lot of interests around the world. Luckily, and I'm using that word loosely, Galina Krause will be coming with guns blazing. Our only chance of breaking in is when she begins her attack."

"Shouldn't we try to get in before it all starts?" asked Wade.

Silva shook his head. "The crossfire will distract everyone. For a short time, anyway. It won't be safe, but it'll be the one shield we're likely to get. A battle waged too soon is a battle lost."

He let that settle in as he drove relentlessly away from the city lights.

Sara looked at the kids. "You probably think I'm going to say we need to bail out of this right now. Believe me, I'm considering it every step of the way. But right now, we're going ahead. Becca knows why. We all do. The horrors Galina will do if she assembles the astrolabe. Still, we should decide on a place to meet in case we get separated."

The Rover began climbing into the foothills south-west of the compound.

"We won't get separated," Wade said. "We promised you and Dad."

Sara cracked a humorless smile. "Uh-huh. But this is different. We need one just in case. Silva, can you sug-gest a good rendezvous?"

He took a breath. The Rover began to slow.

"How about the Pyramids?" said Darrell. "I always wanted to see them."

"They're two thousand miles away with the barra-cudas and the condors," Silva said. "There's a children's hospital, l'Hôpital d'Enfants, in central Casablanca. Very international. On several tram routes. They'll take care of you."

"A French hospital?" said Becca.

Silva turned the Rover onto an upward path toward the crest of the hills. "The French colonized a good part of North Africa. Morocco became independent in 1955, Tunisia the next year, Algeria in 1962, but before that, it was all French. A little Spanish, too. Lots of French still live around here. English. Some Americans. The culture is a mix of African and European."

It was nearing three a.m. Lily breathed in the night.

The cool air rushed in the windows and over her face. The sky above was immense and huge, wide and black. Different. So different. Finally, Silva coiled the Rover up a series of steep roads at the summit of the foothills, stopped, and shut off the engine.

He jumped out and opened a small chest in the rear of the vehicle. From it he took a set of desert camouflage and slipped into it. He fitted a special-forces beret on his head and slung a heavy automatic weapon over his shoulder, an ammunition belt across his chest, and binoculars around his neck.

He gave a low whistle, and a figure trotted down a path along a ridge on the far side of the hill. Silva said, "This is K. K, meet everyone. Everyone, meet K."

K, a scruffy bearded man, bald and wearing no beret, shook hands with them. A walkie-talkie on his belt crackled softly.

"Drangheta and Mistral, the thief, have been home for an hour plus," K said. "No sign of the Order yet. Our man inside, Jibran, tells us the vault room is in the back, or the south side of the house."

"You have a guy inside?" said Darrell. "That's good."

Silva smiled humorlessly. "Until he's discovered." He led them a few paces toward the lip of the hill. "You can see the main room. Use this." He slipped a slender

193

riflescope from a holder on his belt and held it out. "If there's a chance, Jibran will raise the bars on one of the windows."

The main room of the villa that Wade saw through the scope was like an aquarium, glassed in on three sides and barred. The fourth, solid wall was hung with a bizarre collection of weapons, obviously from different cultures and ranging from the antique to the very latest.

"I'm guessing the Order will come in from the north," K said. "The least protected part of the perimeter. It's down there." He pointed to a gap in the foothills, a half mile from where the main driveway snaked onto the estate. "We have men surrounding the property."

Silva nodded and turned to Sara. "The instant the Order makes itself known, Drangheta's men will counterattack and leave the house at least for a short period. If our man raises the window bars, we go in. Five, ten minutes is all the time we'll have. And if Mistral hangs around the vault, we'll probably have to take her on hand to hand. Just saying."

"Until then?" asked Wade.

"Body armor," said Silva, reaching once more into the back of the Rover. "A set for each of you. Sara, we'll need you to go in with us to identify the glasses. Are you okay with—"

"I'll do it." Sara slid her armor over her blouse.

Darrell turned. "Mom, you understand how awesome this is, right? No mom in the history of life ever did what you're doing. You're like . . . Joan of Arc."

"She wasn't a mother," Sara said. "And she was captured."

"Sure, but—"

"And executed."

Darrell took a breath. "Okay, bad example, but still."

"But still," she said, "tighten your straps."

"Listen to your mother," said Silva. "I don't want to lose more than one or two of you."

CHAPTER TWENTY-NINE

For the next thirteen minutes, Wade gazed up at the vast black dome of the sky. It glistened with a sea of silvery stars. He knew the *ocularia* were Becca's thing, but he couldn't stop imagining what the strange glasses might reveal to them.

Would the silvery pages resolve into words and give up their secrets? Would the kids actually discover where the mysterious Triangulum was hidden? Or would they find only more and more riddles to unravel, an endless stream of puzzles?

He allowed his thoughts to shuttle between the excitement of discovery and the frustration of confusion, until even that fell quiet.

He felt sleep coming on, when five or six nearly simultaneous explosions rocked the perimeter of the compound.

He bolted up. Everyone was watching from the hilltop. He scrambled up to them on his hands and knees. K was nowhere in sight.

"Get ready," Silva said.

They next heard the chatter of machine-gun fire. It sounded aimless at first, coming from wildly different directions, as if Drangheta's guards were confused about where the threat actually was. But the firing continued, and Wade realized that the compound was being attacked from at least three positions. The suddenness and ferocity of the attack shocked him.

"Galina's moving in," Darrell said, nudging him. "You hear that, right?"

"Yeah. Gunfire is already pulling away from the main house."

Then came the growling of a heavy vehicle fifty yards down to their right.

"Flatten!" Silva shouted, and they hunkered in a dip in the crest of the hill.

This was too much like war, Wade thought. Hot war, not the covert stuff, the kind they'd seen so far. It was way out in the open. A vehicle, an armored truck, barreled straight for the perimeter fence. It fired a blast, and he saw the fence go slack. The truck drove over the barrier as if it didn't exist. It was inside the compound.

Suddenly, K was back with them, his face poised between fear and opportunity. He tilted his head at Silva. "That was Galina. She's inside. The bars are still down. Boss?"

"We need to be in position in case they go up," Silva said over the popping of gunfire. "I don't want Jibran risking his life for nothing." He turned to them. "There will be a blast in the front of the house. That's the cue for Sara and K to go down the hill toward the rear of the villa and get ready to enter. Once the bars open, you get in there, locate the package, then get out. Understood, Sara? Everyone? The Rover is our getaway."

They nodded, and Sara retightened her armor straps. "Listen, kids. Stay up here, well outside the compound. Don't you dare move. Be ready to jump into the Rover. That's all."

"Mom, you have to be careful," said Darrell. "If I go back without you, Dad will have a fit."

She smirked. "I hope more than a fit, but yes. I'll be careful. I know what we're looking for. We'll only enter the house if the fighting moves away from it."

"It's looking like that," said Silva, finishing a phone

call to his men nearest the point of attack. "Watch over there—"

A flash of white light broke the darkness. It was followed a couple of seconds later by a thunderous blast.

"This is it," said K. "Go, go, go!" A dozen black-clad mercenaries appeared out of nowhere and started down the hill. K and Sara followed. The four kids remained at the crest with Silva.

"Can I use the scope again?" Wade asked.

Silva passed it to him. Its magnification was strong, and once he sighted the house, he could see down inside the glass-walled room and into the central courtyard. He spotted a shape in a side room. "The thief," he said.

She moved across the windows, checking her phone.

"She's nervous. She knows Galina's coming," said Becca. "While the Order's troops fight, Galina will swoop in, grab the glasses, and get out. . . ."

"My men know what they're doing," Silva said. "Once those window bars go up, if there's a ghost of a chance, Sara and my guys will be in and out in minutes."

Wade hoped it was true, but didn't like the word *ghost*.

From her seat inside the lead transport, Galina monitored the global positioning data on the screen to her right. She counted close to two dozen figures swarming the main house.

"Two of them will be Drangheta and the thief," she said.

Ebner von Braun, cringing next to her, didn't reply. There was nothing for him to say. He had spent the last two hours trying to convince her that "going public" this way, with a physical assault on Moroccan soil, was the beginning of a war that could not be retracted.

To which she had said, "We are out of time. Do you doubt that we will win?"

"Not at all, but—"

"Victory has a way of silencing the losers. In a few days, it will not be an issue. You'll see."

Ebner said nothing.

Four minutes later, Galina slid from the transport. One of her men blew a hole through the front door of the house. She kicked aside the splinters, then entered. As he sat in the idling transport, Ebner watched her sidestepping the bodies—through the windows he counted thirteen of Drangheta's guards slain. Galina would follow her instinct and soon find the inner chamber, the vault room, the sanctum. Galina, as ghostly as she was, seemed on fire and unstoppable.

* * *

From the secure position on the hillside, Darrell kept his eyes trained on the compound. Taking the scope from Wade, he watched the progress of his mother, K, and the other troops. At first, they advanced smoothly and swiftly. Then the window bars shot upward, and just when they should have made their final run to the house, a crossfire developed between the Order and Drangheta's soldiers, pinning his mother and the others in a trench between two high-defense walls. They hadn't been spotted and weren't in danger—unless they moved. They were simply unable to advance or retreat while the battle for the villa surrounded them.

Mom, stay put. Stay put!

That's when he spied a slender shape moving against the light inside the house.

"It's Galina," he breathed. "She got in."

Becca stood. "She'll get the glasses. We have to go down there."

"We do," said Lily. "Mr. Silva—"

"It's just Silva, and you're not going anywhere." His face was as impassive as stone.

"Not without you we're not, and you're going down there," Darrell said, surprising himself and wondering if it was okay to argue with a soldier. "This whole thing is about the glasses. You even said we have five minutes before the fighting shifts back to the house and those bars go down. Then we'll never get in. Nobody likes a failed mission. We can do this. Look, it's just Galina and the thief in there. We have the odds. But if we wait, we won't."

Silva stared down at the action.

Darrell knew that as long as the window stayed unbarred there was an opening for a surgical strike. Since his mother and K and his men couldn't get into the house, it was either helplessly watch Galina steal the glasses or intervene.

"We'll have a big price to pay to Sara and my dad," Wade said. "But it's worth getting yelled at, if we can hold up the glasses and say, 'We got them.'"

Silva checked his firearm. "So, okay, then."

"Really?" said Darrell. "We convinced you?"

"Not really, but you said the magic words. Nobody likes a failed mission. Least of all me." He took a small pack of explosives from the Rover and stuffed it into a pouch on his belt. "Everybody stick behind me. Ready? Go, go, go."

They pushed down the hillside and onto level ground in minutes. Silva slid into the bushes outside the house like a snake. Darrell, Lily, Becca, and Wade followed him along the house's westernmost wall toward the south side.

As soon as they were close to the window, Darrell saw Galina's face clearly. It was as pale as ice, almost ghoulish, except for the bright red scar on the side of her neck under her ear, left over from her operation four years ago in Russia.

Whoa.

In the instant it took him to think of that, Drangheta was in the room, his handgun sighted at Galina's head. The thief had vanished. Galina didn't appear to move. Then a burst of automatic gunfire came from somewhere in the shadows behind her. Drangheta leaped back and slipped away, replaced by a troop of his house guards. They tried to surround Galina, but Teutonic agents in body armor lunged out of the shadows and pursued them, firing.

Galina then disappeared into another room.

"She's following the thief into the vault room," Becca said.

"This way." Silva crouched. He moved quickly across a walled terrace.

As they followed, Darrell shot a glance at Lily, who was already looking at him. He wanted to be nearer to her, shield her, even, but that thought went nowhere. Silva raised the butt of his gun and broke the window. Darrell shook like a leaf when he slipped through and set his feet on the floor inside the villa.

CHAPTER THIRTY

Becca tried to hold herself together.

Dead guards and knights lay to her right and left and everywhere in between.

She held her breath, but she'd been doing it too long, and at the last moment was forced to take in a quick breath. It smelled heavily sweet, of desert plants and irrigation, even inside the house.

The soothing scent was worse than smelling death. It meant that people could die and the world would go on its way, not even notice.

"Where's the vault?" asked Wade.

Silva glanced at the schematic on his phone. He

nodded left. "The battle is moving away. Sara and K will join us—"

"We can't take that chance," Becca said sharply. She bolted off, wove through the rooms, the hallways, feeling exposed in the dim emergency lighting. She followed her instincts. Isolated shots and clunks and shouts erupted behind her, but she pressed ahead and found the dark room.

Three shots popped down the hall. Becca crouched to the floor. No more shots. She rose to her feet. Silva was with her. Wade, Lily, and Darrell had fallen back. The two of them were alone in the room; then they weren't. The cat burglar darted through the room past their hiding place. Seconds later, another shape emerged from the shadows at the far end of the room. Galina. She paused in the darkness, completely still. Or . . . not *completely*. She was shivering. Why? What did she see? Becca's muscles ached, but any movement and she'd be seen. Galina turned, awkwardly, against the light of the doorway, and Becca saw the scar on her neck, inflamed to a bright crimson.

Holding her own breath, Becca heard Galina sucking air between her open lips, a habit she recognized, because she'd used it herself lately. Blinding pain could be eased a little by breathing that way.

Then the thief was back in the room, a handgun raised to the darkness. *Where is Drangheta? Already dead?*

Galina burst from stillness, her arms like muscled steel cables. She swung hard at the thief, and something cracked. The gun flew across the room, and the woman's mouth made a sound like water splashing. She fell.

Silva touched Becca's arm, nodding. The vault chamber was across the room. But not yet. The thief was up again. Galina swung her arm back and wrenched a sword noisily from the wall, then slashed it forward across the air. Becca cringed, waiting for the thief's cry, but glass cracked instead. The thief slid a long curved dagger from a display case. The two women began parrying, thrusting, slashing, stabbing. No taunting like in the movies, just swift moves meant to kill.

Galina lunged forward, faked left, and her opponent's blade crashed into a vase, bursting it. It was Galina's chance. She thrust forward; the thief dodged the blade, swung her sword. Galina fell onto her, struggling hand to hand.

Silva pressed Becca's arm. Leaving the fight behind, she slid across the room into the vault chamber. It was cold, artificially refrigerated. There was nothing human about it. Silva moved in front of her and attached the explosive charge next to the safe door. They moved back. A small concentrated blast blew the door from the safe, sending it crashing to the floor. Waving the smoke away, Becca reached into the vault. The small box she had seen in Monte Carlo was resting inside. She tipped open its lid. A bright silvery glow bathed her like a breath of frosty air.

"That it?" Silva whispered.

She nodded. She knew the glasses weren't heavy, but when she lifted the box, her hands and arms felt like lead. The weight of history? Of the Magister's long journeys? Of the horrors?

She swept the box into her bag. They slipped out of the vault room.

Galina was standing, her head hanging low, hair clinging to her face, her sword still in her hand. Mistral was nowhere in sight. Sara, K, and the others were there, their automatic weapons trained on Galina.

"You will regret this," she said. Then, as Becca went past, Galina deliberately brushed her shoulder. "You, especially."

Becca felt her blood turn to ice.

"This way, hurry," said Wade. He helped Becca across the patio and down the stairs. Her bag was growing heavier as she ran. She didn't want to carry it. She already had the Copernicus diary. Having both artifacts was one too many.

"Wade," she started, reaching into her bag for the box, when shots rang out.

They ran, all of them, and ducked through a gap in the wall. An engine idled beyond it. Silva jumped past them all and into the driver's seat, Sara beside him, the others tumbling into the back. Silva hit the gas. The compound was still exploding with gunfire when they roared up the hill to the crest. Becca looked back. Galina was running through the garden, firing back over her shoulder.

"She's getting away. . . ."

"Doesn't matter," said Silva. "We got what we came for."

It was nearly five a.m. The sky was still purple black in the east. For a tiny moment, it was silent in Becca's mind. They had the glasses. *Ocularia arcanum*. She would read the diary as soon as she could. She would—

The thundering of engines broke into her thoughts. She turned back to the desert night.

They were being followed.

CHAPTER THIRTY-ONE

"Ten minutes, are you kidding?" Silva barked into his handset.

Silva twisted the wheel and took the Rover on what surely was not a road. Darrell knew the guy was angry. Was he also afraid? What did it mean when the person in charge was scared?

"The way to the airport is blocked by Drangheta's men," Silva snarled. "He's friends with the police here. We're forced back into the city, at least for now."

"There are two transports after us, maybe more," Wade said, peering out the back. "And I think I see a couple of motorcycles."

"The bikes could be Teutonic Order, the transports

maybe Drangheta. This is a bad-guy sandwich. Hold on!"

By the time the sky in the east began to turn rosy, the Rover reached Casablanca's outer streets, pursued by more vehicles now. Besides the transports and motorcycles, four black sedans had joined the chase, racing after them until they were in the winding streets. The city was just starting to wake up.

"We might have better luck in the medina," Silva said. "That's the older part of the city, lots of narrow streets. The larger vehicles won't follow so easily in there; we'll be down to the motorcycles. I'll drop you at the nearest *bab*—gate. I'll circle back later and pick you up—"

"At the hospital," said Lily. "And I mean that seriously. We'll meet there."

Silva nodded. "Everyone hold on!" He raced along a crowded street, then turned right through a tall archway and into the crowded medina. Even early in the morning, with many shops not yet open, it was jammed with people. The streets were incredibly narrow, and jogged right or left with little advance notice.

"It's too tight!" Lily yelled. "We won't make it—"

The Rover careened into the corner of a blue-walled building, tearing off the vehicle's front end, then swung around and plowed straight into one of the pursuing cars, and turned it over. The black sedan rolled, lifeless, into the front of a deserted café.

Silva backed up the Rover, but the steering was broken. They drove into several empty tables, scattered the men from the sedan. The Rover bounced once, then gave up. It was dead.

"Out!" yelled Sara. "Kids, come with me."

They hurried through a second arched gate and into a world of ever-more-narrowing alleys, crowded with people in flowing robes and scarves, tea tables spilling out of shops, crisscrossing voices, calls, singing, music, and the aromas of dozens of different kinds of food.

Becca slid behind the others, her right thigh aching from when the crash threw her into the door handle. They entered one street, then zigzagged from it to another and another, trying to make it as far toward the other end of the medina as possible.

"We have to pull this off, we have to!" said Becca.

"We will," said Lily.

"Move it!" Silva shot back at them. "Follow me."

They did, deeper into the medina. Then came a sudden blast of gunfire; children screamed. Sara stumbled to a stop and hunkered down. Lily, Darrell, and Wade joined her, but there was nowhere for Becca to hide.

She jumped ahead of them and slid around a corner. More gunfire, she didn't know from where. She ran, then stopped. Where was the gunfire coming from? She couldn't move. The glasses, the diary—both were in jeopardy. Why hadn't she passed one of them off to someone else?

Suddenly, there was Wade, snaking down the alley toward her. "Are you hurt?" he gasped, looking her up and down. For what? Blood?

"No, I'm scared. They're all around us—"

"Not all around. The next street is clear. Silva and everybody will join us there. Come on." He hurried Becca along the winding street from where he'd come. It bathed them in the odor of food and the smell of cooking oil and the coming heat of the day.

"You're a bit slow," he said. "Can you run?"

She shook her head. "Sorry. A minute—"

"In here." Wade slipped into an archway over the door of a small building, and she joined him. Beyond the arch, she saw curling letters painted on the walls inside. It was a mosque.

The sudden buzz of motorcycles was everywhere, roaring loudly over the echo of chanted prayers.

"Hurry," she said.

They rushed down the street and under an arch

draped with carpets and emerged into a small open square. Wade's face tightened with fear and something else. *Indecision?* she thought. *Oh, please, not now.* No, he was checking out escape routes. "This way." He headed left at a fast walk. Her bag suddenly weighed a ton. She hitched it over her neck, away from her left arm to the other side. Not much better.

They pushed out of the square into the first narrow alley they came to. Her thigh hurt more with each jarring step. Wade went halfway, then jerked to a sudden stop, listening.

All at once, a wooden door near the end of the alley crashed open. Two motorcycles bounced in over the scattered planks, then swung around to face her and Wade, revving loudly. Backing up, she spied the top of the passage wall nearest them. It was flat and wide.

"Up there?" she said.

"Yes!"

As the motorcycles accelerated toward them, she and Wade groped up the wall. He got up first and reached down for her. His grip was tight, his arm stronger than she expected. She clawed her way to the top. The bag came loose and slid down her arm. She grabbed it and slung it over her shoulder again just as the first bike roared down the street below.

"Becca!"

She swung around and spotted Lily. She and the others were on the rooftops along the next street. "Wade, we should be over there."

"We'll meet up at the end." Which sounded like something a priest would say at a funeral, but Wade was pointing to where the streets crossed and the rooftops met. "Keep going!" He was being short with her, angry almost.

He's right. I'm slowing us down.

The motorcycles' engines were muffled for a moment. Someone yelled, and Becca heard a crash of pots and pans. Both motorcycles suddenly thundered up a flight of stairs and out onto a nearby terrace, then up to the edge of the wall surrounding the roofs, then toward her.

"What the—" Wade gasped. "Becca, run!"

The motorcycles accelerated along the top of the wall. Wade scrambled on his knees to find a loose brick. He threw it hard at the first bike. It struck the rider, who slowed sharply, then sped up again.

The second rider started shooting.

As loud as the growling engines were, the unsuppressed gunfire crackled across the rosy morning air, bullets ricocheting on the pastel walls around them. More people were yelling from below now. A siren wailed from too far away, not for them. The others scrambled up to the walls separating the rooftops on the other street, but the bikes weren't after them. Becca saw Sara rush ahead of Darrell more quickly than Wade in front of her.

I'm slowing him down. I'll get him hurt—

A spray of automatic gunfire riddled the wall ahead of them. Wade threw his arms around her shoulders and they were flat on the rooftop. Sara, Lily, or someone called out. More sirens wailed in the distance. Help? Maybe. Or maybe Drangheta owned the Casablanca police.

"Do you think you can run?" Wade whispered.

"Yes!"

They hurried across the rooftop walls and slid down the slanted, tile-topped roofs, ran straight across the flat ones. There were parapets on most houses. The sun was very hot now, washing the rooftops in rose and blue and yellow light.

"The bikers know we have the glasses. They don't care about the others."

"So keep running!" Wade snapped. "Don't slow down!"

Releasing her hand, he climbed over the railing and jumped down to the lower roof. He was speeding across the terrace before he realized she hadn't followed him. He whirled around. "Bec—"

Her whole upper arm felt like it was on fire, from the arrow wound outward. So much for antibiotics. It hadn't healed. Not completely. Her arm had no strength left in it. She slid back down the railing to the upper roof.

While one bike sped after Wade, the other bounced over the wall, did a somersault in the air, and landed on the roof with her, screeching to a stop on a single tire. Its rider yanked a pistol from inside his shirt and fired across at her, careful to avoid her bag.

She managed to duck flat under the railing.

Suddenly, there was a crossfire of shots. It was Silva, pumping his gun at the shooter. The shooter fell behind his bike and returned fire. Shots pocked the walls around her. *Pop-pop-pop!* Her brain was firing the same way: *pop-pop-pop*, the diary, the glasses, the relic. She was frozen, unable to move.

Or maybe not.

There was a set of stairs built into the roof some ten, twelve feet from her. Peering down, she saw that the stairs split on the landing below, one way going into the house, the other continuing down to the street. She caught a glimpse of people on the street below. She could get to them if Silva kept the shooter pinned down.

"I'm going to try to make the stairs," she yelled.

"Go for it!" Silva redoubled his attack. *Pop-pop-pop!*

She hurled herself across the open space, then fell down the steps, catching herself halfway, and jumped down the rest. She reached the bottom, didn't see Wade anywhere, and didn't look back, didn't want to see Silva, the soldier who was risking his life for them.

She slid down a narrow alley, her chest heaving with fear and exhaustion. Praying silently that they wouldn't hurt Silva, wouldn't find Wade, that the others would get away, Becca pinned her bag between her arm and her side and padded down the passage. She slipped under a decorated archway along tall blue walls and out into the brightening street.

CHAPTER THIRTY-TWO

Novaya Zemlya, Kara Sea, Russia
June 6
Late morning

Bartolo Cassa, his face and arm bandaged from the attack by the thief in the Hôtel de Paris, exited a jet on the godforsaken island of Novaya Zemlya in the Kara Sea. The place would never be confused, he mused, with Monte Carlo.

"Keep the engines running," he told the pilot. "This won't take long."

"I'd have kept them running anyway," the pilot replied. "They might not start again in this cold."

Drawing his coat tighter, Cassa walked painfully

from the jet to the shore, where he mounted an ice trac-
tor and started across the frozen sea.

Minutes later, he drew up at the excavation site.

A band of fur-wrapped workers huddled around the
drill cap as it was lifted away from the five-foot circle in
the ice.

"You are?" Cassa asked the man with the smuggest
expression, the one in charge.

"Ivanov," the man said. "Konradin Ivanov. You are
from that girl in Berlin, Galinka?"

Cassa allowed himself a quick smile. "Yes. Show me."

The walls inside the hole descended some ten or
twelve feet to a black object of riveted steel. A number
of rivets had been sawed away, and a small portion of
the steel panel pried open. Below that was darkness.

A winch sent down a pair of vice claws.

"The concrete casing was broken," Ivanov said, "but
we believe—I believe—we found the item in time,
before it was degraded."

Cassa knew that if the man was wrong, they would
be dead from radiation poisoning within weeks. Sooner.

When the claw was in view again, it bore in its grip
a blue-gray device the size and shape of a large steel
drum. The device was marked with the red Soviet star, a
series of Cyrillic letters, a small skull stenciled in black,

and the identifying designation K-27. The warhead of a nuclear missile.

"Load it onto my vehicle," Cassa said.

Ivanov nodded happily, motioning his gloved hands as his crew did so. When they were finished, he said, "A good payday for us. My men and me. The girl will be pleased with our service, yes? Where is our payment?"

"Right here." Cassa removed a silenced gun from the pocket of his anorak and shot Ivanov and the excavators once each, for a total of six shots. He removed the clip from his handgun and dropped it into the watery hole, then inserted a second clip.

Back on shore, Cassa supervised the loading of the device into the jet's cargo bay. That was easy—put the big thing into the space. The men were amenable. No one had heard the shots offshore. They were chatting. What he knew of Russian told him it was small talk. Some of them laughed. It didn't take long to secure the warhead in the jet's cargo bay.

"Where is Ivanov?" one man asked.

"He wanted you to be paid now," Cassa said.

"Ah, the Teutonic Order is as good as its word!"

"Count on it," Cassa said, and emptied his fresh clip into them, saving one shot for the jet's pilot, who was using the station's rest facilities. When he saw the bodies, he started to run, but the final bullet stopped that.

After reloading his handgun once more, Cassa boarded the plane and fastened himself into the pilot's seat. He taxied to the runway and left the island, heading for Cyprus.

CHAPTER THIRTY-THREE

"'Follow me,' huh?" Darrell murmured.

The second motorcycle had, of course, gotten tripped up on a rooftop, because motorcycles weren't supposed to be up there. Which was just fine. But when he, Lily, and his mother had escaped down into the streets, they'd found Wade trying to get back to Becca. "Follow me!" he'd said, and so they had, right to where—*bam!*—the black cars were waiting for them.

They were caught. Because of Wade.

"So much for 'follow me'!"

"Give it a rest, Darrell," said Lily.

Darrell had managed to push his mother—he hoped not too roughly—to safety around a corner, while the rest of them were thrown into one of Drangheta's cars. The goons all wore the same tattoo as the dead guy on the train. People in the street were staring, but when Lily stuck her head out the window and yelled a couple of French words Becca had taught her, Darrell guessed that they were the wrong couple of words, because everybody just shrugged and went on with their stuff.

Of course they did. *Drangheta's a local boy. These are his peeps.*

The next thing they knew, the goons had pulled up to a junky building, dragged them all inside, tied Darrell's hands behind his back—in zip cuffs, no less—and chained him to what seemed to be a water pipe.

They did the same with Wade and Lily.

Then they stomped on their phones until they were dust and stole their passports—the fake ones—which was no problem for Darrell, who was happy for Robin to become a thing of the past. Lily groaned when her tablet was cracked under the thugs' heels. The brutes weren't gentle with the kids, either. Darrell's wrists had been stretched and twisted and mangled before they were cuffed.

Is this what Lily feels like when she types too much?
Random thought. Never mind.

Silva, Becca, and his mother were . . . he didn't know

where. He was pretty sure his mother had slipped away. It was just Silva and Becca he didn't know about. And no way to know anything, because Mr. Follow Me had gotten them caught and their phones crushed atomically.

Wade sat moping on the other side of the filthy room, legs crossed, head down. One of the grunts had elbowed him in the side of the face. His cheek was swollen and red. Lily had been thrown down about ten feet from Darrell. They were all pretty quiet at first, but they hadn't heard any sound outside the door for a while, so they began to whisper.

"What are they waiting for?" said Lily. He saw her wiggling her fingers.

"For Drangheta to come and put a bullet in our heads," Wade grumbled.

"Would he?" asked Darrell. "I think he'd want us to talk first. They always want you to talk. Tell them who you're working for. Or *verking for*. Which is how bad guys say it."

"Except that this isn't Germany. It's Morocco," said Lily.

"Still."

"Either way, he scares me," said Lily. She was still wiggling her fingers and now looking up and across the room, as if seeing something no one else did.

Darrell snorted. "He scares you? You think?"

"I *mean*," she said, "we know about Galina. Mostly. She's deadly enough. But this guy? Okay, he's a killer. But of us?"

"Let's not find out," said Wade.

"I'm going to state the obvious here," Darrell said. "I should have led."

Wade lifted his face painfully. "What makes you think you would have done any better than me? Motorcycles chasing us across the rooftops of a strange city. Bullets whizzing all around us. Really, you leading? You ought to be thanking me that you can still thank me."

Lily made a face. "That sounds like a Darrellism. What do you mean?"

"That you *can't* thank me if you're dead, which you're *not*—which is thanks to *me*—so I'll thank you to go ahead and thank me, and we'll call it even."

"Help, I'm in a room with crazies," she said.

"Why don't we just escape again?" asked Darrell. "That way you could all thank *me*, because instead of Mr. Follow Me, I'm pretty sure I'm the one who'll get us out of here."

Wade snorted. "Really, Mr. Zip Cuffs? You can get us out of here? Right now? Because we need to get out of here right now. Becca's alone out there, for crying out loud! To say nothing of your own mother! So can you get us free now?"

"Now?" Darrell twisted his wrists behind him. The zip cuffs were really tight. And strong. "Maybe not *now*. But eventually."

"I thought so."

"Oh, you thought so—"

"Boys!" Lily grumbled under her breath. "I need to think. Honestly, it should be *all* of us thinking, but you can't seem to, so I will. First of all, where are we?"

Darrell snorted again. "North Africa," he said. "You really need a map."

"The humor just never stops," she said with a glare. "I mean what kind of a place is this? We didn't travel far, so we're still in Casablanca. We could still be in the medina, which is the eastern part of the city. I think. Or the western. Or in the center. One of those."

"You *do* need a map."

"Darrell, lay off," said Wade. "It looks like a warehouse."

It looked like a warehouse to Darrell, too.

It smelled of stale motor oil and scorched metal. One wall was lined with rows of oil drums stacked two high. There were things piled up almost completely around them—barrels, crates, stacks of boards, dozens of cardboard cartons, buckets—like a little fort. Or a bonfire waiting to be lit.

Through an upper window they heard a car approach, then idle on the street outside.

"Someone's coming," whispered Lily. "Get ready."

"To do what? Die?" said Wade. "Because that's what—"

The bolts on the other side of the door slid back. There was a jangle of keys and a scrape near the handle, and the door opened.

Ugo Drangheta stepped—*limped*—into the room. The door closed behind him.

Up close, the dark-suited man was far more imposing than they'd previously realized—even wounded. His shoulders were a yard wide from end to end. His left arm was in a sling, his jacket draped over his bloodied shirt. Still, his chest was massive. His face had the look of a boxer's—battered, scarred, dented, with faraway eyes as deep as tunnels. His voice matched his looks, a gravel of words spilling over them.

"You may be curious to know that I cared little for whatever Galina Krause wanted. I wanted solely to kill her. Now I am not sure. Tell me of these relics."

They looked from one to another and back again.

"Define *relics*," Darrell said.

"You are the funny one of the group?" Drangheta said, cracking no smile.

"Just this once," said Darrell. "Usually it's Wade."

"You may also like to know that I care nothing about you. After you help me, I will toss you aside like spoiled fruit."

"Then (*a*) why should we help you," Wade said, "and (*b*) what do you want?"

Drangheta attempted to smile this time. It looked like he was forcing his face to do something it had never done before. "Where is Dr. Kaplan?"

"My mom? You'll never catch her," said Darrell.

Drangheta shook his iron head. "Your father."

The question surprised them.

"I . . . why do you want to know that?" said Wade.

"You are playing a dangerous game," Drangheta said. "A game of vast wealth and power. Your father is an astronomer, yes? A physicist? Galina is interested, and so am I. Where is he?"

Lily cleared her throat. "We forget."

Drangheta closed his eyes for a second, then opened them. "I will take down Galina Krause. I will destroy the Order. You? You are merely pawns in this game."

"Sorry, we don't do that," said Wade. "We don't pawn."

Drangheta pushed his face up to Wade's. "You have ten minutes to tell me where Dr. Roald Kaplan is. Galina Krause wants to know this, so I want to know this. Ten minutes!" He stormed from the room. The door was bolted behind him, his car drove off, and they were alone again.

"What was that even about?" asked Darrell. "Why does he want to know about Dad? And why does Galina want to know where Dad is?"

"Good question, for later," Lily said. "Now we have to get out of here or he'll kill us. You know he will. He doesn't know how valuable I am."

Wade grunted. "This is so not good."

Lily wriggled her wrists. It was painful. Zip cuffs, heavy nylon interlocking bands, seemed easy enough to break free of, except that they were as strong as iron and as hard and sharp as aluminum handcuffs. "Darrell, you're the zip-cuff expert. How do we get out of these things?"

He looked at her. "Uh . . . yell? Yell really loud?"

She smirked. "Ha! I knew it. You're the first person I ever heard who actually used the words *zip cuffs*, and you don't know anything about them. Good thing I looked them up when you first said it and before I became tabletless. I discovered that there are three ways to get out of them. One and two won't work, but three might. I'll free myself first, then help Wade . . ."

Darrell seemed to be waiting for her to finish her statement. She didn't. "What about me? Are you saying you won't let me out?"

Lily grinned. "That depends on whether you agree to let me lead."

His eyes widened. "You?"

"I'll let you think about that while I free myself. Luckily, these are narrow cuffs, and everyone knows that zip cuffs can't stretch when they're stressed to the maximum. It makes it easier to snap them apart. This is where my former gymnastic wrists come in handy."

She clamped her wrists as close together as she was able to, then gripped the end of the zip tie with her teeth and pulled hard, tightening them as much as she could bear. "Oh, oh . . ." Then she flung her arms out.

"Ackk!" Nothing happened except that it felt as if she'd cut her hands off. Her wrists were red, bleeding near the bone. But she had to, right? No choice. Just do it. She pressed her wrists close and jerked out harder than before. The plastic tie snapped under the strain and flew across the room in two halves.

"Yes!" cried Wade. "Lily, you did it!"

"Ow, ow, ow, I'm free!" she said. "I did it! Internet

power! Intelligence officer! Me, me, me!"

"And now—" Darrell started.

"Now I lead." Lily rubbed her wrists while she poked around the room for a knife; she found one, and—*slit-slit*—the boys were free. "Stack some crates under the window. Wade, find me something heavy to throw." They did as they were told. An engine revved loudly and stopped outside. They heard footsteps.

"Drangheta's back to kill us some more," whispered Wade, handing her a large monkey wrench.

"Hide behind the barrels," she said. They were so obedient. She would miss that. She waited until she heard a key in the lock outside the door; then she hurled the wrench at the window, shattering it. The door burst open, and two thick-necked men pushed into the room.

"No!" one shouted, seeing the stacked crates and the broken window. They rushed back out to the car. A few moments later, the kids heard the sound of tires screeching away; then, after waiting another few minutes, they finally crept to the door.

Darrell poked his head out. "All clear," he said. "Let's beat it."

They were out into the hot morning streets, running as fast as they could.

The Day Book of
Nicolaus Copernicus

His Secret Voyages
in Earth and Heaven

faithfully recorded
by his assistant
Hans Novak
Danzig A.D. 1514

CHAPTER THIRTY-FOUR

A s the sun bore down over the narrow alleys, Becca pressed herself into the lessening shadows with lessening success. While she might have been able to proceed in London or even Rome, this was a completely different culture. She was so obviously a pale American teenager, lost in the strange marketplace of Casablanca, which she both couldn't and didn't want to get out of.

My friends are here. They're looking for me. I know they are.

Unless they weren't. Maybe she was the only one who was still free. Maybe the others, the people she loved most in the world . . . That was a dark thought she'd better push off to the side.

Breathe, Becca, breathe.

Long. Calm. Breaths.

She did. It helped. She remembered Galina breathing her pain away. But that was a thought for later. She looked around. The smells, the sounds, the heat, the aridity of the air drying up her nose, sent a sharp pain into her forehead.

She reached up and tested her nose for blood. No. Not that. Not like London.

She took a breath, ready to start off again, when a strange grinding sound came from the interior of her bag. Like metal on metal. And clicking, as if something were striking the teeth of a moving gear.

What in the world?

She slipped behind a row of already-crowded market stalls and found herself in a small shaded alley. She opened her bag and looked inside.

As Becca watched, she felt her breath leave her body. A spark, a speck of silvery light, flew from the diary to the box with the *ocularia* inside, where it sizzled and was returned. Back and forth, forth and back, a miniature bridge of sparkling light formed between the two objects in her bag. It wasn't magic. No. It was electrical. A charge existed between the two objects. Between the silver of one and the silver ink of the other.

"They're connected. They *are*," she whispered. And there, in the quiet of a narrow alley in Morocco, she discovered what she had been hoping to find.

A way to read the diary's silver pages.

Her fingers trembled as she removed the glasses from the box, unfolded them, and gently slipped them on her face. She hooked the curved arms over the tops of her ears one at a time so as not to put strain on them. The last thing she wanted to do was bend the framework of the old device.

I must look silly. Like a character in a comic book.

Blinking through the three-sided, mirror lenses, she discovered that by shifting one or another of them by almost infinitesimal degrees with a dial on each side, you could obtain any number of different combinations. Wade could have told her how many exactly, but with six actual lenses it must be quite a lot.

She turned the diary pages until she found the silvery ones. Even with the glasses, they were illegible.

You have to set the lenses to the right combination to read the silver ink.

She took off the glasses and studied the gears on each side of the frames. They were numbered, so you needed to know the numbers to set them at—three number settings from one to ten on each side. But how did you know how to set them?

The only three-number sequence she had found so far was the five-five-five of the tiny triangle on the Leonardo page. Would it work?

The dials were so small, like watch winders, and so difficult to read that she was forced to do what Lily laughed at, put on two pairs of reading glasses. Squinting through the double glasses, she turned the tiny dials with her fingertips. Five, five, five on one side, five, five, five on the other.

She put the *ocularia* back on and looked at the first silvery page.

Her blood pumped in her ears as letters seemed to float out, finally visible against the tangled mesh of crisscrossing lines. It was handwriting, but the handwriting was not Copernicus's, nor Hans Novak's, both of whose styles she knew. The letters were inked back to front, and they were in Italian.

Everyone knows Leonardo wrote backward! He must have written in Copernicus's diary!

Translating the words as she went along, Becca read the first passage.

Two years ago, in the spring of 1517, I was asked by Nicolo Copernico to create a mechanical arm made entirely of silver.

Inside the arm would be a motor of sorts. I will not say what it was, but it was an engine of power. The arm itself was given to a pirate.

Yes, a pirate! It was Nicolo's friend Baba Aruj, known as Barbarossa. He saved Nicolo's other friend, young Hans Novak, and thus the gift of the replacement arm. Sadly, Baba perished. Well, what do you expect? A pirate's life is a dangerous life.

Now it is 1519, the month of March. I am old and dying myself.

Still, Nicolo has called on me and on Baba's younger brother, Heyreddin, also called Barbarossa. Together the three of us are to bury Baba's silver arm.

I will not say where we bury the arm—that is for Nicolo alone to tell—but it is an arduous procedure to get there, and even more wearying to create the resting place.

Still, my calculations are so precise that all is accomplished in the hours before sunrise. My fine saws nimbly remove the great stone. While Nicolo and Heyreddin do most of the work, I doodle. Finally, I lay my creation within the space they make for it. Stout steel cables are driven deep *below, coiling fast into the bedrock.*

*"The room will flood if the cables are broken," I say.
"The floor will sink. The walls around us will collapse—"*

*There is a sudden sound from above. A stamping horse.
A gruff command.*

*"We are found!" says Barbarossa. "Quickly, withdraw
the three keys! We must run!"*

Then they appear from the shadows.

*Twelve women in death-black robes edged with silver,
hooded to hide their faces from the light. They speak in
unison.*

*"We are the Mothers, and shall evermore be Guardians
of your legacy, Magister. We shall be here, generation after
generation, even unto the end of days!"*

Her breath caught in her throat. "Oh . . . Lily! The
woman in Florida! 'Generation after generation'? She
was one of those Mothers! Five hundred years later,
they're still around?"

*The Mothers reveal swords with wide steel blades and
curving double-edged points, each weapon a wing of steel.*

*"Away!" say the Mothers. Half of them stream up the
stairs before us while the other half show us a different
way back up and out to the shore.*

My chest aches with pain; my head swims. I hear the clash of blades. But soon we are in our dinghy and rowing swiftly away.

Together we three hid the silver arm. But to find the three keys of Barbarossa, you must follow Nicolo himself. For he and Heyreddin must themselves hide them.

Me? Alas, I am not long for this world.

—LdV

That was all that Leonardo had written on the silver page that used the five-five-five combination of lenses. In Nicolaus's hand, however, were three minute scratches:

1′43

These numbers were different. They were the shaking writing of a very old man. "He wrote these later. Much later," she said to herself. "When exactly?"

She then wondered if the numbers were not only the next combination of the *ocularia*, but also a date.

"One, forty-three. January 1543? He died in May of that year. Could this be when he and Heyreddin hid the keys? He was practically on his deathbed!"

She quickly reset the lenses to the new combination

and put the glasses back on. The frames bit into her face, burned her cheekbones like hot wire. But there it was. A second level of the code suddenly became visible.

Only this time it wasn't writing. It was a drawing.

Before she removed the *ocularia* and put them back into their box, she copied the drawing into her notebook as closely as she could. Her heart was fluttering so quickly, she thought she might faint.

Copernicus, da Vinci, and Barbarossa together did this amazing thing. And she was practically there with them, reading their words, their images, their codes. If what had happened in London had changed her in any way, it was this: to know that the past is right here with us, inside us, all around us, everything we are.

Practically laughing, she spoke aloud to the empty street.

"I found the first part of the story. We have the directions to the first key. We're on our way!"

Setting the diary and the glasses back into her bag, she looked both ways and tried to take stock of where she was. Casablanca and the noise of a hot morning. Okay, then—*soon* they would be on their way. For now, she was still very much alone.

Sara Kaplan had no idea where in the medina she was, but she'd never been so terrified in her life. Not even in the coffin. Of course she was scared, and the reason was easy to see. She wasn't an operative, a secret agent, a soldier, or a spy. She'd just been trying to act like one. Yet somehow she'd become the head of a spy unit . . . of children. She was a mother, a stepmother, an archivist, and a wife. But did those things keep her from losing her children?

No.

She ran from street to street, using all the French she knew, but no one confessed to seeing any Western children wandering or running. She hoped Becca was still free, still in possession of the priceless diary—and the stolen *ocularia*—and that Silva was keeping her safe. The others, the others had been swallowed up by a black car. She knew she had to keep herself from being snatched or there would be no hope at all, so when there'd been a chance, she'd slid away. Now it seemed like the stupidest and most careless thing to have done. Not being with her family, even if they were in danger, drove her crazy.

Like a mother should always be, when thinking about her children.

And then, among all the faces in a sea of faces, she spied one she knew. Silva. Alone. Limping, cradling his arm, coming for her, and calling out, "I know where they are!"

The city was coming more and more alive around Becca. The tinkle of tiny bells and a fragrant aroma of cooking floated down from the open windows she passed. There was the odor of exhaust, too, but that was as beautiful in its way as the sunlight and the music weaving through the air.

It was serene, almost peaceful. She moved along the streets, carefully tracing and retracing the same ways, hoping to find her friends. She had discovered a huge clue to the location of the relic. The *ocularia* and the diary *did* work together. It was monumental! It took her breath so suddenly that she had to pause. She leaned against a wall on the shaded side of the alley, and felt the blocks cool her burning shoulder blades.

"*Une matinée chaude, non?*"

Becca looked up. A girl, maybe fourteen, peered down at her from an upper window, a lazy smile on her face. As differently as she was dressed and as strange as their seeing each other was, they both smiled at the same time.

A hot morning? "Oui, très chaude," Becca replied. *"Bonjour."*

"*Vous êtes perdues?*"

Am I lost? Becca wondered. "Yes. *Oui. Un peu. Pourriez-vous me dire comment se rendre à l'Hôpital d'Enfants?*"

The girl's face turned serious. "*Vous n'êtes pas blessées, êtes-vous?*

Am I hurt? "*Non, non. Mes amis sont là.*" *My friends are there. I hope.*

She smiled from the balcony. "*Ah, oui. Je peux vous amener. Il n'est pas loin. Avez-vous faim? J'apporterai quelque chose.*"

"Hungry? Yes. *Oui, oui, merci!*"

The girl vanished inside the room and was out the door on the street in minutes with a small glass of tea and a hot roll wrapped in a cloth napkin, which she gave to Becca. *"Je m'appelle Reyah."* She turned toward the end of the alley. *"Par ici. Allons-y!"*

"Reyah. Reyah. Merci."

Becca tucked her bag tight under her arm and wove with Reyah to the end of the alley and out across the nearest square.

CHAPTER THIRTY-FIVE

The sun was directly overhead now, burning down on the streets.

Wade eventually did lead the way through them, but it was only because Lily let him. She seemed tired. Tired of everything, actually.

When he asked her what was up, she said, "Nothing." A few seconds later, she said, "Well, not nothing. A text from my mom. She wants to talk to me. They both do. Together."

"What about?"

"I didn't get to answer before the goons busted my phone."

"It could be good."

She shook her head. "No, it couldn't. I know why she's calling. It's about how to split visitation. Who I want to live with which days, and who doesn't want me which days. Splitting me between them. Anyway, that is as far away from all of this as possible. I can't think about it. But I also can't lead. These streets all look alike to me. You lead."

So he did.

After a thousand false starts and blind alleys, they finally made it out of the crowded medina and scraped enough coins together to pay for three tram rides, the last of which they left when it stopped at Boulevard Abdelmoumen. From there, a twenty-minute zigzag walk due east brought them to the Hôpital d'Enfants.

Wade ran when he saw Becca waiting for them, and didn't mind what anyone thought when he wrapped his arms around her. She must have felt the same, at least partly, because she hugged him back, then Darrell and Lily, too. Even so, it was the new-style reunion. Short, sweet, back to the business at hand.

"Meet Reyah," Becca said, introducing the girl with her. "She helped me and fed me and brought me here. We can trust her. I think she can help us, too. Sara's just inside—"

"Here!" Sara ran out from an office, dirty, her face

smudged and bruised, but happy to see them together. Silva, suffering a minor bullet wound to his arm, had escaped his captors—who didn't want him anyway—seen the kids on the tram, then had found Sara and accompanied her to the hospital.

Knowing Julian would want the kids and Sara to have new phones, Silva then went out to purchase one for each of them and a tablet for Lily. He also drew on his bank account to provide Sara with a thick pouch of dollars, euros, and Moroccan dirhams.

Lily right away powered up her new phone and the tablet, downloaded her favorite apps, and checked her remotely stored data and found it all there. After that, she texted her new number to her parents, then paused and turned both devices off—unheard of for her.

"They stole our passports, too," said Darrell with mock regret. "I think we should use our real ones now. Galina knows we're in the game. We can't hide forever."

Sara seemed to think about that for a moment, then nodded. "Agreed. There are miles to go before this is over. We'll need to be us again."

"Drangheta asked us about Dad," said Wade. "He's hot to get to him for some reason. And he said Galina is, too. We need to warn him."

Sara asked them exactly what Drangheta had said,

then made the call, while Becca told them what the glasses did and what she had discovered in the diary. She showed them all the drawing she'd made in her notebook. "Reyah, this is what I wanted you to see."

Reyah was bewildered but interested. *"Très fascinant. Il est vieux?"*

"Yes, very old," said Becca.

Wade wanted his brain to piece everything together, but it wasn't all there yet. "In 1517, Nicolaus asks da Vinci to make a silver arm for Barbarossa. But he dies, so they bury the arm with the relic still inside. You can only find it with three keys, which Nicolaus and Barbarossa Two hide when they're old. This drawing tells us the location of one of the keys, is that right?"

"Right," said Darrell. "But how do we decode the drawing?"

After Sara left a message for Roald, she studied the picture. "It's an allegorical drawing. The sun, the ruined columns. The tree coming out of the column. And there are words. Reyah?"

Reyah squinted and studied the tiny writing. She told Becca that the Arabic word beneath the broken column on the right was *Hijri*, which was like a version of "AD" or "BC" for the Islamic calendar. Combined with the number it would mean *Hijri 84* or *Year 84*. She didn't know exactly what that translated to, but it was a long time ago. The word beneath the central column was *Carthage*.

"Which means what?" asked Darrell.

"Ruins. Old city. Very old," Reyah said in English.

"Where is Carthage?" asked Wade.

"Tunis. Coast of Tunisia. Two thousand kilometers, maybe. Far from here."

"We need to get there," said Sara. "We need to get a flight."

"Not at the major airports," Silva said. "Your enemies—all of them—will be watching for you. You have the glasses they both want. You're the target."

"So we need to fly under the radar," Wade said.

"Fly? Plane?" said Reyah, flapping her hands like wings.

"*Oui, mais secrètement,*" Becca said.

"*Voilà! Médiouna. Vous pouvez voler à Tunisie de Médiouna!*" The way she said it, *Médiouna* sounded like a fantasy city in a tale of genies and flying carpets.

Silva frowned. "Médiouna *is* an airfield. That is, it *used* to be one, and I heard about a club of British flyers who used to keep their rigs at the place. I'm not sure if any of them are still there, or even alive, but if they are, Médiouna might be the best field to fly from, after all.

I'll drive you out there—"

"No you won't," said Sara, like a den mother. "You're bleeding. You're going straight into this hospital and, child or not, you're going to get fixed up while we find ourselves a nice taxicab. We're ahead of the game so far, we have the glasses, the diary. Kids, come on."

CHAPTER THIRTY-SIX

One hour, three cab rides, and fifty euros later, the five of them arrived at a ghost town of wooden shacks, broken strips of pavement, and fields of weeds and dirt, which was—so their final driver insisted—an airport.

"Where in the world are we?" Wade asked.

"Is Médiouna!" said the man behind the wheel.

"This can't be right," said Becca.

"Yes, yes, is Médiouna Airfield. You fly from here."

In his mind, Wade watched the relic drift so far from their grasp that it vanished in the sandy distance. How long a journey did they have ahead of them? They didn't even have the first of the three keys. Did Triangulum still exist? Plus, where in the world *were* they?

"Médiouna!" said the driver. He took their money and left.

"Seriously, there's nothing here," Darrell said. "I mean no . . . thing."

"There's flat . . . ness," said Becca.

"No, you know, this is good," Lily said surprisingly. "If the first of the keys is in Tunis, then we need to get there before Galina does. She doesn't know where to look yet, so we have a real chance. Either way, we shouldn't waste any more time."

Wade was glad to hear Lily step up. She was feeling bad about her parents, but she had a spark. It was enough to get them moving.

They hiked through the weeds and outlying sand to the only hangar that had a sign of life. A transistor radio was playing. Darrell identified the tunes as British rock from the 1960s. Maybe that was new music here. Half in and half out of the hangar stood what appeared to be a broken-down wreck of an old single-wing cargo plane. A wrinkled man sat at a small desk just inside the doorway. He was bent over it, doing paperwork. He wore a desert cap with a flap down the back to protect his neck from sunburn. A large dog lay sleeping at his feet.

"Excuse me, we need to fly to Tunis," Sara said. "A

friend suggested we might get there from here?"

The man raised his face. He had, Wade estimated, a good twenty years on his stepmother, or may simply have been in the sun too long.

"Tunis, is it?"

He spoke like an English actor.

"We need to get there in a hurry," Becca added.

It was as if the man suddenly woke up. "Tunis? In a hurry? Do you, by Jove?" he said, bolting up from the desk and extending his hand. "Welcome! I'm Pinky Chamberlain. My partner, Bingo, will fly you to Tunis, every single one of you. If you can pay, that is."

"We can pay," Sara said. "But we need to get there as soon as we can."

"You're on desert time now," Pinky said, waving them inside the hangar. The dog followed, wagging its tail slowly. "Tunis is quite a jaunt, after all. You didn't happen to bring your own plane, by any chance?"

They stared at him.

"No? Well, no problem. We do have one, of course. It's just that it's a bit . . ." He trailed off. "I say, Bingo. Customers! You'll love Bingo, you will. He'll have the plane up and running in no time. Or, rather, running and *then* up, if you see what I mean. Oh, Bingy, do be sociable!"

The man named Bingo removed his head from an open panel under the engine of the cargo plane. He was tall and sticklike, and his hair, what there was of it, flew away from his head in all directions as if it didn't want to be there.

Pinky explained what they'd come for, while Bingo shook their hands.

"Really?" said Bingo, his eyes wide with surprise. "Fly the old deathtra . . . mail plane, eh? I'd be delighted. Delighted, I say! You have life insurance, yes? No matter, let's just be off! But seriously, we'll need a list of next of kin."

"We're pretty much all here," said Sara, introducing them all.

"Well, I call this a party!" Bingo boomed. "Last one on board is copilot." When Wade laughed, he added, "No, son, I'm serious. Someone really will have to help with the whole mappy thing. The sand all looks pretty similar to me."

"Oh, he's just joking, of course!" said Pinky. "But if you could help him, naturally, it might make your trip a bit more . . ." He didn't finish.

It was settled quickly. The only plane, a Piper J-3 Cub, had a normal range of a hundred and fifty miles. The distance to Tunis was "somewhere around a thousand miles." But this "original Flitfire," as Pinky Chamberlain proudly called it, had been equipped with two extra fuel tanks for long-distance mail service. "Which makes it pretty cramped inside, but it can make it to Tunis in five hours, including only one refueling stop. Or more, at the most."

Bingo quickly finished working on the plane, then Pinky joined him, wielding a pair of hammers to help get the engine panel back into place. The dog barked with each rap of the hammer.

"All aboard!" said Bingo, and he and Pinky embraced as if it was the last time they'd see each other. It was a long hug. You could barely tell where Pinky ended and Bingo began. Finally, they pulled apart.

"Woof, woof, Gussie," Bingo said, and the dog echoed him. "Off we go!"

With a symbolic point of his finger to the east—the direction they were flying—Bingo climbed into the pilot's seat, lowered his goggles, and set the controls for starting. They piled into the cabin after him. It was even tinier than Wade expected. The six of them were jammed into one another, even when Wade decided to take his place up front in the copilot seat.

Meanwhile, on the ground, Pinky gripped the propeller with both hands and swung it down with a grunt. Nothing. He did it again. Nothing. Again. Again. Nothing. Nothing. Neither Bingo nor Pinky seemed surprised.

The seventh time, it caught.

It caught, but the engine at full power sounded like a cross between a go-kart and an electric can opener. It vibrated though the frame and rattled the fuselage. The way the plane tumbled out of the hangar was also not inspiring. Pinky waved exaggeratedly with one hand, wiping his cheeks with the other.

"We'll make it, won't we?" asked Lily.

"Sorry, headphones, can't hear you!" said Bingo. He wasn't wearing headphones.

And they were off. Mostly off. The airstrip was half smothered in drifted sand, and its borders were difficult to make out, even for Bingo. Until he lifted his goggles off his face. "Ah, there it is," he murmured.

With the engines screaming like a chorus of cats, and the soft wheels bouncing like beach balls, the plane finally dragged itself up from the ground. They banked once over the airfield, where they saw the tiny form of Pinky waving both arms, and Gussie running circles around him, then headed east. Soon they were over the desert—the real desert of sand dunes rolling to the horizon like golden waves.

CHAPTER THIRTY-SEVEN

The noise was horrendous. Lily blocked her ears, but that didn't do much. Everything around her hummed and rattled and shook. At least it was distracting. Only Bingo and Wade had normal seats. The others sat on three buckets turned upside down, while Sara clung to the rearmost contraption, which was a thing apparently made of bent rods with a "cushion" cut out of two slices of plank nailed together.

No one was anywhere near comfortable, but they were moving over the desert.

"Bingo, what do you know about Carthage?" asked Wade.

"Garbage?" he said. "Just chuck it in the back. But

don't hit your mum."

"No!" he yelled. "Carthage!"

Bingo pulled back on the engine. The volume of noise lessened a decibel. "Ancient. Nothing much there now. Home of just about every civilization for a while," he said. "You can check the book."

"The book?"

"Behind Miss Rebecca's seat there!"

Becca smiled, surprised to hear her full name. She reached behind her seat for a book, which she found sitting on top of a metal cash box. Once she grabbed the book, the box popped open, something slithered out, and she jumped off her bucket, screaming.

"A snake! A snake!"

Bingo half turned around. "Oh, that's just Corky. She's harmless. I say, Wade, take the control stick." Bingo slid from his seat, leaving Wade to hold the plane steady. "Here, Corky! Cork, oh, do come on!" Using the cash box as a trap, he coaxed the wiggling brown snake to him, scooped it up with the jaws of the box and lid, and snapped it shut. "Sorry about that. Corky's just a harmless little carpet viper."

"Is she defanged?" asked Sara.

"Defanged? Is that a thing?" Bingo slid the box back behind Becca's bucket. "Well, then, perhaps Corky's not so harmless." He took the control stick back from a terrified Wade and settled back in his seat, whistling to himself.

Soon they had left any grassy hills behind and were flying low over the sand, with great humped dunes loping one after the other as far as they could see.

The book, which Becca had dropped on Lily's lap, was a beat-up copy of *The Barbary Coast: Sketches of French North Africa*. It was written by Albert Edwards and published in 1913.

"You don't have anything more, uh, recent?" asked Lily.

"The past is the past," he said over his shoulder. "Maybe there's an eyewitness account of Carthage in there. Why are you interested, if I may ask?"

They told him in basic terms what they were looking for and showed him the drawing in Becca's notebook.

"An ancient key? Well, that's just spiffy!" Bingo said. "I'll get you to Carthage as quickly as . . . as . . . " Like Pinky, he didn't quite finish his sentence.

After skimming the table of contents, Lily found a page with one paragraph about Carthage.

Three quarters of an hour's ride from Tunis is the place where Carthage stood. A strange fate has overtaken the ancient city. The vengeance of Rome was complete, no one stone was left in place upon another. The site was sown with salt. A pagan Roman city, a Christian Roman city, a Vandal city, and an Arab city have been built on the same site and have passed away. The archaeologists have not discovered with any certainty where a single one of the buildings of Punic Carthage stood. But beneath the many strata formed by the ruins of vanished civilizations they have come upon the graveyards of the ancient city.

"Graveyards of the ancient city," said Darrell. "Great. Grab your shovels, folks."

"I do not dig in graveyards," said Lily.

For some reason, reading that aloud made her very sad. Nothing lasted. Everything went away. Even great things ended. She passed the book to Becca.

"Okay, but if Carthage was already a ruin when our friends went there in the sixteenth century," Becca said, "why would they hide a precious key there?"

"Exactly," said Wade. "People rebuild over ruins and probably cart the really good stuff away and reuse it anyway."

"The book says the Arabs conquered it last," said Sara, peeking over Becca's shoulder. "Maybe that's a clue. The ruined columns in the drawing might signify

Carthage after it fell. And trees mean growth."

"Good," said Darrell.

"The year," said Wade. "Hijri 84, or 84 Hijri. When is that, Bingo?"

"I say, this is fun!" he said. "If I remember correctly, year one of the Hijra is the first year of the Islamic calendar. It's somewhere around our year 622. So add eighty-four to that and you get 706 or so. Ballpark, anyway. Hold on! It's coming back to me now. According to whom you read, Carthage was destroyed by the Muslims anywhere from 698 to 703 or so. Your drawing could very well be about the fall of Carthage!"

While the others started debating that, Lily realized that she had was zoning out. She needed a break from head games. There was no service for the brand-new tablet Silva had picked up for her, it was only half charged anyway, and she didn't want to risk having to answer—or ignore—a call from her mother on either the tablet or her phone, so she didn't bother firing either of them up. Instead, she glanced out the rattling window next to her.

The sun was bearing down on them, making the plane hotter with every mile. Still there was something soothing about the engine's rumbling around her, and once she let go of the possibility of talking with her parents, she found that flying a few dozen feet over the desert, skimming the grassy plains, then the dunes, was more freeing than anything she'd experienced before.

While the others kept up their humming conversation about Carthage, Lily wished she could just dip her hand out the window and skim the sand as if it were water outside a canoe. Just watching the ground flash by, her whole body throbbing to the grind of the primitive engine through her bucket, she'd never been so happy to be disconnected from the rest of the world. Being as far away as she could possibly be from the situation back home made her chest flutter, then pound with excitement. She dismissed her life, all of it, every bit, for this. Just *this*.

This was living: feeling the world move by, much more slowly than she had ever thought it could from a plane, riding the sand at a height of fifty or sixty feet, sweeping past the foothills of a range of mountains arcing to the north. The anger and the fighting and the emptiness had gone.

"What are those called?" asked Darrell. "Those mountains up there."

"Those are the tail end of the Atlas Mountains, the ones that started all the way back in Casablanca, though we're nearly in Algeria now," said Bingo. "You know Atlas, the sorry chap who was cursed to tote the world around on his back? Well, those mountains are his backbone. They have marble quarries in there like you wouldn't believe. Black marble and yellow marble. Famous the world over, as they say."

"Marble," said Wade softly, turning around to face the others. "Columns are made of marble." He nudged Darrell aside, pinning himself between Becca and Lily. "Let's say the drawing shows Carthage after the battle in 703. What happens to ruins? Trees don't grow out of them, do they?"

"There are places so ancient that the stones and the trees become twined together," said Sara. "Like at old temples in Cambodia. Other places, too."

"Good, good," Wade said. "Anybody know what kind of tree this is?"

"A *tree* tree," said Darrell. "With a sun growing in it."

Keeping one hand on the controls, Bingo turned nearly completely around to examine Becca's drawing. "That there's an olive tree," he said. "*Sol* is Latin, of course, for sun."

Wade chewed his lip, then shook his head. "So how about this? The ruined city becomes like a quarry. I mean, we do this in Texas and everywhere. People reuse stuff all the time. Well, if Carthage was such a great city, it must have had great stuff. Marble columns and all. What if this picture means that we should be searching for what *grew* out of Carthage?"

Becca turned to him. "I like that. Maybe what we're looking for is a place that used the *ruins* of Carthage. A place that has something to do with an olive tree and a sun. And the outline. Bingo, what does the crescent moon on top mean?"

He glanced back at it. "Well, anything Arabic or Ottoman, I suppose. But the shape of the outline is like a doorway. A mosque, maybe?"

Wade was getting antsy now. "So after Carthage was destroyed in 703 or whenever, the stones were used to build something. Maybe a mosque. And if it *is* a mosque, the olive tree and the sun are the clues to tell us which one."

They all sat there. No one seemed to have any more to add.

Not bad, thought Lily. "It could use some fine-tuning. We'll get there. In the meantime, let's just look. It's beautiful out there."

"It's why I stayed," said Bingo. "I love the desert. Well, that and Gussie and Pinky, of course. Love Pinky."

"I think he loves you, too," said Sara.

Bingo dipped even lower over the dunes. "And we all love all of this."

Gazing at the rolling sand, Lily thought of where their journey was taking her, farther from her home than ever before. Especially now that her home was a question mark. She knew, she just knew, that there would be a message waiting for her the instant she turned on her phone. *Lily, please call! We have to talk!* She didn't want to talk. Not now. Not yet. She was too busy being herself. In this otherworldly place, doing strange and wonderful and dangerous things, she was becoming someone new, and that was what she really needed now.

Finally, as the distance between her and them grew and grew, Lily wondered if she'd ever see her parents together again and what it would mean if she never did.

It was a question she couldn't answer. She didn't want to. All she wanted was to watch the dunes roll on and on.

CHAPTER THIRTY-EIGHT

Central Italy
June 6
Early evening

After waiting most of the day for Paul Ferrere, who was unavoidably detained in Paris, Roald and Terence made the decision to head to the immense facility at Gran Sasso without him. The both hoped it wasn't a dumb move, but after yet another call from Dr. Petrescu, there seemed little choice.

Seven miles outside the underground laboratory, Terence pulled their rental car up to the first of several checkpoints. Four security guards came out of a pair of roadside buildings.

One said, "Please shut off the engine and leave the keys inside."

"We will park it for you," said another. "You will take an official car inside."

Roald shared a look with Terence. "All right," he said.

A few minutes later, a gray car appeared. A short middle-aged man got out of the rear and put on a large, nervous smile. "Dr. Roald Kaplan! And friend?" He extended his hand. "Pleased to meet you both."

Roald tried to read the man's face, but he couldn't tell much. Dr. Petrescu seemed to be trying too hard to smile, but it was difficult to tell for sure.

"We must enter, but first security photographs, yes?" the man said. "In the hut." He briskly led the way inside one of the checkpoint buildings, where both Roald and Terence stood for individual and joint photographs.

"Perfect, perfect," said Dr. Petrescu. "And now, we enter."

The man was pleasant enough, but something was off. Roald didn't like the feeling. "Doctor, your phone calls—"

"Not now," he said, narrowing his eyes. "Please. The car."

A uniformed driver drove all three of them into an immense complex of buildings at the foot of the large forested mountain. There they entered a steel doorway, which closed behind them, and drove another twenty minutes, coiling downward, until they arrived at a subterranean parking garage.

"This way, gentlemen." Dr. Petrescu used a card-access terminal and took them into an elevator, pushed a sequence of numbers, and had his handprint scanned. They descended several floors below the garage and exited into a long hallway.

Roald felt his senses go on alert. He made a note of everything, aware that Terence was doing the same. The walls of the hallway were brushed aluminum, the lighting recessed, the carpet beneath their feet dense and noise-suppressing. Roald shot a look at Terence. His friend's face was grim.

Dr. Petrescu's office was large, with a wide interior window overlooking a very large laboratory below. It was like something out of a James Bond film—a pristine lab bustling with activity—except that in this case, instead of a villain out for world domination, their host was a highly respected nuclear specialist.

Something was definitely off.

Roald's senses tingled as they did when he felt the presence of one of the Order's agents. The Order wasn't there, at least not visibly, but something of Galina's presence seemed to assert itself, and it worried him.

"You will see that we are nearly ready," Dr. Petrescu said. "Some five of your colleagues are only hours away. Beyond them, I am awaiting only three nuclear physicists who had to alter their plans, you see."

Dr. Petrescu looked around his office in a distracted manner.

"Doctor, please. Is everything all right?" Roald asked.

"Oh?" He turned to him as if he had just realized there were people in the room with him. "Oh, yes. Of course. Certainly. It's just that . . ." He trailed off and didn't finish, his fingers drumming the armrest of his chair.

He's waiting for something, Roald realized. *Or someone.*

"Dr. Petrescu," Terence said, picking up on the same feeling, "you seem distracted. Are you in trouble? Or not *trouble*, but, perhaps, danger? Is there something we can help you with?"

"I . . ." Petrescu tapped a gold letter opener on the rim of his coffee cup, seemingly unable to make his fingers do anything else. "Let me put it this way. Galina Krause. The young woman with the eyes? You know her, certainly you do. That is why I asked you here. Well, she knew about my little meeting."

"Wait. Are you saying you've seen her?" Roald asked.

"That is why I changed the time and place! And still I fear I will not be able to tell you all I have discovered. Temporal disturbances that cannot be reversed! Already perhaps it is too late."

"Tell us," Roald said. "Dr. Petrescu, you must."

"How did Galina Krause know about my meeting? I have no idea."

"I don't like it," said Terence. "We're not equipped for this, Roald."

"There is something the woman is trying to do," Dr. Petrescu said, setting the letter opener down. "Something terrible will happen. A disaster. A flood. She spoke of a flood. I hope we are safe here. But this is why I changed the place and time of the meeting. She was going to push her way in. I have fooled her, but I don't know for how long."

A flood? It sounded like the disasters Copernicus had told Becca about in London. "Can you be more specific, Doctor?" Roald asked. "I'm more sympathetic than you might guess. I know a lot about Galina. I've seen her power and the evil she's capable of."

"Dr. Petrescu, has Galina actually threatened you?" said Terence. "We can go to the authorities."

"Me? I care not for myself." Dr. Petrescu shook his head firmly. "We cannot risk angering her. No. I have arranged with a private security firm for our protection. We may not need it, perhaps, but there you are. The firm is said to be very fine. They have sometimes worked with the Vatican." His expression was a mixture of fear and desperation. "Perhaps you had better follow me to your rooms, Dr. Kaplan, Mr. Ackroyd. While we await the others to arrive."

As they followed Dr. Petrescu from the office, Roald saw Terence slide the letter opener from the desktop and slip it sideways into the lining of his coat.

CHAPTER THIRTY-NINE

"Where are we now?" Becca asked. "The sand is so red."

It was solidly afternoon, and the sky was a cloudless dome of white heat. The desert had changed color, darkening over the last hour.

"Ah, deep in Algeria now," said Bingo. "Red sand is one of the peculiarities of the Algerian desert. And now"—he pushed the control stick forward, and the nose of the Flitfire dipped—"it's time to refuel."

Becca clung to the struts framing the inside of the fuselage. The plane banked gently over a flat stretch of sand. Approaching below was a collection of little shelters made of tin. Two or three battered cars stood in haphazard relation to one another. Bingo identified a large fuel pump near a vintage gray plane that was parked outside one of the buildings.

"That old Spartan down there may have just arrived for fueling, too," he said. "You can still see the imprint of its tires in the sand."

Their landing was rough. The tracks that rutted the flatness of the ground were by no means a proper airstrip. The plane nearly tipped over twice on its way to a standstill. The boys seemed to love it, while Lily grumbled to herself.

Becca glanced over her shoulder. Sara sat in her makeshift seat, gripping the sides to keep from falling forward. She gave Becca a tight-lipped grin. "I'll be okay. Once we're on solid ground."

Sara was putting up a good front, but Becca saw the worry about Roald etching her features. During the flight she'd tried several times to contact him, and the uncertainty of no reply was taking its toll on her. Becca knew Wade felt the same. They all felt it.

"A half hour to get topped up, people," said Bingo. "Then we're off again."

Attached to the largest building, which seemed a hangar of sorts, was a low structure, tilted away from the roadside, with a broad awning supported by two stacks of crates. When they hopped out of the plane, the breeze blew at them like a constant hot exhaust, a wall of white sand-filled air. The low structure provided shade, but the moment they entered it they realized that the corrugated tin roof acted like a pot lid. It was stifling inside.

The place was empty except for a stick of a man behind a café counter, and two men in crumpled suits made of linen that had once been white. They sat at a small round table in the back of the room, a bottle of something brown on their table, surrounded by tiny glasses.

The smell of the café was wretched.

Becca felt the acidic contents of her stomach rising up her throat, burning it. She only kept herself from vomiting by pinching her nose tight and breathing through her mouth.

A tinny melody just shy of complete static surged in and out of a radio powered by an electric cord dangling from the ceiling fan. The fan rotated as slowly as possible.

"I say, chaps, need to fuel up my Piper," Bingo said to anyone listening. "Is Freddy still around these parts? We're rather in a rush."

"And water?" asked Darrell. "Do you have water?"

The man behind the counter, who hadn't moved except to watch them stumble in, opened his mouth as slowly as possible. "Freddy gone. Water, twenty dollar."

"Seriously?" Becca snapped. "We're dying here. Twenty dollars?"

The man shrugged. "Twenty-five."

There came a chuckle from the back of the room. The far larger of the two men fanned his wet face with a grimy straw fedora. He set it back on his head for a moment, then removed it to fan some more. He had a face completely without wrinkles—boylike, thought Becca—and she guessed that Lily, if she hadn't been so quiet for the last hour, would give him the name Bigboy, so that's what she called him in her head.

"Some vater for our guests, Prince Ali," Bigboy said unpleasantly in a Northern European accent that Becca guessed might be Dutch. "Put it on the company tab, along with the petrol for our Spartan out there. Chop-chop."

It was insulting and racist, thought Becca. Bigboy was like a throwback to a nasty old movie about linen-suited jerks in Africa. The man behind the counter shrugged and produced a plastic jug of warm water. Darrell took a cup of it to his mother, while Bingo went with the counter man outside to supervise the refueling of their plane.

"Thinks are different here," Bigboy said, without explaining what he meant. He seemed of indeterminate age. His skin was pink and very smooth with a hint of fuzz above his upper lip. His suit consisted of yards and yards of fabric.

Wade turned away from them and whispered to Becca from the corner of his mouth. "Do you think, I mean, that they were waiting for us?"

Becca frowned. "Except who knew we'd be landing here?"

"They always know," Darrell said under his breath. "*She* always knows."

Which was normally true. But here in the middle of the Algerian desert? Was it really possible that they'd known of their arrival, had flown here to be on-site when they arrived? Even Galina wasn't that clever.

The man with Bigboy was his complete opposite: a slender, almost two-dimensional guy with no waist or chest or shape at all, but whose face was stubbly and brown and as long as a sad mask at a theater. He wore a pair of goggles pushed up on his tall, sloping forehead. His mouth remained open the whole time, as if he were singing, "Ohhhhh."

He was Fish.

Bigboy rose nimbly from his chair—weightlessly, Becca thought—and wove between the tables over to them, while Fish just leaned up against the wall, picking his teeth with what appeared to be a needle.

"Hello, my frents," Bigboy said to them. "I say to myself, it is odd to espy such a grouping as yourselves in the desert, is it not? Then I realize. Of course! You are the Kepelens, yes? You are. You would like to esk me how I know? I will tell you how I know. My name is Hendriks. Dutch, yes? Dutch, of course. My colleague here is Emil. You will never guess what."

"Guess what?" asked Darrell.

Bigboy laughed. "Emil is Polish! Just like your Magister Copernicus!"

The room went silent, except for the radio's crackling static.

"Your expressions tell me you *are* the Kepelens! Emil, we were correct."

Fish spoke. "We were."

"You're with Drangheta?" said Sara. "Or the Teutonic Order?"

"This name Drangheta we do not know," Bigboy said with a wide grin that produced no wrinkles in his face.

"But yes, Emil and I are knights of ze Teutonic Order. Naturally, we will kill you ze moment you try to exit outside zis café."

Becca looked at Wade and Darrell, then at Bigboy. "Really?" she said. "You just come right out and say it? That you're a killer with the Order?"

Emil paused from picking his teeth. "It is too hot for banter."

"Ha! Ha!" Bigboy said, his brow pouring sweat into his eyes, which he wiped almost constantly with a splotchy brown handkerchief. "My colleague spiks the truth. It is too hot to beat round bushes. Beating round anything is *très* exhausting. So let us just come out and say it. We all relax sooner when you are dead."

"Not us so much," Darrell grumbled. Becca saw his eyes searching every inch of the café. Probably to find something to throw at these two goons.

"The genius of Galina Krause," Bigboy said, "is that she alerted everyone in North Africa. Agents are strung from city to city along the entire Mediterranean. She knows the next relic is near. When you left Casablanca, we were notified. We were *all* notified. If you are not tracked, your plane was."

Lily laughed wickedly. "City to city, huh? So how did you rate this dump?"

Bigboy's fat grin died in an instant. "I *could* just kill you now—"

"Hendriks," said Emil. "Remember."

Bigboy growled to himself. "Ah, yes. The telephone." He lumbered over to the counter and fished beneath it. He pulled up an old telephone and dialed it.

Becca had an idea. It wasn't much, and it depended on all of them picking up on it without her being able to tell them. There was no finger clue, so she made one up. She held up the index finger of her right hand, and drew a slithery line across her forehead. *Snake, get it?* She hoped they would.

She moved slowly in front of the others, nudging Wade in the process.

"I'm sure we can resolve this," she said softly. "Your boss . . ."

"Miss Galina," said Emil, his eyes lighting up as he spat blood onto the floor near his feet. "What about her?"

"We have something she wants. It's in the plane."

"Becca," said Sara.

At that moment, the counter man reentered the saloon, leaving Bingo outside to finish the refueling by himself.

Lily stood up. "Becca, what are you doing?"

"It's in a tin box under one of the seats," Becca said.

Wade raised his eyes to her. He'd understood, even if Lily hadn't yet. "You can have it," he said. "As long as you let us go free."

"You guys are crazy!" said Lily. "There's the—"

"Relic in the tin box," Wade jumped in. "Yeah, we know. But we have to, Lily. To save ourselves."

Lily got it. She looked at all of them, one after the other, and pretended she was shocked at their betrayal. She put her head in her hands and began to fake-sob. "I can't believe . . . the relic that we've been searching for . . . and we're just giving it away!"

"Becca, it's too precious." Sara was in on it now, too. "You can't. We can't."

"To delay your deaths, you will!" Bigboy said with a chuckle. "But it is true. The slightest pressure of the Teutonic Order gets results, does it not, Emil?"

"Mmm," Emil grunted. "It's that Galina. She scares people."

"As do we, Emil. As do we."

"Let me get the box for you," Darrell said. He stepped toward the door.

"Ha!" Emil growled. "Nothing doing. You'll alert your pilot. The little girl leads. I go with."

"While I," added Bigboy, "hold the rest of the family

hostage." He removed a handgun, which, by the look of it, hadn't been fired in years. "No moving. You, either, Aladdin." He referred to the counter man with another insult.

A few minutes later, Lily stumbled back into the room, followed by Fish, who held the dented tin box in both hands and said, "Guess what? They have a book open to a page about Carthage!"

Bigboy beamed. "Galina, she will love us. Now, bring me the relic box!"

"I'll open it for you," said Sara, reaching for it.

"Ha! Not!" said Bigboy. He pranced over to Emil, undid the latch, and lifted the lid. Corky hissed and sprang out of the box. Bigboy screamed. He clutched his face, and Emil lurched forward. Darrell pushed Fish at Wade, who kicked him behind the knees. Both men were now on the floor with Corky, screaming at the top of their lungs.

Bingo rushed in. "Out!" he yelled, shooing the kids and Sara to the plane.

They scrambled into the Flitfire, all of them, and Darrell spun the propeller. It caught the first time. He swung in through the cockpit door as the plane started to roll, and they sped down the airstrip, finally skimming the crests of the dunes in a zigzag pattern to evade any retribution.

Wishful thinking.

The distinctive *pop-pop-pop* of gunfire crackled in the air, and there was Bigboy holding his face with one hand while he fired at them like an angry brat.

The engine sputtered.

The old Flitfire dipped.

The desert came rushing up at them.

CHAPTER FORTY

"**B**last it all!"

Bingo wrenched the stick back, but the plane lost altitude so fast, Lily's empty stomach slid into her throat.

"That baby-faced blighter hit our engine and our lovely fuel tank. Sorry, chaps and ladies. You'll have to catch another sort of ride from here. Hold on!"

The engine continued to sputter until it died out, then caught again, then sputtered. The sand Lily had found so exhilarating before was getting way too close. "Should we bail out or something?"

"I'd pray or something," said Bingo. "We're fresh out of parachutes."

After a few miles, the Flitfire finally dipped too low to stay aloft. It bounced down onto a flat stretch of sand and grass, skidding roughly and nearly tipping over twice, but Bingo held it more or less steady until it jerked to a violent stop. The engine gasped out a puff of black smoke and died.

They climbed out. Bingo inspected the engine and the fuselage, but the plane was essentially finished, because the tank was, as he said, "Swiss-cheesed!"

"Bingo, can you tell where we are?" Sara asked, unfolding a map that had tumbled out from under her seat during landing.

"Well," said Bingo, looking in every direction, then at the map. "The desert, for sure. But to be more accurate, I'd say we're . . . here!" He pointed to a large unmarked area between Casablanca and Tunis. "Which is to say, nowhere in particular, but we're not back there with Babyboy and the Edge, and that's progress!"

"They have a plane," said Darrell, "and are probably already on the way to Carthage."

"But they don't need to see us. Help me drag the mesh over the plane," said Bingo, climbing back into the cockpit. He tugged out a large folded tarpaulin that had the mottled look of desert camouflage. With all of them helping, and Darrell and Wade balanced on the wing, they were able to shroud the plane enough, Lily hoped, to obscure it from the air.

"Do other planes land here?" asked Sara.

Bingo consulted the map again, frowned and scratched his chin, and finally grinned. "By Jove! We're actually in Tunisia, after all. Crashed, of course, but alive. I think I can get us out of this mess. Eventually." He hauled himself back into the cockpit and cranked up the radio. He soon raised a signal from Médiouna.

"Oh, I say, Pinky? We've encountered rather a spot of bad luck here. No, no, safe and sound. And not far from Tunis as it happens. But listen, can you send a car, a large toolbox, a new fuel tank, yourself and Gussie, and a snake rope to these coordinates?"

He glanced at the map and gave the numbers to his friend. "Splendid! And ring up Jendouba for any old thing that rolls. Our passengers need to keep moving pronto. No hurry for me! Oh, and bring a pile of sandwiches and maybe a pistol or two, would you? There's a good chap."

Bingo settled himself on the sand in the shade of the wing to wait. "I suggest you get out of the sun, too. There are birds, you know. They sniff folks in trouble."

Darrell snorted. "Let me guess. Egyptian vultures?"

"You're quite the naturalist, you are!" Bingo said, as

they all crawled in under the net. "Yes. Big red birds. Rather like condors."

Even in the shade the heat was stifling and heavy. Lily closed her eyes, felt herself drifting off. For nearly two hours, she slept. They all did, apparently. It was finally deep afternoon when they woke up to the sound of a rumbling motor. An old fenderless, roofless Jeep bounced over the dunes toward them. Driving it was a woman in colorful scarves that flew behind her like a hundred banners. She wore a scarf draped tight over her face.

"Oh, what luck! It's Alula!" Bingo waved her down. "She's a dear. You'll be in old Carthage by whenever she gets you there. I'm sure of it!"

Sara quickly negotiated a ride with Alula, who promised to drop them in Tunis, "in two hour, no less, maybe more."

"We really want to be there by nightfall," said Darrell.

"Certainly, maybe. Come!"

They crammed into the Jeep, Sara in the passenger seat, the rest of them in various positions in the stripped backseat. Because the Jeep was open, and the sun still high, the heat was incredible, but Darrell noted that it was "dry heat, so we don't sweat so much, except for maybe Wade because he's got such a head start on the rest of us," a remark that made no sense to any of them.

They did need to drink as much as they could, and Alula had stocked plenty of water bottles for them. When a hot wind blew at them out of the northwest, she began to tell them about desert winds. Lily loved their romantic names.

"*Simoom* is one," Alula said musically. "There is also the *harmattan*, and the dry *ghibli*, and the sweet and salty *imbat* that comes mostly from the water. There is the *solano*, too . . ."

The first hour came and went. They were quiet, exhausted. Lily ached all over. The attack at the villa, their chase through the medina, the terror at the desert café—they were wearing her down. But more than everything else was the persistent worry about the phone call she'd have to make but couldn't bring herself to face.

Whatever her parents said would change everything.

To Becca, the terrain in Tunisia was so different from the dune-filled deserts in Algeria. Here there were waist-high grasses and weeds, wind-tossed flowers, and the remains of what looked like stalks of wheat. The landscape greened up the farther east and north they drove, reminding her of the olive tree in the drawing.

She slid on the *ocularia* and tried to read more words on the silver page, but no matter how she arranged the lenses, the rest of the story was locked away.

"These glasses are like a key, too," she said. "Or many keys. There are so many combinations of the lenses, but only one that will unlock the next passage. Something in Tunis may tell us. I hope."

"Not long to Tunis," said Alula. "One hour. No less."

Soon the land began to slope down to the sea, the day faded, the white sky turned blue and purple in the east, and the kids finally spotted the outskirts of the sprawling metropolis of Tunis. The giant Mediterranean beyond lay out to the horizon like a great flat darkness.

They stopped to get gas, which Sara paid for. While they were waiting, Becca had one more idea and drew the diary from her bag.

"Alula, excuse me, but would you have any idea what this means?" She opened to the page with the drawing of Carthage. "We know it says 'Carthage,' and that it's probably about when the city was destroyed. But the olive tree? And the sun? Do you have any idea what it means?"

The woman leaned her head over the picture. "Well, it is an olive tree. It's growing out of a column. They say that all the marble from Carthage was used to build new things."

"I knew it!" said Wade. "That was my idea. But what did they build?"

Alula shrugged. "Old things in Tunis. I don't know. But look. I show you the word of *column*. Here." She wrote it down in Becca's notebook. "The word for *sun* is this. And *olive* is this."

Becca studied Alula's fluid finger motions as she wrote the words in her notebook, although she realized that "wrote" was hardly the correct word for what she had done on the page. It was painting. "That's beautiful. Thank you."

"I hope it helps," the woman said.

"It all helps," said Sara. "Very much. If you can, would you please drop us off at the American embassy? I'll call my husband from there, and we can use their services to narrow our search even more."

Alula smiled. "It is but minutes away. No less." Ten minutes later, she left them outside a gray building complex in a large fenced-off area.

"Here. American embassy. I hope you find what you're looking for."

"Thank you, so much," Sara replied.

"That is *shukran jazeelan*, in Arabic," Alula said.

"Thank you for an adventure!"

Once they were inside the embassy—using their real passports for the first time in days—Sara placed a call to Roald while Becca and the others searched out the tiny library. Since the outline of the allegorical drawing led them to think that what they were looking for might be an old mosque, Becca asked the young man behind the counter for information.

"As you can guess, we have several very old ones," he said, setting them up at a computer. He unfolded a map of the city. It was printed in both English and Arabic. He circled the many mosques. Lily slid into the seat in front of the computer, Becca spread out the diary and her notebook, and Wade brought out his own notebook, with Darrell leaning over his shoulder.

They began to work.

"Out of the seventeen mosques," Becca said, "two are modern, and eight others were built later than the fifteen hundreds. That leaves seven."

Seven mosques.

Between yawns, Lily dug at the internet, following one link, finding nothing, backtracking, then moving forward again. She followed *olive* and *olive tree*, then *allegorical drawings*, which only made her crazy. From there, she jogged back and forth between *Carthage* and *marble*, until she found actual internet confirmation of what they had guessed.

"A lot of building material from Carthage was brought to Tunis," she said. "They built some of the oldest buildings built. Some of them are still standing."

"What about buildings from Hijri 84?" asked Darrell.

"That's a little harder to find," she said. "It's not like they have a list of the year a building was born. Built. Whatever. I'm so tired."

"I can take over, Lil, if you want," Wade said.

"Please," she said. "I'd better call home."

She turned her phone on for the first time since Casablanca, wondering if it would ring the moment it powered up. It didn't. But there were three text messages waiting for her. They were group texts, sent from two phones to all three of them.

The first, from her mother, said, *Please call, dear.* Then her father texted, *Good news.* Finally, her mother added, *We think it's good news.*

She nearly dropped the phone, her hand was trembling so violently. The roller coaster of it made her want to scream. She drew a long slow breath and started to tap in her mother's phone number. There was every reason to call home now—*right now*—and only one reason not to. She was afraid of what "good news" could possibly mean, and who it was good for. She glanced over at the others. They were all bent over books and maps, absorbed in deciphering the drawing. Darrell flicked his eyes over at her, then buried his head again. She drew another breath and blinked her eyes dry. She disabled her phone from accepting incoming calls—an easy hack, after all. She powered off the phone and went back to the others.

"So, what did you find out?"

Darrell grumbled. "Not much. If we're right that the drawing refers to a mosque near Carthage, we still don't know what the olive tree and the sun are supposed to mean."

"We're going around and around, hoping to get closer, but not hitting on the critical clue," Becca said, rubbing her eyes. "We need help. Human help."

"I have an idea," Lily said. She slid Becca's notebook off the table and marched over to the clerk's desk. "Excuse me, we have this picture that we're trying to figure out. . . ."

He brightened as he looked at Becca's rendition of the drawing. "Mostly I research passports and things. I rather like this." He glanced at the drawing and spoke the same words Alula had, as he looked at the picture. *Column* and *sun*, and then he came to the olive tree.

"The Arabic for *olive*," he said, "is pronounced 'zy-toon.'"

Lily nodded. "Okay . . ."

"'Zy-toon,'" he repeated, coming out from behind his desk. "Didn't you see? The mosques I circled for you on the English map." He led her back to their table, scanned the map, then tapped his finger on one of the circles he had drawn. "Al-Zaytuna Mosque," he said. "The mosque of the olive tree. It is one of the oldest in Tunis. And yes, it was built with marble from Carthage. The guides always tell you so!"

Becca jumped up from the table. "Thank you! Thank you!"

Lily took a breath. She had to keep going to keep her mind off . . . the other thing. "Intelligence officer coming through," she said, nudging Wade from the computer. Her fingers blurred over the keyboard; then she punched the Enter key.

"Okay. Al-Zaytuna. Something, something . . . The marble of the columns and the arches and the main courtyard, as well as—ha!—a famous *sundial*, were built with marble from the ruins of Carthage." She spun around in her chair and faced them, beaming a big smile. "The first Barbarossa key, the first key to Triangulum, is in this mosque. Copernicus and Barb Two hid it there. And that's where we're going right now!"

"Yes! Good work, people!" Darrell hurried into the office to tell his mother. Lily and the others followed and found Sara sitting in the desk chair by the phone, staring at it. Her face was tense and tight. Her eyes were red.

"Mom, what is it?" Darrell asked.

Sara looked up at them. "It's Roald. I couldn't reach him for the longest time and kept trying. When I finally got him, he was breathless, as if he'd been running, or was running while I was talking to him. There were echoes. He was inside. In the underground lab, I guess. I asked him what was going on, what about the meeting, but he said the strangest thing. He said, 'A flood. There's going to be a flood.' When I pressed him for more, the line went dead. I couldn't reconnect. He was gone."

CHAPTER FORTY-ONE

The relief Wade had felt at finding a real clue to where the first of the keys was—they'd had little but guesses so far—crashed and burned after Sara's weird phone call with his father.

His father. Running. His father, afraid. *There's going to be a flood.*

Wade felt he could easily spiral into some pretty dark thoughts.

"Kids, we don't know . . . ," Sara began, then stopped.

So she felt it too. This might be as bad as they imagined. *A flood.*

Wade took a moment. He pressed himself to look at the call logically, not emotionally. Emotionally, he wanted to scream and hit something and get to Gran Sasso as soon as he could. Logically? Logically, there was next to nothing to go on. *There's going to be a flood.*

"What kind of flood?" he asked, a shiver running up his neck. "Where? How? You can't *predict* floods, can you? Not like that. Is he talking about a flood there in Italy? The weather's good there. And there are lakes near him, not oceans. Lakes don't flood, not in good weather. So what, then? Galina can't make a flood happen, can she? Seriously? How do you do that—"

"Wade," Sara said. "We don't know."

"Uncle Roald's great at codes," said Becca. "Maybe it's a code, a message."

"But he never talks to *us* in code. Not like that." Wade was getting hot all over. He went back to the table, but the map no longer interested him. He always trusted his father to be careful, but if Galina was doing something . . . *A flood?*

"It could be Drangheta," Darrell said. "He was after Dad, too. Drangheta owns ships, remember. Ships, water, floods."

"Darrell," said Lily.

"Kids." Sara held up her hands and stood up, and they went quiet. After almost a solid minute of watching her face, Wade saw her pull it together like she usually did, doing the parent thing, keeping her suspicions in check. "Let's put our brains to it," she said, not looking at anyone specific. "And be smart. Keep our worries on the side. A flood. So, okay. Something bad. We're always ready to fit that into what's going on. But we don't know anything real yet. Just add this clue to the others and keep moving."

Then, still looking as if she could crumble if she let herself, she simply didn't. She drew in a long breath and coolly arranged for a taxicab to drive them to the mosque.

So. Okay. Keep our worries on the side.

A somber ride later, through the slow, thick evening traffic, the harsh blaring of horns, and the over-revving of motors, they stood at the end of Rue Jamaa Ez Zitouna, looking up at the main entrance to the Zaytuna Mosque.

It was a vast walled structure—"Over an acre," Lily told them—surmounted by a tall, square minaret with a crescent at the top. Floodlights lit up the sides of the tower. The mosque bordered on Tunis's medina, the now-familiar narrow-streeted old section of the city.

"We want the courtyard inside," said Darrell. "It's called the *sahn*. That's where the sundial is. We'll have to search every inch of it for the key."

"If the mosque is still open," said Becca. "Evening prayers are over now."

Wade liked that she knew stuff like that, but barely found any space in his own head to think of anything besides his father.

They ascended the stone steps. Inside a tall arch, whose frame was very like the outline in the diary's allegorical drawing, was an only slightly smaller pair of wooden doors. Sara tried one. The doors were unlocked. Together, the five of them entered under the main ornamental archway. The instant they set foot inside the walls and the doors slowly closed behind them, quiet descended over them like a heavy shawl. But it wasn't a tense quiet.

It was peaceful, and time slowed in that way it does when the noise of the world is shut away. Their own breathing and the sound of their footsteps were hushed in the dense darkness and the quiet of the stones.

Of course, Wade thought. *When you're worried or afraid, you find a quiet place and pray. Protect my dad. Protect Terence, too.*

The vast open courtyard lay ahead, but no one entered it.

"Now what?" whispered Darrell.

Only a few seconds passed before a slender older

man moved toward them out of the shadows to the left. He wore layered robes of different colors and a short, tight-fitting hat, and as he approached, the fabric of his garments floated around him.

"My name is Abul-Qasim," he said.

His words, spoken deeply in perfect English, also seemed to float.

"I'm one of the caretakers of the mosque. It's late for visitors. Still, how can I help you?"

Wade noticed what he took to be expensive jeweled stitching on the collar of the man's robe, while his hat was old and frayed. His gray hair was short beneath its worn velvet seam. His beard was stubbly, also gray.

The fabric shoes he wore—which Wade later learned were called *babouches*—were little more than rags with leather soles stitched to them.

A boy trotted out of the shadows and stood by him. "My grandson, Karim."

Karim was around eleven or twelve years old, and his dress was a smaller version of his grandfather's. He smiled at them. "Hi. You're Americans?"

Sara smiled back. "Yes. Please forgive us, but we're looking for something. We believe it could be in your mosque. It would have been hidden here a very long time ago. In the sixteenth century."

The man raised his eyebrows. "In the sixteenth century we were here for hundreds of years already." He smiled. "Tell me, and I'll try to help."

Something about the man reminded Wade of Brother Semyon at the monastery of Saint Sergius in Russia, although the two men couldn't have been more different. Semyon was young and tall; Abul-Qasim was older, grayer, shorter. But they both exuded, if that was the right word, the same aura of good feeling, of kindness, of trust. It was a feeling Wade sensed from their faces, the way they looked at him and the others, and from something about their eyes. The words *holy men* seemed a perfect way to describe both of them.

Abul-Qasim was plainly someone you didn't keep secrets from, and the others must have felt the same, because they told this man as much as they dared in as brief a way as they could.

As he listened, he startled them by knowing some of the story.

"The elder Barbarossa's name was Baba Aruj. Yes, he was a buccaneer, but also a people's hero in North Africa. As for finding an object secreted here, well, as you see our mosque is very large. Even if you go back five centuries, there are still a thousand places your object might have been hidden."

He stopped at the entrance to the giant prayer hall, a tall room of chandeliers and dozens of thick columns arranged in bays. On either side of the entrance to the room were empty racks. *For shoes,* Wade thought. He wondered whether they were supposed to remove their shoes now.

"Can you show us what you have?" asked Karim.

Becca slid Copernicus's diary and her notebook from her bag. "There's a passage in this diary that says that Nicolaus, and Baba Aruj's younger brother, Heyreddin, hid three keys to something very precious. The first key is hidden in a place described by this drawing in my notebook. It's an allegory."

Abul-Qasim studied the drawing, listening as Sara and the children told him how they came to believe the key was in the mosque, ending with the notion that the key was hidden in a sundial.

"You've been clever," he said. "I find allegorical art difficult, but I believe I'd have come to the same conclusion as you. The face of the sun in the olive tree would seem to indicate that our sundial is what you're looking for."

But Abul-Qasim didn't move from his position in the hallway, either to the prayer hall or the courtyard, and it was soon clear that while he was sympathetic, he couldn't allow the tampering with and removal of any object from one of Islam's holy places.

Even when Sara explained the mission of the Guardians, *their* mission—"it's vital that we find the object, and many lives could be at stake"—he shook his head.

"I sympathize, of course. But I'm afraid it's not possible."

"What if we can prove that the key actually belonged to Copernicus?" asked Wade. "I know some astronomy, and believe us when we say that what Copernicus was hiding with this key is really important. It was made for him and the Guardians, not really for Barbarossa or the Ottomans. And it was meant to be found . . . by us."

Abul-Qasim tilted his head from one side to the other, his smile neither increasing nor fading. "The astronomer is certainly a hero to all people of science, no matter where they live. Even supposing you can show me—if you can *prove* to me—that Nicolaus Copernicus entered these walls, *and* that he hid something here to be found by the keepers of his memory, I would not be able to convince my fellow stewards of the mosque to allow you to leave with it. Certainly not in any reasonable time."

To Wade, Becca looked as if she were going to blow to pieces, and Sara didn't look much different, but she put her hand on Becca's arm, smiled grimly, and said, "We understand, of course, sir, and we thank you for listening to us."

"But, Sara, please . . . ," Wade started, then paused. They had no right to mess around here.

Even if Galina ripped the place to shreds looking for it, they themselves would not. The mosque was holy. A shrine and a place of worship. He'd felt it the minute they entered. Since he and his family weren't Muslim, they had little right to be there at all. Wade felt Abul-Qasim would kindly shoo them out, case closed.

Instead the man held up his hand as if he knew what Wade was thinking, and right then another, different tone entered the conversation.

"I understand your desires," he said. "And how strong, and perhaps, good, they may be. But you must realize that I have a very important . . . phone call."

Abul-Qasim then fixed his eyes on his grandson. He put his hands on the boy's shoulders. "Karim, if you would be so kind as to show our visitors the way? I may be gone some minutes. On my important phone call. Ten minutes."

Then Abul-Qasim looked at Wade, his mother, and the others. "Perhaps even longer. It may be a long call. Now, please forgive my rudeness as I take my leave of you. Karim will show you the way. . . ."

He slipped off his shoes, turned, and strode off quickly across the matted floor of the prayer hall. The room was dusky with candlelight. He was gone.

"What just happened?" Darrell whispered.

"You mentioned his name," said Karim, smiling.

"Barbarossa?" said Lily.

Karim shook his head. "Copernicus. My grandfather is, or was, a scientist. He knows all about time and space and physics. He taught cosmology. Besides, you heard him. He asked me to 'show you the way.' Not the way *out*. Just 'the way.' We live in different cultures, but I'm pretty sure that means the same to both of us. Wink, wink. So. Let me show you the way . . . to the sundial!"

"You are awesome!" said Wade.

"Everything around here is. Come on."

CHAPTER FORTY-TWO

Wade and the others followed Karim, backtracking along the gallery to the main entrance. They passed through a pair of wooden doors set into a low wall and entered a large open courtyard—the *sahn*.

The instant they did, a great flock of pigeons swept up from the stones and circled the floodlit minaret.

"Like Saint Mark's Square in Venice," said Lily.

"Yes!" said Karim. "Well, I've seen some movies of it."

The sun had dipped below the horizon, and the sky overhead was dark, a deep purple splashed with flickering stars, but waves of heat still rose up from the tiles as if the entire space were underwater. Some of the pigeons settled back on the stones.

In the center of the yard three stone discs were set on low pediments some ten to twelve feet apart. A higher, rectangular column of stone on which four iron gnomons jutted up like blades stood in more or less equal distance from the discs.

"Are there three sundials?" Lily asked.

"No, no," said Karim. "The three pediments are openings to wells. During prayer times, when the courtyard is full of people in the middle of the day, it gets very hot. So, there is water. This sundial, however, is far older. My grandfather knows his astronomy. He taught me a lot. Show me what you have."

Becca took the mirrored spectacles out of their case, adjusted them, and read the passage in the diary, translating it to him.

Karim frowned. "So, you're really looking for a number. The letters you read at the end. *LdV*? I wonder if this is a clue also."

"It stands for Leonardo da Vinci," Darrell said.

"But could *LDV* also be a Roman numeral?" asked Becca.

Karim shook his head. "The letters, yes, but not in that order. The proper way to say it is *DLV*, which equals five hundred fifty-five. A number that does not occur on any of these sundials."

"Five hundred fifty-five." Lily looked directly at Becca. "Five-five-five."

"It could be right," said Becca.

They checked the number five on the sundial, but there was nothing to make it seem as if something was hidden there.

"Maybe he means to add them?" asked Lily. "Fifteen?"

"Possibly." Karim asked to see the drawing again. He pointed to the word *Sol* beneath the face on the olive tree. "Did Copernicus write this word?"

"It's not his handwriting," said Becca. "I'm guessing that since most of the words are Arabic, they were written by the younger Barbarossa brother, Heyreddin. We call him Barb Two. They were both very old at the time, and Copernicus was ill. He died just weeks later."

Karim smiled. "That's it, then. *Sol* is the answer."

"*Sol* is Latin for 'sun,'" said Sara.

"Of course it is," the boy said. "But if this is Heyreddin's handwriting, the clue is not in Latin, although the letters are. He was an Ottoman and a Turk. It is Turkish. *Sol* means something quite different in Turkish, the language that Barb Two knew best."

He folded his arms across his chest and kept smiling.

"Uh . . . Karim?" said Darrell. "Are you going to tell us?"

"*Sol* means 'left'!" he said. "Your clue means to search the left of the sundial!"

They stood in front of the sundial and went over every inch of the left side, particularly the leftmost of the four gnomons, but they could find nothing there.

"What did we get wrong?" said Wade.

"What if . . . ," Lily began, "what if the five-five-five has to do with the time of day? Five o'clock, ten o'clock, and maybe fifteen hundred hours, three o'clock in the afternoon. I don't know . . ."

Karim smiled. "Yes, yes! Where would the left gnomon point at those times of day? Let's try." He ran his fingers along the outer edge of the sundial and suddenly stopped at the tile marking the five o'clock position. It sank below the surface of the sundial. "Oh, yes!" The same thing happened at the ten o'clock position, and again at three.

The moment the last tile sank, they heard the sound of stone sliding against stone on the left side of the sundial near the base. A portion of the column had slid outward.

Darrell laughed. "You found it!"

"See what it is!" said Karim. "Miss Sara, please."

Sara knelt and drew out the stone. Behind it lay a slim box of marble approximately two inches wide and six inches long. It had two small openings, one at either end, which appeared to be finger holes, allowing the marble piece to be lifted out.

Wade's heart was thumping. "The first key is in there."

"We hope," said Becca.

"Karim?" said Sara. "I think it's most proper for you to do this."

He beamed at them. "Thank you for the honor." He inserted his small fingers into the holes and pulled up on the lid.

Inside, fixed tightly within the walls of a shallow indentation, was a large key, nearly six inches long and made of rough, thickly cast iron.

The entire surface of the key was engraved with interlocking loops and delicate swirls of ornamentation. They were the marks of a key made by da Vinci.

The shaft was more or less plain, even rugged, and the bit—the part that fit into the lock—was thickly made, with a complex arrangement of angled parts. But it was the bow of the key, the part you gripped when you turned it, that was the most amazing and intricate. Wade took a photograph and enlarged it on his phone.

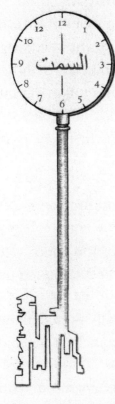

The face of the bow was wide, perhaps two inches across and a quarter-inch thick, and it was incised with numbers all around the perimeter, in the manner of a clock. There was an Arabic word scratched into the center. The back of the bow was coated in silver.

"The numbers around the edge are wrong," said Darrell. "There are two twelves."

"Karim, what does the word on the key mean?" Sara asked.

He studied it, pronounced it silently with his lips, then asked for something to trace it on. Wade gave him his notebook. Finally, Karim said it aloud. It sounded like "ascent."

"I would translate it as 'azimuth,'" Karim said. "It's the direction between one point and another. Wade, you know astronomy, so you know azimuth, yes?"

He nodded. "Not well. I have to refresh my memory, but I think it's the degree of an angle from a vertical line, isn't it? The way to measure the position of stars?"

"Yes, but it's also used in navigation. Seafarers used azimuths to keep on course. There are three hundred sixty degrees in a circle, with zero and one hundred eighty as the north and south poles. The numbers on this key would seem to give you a direction. Not a distance, but a direction."

"So the total of all the numbers should give us the degree, right?" asked Darrell.

"Already got it," said Lily. "The numbers from one to ten, with two twelves and no eleven, equal seventy-nine. So what is seventy-nine degrees from here?"

"I have to find true north first," said Wade.

"What's this line?" asked Becca, pointing to a straight line of stones that ran from one side of the courtyard to the other. "Is it north?"

Karim shook his head. "No, no. That is our *qibla*. You see the cupola in that wall? That is the entrance to the prayer hall. Against the back of that is our qibla wall. It is the direction to Mecca in Saudi Arabia. We pray facing Mecca. It is one hundred twelve degrees from true north."

"Which is that way," said Wade, lining up his phone's compass. "Seventy-nine degrees would point somewhere east-northeast of here."

"You'll need a map and a calculator," Karim said, "but it could be somewhere like Istanbul. On the other side of the Mediterranean. In Turkey."

"Which makes sense," said Becca. "Heyreddin lived there later in life, and he probably started from there when he took the journey with Copernicus. Sara?"

Sara drew a long breath. It was plain to Wade that she was worried about the next leg of the journey without his father. "Istanbul . . ."

Abul-Qasim raced into the courtyard, his robes flying. The pigeons fluttered off again. "You must leave! They have found you. Don't ask me how. There is an exit to the streets in the medina."

"Who is it?" said Sara, as they rushed across the courtyard to the far side.

"A large man, and his slender companion who looks like a—"

"Fish!" said Becca. "It's Bigboy and Fish!"

"Are you serious?" said Lily. "They must have tracked our new phones. They flew their plane after us. It's the only way they could have found us so soon! Hide the key!"

Darrell pushed it deep in his pocket and ran for the exit.

A shot boomed across the courtyard, and the pigeons

swept up again, a wall of wings and feathers. The fat man from the desert rushed under the qibla colonnade toward them, waving his pistol like a madman. "Shtop right there!" Fish was racing around the other side. He had a long dagger gripped in his hand and held it out straight like a sword. Abul-Qasim swept his arms around Karim and pulled him back behind him.

Bigboy's next shot struck the stones near Wade. He jumped out of the way, lost his balance. When he fell, his phone crashed out of his hand to the ground and clattered across the stones out of reach. Darrell was suddenly there, pulling him away before he could crawl for it.

"The photo! The photo of the key is on there—"

"Doesn't matter," said Darrell, as bullets crackled over his head. "You do."

Karim tore out of his grandfather's grasp and sprinted across the courtyard. He scooped up the phone, ran between the columns toward the prayer hall, but Fish bolted after him like a rocket and wrenched the phone from him. Abul-Qasim leaped across the stones toward his grandson, but Bigboy twirled around and grabbed him with one hand and pressed his gun into his ribs. Abul-Qasim yelled over his shoulder, "Go! Go!"

Wade wanted to rush to their aid, but Darrell

wouldn't let him into the line of fire. He yanked Wade's arm until it felt as if it were going to fall off, and they were out, racing under the colonnade and down the steps into the bustling street.

CHAPTER FORTY-THREE

Night had fallen heavy, fast, and hard.

Lily powered down the street ahead of Sara and Becca, with Darrell and Wade right behind. She hated being breathless, shaken, afraid because of Galina and her assassins. The crazy woman would find them wherever they went. As soon as Lily and the others woke up in the morning, Galina's knife was already at their throats.

Sara waved down a taxi, and they threw themselves in. "Airport! Please. Fast!"

"Oui, oui!" the driver said, jamming the engine into gear and flying off into the traffic of a wide boulevard.

"Those creeps are minutes behind us. We need a

map of the Mediterranean," Becca said, almost choking on her breath. "Double-check if we're really going to Istanbul."

"And I know the phones are compromised, but I need one for a second," Wade grumbled. "I have to determine an azimuth. Once I find north, or zero degrees, we'll know where the angle of seventy-nine degrees actually points to."

Lily brought up a map on her tablet, but Sara shook her head. "No. A map of the Ottoman Empire is what we need. The world in 1543, the year of Nicolaus and Heyreddin's journey to hide the keys."

Lily shook off a shiver and tapped her fingers ferociously on the tablet's screen. "The closest I can do is 1580. Wade, here."

"Thanks," he said.

On the screen was the familiar Mediterranean region, outlining the usual countries, but highlighting the extent of the Ottoman Empire in North Africa, the Middle East, and Europe at the height of the empire's dominance.

Using the compass direction in the map's legend, and from a starting point of Tunis, Wade traced the azimuth of seventy-nine degrees from true north. "It could be in Greece," he said, "but the city it points to directly is what Karim said: Istanbul, Turkey."

"They were hiding the keys in Ottoman locations," said Becca.

"And right where I pointed Bigboy and Fish," he groaned. "Because of the stupid, stupid, stupid photo I took and practically *gave to them*, they'll discover the location of the second key and tell Galina, and they'll all get there before us, and snatch it up, and we'll be left with nothing!"

Darrell held the key tightly in his hands, trying to close his ears against the rush of noise and danger and open them to what Wade was saying, but something else was going on. The key was going on. It was going on his fingers.

"My fingers are turning silver. What is this stuff? Paint? Ink? Whatever it is, it's coming off on my hands. There's a triangle on the back of this key. Becca—"

"Becca, the glasses, hurry," whispered Sara, with an eye on the driver to make sure he wasn't looking. "Maybe there's something to read."

"Before Darrell smudges it to oblivion," said Lily, taking a picture of the back of the key and enlarging it. The numbers inside the triangle were three, six, and four.

Becca adjusted the *ocularia* and, holding her head

down, slipped them on. She blew the crumbs of silver ink away.

"More Arabic. How are we . . ." She quickly traced the characters as accurately as she could in her notebook and leaned over the backseat to the driver. "Excuse me, sir? Can you read this?" She held the notebook out to him.

The driver slowed the cab, glanced at it. "Is two words," he said. "It says 'from qibla.' You know what is qibla?"

"We do!" said Sara. "Kids, do you know what this means?"

"Not exactly," said Becca.

"That it's not seventy-nine degrees from true north," she said. "It's seventy-nine degrees *from* a hundred and twelve degrees. It's not Istanbul at all. Wade—"

"That's . . . thirty-three degrees from north," he said. Using the phone's compass again to estimate the direction on the map on Lily's tablet, he traced his finger along a much narrower angle, northeast from Tunis, across the Mediterranean.

"It's not Italy," said Becca. "The Ottoman Empire didn't extend to Italy."

A line drawn at exactly thirty-three degrees clockwise from north of al-Zaytuna mosque in Tunis pointed directly to one great European city.

"Budapest?" said Lily. "The Ottomans really went all the way up to Hungary? Is there anything left there from the Ottoman days?"

"Hey," said Darrell. "Instead of Turkey, it's Hungary? Am I the only one thinking of food right now?"

"Voici l'aéroport!" barked the driver, pulling up to the departure terminal.

After paying and dragging everyone out, Sara took over the tablet from Wade and scoured the internet even as the rest of them cased the outside of the terminal, then they quickly entered the building.

"Some things are still around from the sixteenth century," she said, one eye on the crush of people inside. "And that's where we'll have to start looking. Becca, can you read the next silver passage in the diary? You have the numbers."

"As soon as my head stops spinning," Becca said. "But Wade, you know, it turned out all right anyway. You only took a picture of the front of the key. Bigboy and Fish—and Galina—will think the second key is in Istanbul. We're pulling away. We'll find the relic!"

Wade grumbled under his breath as they headed to the ticket counter. "Thanks, but it was still a dumb move. And Galina's smart. She'll figure it out. She always does. She's only a half step behind us."

The next available flight to Budapest was on Air France the following morning. So they stayed under false names at one of the airport hotels. After a two-hour stopover in Paris, their jet would arrive at Budapest Ferenc Liszt International Airport by late afternoon of the next day, Saturday, June seventh.

Budapest.

Where they hoped to find the second Barbarossa key.

CHAPTER FORTY-FOUR

Ebner found Galina standing alone, head bowed, under a partially crumbled archway on the fringes of ancient Carthage. Harsh spotlights on the ruins of the old Punic, Roman, Vandal, and Arabic city put her in shadow. So ghostly. So thin.

"Galina? Miss Krause?"

Five minutes before, she had ordered the driver to stop the car on the way to the airport and had frantically bolted out. Now he understood why. As he drew nearer, he smelled the odor of sickness. She lifted her head slowly, cupped a hand to her mouth, then threw her head back. And that was a motion he knew all too well. Pills. Medication. No, her last treatment had been far from successful. His mind wandered briefly to Olsztyn, when she had fainted into his arms.

"Speak," she said softly.

"Alas, we believe the Kaplans have already left Tunis by air. Our people are scouring the airline ticket databases as we speak and will soon know where they are flying to. In the meantime, our agents have arrived." He glanced back. The insanely odd pair was waiting by their car. "They have something for you."

She turned, steadied herself on her feet, and looked out on the night, the pale spotlights, the dead culture. She held up her hand.

"Ebner, it took me far too long to understand what the serpent was trying to tell me." She pulled strands of her long dark hair one by one from her face. "Serpens was not pointing me toward the relic. The *relic* is not in several different places. The *clues* to the relic are. I predict we shall travel three or four times before we find the relic's true location."

"Precisely," he said. "This is why our agents are anxious to see you."

Ebner turned his face and prepared himself to view once more the overweight baby of a man who was on their payroll and who slid uncannily over the ancient stones like a dancer. Following the baby was a man of two dimensions, next to whom Ebner felt overweight.

The fat one—*yes, let us say it outright*—slid his massive paw into a pocket of his grimy suit coat and withdrew a battered cell phone.

"It belongs to one of the Kepelen boys, Wade," he said, then added with a smirk, "We wrestled it from Ali Baba's grandson."

Galina swung around and slapped him across the face. "You're a racist and a fool, you fat man! You should have followed the Kaplan family."

"It has a photo of a key!" said the other man, Emil.

Galina snatched the phone from the fat agent and studied the image. "A key? A key. So. *This* is what the Kaplans have been searching for. Ebner, you remember the places Serpens took us toward? Eastern Europe. Syria. Perhaps a second key and a third key await us there."

"I know a word or two of the local gargle," Emil said, mouthing what appeared to be a needle between his lips. "That word on the key is 'azimuth.' It's an angle or something—"

"Galina Krause knows what an azimuth is!" Ebner said, leaning over her to examine the image on the phone. "Ah. Definitely of Leonardo's making, but the clues are by Copernicus and the pirate on their later journey. So, seventy-nine degrees. From Tunis that would be . . ." He opened his own phone and tapped the number into an app. A moment later, he turned his phone to her. "Istanbul?"

Galina frowned. "Perhaps. Perhaps there exists another clue to tell us exactly where. Fat man, get out of my sight. Go to Istanbul with your shadow and wait for instructions."

As the two mismatched men left together, the fish-faced Emil tossed his needle onto the ancient stones. Ebner cringed. It was soiled with bits of food and blood.

"Ebner," she said softly, "this phone is not as protected as their usual phones are. Establish a connection between it and the Copernicus Room. Have them trace all the Kaplan numbers. If even one of them can be cracked, our servers will triangulate their location."

For seven minutes, neither of them spoke. Galina moved among the fallen stones. Slowly. Unsteadily. Ebner wondered how ill she was. Had her latest doctor given her an all-too-hopeless report? Was that why she'd killed him?

Ebner received a text from the Copernicus Room. "They have purchased tickets connecting to Budapest."

She nodded. "So, there was an another clue relating to the key's numbers. Let the agents proceed to Turkey.

We may need them there."

"As you say," said Ebner, "but the servers also report that Dr. Roald Kaplan is not in Geneva. The family plays this game well. He is heading here."

He showed her his phone.

42.454°N
13.576°E
Laboratori Nazionali del Gran Sasso
L'Aquila, Abruzzo, Italy

Galina glared at the screen. "Petrescu moved the meeting from Geneva. Even better. Alert the colonel. Tell him to deliver Aurora *there* as quickly as possible, and alert us when he is within fifty kilometers of the laboratory. In the meantime, we fly to Budapest."

Just before dawn the next morning some two thousand kilometers northeast of Tunis, Ugo Drangheta and his partner, Mistral, both wounded in Galina's bitter attack on his compound, slowly approached the walls of Olsztyn Castle, where his sister had perished.

Mistral nursed a broken hand and a deep gash across her forehead. He had a bullet wound in his shoulder, a fractured shinbone, a battered kneecap. Ignoring their pain and the drenching downpour, they made their way across the lawns to the cordoned-off construction area beneath the castle's northeast wall.

Ugo stared at the hole in the ground and began to weep. "Uliana . . ."

Mistral put her arms around him. "Yes, Uliana, always Uliana, but why this interest in Roald Kaplan?"

He took in a long breath. "At first, I wanted only to kill Galina Krause. But you yourself introduced the notion of the astrolabe. The time-travel machine. The Kaplan father is an astrophysicist. He knows what the woman is doing and if the machine is real. We will join him, aid him. I will be his ally."

She removed her arms. "What if all he sees in you is another enemy?"

Ugo stood at the edge of the pit, staring into the darkness. "I will make him believe. For Uliana's sake."

There was the sound of footsteps in the soggy grass.

"Her husband has come," she whispered, as a man of about thirty years old approached out of the rain. She slid a knife from her belt.

Ugo raised his hand. "Not yet."

The man stopped. He had obviously shed tears recently; his face was hard, angry, resolute. "I am Vilmos Biszku," he said, his voice steady. "Uliana was my wife for two years. I cannot live without her. You are Ugo Drangheta?"

Ugo nodded. "If you loved my sister, tell me what you know about the Teutonic Order and Galina Krause."

The man quivered, shook it off. "Just before Uliana died, she told me that Galina Krause was searching for pieces of some old machine. Uliana didn't know where the pieces were supposed to be, but she heard places named. Kraków. Prague. Salzburg. I loved Uliana more than the world. Tell me what you want of me. I cannot rest until Galina Krause is dead."

Ugo breathed slowly to calm his heartbeat. "Mistral, the knife."

With it, Ugo cut a mark into the young man's forearm.

Wincing, shivering, the young man said, "Command me, Sir Ugo."

In his mind, Ugo grew to massive size. "First report to my office in Warsaw. They will equip you. Then go to Prague. Discover what you can about the machine. Report all to me."

Vilmos Biszku turned and walked away, blood from his arm staining the rain-drenched lawns.

"And for us?" Mistral asked.

"Kraków."

Chapter Forty-Five

Budapest, Hungary
June 7
6:17 p.m.

After a delay on the tarmac in Paris it was early in the evening of a foggy day when they finally reached Budapest, a city divided by the wandering Danube River. Wade knew there were songs about the Danube but couldn't remember any of them.

He had done something monumentally dumb in losing his phone. It didn't matter that the loss might actually have thrown off Galina and her goons. It was amateur. He tried to make up for it by suggesting they put the key in an airport locker to keep it secure while they searched for the next one.

"We'll be back at the airport anyway to search for the third key," he reasoned.

"I agree," said Lily surprisingly. "I feel someone's watching us. He—and I'm assuming it's a man, because they're the ones who make a mess of everything in the world—saw us get off the plane, exit the arrival gate, and go through passport control. I felt his beady little eyes on us every moment. But of course each time I looked around, all I saw were passengers, regular people, no obvious Teutonic agents, so he must be there."

"Hard not to agree with that," said Darrell.

Of course it wasn't, thought Wade. What she'd said was pure Darrell. "I agree, too," he added, "but I don't know about the 'man' idea. There's Galina."

"And she's not a man," Darrell actually said aloud.

Lily flashed him a look. "Maybe. But she's a totally different story."

"Oh, yeah, she is," Darrell said, digging himself in deeper, although Lily didn't take the bait.

The air outside the airport was unseasonably cool, the sky was heavily overcast, and it felt like rain was on the way.

"We have to assume that they'll find us," said Sara as they entered a taxi. "So it is a good idea that we're

keeping the key locked up. Becca, have you found anything?"

On the flight, Becca had been careful not to let anyone see her using the strange-looking *ocularia*. The new
silver number code they'd found on the back of the key
proved to be the same one that unlocked the next portion of the diary. This was not a passage of the 1519
story, but a series of shaky lines written alternatively by
the two very old men, Copernicus first. She read from
the translation she had written in her notebook.

> *Baba's hand is silver; his beard is red.*
> *Baba's fingers are black; his head is bald.*
> *Baba sleeps in a tomb.*
> *Baba sleeps in a turban.*
> *Baba is dead.*
> *And Baba is dead now, too.*

Darrell frowned. "Is this a turban joke? Because if
we're doing Ottoman turban jokes now, I think we're
pretty sunk."

"There's nothing else?" asked Lily.

"No," Becca told them. "I can't read the next passage.
It must rely on another combination of lenses. There's
nothing now but these six lines."

Sara shook her head. "Turbans and tombs. There's a lot to work with. Maybe too much. But let's get started."

Lily gazed out the cab window. She had slept, but not well. All night she'd twisted in her cheap airport hotel bed, dreaming of arguing with her parents, who were sometimes walking toward her as she argued, sometimes away. Maybe that was because she'd disabled incoming calls and hadn't heard a word since Tunis's "good news." Now she was in a cab. Another cab. It was early evening; everything was gray: the cars, the buildings, the people, the sky. It always seemed to be nearing the end of the day that, even so, would go on for another few hours. Lily felt she hardly knew *where* or *when* she was anymore. She guessed the fraying of her home life—*fraying? It's exploding*—was hitting her hard, making her mad at everyone. She glanced at her black phone screen. Would hearing the news help or hurt?

She thought of the hot desert winds, the rising and falling dunes. In gray Budapest, the desert seemed no more than a dream.

She wanted . . . what did she want?

She wanted to be alone. To think her own thoughts by herself.

Looking out at the streets the cab was whizzing by, she wondered what it would be like to walk down one of them by herself. To hear nothing but the clicking of her heels on the sidewalk, not all the noise. Hadn't both Wade and Sara used her tablet at critical moments and found the clues they were looking for? She was totally replaceable. Lily searched her heart for a magnet that might keep her on course and didn't find one. She'd miss them, if she wasn't here, of course. Becca the most. Darrell, too. Wade, too.

She'd miss them, being alone, away from the noise.

Lily is brooding more and more, thought Darrell.

I know why, of course. But she always pops out of it. She's Lily. So she will, this time, too. She's just too perky not to.

He knew *perky* was a dumb word, and he quickly brushed it from his mind and looked out the window. The gray streets were darkening, night rolling in; the city was now starting to sparkle with lights. It was hard for him to imagine this obviously European capital of churches and bridges and castles and little old peaked houses being ruled by a Turkish emperor.

It didn't fit in the neat little box of what he knew of world history. Turkey was in the Middle East. Hungary was deep in Europe. And yet Ottomans had lived in

Hungary. Had they worn their robes and scarves when they were here? Or was that a stereotype, taken from bad Hollywood movies? Maybe.

Of course it was true, as Becca had told them, that the Romans founded everything, not just Nice, and Romans wore togas, but maybe not in the colder parts of Europe? He was going way beyond his comfort zone in thinking of all this. One thing he did know: the Romans had founded just about every city east of New York.

Wade was mumbling something.

"We have to look at the riddle," he said, "both from now *and* from five hundred years ago. The first key tells us that Copernicus and Barb Two hid the second key here. That was 1543. If the place they hid it *doesn't* exist anymore, then we're back at square zero, as Lily says. But if it *does* exist, then what?"

"Then there's a place four hundred and sixty years old that is still around," said Sara.

"Exactly," said Wade. "And if you're the Guardian of that key, you make sure that it's protected there. That's Guardian 101. Now, because of Barb Two, *and* to honor Barb One, let's assume it's some special Ottoman site. So, one thing is, how many Ottoman places are still around in Budapest? That's one thing to find out.

But there's something else. It's sort of logical and sort of not."

"Like you sometimes," said Becca.

He grinned. "True. But I can't work it all out by myself."

"Keep going," Sara said.

"Okay. When the riddle says, 'Baba is dead. And Baba is dead now, too,' it sounds like they're talking about two different people, both named Baba. And while one Baba sleeps in a tomb, the other sleeps in a turban."

"Where's the logical part?" asked Darrell.

"The logical part is this," Wade said, taking a breath. "*Both* Babas are dead, so they're *both* in tombs, but one of the tombs is, I don't know, a turban, or *like* a turban. You know, maybe it has a domelike shape."

It wasn't all that much, but it might be enough for Lily, if they could drag her out of the hole she was falling in. "Lil," Darrell said. "Lily?"

She turned to him, her forehead creased, her eyes moving across his face.

"I know. Me. I'll look it up." She swiped her tablet on.

The cabdriver drove slowly into the heart of the city, around and around the old streets, because they had told him to keep doing it until they knew where to stop.

The cabbie told them in French—he didn't know English or German—that he didn't care as long as they paid.

"Nous allons vous payer," Becca said, and that settled it.

Darrell saw towering spires everywhere and old stone churches and ancient neighborhoods and so many stone bridges as the cab drove from street to street that the general feel of Budapest for him was of a dark old medieval city, like something out of a fairy tale.

Lily looked up from her screen. "I searched on Baba and Budapest and found a guy named Baba who wasn't Baba Aruj. He was named Gül Baba. He was an Ottoman from Turkey, but he's buried on a hill here. By the way, apparently *türbe* in Turkish means 'tomb' . . ."

"Then that's it. Holy cow, Lily," said Darrell. "Good work."

"Sara, could you take over again?" Lily said, turning to the window.

"Sure." Sara gently slipped the tablet away from Lily and read from it.

"Gül Baba was a Turkish poet," she read.

"Black fingers," said Wade. "From all that ink he used for writing."

"He died here in 1541, during the Ottoman reign," she continued, "and his tomb was built two years later in 1543—the year of Copernicus and Heyreddin's journey, the year Nicolaus died. Actually, the tomb still belongs to Turkey. It's on a hill overlooking the river, called Rose Hill."

"Good work, Lily. You found him," Darrell said again. He smiled, but she sat expressionless, looking out the cab window. Was she crying again?

"Pourriez-vous nous emmener à Rose Hill, s'il vous plaît?" Sara asked the driver, speaking French, which Darrell remembered his mother knew pretty well. *"Le tombeau de Gül Baba?"*

"Non," he said. *"Non!"*

"Excuse me, why not?" Sara asked.

When Darrell saw the driver's face in the rearview, the man's eyes were riveted on the traffic behind them. He swung around. "Someone's following us," Darrell said, spotting two blue cars, one close, one farther back.

"Oui, following!" the driver said.

"Essayez de les perdre, s'il vous plaît," said Becca. *"Et rapidement!"*

"Ah, certainement!" The driver punched his foot on the accelerator, and Darrell watched the two blue cars speed up, too.

CHAPTER FORTY-SIX

Galina Krause's private jet touched down minutes after the Kaplans arrived in Budapest. Her agents on the scene were instructed to follow, but not to intervene, not yet.

"They are in Buda, near the river," said an agent named Istvan who met her at the airport. "We can be there in ten minutes. Operatives are already on the scene."

"Make it five minutes, and tell the others to wait for me."

"Yes, Miss Krause."

Her phone rang. It was Ebner. "Yes?"

"There is something new," Ebner said. "Ugo

Drangheta and Mistral the thief were sighted driving south across Poland. They were at Olsztyn Castle. Galina, he learned something there."

Galina closed her eyes. "Alert the colonel. Have him intercept the couple."

Four hundred kilometers north of the Hungarian capital, Marius Linzmaier downshifted the armored transport disguised as a delivery truck. They approached Nowa Huta, the easternmost suburb of Kraków, Poland. He was to make another pickup. Pickup? Yes, but of what, exactly? He had never actually seen his cargo, but it was heavy, he knew that. Their driving progress was being monitored; he knew that, too. His front-seat companion certainly didn't tell him any more.

The grim-faced military man hadn't actually said anything at all for the last nine hours, and the cabin seemed to be getting smaller by the minute. The fifteen paramilitary agents of the Teutonic Order stuffed in the truck's rear compartment guarding whatever it was didn't know how well they had it.

"Colonel," said Marius, "we will arrive at the Lenin Steelworks in eighteen minutes." He knew it hadn't been called the V. I. Lenin Steelworks since the fall of Communism, but perhaps to get a reaction from the stone sitting next to him?

No such luck. Nothing.

"Then shall I notify our men in Building Forty-Three?"

Without changing his expression, the colonel nodded once.

And that was the whole of it. The man simply never spoke. Not so much as a word issued from his lips, as though his breath were too valuable to share with a commoner. Marius had to admit that there was something regal about how the fellow sat for hours without moving. As regal and uncommunicative as a statue of a German prince. The Teutonic Order, thought Marius, had been born in Germany, had faltered in Germany, had nearly disappeared in Germany, and since Galina Krause, had been reborn in Germany.

The colonel was not German.

That, if nothing else about the silent man, was plain to see.

CHAPTER FORTY-SEVEN

Forty minutes of swift driving by the cabbie back and forth over several bridges between Buda and Pest seemed to have confused the drivers of the blue cars enough to lose them—nearly also losing Wade his lunch—but the family had lost valuable time, too. When they finally arrived at Gül Baba Utca, a winding, steep, moody, medieval lane on the western—Buda— side of the city, their cabdriver didn't waste any more. He accepted the fare, told them in French the way up to the tomb, then tore off before any more blue cars could appear.

"Just because we lost those cars doesn't mean Galina won't figure out where we are or where we're going," said Sara. "So let's move it."

It was nearly seven p.m., the sky was still heavily overcast, and night was settling more and more over the city. A cool wind swept up the hill from the river as they began their hurried climb.

Sara took the lead with Becca. Wade and Darrell followed, Lily trailing behind. She was in her own space but keeping up. Right now that was good enough for Wade and the others. His father, her parents. They couldn't let anything more distract them.

"When Gül Baba died," said Sara, as they hurried upward, "they carried his body up to the top of this hill. One of the pallbearers was Suleiman the Magnificent, the Ottoman emperor."

Darrell liked that. "So cool."

"Copernicus must have come this way, too," Becca said. "And Heyreddin. Probably with Albrecht's knights on their tail."

Wade imagined those knights on horseback or on foot treading up the street, clopping over the cobblestones, swords drawn as they climbed each breathless step up the uneven street. He looked back nervously. What he saw was a vast lighted city spread out on both sides of the river. Colored coral and pink, yellow, gray, and black, the houses on both sides looked as if they had changed little in centuries.

"Searching for a tomb," said Darrell. "There's so much death on the hunt for the relics, we're probably the experts on death."

Wade flashed on his father's face for an instant, but pushed it away. *Get to the top. Find the second key.* His legs ached as they climbed a final, narrow stairway from the end of the street up to, of all things, Turban Street, another part of the diary's joke.

Türbe means *tomb* means *turban*.

At the top, they hurried along a short street, then entered a garden surrounding a small octagonal tomb. It had a shallow dome on top, made of iron and painted wood. Standing outside was a statue of Gül Baba, slightly animated, as if caught at the moment of poetic inspiration.

Sara kept watch. "The tomb is closed, and we're not breaking in. Not this time. Gül Baba was a poet, not a dictator like Lenin, which was still wrong."

"We know," said Wade. "And we won't. . . ."

They approached the tomb slowly. The breeze was constant, damp, and cool, with a fragrance of bitter coffee and wood smoke mixing with tens of thousands of blossoming roses surrounding them. The combination of dim spotlights, the overcast sky, and general darkness cast the structure in an eerie glow. In the momentary quiet, Wade heard the muffled striking of metal on stone. They froze. The sound continued for a minute or more before it stopped.

A few seconds passed, then the sound of boots on the ground echoed from every direction, louder and louder, until a troop of armed men swarmed out of the trees and surrounded them.

"No one move!" grunted one of the men. He took Sara roughly by the arms.

"They were waiting for us!" said Becca. "How on earth—"

A figure emerged from behind the octagonal mausoleum, silhouetted against the lights from the city below.

Galina Krause. She had a gun in her hand. In the other . . . a large iron key.

"How could you possibly have—" Lily started.

"I can discover the smallest detail about you in moments," Galina said, her voice low and hollow. "It was not difficult to determine that you had come to Budapest. After that, simple surveillance. Still the best way to leap ahead of someone. Once we identified your taxi and where it left you, we moved in. Strange you do not expect me to be several steps ahead of you."

Wade knew she hadn't been ahead of them. She'd

been following, but then had done an end run around them. They needed to improve their game.

"We don't have the first key with us," he said. He might actually have done the right thing by leaving it at the airport. "That would be stupid."

"Search them anyway," Galina said.

The manhandling was rough and thorough, but her rude agents found nothing.

"A pity," she said. "Now, what on earth will I do with you?"

From somewhere behind and above everyone came a single warning shot. It struck the stones at Galina's feet. The goons swung around, trained their weapons on the source of the shot. A man yelled out from the woods surrounding the tomb.

"In Ruhe lassen, Schlangenfrau! Sie haben was Sie wollen. Ich halte dich im Auge!"

Leave them be, snake woman! You have what you want. I have you in my sights!

Galina raised her hands as if in surrender, then pumped eight shots into the trees. There was a cry of pain. Her agents flew into the woods, their flashlights crisscrossing the darkness.

"Run!" Sara dived for cover behind the stone ramparts surrounding the tomb, bringing Lily and Darrell with her. Becca and Wade jumped after them. Several shots thudded from the trees; then they heard shouting, another shot, then nothing, no sound at all, except for a lone siren wailing in the distance.

Then Galina. "Leave them. We have the key. Go!"

Seconds later, they heard the shriek of cars roaring away from the hilltop.

After making sure the garden was clear, they bolted into the trees and found a young man in his twenties lying on the ground, one hand clutching his right side. He grabbed Lily's arm and drew her nearer. Wade knelt, too. The man's voice was barely audible. Whispers, syllables, a word or two.

"I em Guardian," he said softly. "We watch every night at Baba's tomb. Go, sixty-two Nagymező Street."

"Sixty-two," said Lily. "Becca, write this down."

"Is it about the third key?" Wade asked. "Is that where it is?"

The young man shook his head. "Two-four-zero-five. Not before, not after. Another will be there, waiting for you. Turn off your phones. They are not secure. . . ."

His eyes went glassy, but he kept breathing.

While Sara and Wade helped the man keep pressure on his wound, Darrell dashed around to the back of the tomb, but returned seconds later. "It's gone. You can see silver marks on the stone and loose bricks."

The sirens were louder. Sara stood, her hands bloody and shaking. "We have no way of explaining this. We can't be here. The ambulances will take care of this man. We go through the garden and over the wall, then down to the river. Does everyone remember the street? Nagy . . ."

"Nagymező Street," Lily said.

"Then, come on," Sara said. "Make sure your phones are off. Galina may have the second key, but we're still a target. Make no noise. . . ."

Wade and the others followed Sara between the rosebushes, scrabbling over the top of the wall before the first officers and emergency personnel entered the garden and the whistles began to blow.

CHAPTER FORTY-EIGHT

Nagymező Street was only two miles away in Pest, across the Danube from the Turkish poet's tomb in the Buda hills, but they didn't want to be on the streets any longer than they had to. So they hailed a cab. Becca knew she made a hash of the street name—"Naggy Metzo, Nazsh Meza, Neggy Mezoo"—but the driver eventually waved them in. He had understood. It wasn't far, but he would take the American family. When Sara asked to tour the streets around it first, he understood that, too.

Except for Wade, who was running numbers aloud, they were all too shocked to speak, but Becca couldn't stop thinking about how Galina shot the young man so viciously and emotionlessly. There'd been a glint in the young woman's eyes outside the tomb, which maybe was only the glare from the streetlamps, but it had made Becca's blood run cold. Galina was different somehow since the last time they'd seen her. Thinner and more electric, sure, but something else was going on.

The woman was more direct. Less elegant.

Just shoot, then shoot again.

Not them, though. That was odd and confusing. Not them. Galina had had a gun, but not for them. To not kill people when you had the chance was to keep them alive. Galina wanted them alive.

Why?

After zigzagging the neighborhood and seeing no blue cars, they asked the cab to stop two streets away from their destination. The driver hadn't seemed the least bit interested in why they wanted a roundabout way of getting someplace at night. He was tired, probably of Becca's lousy Hungarian, and didn't respond, even after she said, *"Köszönöm"*—thank you. He just looked at Sara's fingers as she dug into her wallet and paid him. Then he was gone.

Well, not the friendliest guy in the world, but he'd done what they wanted, and it was over soon. They walked to the corner of Nagymező and waited.

A few pedestrians were visible on the surrounding streets, but not many. It was dark, and only some of the streetlights were lit. It was now close to nine.

"At the poet's tomb, did anyone else notice the scar on Galina's neck?" said Darrell. "It was really red, all inflamed. It didn't look good. I mean, she looked all right, because she always does, but that scar didn't. I think maybe she's sick."

Becca glanced at Lily. She'd normally snap at Darrell for something like that, and he'd probably said what he had so she would respond, but she didn't.

She just kept looking at her phone, which Becca knew was not on.

"You'll answer them, right?" she whispered. "I mean, when we get better phones?"

"Don't tell me what—" Lily stopped. "I'm sorry. I'll call. Just not now. There's too much happening. That's all so far away from us, from this."

Becca let it go then, just smiled at Lily, put her hand on her shoulder.

"Let's move closer." Sara led the way down the opposite side of the street and found an alley not quite straight across from number 62, but with a full view of the front door and the windows.

The house was dark, no lights at all. An arched

doorway was inset in the pink facade, next to two arched windows that had bars over them. There was a balcony on the second floor over the windows. The facade was narrow. There might have been rooms above the third floor—the roof was peaked—but you couldn't tell.

"I think I've got it," said Wade. "The Guardian at the tomb said 'two-four-zero-five,' or twenty-four-oh-five. Which is . . ."

"Nicolaus's death day," said Becca. "May the twenty-fourth."

"Right. But the man also said 'not before or after.' So I think it's also a time. The problem is that twenty-four hundred is midnight, so there *is* no twenty-four-oh-five. Unless it's supposed to mean five minutes after midnight."

Darrell checked his watch. "Three hours from now."

Becca looked up and down the dimly lit street. "Let's just keep our eyes on the house and wait. See if anything happens."

A cool breeze smelling of the river came down the street. They settled down to wait. Darrell sat against a wall with his legs outstretched. Sara and Wade were speaking low to each other. Then Becca felt a pang when she realized they weren't talking to each other but leaving a message for Roald from Sara's phone. *Poor Wade. Poor Sara.*

Families and the relic hunt. Talk about crazy.

And Lily. Lily leaned on the wall across the alley from Darrell, not looking at him or at anyone, staring up between the houses at the sky. A horrible thought flitted through Becca's mind then.

What would all this be like without Lily? Could her parents tell her something that might change what we have here? Is there a relic hunt without Lily?

Thinking about that now probably wasn't helpful. Becca tried to empty her thoughts. Everyone had gone quiet. The hours passed. They rested, they paced, they said nothing for a long time, drifting down dark streets in their minds, until finally Darrell pushed himself away from the wall, his eyes on his watch.

"Seven minutes. Get ready, everyone."

Those seven minutes dragged on and on, until, at precisely 12:05 a.m., the light in the middle window of the second floor of 62 Nagymező Street flicked on for a second, then off.

If you weren't watching, you would have missed it. They were all watching.

While the light was out, the curtain ruffled briefly, then stopped, and the light came on again. This time, they saw a face framed in the window. The wrinkled face of a woman, like something from an old-master portrait. She was very old and had little or no hair on her head. She looked from the window the way you might expect a sightless person to, touching the glass with her fingers as if feeling the air in front of her face. The curtain ruffled back across her face.

The light went out and stayed out.

They stared up at the window. There wasn't any more movement.

"Was that the signal?" Wade whispered. "Just that little thing?"

"I think it may have been," said Becca.

"Then it's our cue to go in," said Darrell. "The man in the garden said she's a Guardian. Why are we waiting?"

Sara didn't move. She scanned both sides of the street, looked at her silent phone, but didn't move a step toward the house. "I hear you. I suddenly like it a lot less than I did before. People sending us to places. On the other hand . . ."

"Right," said Wade. "What choice do we have? Besides, it's not really Galina's style. We all see that, right? The creeping in shadows. She doesn't do that. Even her agents are all, 'We kill you now.' Plus, she had a chance to do something at the tomb. I think she's on her way to find the third key—"

"If there is one," said Lily.

"There is, and she'll find it," said Darrell, getting agitated. "Unless we follow up on this. I agree with Wade. Can we just go and get the next clue?"

"Darrell, cool it," said Sara sharply. "You're not bulletproof, you know; none of us are." She cased number 62 up and down, then peered out of the alley both ways down the deserted street. She slipped her phone into a pocket.

"All right. Quietly. Behind me."

The front door was not locked. A musty smell blossomed over them when Sara pushed it open. The stairwell was dark and heavy and utterly silent until the sound of heavy bolts and locks drifted down from upstairs. They climbed up the narrow, black staircase, Sara leading slowly. Slow was good, Wade thought. She was right. *At the very least, she's seen more spy movies and crime shows. She gets it.*

A door on the third floor opened as they reached the landing.

The light inside was on again. It cast a narrow yellow glow down the steps and over them. In the door frame stood the squat silhouette of the elderly woman they'd seen from the street.

"Idiots!" Her voice was angry and sharp, like two pieces of sandpaper scraping each other roughly. "So *you* are the ones who killed my son."

Sara stiffened. "Excuse me—"

The woman flung the door wide. "Get in! Unless you want to kill me, too."

Visibly shaken, Sara entered; the others followed. Darrell closed the door timidly behind him. The large front room was bare except for a small desk, a chair, and bookshelves lining the walls.

The old woman didn't look at them, as if she couldn't stand the sight of them, but she didn't speak, either. Finally, Sara said, "Is he really dead? Your son?"

"What! No! I have no son, except that all Guardians are my family, and no, he is not dead. He was taken to the hospital. He called me from there to expect you."

"Do you have a secret for us?" Wade asked boldly.

"Secret? Secret!" she boomed. "You fools leave a trail of blood wherever you go! You are pathetically unprepared for the heavy work you have undertaken."

They were stiffened to silence. The lady barely kept herself from exploding all over her little room.

Her words and her tone reminded Wade of the poet

known as Papa Dean, the Guardian of the Scorpio relic in San Francisco, or rather, the decoy of Scorpio. To put it mildly, Papa Dean didn't think much of the Kaplans, either. He hated them.

"Maybe we're not the greatest Guardians who ever lived," said Lily, who seemed to be fired up for the first time in hours. "But Carlo trusted us, and we're doing what we need to, to protect the Legacy. Plus we're in a hurry, because Galina just found the second key. If she somehow finds the third one, she'll know where the relic is. So you don't have to be so mad at us. If you have a clue that we can—"

"Silence!" the old woman shouted. "I am angry because you are so late. You must fly like the wind to ever hope to catch up to the demon woman. Guardians are few and we are dying. Since Galina Krause killed Heinrich Vogel, more than fifty of us have perished around the globe to protect the Legacy. You could easily add yourselves to that number if you are careless!"

Fifty? Wade thought. That many? The number was horrendous.

"I believed that there would be others, stronger than we are, to take our places. But . . . children?"

"And my mom!" said Darrell. "And my stepdad, who's finding out about Galina right now. Her weird plans. Plus, what about Hans Novak? He was a boy. He helped Copernicus more than you ever did."

"Darrell," Sara said, her hand on his forearm.

The woman's sunken cheeks reddened, and her eyes welled up. She stared at them for a long time, saying nothing.

"We're called the *Noviszhny* in Russia," Becca added, softly.

Finally, the old woman turned to the bookcase and removed a large antique book and set it on the table in front of them. Opening it, they saw that it was a fake, and that a section of its pages had been cut out. In the cutout was an octagonal object about five inches long and three inches from side to side. It was constructed of multiple pieces of burnished wood that were inlaid with semiprecious stones and designs made out of the thinnest impressed wire.

The woman removed it from its hiding place. "This is the clue you are seeking." She handed it to Sara. "Sometimes there is a second clue, because of the fear that one clue will be lost. This is your second clue. There will not be a third."

"It's heavy," said Sara, turning it slowly in her hands.

Becca removed the *ocularia* from their case and slid them on. "There are marks in silver here and there on its surface. Numbers. They could be the lens combination to the next part of the story."

"Are the wooden pieces movable?" asked Wade, taking the object from his stepmother. Something rattled when he moved it from side to side. "There's something inside. It's a puzzle of some kind. A puzzle box. Is that right?"

The woman toddled over to the window and looked out. "It is a clue to the next key. Other than that, I know nothing. If Galina Krause has the second key as you and tonight's tomb watcher reported, then you *each* have a message telling you where the next key is. Go. You are out of time. Morning will arrive all too quickly."

"What about you?" asked Becca. "What will you do now?"

"Remain at my post. The Protocol demands that I stay. And that you go. Now!" She rushed for the door, threw them out, and slammed and bolted it behind them before anyone could say a word.

CHAPTER FORTY-NINE

Darrell shivered. It was in the small hours of Sunday morning, and Nagymező Street was silent, still, completely deserted.

Not a soul moved on either side of the block. A flag hanging from a window opposite rippled lightly in the breeze. Traffic moved sparsely on the far cross street, but no one entered Nagymező. Nothing moved there.

Darrell tapped Wade's arm. "What do you think? Can you solve it?"

Wade shook his head as he held the heavy cylinder of red wood. It was divided into three sections, each one exactly a third of the cylinder's length. There must have been something like an axle running through the center of the pieces because Darrell watched him turn the sections back and forth like the faces of a Rubik's Cube.

"I don't know . . . yet. I really need time."

One end of the puzzle was flat. The other had little cutouts along the rim—he counted over twenty—like the crenellations at the top of a tower.

"Is it a model of an actual tower somewhere?" said Lily. "And once you solve the puzzle does the thing rattling inside show you *where* in the tower the key is?"

"That's clever enough for Copernicus," Sara said. "And Ottoman puzzle makers."

They were moving slowly along the dark street, Wade turning the octagon, when Becca stopped him. "Wait. I see a triangle. I think that's a triangle." She took a quick picture of it with Sara's phone and enlarged it. "Yes. It's marked with the numbers four, one, four. I think I can read the next silver page."

Darrell watched her adjust the *ocularia*'s lenses to the new combination. She closed her eyes, breathed in. She slipped on the *ocularia*, and he saw her face tighten from the instant pain of looking through them. Ignoring it, she read the next passage of the hidden story, and translated it in her head as she went along. "It's from

Leonardo, again." But it wasn't what she or anyone else had hoped for. After writing it in her notebook, she read it to them.

We insert our keys, first the astronomer, then the pirate, then myself. The stones revolve and lock into one another. The silver arm of Barbarossa is hidden.

After it is done, we each withdraw our key. "The three keys of Barbarossa."

But Nicolo is the first to see my little secret. "Locking the stones has revealed a fourth keyhole. Leonardo? Three keys to lock it, four keys to unlock it?"

"An extra precaution against thieves," I say. "The room will be destroyed if the lock's steel cables are broken. The floor will sink. The walls around you now will compress. None can retrieve the relic without the four keys."

Heyreddin Barbarossa gives me a stare. "And where is the fourth key?"

I smile. "The fourth key does not exist."

"Leonardo?" Nicolo says.

"It will never be found. Not without the lantern that lights my final days."

"No more riddles!" they chime. "Tell us!"

I do not. Instead I lock my lips with my fingers, signaling I am done.

Darrell groaned. "Seriously, there's a fourth key that doesn't even exist? A *fourth* key? That doesn't *exist*?"

"It has to be a riddle," said Sara.

"It better be," Darrell said. He wanted to scream or hit something, but then, they probably all did. He turned to Wade. "Well?"

Wade pulled at the object's various surfaces and turned each of the three parts clockwise and counter-clockwise at different increments, gently, near his ear, trying to hear or feel an inner movement that would release the puzzle.

"Just keep moving," Darrell said. "Wade can't do anything if we look at him."

"Good," his mother said. "Good idea. Let's walk to the river."

Lily said nothing, just pushed ahead of everyone else.

We're really fraying, Darrell thought. *Everybody's pressed to the limit. Can the relic hunt keep on like this? Will we survive the quest all the way to the end?*

While they walked from street to street toward the Danube, Becca and his mother fell to whispering about what their next move should be. He saw his mother pause once to check her phone, but there had been no message.

"Dad's with Terence," Darrell said. "Between them,

they'll know what to do."

He didn't want to let his mind go where it had gone when they couldn't reach his mother for days, only to discover that she'd been kidnapped.

Even though they knew the phones were compromised, Becca put in a call to Julian, who hadn't heard from Roald or Terence, either, but would arrange to come to them "once you know where the next key is hidden."

Darrell nudged Wade. "More pressure for you, bro," he said. "But, you know, no pressure or anything." Wade gave him a look and edged away.

We're all at our limits.

Then Becca stopped short. Lily did, too. They stared down the street.

Silhouetted against the streetlamp was a figure that might have been a woman or a man wearing a long robe.

"Lily," Becca whispered. "It's like the old woman in Austin."

But no. When the figure came slowly toward them, limping stiffly with every other step, it moved like a man. A smaller figure appeared by his side, helping.

"Holy cow!" said Darrell. "Is that . . . it's Abul-Qasim and Karim!"

They rushed to them, but when they came under a streetlight, they could see that Abul-Qasim's cheeks and eyes were scraped and bruised, there was a bandage on his forehead, and he grimaced with each step toward them. Sara urged them to sit on a nearby bench.

"It was Fatboy, wasn't it?" Lily said angrily.

"Bigboy," said Becca.

"Not anymore."

"Yes, the two men," said Karim. "They found me hiding, took your phone, Wade, then made us tell them what we knew."

"As soon as the men left, we determined to study the information you had uncovered," said Abul-Qasim.

Karim nodded. "I have a good memory. I remembered the numbers on the face of the key, and suspected Istanbul. But Granddad wondered if our qibla was part of it. He was right. Putting it together, we made the same leap that you must have made. The Ottomans were here, so we said, 'Budapest!' We flew here as soon as we could."

"How did you know we were right here?" asked Darrell.

Abul-Qasim smiled. "Knowing the ruthlessness of the Order, we checked the hospitals and found a young man who had been shot. I persuaded the police I was his spiritual adviser. The man understood at once that we knew you."

Karim let out a quiet breath. "He told us where he had sent you. So we've come to help."

"Help?" said Sara. "But you're in more danger now than you were before."

"Helping is what Guardians do," said Abul-Qasim.

"I knew it," said Becca. "You're Guardians."

"Only if you allow us to be," the man said. "After those two agents left us, we spoke, Karim and myself, for a long time. We don't know the whole story, but we feel we know you, and would like to join you on your mission. Between Karim and myself, we know something about history, astronomy, geography. Let us help you."

Lily turned to the end of the street. "Let's go somewhere. I still feel the creepy Order creeping around."

A few minutes' walk brought them to an all-night *kávéház*—coffeehouse—not far from the river, where they huddled together at a worn table.

"Galina found the Budapest key," said Darrell. "We think she's already gone to the next location. But there's this. Wade?"

He showed them the wooden puzzle. "We don't know what it is. I mean, we know it's a puzzle, but we don't know what the shape of it means."

"We think it could be a building of some kind," said Sara. "But we have no idea." She shot a glance at Lily. "It's hard to search the internet for something when you don't know what it is."

Abul-Qasim took the puzzle in his hands and turned it from side to side. The object hidden in the middle of it clicked with each movement. "This is very much like some old Arabic puzzle boxes I have seen, except that it's not Arabic. It is Ottoman. Karim?"

The boy took the puzzle and held it to the light. "Yes, the markings. Turkish?"

Between the two of them, they began to assemble a handful of clues. Finally, Abul-Qasim sat the puzzle upright on the table. It stood like a squat tower. He closed his eyes for several seconds, then blinked them open.

"Someone please look up *Kizil Kule*."

Lily didn't. She couldn't bring herself to search and link, search and link. She let Sara do it. For the last ten minutes, after seeing what their two friends from Tunisia had gone through to get to them, Lily had felt the brutality of the relic hunt steal something from her. She watched them all going at it, trading clues, making fresh connections. Was she already out of the hunt? Maybe, she thought. She'd answer her parents soon. She felt it coming, was almost ready to hear the "good news."

But one thing bothered her.

She borrowed Becca's notebook and turned to the passage Becca had read them. Something unsettled her about the passage, and she'd been around Becca enough to know that what bothered you just might be what gave you the answer.

It was da Vinci's snarky response to the question of where the fourth key was.

> *It will never be found. Not without the lantern that lights my final days.*

That was the riddle. Fourteen words. But she wasn't bothered by the first five. It was the last nine: *Not without the lantern that lights my final days.* And of those, she felt there were two parts.

Not without the lantern.

And *that lights my final days.*

While the others puzzled over the puzzle box, she started on the first four words. *Not without the lantern* could simply mean "you need the light of the lantern." But maybe *without* meant "outside." You'll never find it *outside* the lantern. You'll find it *inside* the lantern. Okay. But it didn't seem to mean any actual lantern he might have had at the moment, because Nicolaus and Heyreddin would have searched it and found the key right there. No, he meant another lantern. Plus he also said the key didn't even exist.

That's where the last five words came in, and of those, the last three were the riddle. *My final days.* They already knew that Leonardo died in France. Sara had said that his last house was the Château du Clos Lucé in central France.

Something about the château's name bothered her now.

She asked Becca for her phone and went to a trusty translation site. *Clos* meant "closed." "Walled in." A *close*, or a walled-in place. *Lucé.* Nothing from the translator, but those letters. *Lucé*, as in trans*luce*nt? Something to do with light?

Closed light?

Lantern.

She felt a tingle in her neck. "Um, I think I have something."

They turned to her. Wade nodded. "Go."

"I don't know about the fourth key not existing, but if it *does* exist, I think I know where it is. His home in

France. Clos Lucé. It kind of means 'lantern.' I think we should check it out."

"But Kizil Kule," said Darrell. "We have to go there, too. Look."

Sara turned the tablet around for her. "Kizil Kule means 'red tower,'" she said. "It's on the coast of Turkey in a city called Alanya. It's a hundred feet tall and was built in the thirteenth century to defend the Ottomans from invaders. The picture of the tower exactly matches the puzzle."

"I'm willing to bet that the third key is in the red tower," Wade said. "And that the bean rattling inside tells which room the key is hidden in."

"We all think so," said Becca.

"Fine," said Lily. "But we'll still be missing the fourth key, and it may be the most important of all. Listen to this."

She went through the riddle step by step with them.

After she was done, Abul-Qasim nodded slowly. "I think Lily may be right. In saying, 'The lantern that lights my final days,' Leonardo appears to be pointing you to his home at Clos Lucé. Leonardo was practically on his deathbed when he hid the relic with Copernicus and Heyreddin. Clos Lucé could very well be the lantern he speaks of, and some of you may have to go there."

Darrell stood from the table, a grin spreading on his face. "This is so good. I like this. Guardians at work. We can totally do this."

"We can," said Sara. "Thanks to you, Abul-Qasim, and to you, Karim. Now both of you *have* to get yourselves back to the hospital to visit the young man who was shot. You've done enough Guardian work for one day. Two days."

Karim smiled. "Remember, you have friends in Tunis, if you ever need them."

"Not just friends," said Becca. "Guardians."

Abul-Qasim rose to his feet, steadier than before. "Good luck. *Ma'a salama. Allah yusallmak.*"

"In other words," said Karim, "Good-bye, and may Allah go with you."

Becca used the words Alula had told them. *"Shukran jazeelan."*

Abul-Qasim and Karim bowed to them. A few minutes later they were on the street, in a taxicab, and gone.

"We have to go, too," said Sara, removing her phone from her bag and turning it on. "I'm calling Julian to ask him to meet some of you at Clos Lucé. The others will come with me to Turkey. Who wants to go where?"

CHAPTER FIFTY

"Idiot!"

As the nameless driver screeched into the Order's hangar at the Budapest airport, the short, rumpled man in the corner watched her storm out of the car, leaving the door swinging. She was angry. He hoped only at the driver, not at him.

"Gerrenhausen!" she screamed.

She wants me. Oskar emerged from the shadows of the hangar, wrapped his open trench coat around himself, and trotted over, hoping his face showed less fear and more an eagerness to please.

"Yes, Miss Krause? How may I be of—"

"This key was crafted by Leonardo." She handed it

to him. "But the engraving is so much cruder, it must be the work of Copernicus or Heyreddin Barbarossa. What does the design mean? Is the double *K* the Russian letter *zhe*?"

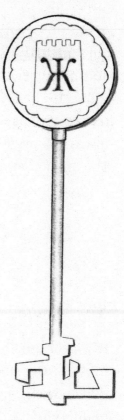

Gerrenhausen took the heavy object into his hands. "Yes, yes, Leonardo. The letter, perhaps Russian, perhaps not. And silver marks here, likely readable only with the stolen *ocularia*"—he did not look at her as he said that word, knowing it was partially his fault the children had it—"but we can determine one or two things. . . ."

He trembled to imagine her anger if he should come up with something wrong or, worse, nothing at all. He thought of stepping out of reach, when his senses tingled excitedly. Recognition did not surface, but something else did.

"Look here. There is the barest tab, a lever of sorts, on the edge of the back side. My fingers, you see, are so very sensitive."

He pressed the lever gently. It pushed in, then fell out onto his palm. The lever was actually a tube, hollow and no wider than a needle. And it contained something. He held it up to his lips and blew hard. A tiny fragment of paper fell out into his palm. He unrolled it. It was a quarter-of-an-inch square. One side was blank. The other contained a very small colored image.

"A compass rose," Galina said. "But no map to identify its origin."

"No," Gerrenhausen murmured as he closed his eyes and moved the tiny paper gently between his thumb and forefinger, "no map . . . but the cartographic paper it is painted on—that, perhaps, is the clue. My fingers know it. The paper is not European, Miss Krause. Not Western European, at least."

"From Budapest?"

He brought the fragment up to his nose and sniffed it several times. "No. Beyond. It is Greek, perhaps. Or Egyptian. No . . . Turkish."

"Ottoman!" she said. "Yes. And what else?"

He nodded, a smile teasing at his lips. He was on home ground now, she in thrall to his peculiar mastery of the history of paper. "It is a compass rose from a Turkish map produced in the first part of the sixteenth century. . . ." He handed the paper to her, then withdrew a narrow notebook from the breast pocket of his coat. He consulted page after page and then stopped. Holding it up, he took the cartographic fragment back from Galina and held it next to the notebook page. "Ah, yes. Piri Reis. A cartographer for Suleiman the Great of Istanbul. This is a fragment of a printing of maps he made of the coast of Alanya, a port city in the Antalya Province of Turkey."

Galina breathed. "Excellent. Anything else?"

"With that as a clue," the little man went on, "I can now offer a guess as to the image on the front of the key. The back-to-back double *K* emblem is not the Russian letter, but identifies the octagonal building as the tower of Kizil Kule, a formidable structure that guarded that same portion of the Turkish coast for over eight centuries. That, my dear Miss Krause, is where another Barbarossa key is located!"

She turned immediately from him. She seemed happy with his work. Perhaps now she would reconsider her threat to his grandson.

"Gerrenhausen, come. You are needed."

The words were music to him. He followed Galina across the hangar to her jet and watched her press an icon on her phone. Ebner von Braun's face came up, the blue of ocean water behind and below him. He was on the deck of a ship. The tumblers in Gerrenhausen's brain turned. *He is on her yacht near Turkey.* Ebner was very near the next key.

"Ebner, the third key is hidden in the tower of Kizil Kule in Alanya," she said. "Notify our newly arrived agents in Istanbul to meet you there. Direct others to the nearest airport. I am sending Gerrenhausen with the second key."

This was unexpected. "Me?" he said.

"The relic may be close by. We must be ready with the key. Ebner, the Kaplans could have beaten us there. Descend on the tower now!"

"Of course," Ebner said. "And will you join us, Galina?"

"Once my other business is done," she said. "Do not fail me!"

CHAPTER FIFTY-ONE

Hong Kong, People's Republic of China
June 8
7:28 p.m.

In the Marco Polo suite at the Peninsula hotel, Markus Wolff looked up from the desk and out across Victoria Harbor at Hong Kong Island.

Twilight was coming. The mix of yachts, tall-masted sailing craft, traditional junks, and assorted barges and dinghies streamed in and out of the wharves even at this late hour. It was a scene he had viewed nightly for the last two days, and now it was time. He glanced at his phone: 7:28 p.m.

At seven forty-five, with dusk finally settling over

the harbor, he would board the Star Ferry for the island. From the dock he would then walk to his appointment on Wing Lok Street. Strange, he thought, having an appointment with a man who expected someone else. Feng Yi was a traitor to the Order, a clever man so obsessed with the authentic Scorpio relic that he had finally located it, after killing nine people who stood in his way. He was now arranging to smuggle the relic into North Africa. To a buyer who had expressed sudden and lucrative interest. A man by the name of Ugo Drangheta.

The alarm on Wolff's phone rang. It was seven thirty. Time to go.

Wolff closed his edition of the late poems of Emily Dickinson and rose from the desk. He arranged the items on it as they had been before he took the room. He slipped on a pair of tight gloves, entered the bathroom, and returned with a damp hand towel, which he used to wipe down the surfaces he had touched. As the hotel's recycling notice suggested, he tossed the towel on the bathroom floor.

After picking his satchel up off the bed, he smoothed the bedspread with the flat of his gloved hand. One more look around. He left the room. In the lobby, he nodded once at the concierge, who returned the nod and said, "Good day, Mr. Ambler." *Ambler* was an identity Wolff used often in the Far East.

On the street, he took his bearings, walked to the ferry docks, boarded the seven forty-five, and was on the island by eight. A ten-minute stroll brought him to the corner of Wing Lok and Man Wa Lane, where he waited under an awning behind an illegally parked van.

Last night, he had sent Feng Yi a text from a burner phone:

Central Island Exports, 71 Wing Lok St., 8:30pm. Bring package. Transport arranged, destination Casablanca, 48hrs. 2mill euros. Come alone.

Feng Yi had responded. *Prove you represent who you say.*

Wolff had then transferred a photograph from his phone, as if it were a picture of his own wrist, an image courtesy of Oskar Gerrenhausen.

Ø

He had repeated the message. *Come alone.* This received no response. So now, under that awning, Wolff waited to see if his trick had worked.

At 8:28 p.m. a taxi rolled quietly to a stop at the far end of the street. A man struggled out of the back-seat. He held a small brushed-aluminum briefcase. He said something to the driver, closed the door behind him, and began to limp toward number 71. The man had long black hair, much as he had in San Francisco, where Wolff had shot him for trying to steal the Scorpio relic. But like all failed seekers of that poisoned device, Yi had succumbed to a death lust. He had become ill from the radiation, and still he couldn't drag himself along the sidewalk for a minute without rechecking the radioactive contents of the suitcase.

When the moment came, Wolff could say something clever to him, but with the end so near, the words one said had to bear so much more weight than mere cleverness. A soul would die soon, leave the world, his journey done.

He thought again of the words he had been reading in the hotel.

He lived the Life of Ambush
And went the way of Dusk

Wolff wondered which of the two of them the poem might refer to.

But there was no sense in waiting. The street was quiet. He wouldn't break the air with the concussion of an unsilenced gunshot. He drew the noise suppresser from inside his leather coat, screwed it onto the barrel of his Walther, took seven steps, and raised it at the limping man.

"Mr. Yi."

Feng Yi raised his face. "You? But no—"

The report from the Walther was quick, dense, dull. Feng Yi fell to the street with a groan, his expression puzzled, his face a question, a worry, as if he didn't quite understand his own ambush and was unable to comprehend what had just been done to him. The second shot removed the worry, removed everything.

At the far end of the street, the taxi backed up, drove away. Wolff stood over the body, watched its stillness for a few seconds. Dusk fell into night.

He removed the silencer, pocketed both it and the gun, then opened the suitcase for a fraction of a second. The jade scorpion lay fitted tightly inside.

"And that is done."

He snapped the case shut. "Dear Galina, the scales are even once more."

Some nine thousand kilometers to the northwest, an armored convoy approached the route to the central

Apennine range called the Monti della Laga, the mountains of the lakes.

Marius Linzmaier glanced out of the corner of his eye. The colonel sitting next to him had worn the same somber face the entire trip.

"Pull over," the colonel said, his first words since before the Austrian border crossing. Linzmaier slowed and parked on the shoulder, and the following vehicles did the same. They idled there while the colonel removed his phone from his jacket pocket and placed a call.

"We are one and one-half hours from arrival," he said into the phone. There came a few words of response the driver couldn't hear. The colonel nodded and hung up.

"We wait here."

Linzmaier turned off the engine. "May I ask for what?"

"Our people at Nowa Huta report seeing a man and a woman surveilling the steelworks."

"Did our people intervene?"

"No. That will be our job. We wait here."

Confused as he was, but knowing that the conversation with the colonel was unlikely to continue, Linzmaier left the cabin, went around to the rear compartment, and unlocked the doors. One by one a troop of armed guards left the compartment and stood by the side of the road, stretching, smoking. The driver studied what he had been transporting: a monster of unconnected fragments, a skeleton of girders, rods and struts coiled into the shape of claws, levers and pistons and pipes and gears in frightening disarray—a thing unbuilt, unformed, unborn. It terrified him. The looks on the guards' faces told him they felt the same. They were gray and grim and, in a word, horrified to have been locked up with that mess for so long.

The one thing that joined the pieces in some kind of symmetry was that down to the very last bolt and gear, they all seemed to be crafted of a single substance.

Gold.

CHAPTER FIFTY-TWO

Tours, France
June 8
Late afternoon

Becca was the first to spot Julian outside the Val de Loire airport in Tours, waving to them from the driver's seat of a rental car.

In Budapest, they had decided that Sara would go to Turkey with Lily and Darrell, and that Becca and Wade would meet Julian in France as soon as they were able to get there—which was Sunday afternoon. They would have with them the *ocularia*, the first key, and the diary safely in Becca's indestructible go-bag. As usual, Julian would provide a new set of secure phones for them.

Sara had also called Silva, asking him to please meet them in Turkey, if he was able to. She told Silva that since Galina possessed not only the second key but also the powerful resources of the Copernicus Room to assemble the tiniest fragments of data, it was practically ensured that the Order would be waiting for them. Silva told them he would meet them as soon as he could.

There was no reunion chatter when Becca and Wade got in the car and Julian started it up. "Still no word from my dad," he said. "Paul Ferrere's on-site now but so far as he can tell Roald and my dad are already inside, and Paul can't get near the facility. One more day, we're going to the police."

Wade nodded, then shared a look with Becca.

She knew what he was thinking. Sara was great, supersmart and careful, but with his father unreachable, at best a critical member of the team was out of action. At worst, his father was in grave danger.

Julian drove speedily onto the highway and headed southwest toward Château d'Amboise, on the grounds of which stood Leonardo's smaller house. "It could simply be that the mountain lab is out of range of phones, for security reasons. Paul doesn't think so, but I'm hoping that's all it is."

"Us, too," Becca said. "Your father and Roald are

smart. They can deal."

"They can. And my dad can make a deadly weapon out of a toothpick, so there's no reason to panic. Still . . ." He didn't finish, just let it end there, and concentrated on the driving.

After one quiet roundabout hour they drove through the gates and up a winding road to the main château.

From where they parked outside a sprawling complex of ornate stone mansions, it was a brisk seven-minute walk to the much smaller Château de Cloux, now known as Château du Clos Lucé.

"I'd always thought that Clos Lucé could mean something like the 'castle' or 'keep' of 'light,'" he said. "It was really no stretch at all to think of the château where da Vinci died as a lantern."

"A big lantern," Wade murmured when they finally saw it.

True enough, Becca thought. The house was small only when compared to the city-size immensity of the nearby Château d'Amboise. Da Vinci's mansion was three stories of red bricks, white limestone, and tile set in a sweep of rolling lawns. Leonardo died when he was sixty-seven on May 2, 1519, a little over a month after he returned from . . . wherever it was that he and the others hid Triangulum.

"I love these quiet places," Becca said. "Like Bletchley Park in England. Quiet places where we learn incredible things."

"Maybe not so quiet," Wade whispered, pausing on the path toward the house. "Julian, I maybe see an agent. Bearded, tall. On the left. His hand is buried in his jacket pocket."

"He could be château security," said Becca. "Or not. I see his short friend."

Julian pulled out his phone and brought it to his ear as if receiving a call. "Pretend you don't see them. We'll have a tiny advantage."

"We could take them," Becca whispered, only half joking.

"Oh, I know," Julian said. "We totally could. But we don't want to scare the museum guides, do we?" He turned away as if to speak on his phone. "You go on the tour. I'll try to lead our friends on a little chase. Remember to find the key."

"That's the idea," said Becca.

Julian slipped away, still pretending to be on a phone call, and in a matter of seconds had gone around the side of the house. The taller of the sketchy men pursued him, followed a few moments later by his shorter colleague.

"Julian's good," said Becca. "Professional."

"Yeah. Easy to forget he's only seventeen. Come on."

As soon as they identified themselves inside the house as Americans, a perky young woman trotted over to them, a student intern from Massachusetts named Lucy. Which seemed appropriate to Becca, because, after all, the intern's name meant "light," too.

After giving them a solid overview of Leonardo's last years in France, she swished them through several rooms and finally into the master's final workshop. Because the tour was near the end of the day, Lucy's presentation to them and the three other visitors became more relaxed and informal, and more informative.

"We're interested in Leonardo's work while he was here," Wade said, during a gap in the discussion.

"Especially his work with silver," Becca added. "And especially from 1517 to the end. Kind of specific, I know, but . . ."

"Well, he was a renowned silversmith," the guide said. "And in the last years, he was deeply into the study of mirrors. Mirrors use silver, of course, for the reflection; they always have. But Leonardo worked on, or wrote about, what he called a three-sided mirror, or *lo specchio con tre lati*." Her accent was good.

The two shared a look. They knew exactly what that looked like.

"Interesting," said Becca.

Lucy smiled. "You probably know that Leonardo was a hopeless experimenter. He sketched out thousands of proposed plans and never went through with them. I think he simply *had* to understand how something worked, but then became bored when he figured it out. Who knows how the mind of a genius works?"

"They called him the spy of nature, didn't they?" said Wade.

"Exactly!" Lucy said. "Well, feel free to look around, but obviously don't touch anything. Wouldn't want to break an original da Vinci!"

As the intern wandered off, Wade and Becca scoured the workshop for anything that might be a clue to the location of the last key. While no one was looking, Becca took the *ocularia* from her bag and slipped them on, hiding them under a pair of dark glasses.

As he usually did, Wade seemed to need to talk out everything they knew so far. "Leonardo and Copernicus met here in 1517—that much we know," he whispered. "Copernicus asked him to be a Guardian, but Leonardo was too old. So Nicolaus looked around, saw all the silver, all the mirrors, maybe he saw designs for armor; whatever it was, something clicked in his memory. He remembered his old pirate friend, the man who had lost his forearm saving Hans Novak. It all came together for him. He asked Leonardo, 'Make a silver arm for my friend, the pirate Baba Aruj, called Barbarossa.'"

Becca liked the way it all sounded, laid out like that. It struck all the right notes. "Leonardo used his knowledge of silver and mirrors, and he made a new arm, a silver arm, with Triangulum inside to power the fingers like a motor. It was the first mechanical prosthetic arm."

Wade looked at her. Becca liked that he was smiling. The two of them together had pressed at the problem until it gave up an answer.

Part of an answer.

"But there's still a question," said Wade, looking out to the garden from a window made of wavy glass. "If Leonardo said that the fourth key doesn't exist, why would he tell Guardians to come here to his lantern? What did he mean?"

Becca imagined the scene in the stony place where the silver arm rested. Leonardo was there. Copernicus. Barbarossa Two. She suddenly felt a wave of awe fall over her. "These men, three famous people in the same place, talking as friends, trying to save the world, protecting something of great power from falling into the wrong hands . . . oh . . . oh!"

He smiled at her. "What is it?"

Her eyes were wide, staring at him through the shaded *ocularia*. "Wade!"

"What?"

Without taking the glasses off, she started scanning the room. "It's not just that the fourth key doesn't *exist*. Wade, what if . . . what if . . . Leonardo *never made* the fourth key? That could be why no one would ever find it. That's what his riddle is. Three keys lock the relic away, but you need four keys to unlock it. So why didn't he make the fourth key? Because he didn't need to. Only the Guardian who collected the relic would need to. That's us! We need to make the fourth key! It's totally the best kind of security!"

Wade looked at her through the glasses. Her eyes must have seemed all broken up into fragments. "Okay, Becca. That's actually kind of brilliant. But how does it help us find it?"

"Because the fourth key *is* here!" she said. "It's like Lucy said. He designed it, he drew it, but he never made it. We need to find his design. And then we need to find someone to make the key for us. That's what any Guardian would have had to do!"

He looked straight through the silver lenses into her eyes.

"You're pretty amazing," he said. "You know that, right?"

CHAPTER FIFTY-THREE

Searching frantically in every room in the château that was open to the public, Becca felt her heart ready to explode.

"Even assuming we're right," she whispered to Wade as she peered through the *ocularia* hidden under her dark glasses, "and the fourth and final key has to be made from scratch before we can unlock Triangulum, how are we actually going to make it? Could Julian help us?"

Wade looked out the nearest window to the garden, then turned to her. "I hope so. Should I call him? Maybe he's in trouble."

"Let's find the design or whatever it is first," she said.

That's when she realized something she hadn't before. "Galina's not as light on her feet as we are."

"What do you mean?"

"That we're a team," she said. "We can spread ourselves across countries and work independently and at the same time. While Lily and Sara and Darrell are off in Turkey finding the third key, we're finding the fourth."

"Galina has the Copernicus servers," he said. "And Ebner and Wolff."

"But she doesn't trust anyone, not really. You see that, right? And she's not well. That's easy to see, too. Galina has a serious weakness. She's alone."

Wade nodded. "You're right. Being alone isn't the way to find the relics. You need a team. We have a team. You, me, Lily, Darrell, Sara, my dad . . . when he gets back . . ." He trailed off, then added, "*And* Julian and Terence, Silva, Karim and Abul-Qasim, Carlo, and Bingo and Pinky and Alula. That's how we find the relics. That's the way we'll win."

An image of Lily's face flashed into Becca's mind. Her best friend was hurt. She should be there with her. "Let's find this thing."

Wade headed back into the workshop. "Except that I don't know what we're actually looking for. Even if

Leonardo was making a pun on *lantern*, maybe he really means *lantern*. But I don't see any. At least not one that could be from the early sixteenth century."

"Keep at it." Becca entered the bedroom where Leonardo died. She hoped to find a crusty old lantern overlooked in a niche in the wall. Maybe it no longer held a candle, but in its secret compartment were the designs for the final key.

No such luck.

Becca felt her excitement slipping away, like the sun was doing right now in the late afternoon. The sky was clouding up. The museum would close in less than half an hour, and they had nothing. Julian was still out there running interference—she hoped he was, and hadn't fallen into the clutches of the Order.

"Let's . . . let's look at the drawings and paintings. Maybe there's something there," she said. "A lantern in one of his paintings. It could be a code. Maybe?"

The museum shop had a good selection of art books covering the full range of Leonardo's drawings and sketches. They each took a massive collection and scanned it for work done after 1517. Nothing, nothing, nothing.

Then, something.

Wade leaned over a page in a catalog of late drawings.

"Bec . . . look at this. It's from one of his famous note-books of sketches and writings called *Codex Atlanticus*. A drawing from 1515 or later."

It was a lantern, but not the usual type of lantern. The caption noted that it was a kind of primitive slide projector called a camera obscura or a magic lantern.

"I don't get that it's a design for a key, though," he said.

She lifted the *ocularia* and sunglasses off and replaced them with her reading glasses. She studied the drawing. "Leonardo said, 'not *without* the lantern.' Like Lily said, 'not without' could mean 'within.' The lines inside the lantern aren't very clear. They might be different when you look through the *ocularia*. I'm going to use the combination five-five-five. It's Leonardo's number, after all."

"Go for it."

Making sure no one saw, Becca adjusted the lenses as she had before—five-five-five on one side, five-five-five on the other. Taking a breath, she slipped them on.

Under the lenses, the crosshatched lines inside the lantern reformed themselves and took on the look of a schematic. It was the design for the fourth key. She took off the glasses, held her new phone behind the lenses, and snapped a photo. Then another. Six photos in all.

What she saw in the decoded lines was a clear image of a key.

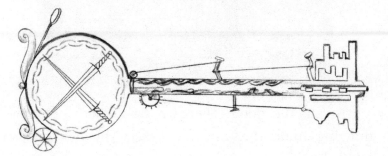

A key. Similar to but more intricate than the others. It bore the same telltale ornamentation on its shell, but it also had gears and struts and linkages and silver wires extending from it. It almost looked like a weapon or an engine, and reminded her that Leonardo had designed many military machines in his career.

"The fourth key," she whispered. "We found it!"

But Wade was fixed on another page in the book of drawings. He turned the book around to her, to one of several sketches depicting a cataclysm of water.

"Becca, the flood. There's a whole series of these drawings under the same title: *Deluge*. The flood my dad told us about . . ."

"What's the date of the drawings?"

He read the caption. "Between 1515 and 1519."

She shivered in the sunlit room. These drawings from five centuries ago seemed as fresh and terrifying as if they had rendered something that had just happened today. Or would happen tomorrow.

Or . . . at whatever deadline they knew Galina was obsessed with.

"What if Leonardo drew these because Copernicus told him about the horrors of time travel?" she asked. "The ones he told me about in London? Wade, maybe Copernicus saw a flood and told Leonardo. But it hasn't come yet. It's coming now. Your father knows about it, and it has to do with Galina."

Wade pulled out the phone Julian had given him. "I'm calling Sara—"

Julian raced in, followed by the intern, who was angry. "There's no running allowed in Leonardo's house!" she said.

"Sorry!" said Julian. "If I break something, I'll buy it." He drew Wade and Becca quickly from the room. "I threw off our friends—finally—but a couple of black cars just pulled into the lot. You know what that means. I hope you found what you were looking for."

"We have the design for the fourth key," Becca said, pocketing her phone.

"And that's not all," said Wade. "But first, we need the best jeweler you know!"

CHAPTER FIFTY-FOUR

Alanya, Turkey
June 8
Evening

Because of all the near-death experiences they'd racked up so far, the uneventful flight to Antalya airport was just long and boring and foodless, but Darrell couldn't care about any of that after he deplaned and got Wade's call.

"I have good news and bad news," Wade had told him.

And as good as the good news was—"Becca and I found the design for the fourth key"—the bad news was crazy bad: "We also found a bunch of flood drawings."

Darrell told Lily first, hoping she would actually talk with him. She was quiet to begin with. "Hmm," she said. Then she got quieter.

His mother was quiet, too, but for a different reason. "I keep thinking about your stepfather's secret meeting," she said softly. She was going to say more, he was sure of it, but she swallowed the rest. "But first, we get the third key."

"You bet we do," he said. He glanced over at Lily, who just nodded, which was better than nothing.

Of course, it made sense to Darrell to connect the Copernicus horrors—*we should have a better term for that*—with the flood that his stepfather had told them about. But it was a kind of grim, end-of-the-world sense. The bad news was drowning the good news.

His mother had sat next to him all through the flight, trying, hopelessly, to unlock the secret of the puzzle box of the tower, to find the exact location of the third key, but she was getting nowhere.

When he'd tried to be polite—"Don't drive yourself crazy with it" and "Do you want me to try?"—she shook her head. "I just want to try one more thing." So he'd turned to Lily, but every time he looked at her, he'd found himself tongue-tied.

His mom and dad had broken up, so he *kind of* knew

what she was feeling, but he'd been a lot younger when his father had drifted out of their lives, and Darrell and his mother had always been together, so yeah, he didn't *really* know what she was feeling at all.

Maybe I can just tell her that. Maybe someone can let me do something!

"Ladies and gentlemen," the pilot announced, "we have begun our descent into Antalya airport and will arrive in approximately twenty minutes. Flight crew, please begin your cross-check and prepare the cabin for landing."

He glanced at Lily. *Say something neutral,* he thought. "I hope Silva is there," he said. "Or a hundred of his friends. I think we'll need protection."

"Well, *you* will," she said.

Ah! Good old Lily! He decided not to wreck it with a quip. He just laughed.

Turning to the window, he saw how the ultramarine blue of the sea contrasted with the brown earth and beaches of the coast that spread out beneath them.

"It looks like a vacation place," his mother said, still fiddling with the puzzle.

"That's what makes it so dangerous," he said.

"Meaning what?" asked Lily.

"I'm not sure." But he made a mental note to use it on Wade.

The airport was large, but not jammed at that time of day. Because Becca and Wade had the first Barbarossa key, Darrell, Lily, and Sara didn't need to hide anything in a locker, but he came up with the bright idea to rent one anyway, just to have a decoy locker key.

"Uh-oh," Lily whispered. "Some guys just walked into the terminal. Not the good kind of guys."

Darrell saw them. A trio of plainclothes Europeans, beefy, hands in pockets, on phones, obviously packing sidearms, heads swiveling around the room. He didn't want to be seen watching, but he couldn't wrench his eyes away. Big mistake. His stare connected with one of them. There was a flash of recognition.

His mother saw. "Get out of here!" She rushed them both back through the crowded concourse, searching for the nearest exit. Darrell "accidentally" dropped the locker key, and Lily "accidentally" kicked it across the floor, sending one of the agents skittering after it.

"Good fake," she said. "Now run!"

They were out on the sidewalk before the men, and bolted into the car at the head of the taxi line. Darrell said, "Driver, please get us out of here. We're being followed!" But the driver apparently wasn't familiar with spy movies, because he just turned in his seat and shrugged, until Darrell's mother held out a huge wad of euros. The man grabbed the bills, punched the gas, and the cab screeched away from the curb. Two of the three agents stumbled out of the terminal, shouting. The third was probably checking the lockers, Darrell thought. So there!

When Sara told the driver their destination, his foot lifted off the gas pedal.

"Kizil Kule? Is over hour away." The man sighed, as if he'd heard the request a billion times before, but Darrell's mother folded over another few euro notes, and he was all smiles. "Yes, yes." He pressed his foot on the gas again and got on the highway.

It *was* over an hour away. Not less. Close to two hours after the airport-key incident, the driver dropped them at the water, stuffing the remainder of the fare into his pocket and shaking his head as he left.

Kizil Kule was a squat polygon, and the model in his mother's hands right now was indeed accurate. Darrell thought its many sides must have helped deflect direct artillery strikes, like the angles on a stealth fighter deflects radar. It was, even after seven or eight centuries, fresh and stout, and a perfect place for Copernicus and Heyreddin to have secreted the third key to Triangulum.

In fact, because of Heyreddin's high esteem and position in the Ottoman capital, it probably meant that the hiding place was especially clever.

Great, Darrell thought. *Another challenge.* His mother had relinquished the puzzle to him, and he realized why she hadn't been able to solve it. It was a heavy block of wood with a taunting little rattly thing inside. No matter how you rotated its moving sections, the only thing that happened was that the rattle kept rattling, and the puzzle kept its secret.

"Better go in," his mother said. "Maybe inside the tower there's a clue to the puzzle that will give us a clue to where the key is inside the tower. In other words, a clue to the puzzle, so the puzzle can give us a clue."

"A Darrellism," said Lily. "I fear for you, Sara Kaplan."

Lily found a few Turkish words on her phone and, after guessing how to pronounce them, told Sara, who bought three tickets into the tower museum. Ten minutes later they entered the cool air of its lowest level, the bottom of a labyrinth of stairways and ramps and levels and shadows. Plenty of shadows.

* * *

After escaping from Clos Lucé, Julian, Becca, and Wade jetted to Rome, where, hours later, they found themselves hurrying down a warren of narrow passages off the Via Borghese.

Julian had earlier linked to his father's computers in Nice and dug up the name of a black-market jeweler his father had interviewed for one of his novels, *The Vatican Directive*, a book Julian thought deserved a far more exciting title.

"Her name is . . . ," Becca said.

"Adriana Nissi," said Julian, searching the street. "Via della Torretta. Number sixty-nine."

"Does 'black market' mean she's really good, or really bad?" Becca asked.

"A little of both, I think," said Julian. "We'll find out soon."

Entering the ground floor of number 69, they found the jeweler listed as residing on the top floor.

They rang for her. No answer.

"We can't wait." Julian bounded up the staircase from the street.

The door to the flat was open. The interior was illuminated by a bank of open windows along the rear of the building. A warm breeze blew out to the landing.

Julian knocked. *"Ciao? C'è qualcuno?"* he asked.

"*Sì. È aperto*," came the muffled reply. "Come in, door is open."

They pushed in and found a tattooed middle-aged woman wearing goggles, a halter top, low-slung work pants, and no shoes, leaning over a high bench. Her tattoos, Julian noted silently, seemed to wander from her neck to her toes, and might have been everywhere in between. A long blue snake coiled down the outside of her bare left arm, its bloody fangs inked out over her two middle fingers. She held a miniature blowtorch in one hand and was alternately dipping it at and removing it from a length of gold pipe. An electronic cigarette hung from her lips, and she wore a jeweled nose ring and earlobe studs. Looking over her shoulder at them, she extinguished the blowtorch. The snake rippled when she moved. She removed her goggles, then blinked. "You are Julian!"

"Yes!" he said. "Thank you for seeing us."

"But of course. I know your mother from pictures."

This surprised Julian, and for a moment he brought up his mother's face. "Did you really?"

"*Sì, sì.* You look so like her. I am sorry you lost her very young. Come for kiss." He didn't have to because she lunged across the floor to him and kissed both his cheeks. He turned red instantly.

Shaking the kids' hands, she added, "So, *amici miei*, what can I do for you?"

Her eyes lit up like a child's when Wade said the name Leonardo, and she gasped repeatedly when Becca showed her the photos of the key she'd taken through the *ocularia*.

"*O, dio mio!*" she said under her breath. Pressing her temples, she walked over to her workbench and studied the phone under a jeweler's loupe as if she were holding a priceless artifact and not a digital copy of one. She sent the best image to a computer across the room, and printed an enlarged photo of the design. She taped it in place on the workbench.

"I suspect you need this key *pronto*?"

"*Sì*," said Wade. "If you can."

Adriana Nissi smiled. "I can. You wait."

She quickly assembled tools and materials from all over her workshop, bringing them to the bench. When she finally dropped her goggles back over her eyes, and the blowtorch flashed, her toned arms flexed and her biceps bulged.

Julian swore he saw that blue tattoo snake slither slowly down her arm as the sparks flew like stars to the studio floor.

CHAPTER FIFTY-FIVE

Central Italy
June 8
Evening

Ugo Drangheta powered his SUV swiftly down the Vocabolo Angelica, just north of the well-known hairpin between Papigno and Marmore, where the road sank in a sharp V, changed its name to Vocabolo Rancio, and drove sharply north. His rage had boiled for so long, it was now seething in his blood.

Galina Krause would die, and he would have her empire.

"How far behind are we?" he asked his passenger. He was on the trail of a convoy of five black vehicles, including one large transport, that his brother-in-law had spotted leaving Salzburg, Austria.

Mistral glanced ahead, then checked the message on her phone. "Less than an hour. Are you certain we are following the astrolabe?"

"We will find out. In less than an hour."

He was downshifting in anticipation of the famous hairpin when he caught sight of a large truck with German license plates parked in the otherwise deserted lot of Ristorante il Focolare, a boarded-up pizza restaurant situated at the very apex of the hairpin.

"Ugo? No, no. It cannot be."

He braked to a crawl, snarling the traffic behind him. His suspicion kicking in, he drove slowly past the lot, saw that the truck's cabin was empty, and continued up the road. A half mile or so later, he pulled over, let the traffic by, and reversed. He carefully returned to the restaurant and pulled into the lot. Mistral removed two pistols from the glove box in front of her. They were for her. Ugo had his own brace of handguns and pulled them out from under his seat.

"Wait here."

"No, Ugo, I am with you in everything."

He looked at her, kissed her, and exited the car. She went out her side. They rounded the large truck. It was indeed empty, though the rear compartment was locked.

"Shh, listen," Mistral whispered.

He froze. Someone, a man, laughed inside the abandoned restaurant. Another two or three men answered with more laughter.

"They're taking a rest," he said, his heart pounding. If he could stop this, if only he could . . . Ugo didn't know what. His plans had not yet had a chance to form themselves, except to insist that any disruption of Galina's plans was good.

He raised both guns—she did, too—and he nodded to her to go around the patio to the right of the parking lot. "On my signal," he whispered.

There was more laughter and the sound of glasses clinking as she scurried past the boarded windows around the corner, then peered back around—her beautiful face—giving him a nod.

He drew a breath, waited three seconds, and returned the nod. Both firing, they blasted open the doors and burst into the restaurant, to be confronted with what could only be described as a firing squad of two dozen men. The barrage was horrendous: Ugo fell to the ground outside, struck in the face, the torso, his already wounded arm. In desperation, he fired back

411

into the restaurant doorway.

He watched Mistral fire over and over, then disappear back out the side door onto the patio and into the valley below, pursued by ten, twelve gunmen.

"Mistral . . ." His voice was a whisper. He heard the woods erupt with a chaos of bullets, hundreds, thousands, then stop abruptly. *My Mistral. She must be dead.*

Ugo crawled back to the SUV, dragged himself to its footrest, to the door handle, to the seat. He slid painfully behind the wheel, bleeding from his head, his stomach, his arm. He saw—or thought he saw—a khaki-wearing Asian man with a black pistol standing in the doorway of the restaurant, his face a thing of stone.

Ugo pressed the ignition, blood streaming down his hand; then a resounding blast came from the doorway, and the windshield exploded into his eyes.

After trudging up the endless stairs to the open roof of Kizil Kule in Alanya, Turkey, Ebner von Braun, trailed by Oskar Gerrenhausen and the skinnier of the two unspeakable agents from Tunis, felt his stomach tumble. He had tinnitus, a constant ringing deep in his ears like a horde of cicadas living inside his head. Here, with the ocean grinding below and the wind screaming across the bricks at such a pitch, he felt nauseous.

"Some view," said Emil, who had
replacement needle to pick his teeth v
encrusted thing around like a point

Ebner wheeled away from him,
the love of Albrecht!"

"Take these," said the bookseller, opening to him a
tin of small white pills. "For seasickness. I, too, suffer."

Remembering Galina in the ruins of Carthage, Ebner
drew out several of the pills, popped two, and saved the
rest for later. "It is all this running around, you see."

"I do," Gerrenhausen said to him. "It was I who
identified this tower to Miss Krause as the location of
the third Triangulum key."

"Care to narrow that location down a little?" Ebner
replied. "It's rather a big place. We are but several feet
away from discovering the key, but several feet in which
direction, my little friend?"

"Alas, the key was not that specific."

"You two talk like a book," said Emil, who broke
wind loudly and walked away.

It was absurd to Ebner, their need to rely on the
blasted Kaplan family for clues. All this skulking around,
waiting for "breaks." Galina's two-month absence had
created a situation that was cosmically unnatural. Back
in March, the order had been simple: Kill the Kaplans.

413

n the mess in London, Crux, the old church, evidence of time travel, the death of Archie Doyle, all led to the command being rescinded. The waffling bred its own kind of seasickness. And yet . . .

The family's record of success was dismally clear. After locating two relics already, they were well on their way to finding a third. Was it partly because of the poor quality of the Order's far-flung agents? Of the sort exemplified by the fat man and this *thing*? *My Lord,* he thought. *Give me Helmut Bern or even the late, lamented Archie Doyle over these creatures.*

Gerrenhausen held out the key. "Perhaps a new set of eyes will find a clue?"

Ebner was reaching for it when someone screamed from below. Moments later a young French boy, perhaps five years old, rushed up the stairs to the roof, crying, "A giant fat man is chasing people with a gun!"

So. The Kaplans had been found.

Eight minutes before the screaming boy, Darrell's head split in half because he wasn't Wade. Wade would have worked on the puzzle until—*voilà!*—he found an elegant and stunning way to open the priceless puzzle box and reveal the actual location of the third Barbarossa key. But, no, Wade was in France, which left Darrell to make do with twisting and turning and shaking and rolling the stupid thing in every conceivable way, while it just looked back at him smugly and said, "Ha!" So while his mother was on a lower level, and Lily on the level above, Darrell gripped the puzzle and smacked it lightly against the nearest wall. Nothing happened. He hit it again, a little harder.

Twice. Nothing. Nothing.

Finally, his anger took over, and he slammed it at the wall hard. It split.

"Uh-oh."

He'd just destroyed a work of sixteenth-century Ottoman craftsmanship. That was probably a sin, at least a crime, at best unforgivable, but . . . the bead, a small wooden ball painted silver, of course, rolled across the floor and bounced away down the stairs. And there in the broken fragments of the puzzle were tiny silver paint marks that the rattling bead had made.

Darrell knew where the third key was hidden.

He breathed out. "Okay, then. Okay—" He listened. Footsteps were coming up the stairs from below. Footsteps he knew. Not his mother's. She was down on another level somewhere and, he hoped, safe. No, these were the light, dancing footsteps of a very heavy man.

"Lily, get down here!" he cried overloudly. "The key's

in a chamber on the lowest level of the tower!"

Lily rushed down the stairs to him. "Really, you solved the puzzle?"

"Sort of—"

She spied the splintered wood. "Darrell!"

That's when some French kid started screaming. He tumbled up the stairs inches from Bigboy, who pranced nimbly up after him, waving his pistol around. Darrell jumped away from the stair opening as the gun went off. The centuries-old brick exploded behind his head. Darrell pushed Lily back toward the upward steps. Another shot exploded on the wall next to his face. He was terrified, moving without reason, just moving.

Lily scrabbled around on the steps and suddenly hurled a five-inch square of broken brick right past Darrell's head. It struck Bigboy in the face, tearing open his wide pink cheek. The guy squealed, slapping his bloody face with one hand as he tumbled to the stone floor, falling forward like a whale. The gun went off beneath him, and he let out a horrible groan.

Lily went white in the face, faltered as she tried to get up. "What did I do—"

"Lily, come on." Darrell jumped two steps up the staircase.

"But you said it was downstairs!" Lily said.

"I lied. I guessed someone was listening. It's near the top of the tower—"

Lily leaped past him up the steps, then without warning pushed him backward into a deep cutout in the side of the wall and slapped her hand over his mouth. It was close in there. She was very close to him. He felt her breathing as if it were his own lungs doing it, but when he tried to shift away, she pressed against him harder, pinning them deeper in the shadows, until he saw why.

Fish leaped down the stairs right past them.

Ebner trailed him down the staircase, pushing screaming tourists out of the way with the barrel of his gun. He was on the phone, muttering and spitting in German. The bookseller skipped down after Ebner.

Darrell and Lily waited in the scanty shadows, pressed against each other until the three men had disappeared onto the level below.

"Uh . . . ," Darrell said.

"Just come on," she said as she jumped up the stairs. "And don't say it."

"Say what?"

"Anything." She shook herself as if shaking off bugs. "Now go!"

Darrell took the lead, bounding up to the second-highest level. Holding the important piece of the

shattered model, he veered left at the top of the steps and pushed through to one of the outer chambers. There was a cutout in the brick with a view of the sea. He lined it up with the model. He ran his finger down the wall from the sill until he saw a tiny silver mark on the corner of one of the bricks.

"Whoa, Darrell . . . ," Lily whispered.

He smiled. "Come on. Help me."

Together, they pried the brick out.

The third key was lodged securely behind the brick. As with the one they'd discovered in Tunisia, the dense design work identified the key unmistakably as the work of Leonardo da Vinci.

"There's a big *M*, and writing on the shaft," Lily whispered. She traced her fingers over the inscribed letters. They were crudely written, identifiable barely as letters at all, and were strange: partly Latinate, partly something else. The accents were ones that neither of them had ever seen before.

L-aḥḥar gḥargḥar

As usual with Darrell, he had to speak them aloud—
try to speak them aloud—the way a child might try to
sound out unfamiliar words.

"Lahar garrr gahhh rrrr," he said. "El ahar gargar?
What kind of language is—"

Lily started shaking. "Darrell . . ." She closed her
hands over her face, then dropped them. "Darrell, this
is what the old woman said to me and Becca in Austin.
The Mother. She said, 'Lahar gaharr.' We thought she
was just trying to breathe, but she was saying words.
My translator. I need my translator!"

"My phone?" he said. "Or yours?"

"Mine. My apps. But my fingers are shaking—"

He took her phone. "What's your pass code?"

"Zero nine two three."

He started to tap it in. "Wait. September twenty-
third? That's my birthday—"

"So?"

"And you disabled your phone and messaging?"

"Just do it!"

He did, finally hitting the translator app on her home
screen. There were noises on the level below. "This is
dumb," he said. "We need to get out of here."

"If we lose the key, at least we'll have one clue. Hurry up!"

"Got it. But how do I do this. I can't key in those accents."

Growling, Lily took the phone from him. "If we're lucky, it'll still translate it."

Selecting the button that read *detect language*, Lily typed in the letters in English—*L-aħħar għargħar*. A few moments passed before anything happened; then two words popped up.

Maltese detected

"Maltese!" Lily said. "Darrell, the old woman was from Malta. The women Leonardo talks about. The one who came to us. The Mothers who protect the relic. That's what the *M* on the key means. The Mothers are in Malta! Guarding Triangulum!"

"Lily, look at what the words actually mean," Darrell said. *"L-aħħar għargħar* means 'the final flood.'"

She was staring at the screen, her mouth open, when his mother suddenly appeared. "I managed to slip past them, but there are more now. At least ten of them entered the tower, and they're clearing it, floor by floor. We need to go up."

"Is there a helicopter up there?"

"No, but there's no going down," she said. "You found it?"

"Here." Darrell gave her the key. "Come on."

Lily outpaced them both, rushing up the steps two at a time.

It was hot on the roof of the tower, but there was a haze darkening the sea.

"Now what?" Lily said.

All Darrell could think of was the flood. The deluge. The Mothers of Malta. "The key tells too much. The words. If Galina finds out . . . Mom, the key."

Before she could actually release it, he snatched it away, went to the parapet, and scraped the shaft across its sharp stones, wearing down the words.

"That's an original da Vinci you're defacing!" said Sara.

"And it breaks my heart."

Ebner von Braun flew up the last stairs and was on the roof of the tower with them. He wasn't alone. Ten, maybe twelve others, as well as the two thugs from Africa and the little antiquarian bookseller, surrounded them.

"You will give me the key," Ebner said, waving his pistol to shoo the children to the edge of the roof.

Meanwhile, Bigboy, breathless and sweating, with a large bloody stain on his vast shirt, dragged Sara roughly from them. Fish raised a surprisingly wide butcher's knife to Sara's neck.

"You see? No choice." Ebner approached. "Galina wants what she wants."

"He is correct," the bookseller said. "She always gets it, too."

Ebner set the end of his pistol barrel against the center of Darrell's forehead and slid the key from his hand. He glanced at it and handed it to Gerrenhausen.

The bookseller studied it, then smiled. "Yes, identical craftsmanship. It is of a kind with the Budapest key. We now have two of the three."

Of the four, thought Darrell.

Ebner took it back and slipped it into the pocket of his coat. "Hendriks, Emil, detain them."

"Kill them?" said Bigboy.

"Alas, not yet. Detain them only."

Ebner and the bookseller stormed out of the tower into a waiting car. It took them to the dock, where they boarded a motorboat that took them in an hour and a half the fifty nautical miles south to the yacht of Galina Krause.

Galina, he thought. *Galina, we are nearly there.* He was about to place a call to her when his fingers felt the shaft of the key in his pocket. Yanking it into the daylight, he spied the horrifying defacement.

"What the devil! They know where the relic is!"

"The boy mangled a genuine Leonardo!" Gerrenhausen cried, pounding his fists on his thighs. "I should have shot him on the train when I had the chance!"

All at once, Ebner's phone tinkled with a harp arpeggio. *Galina!* He could decline the call. No, he could never. Dreading the coming conversation, he swiped the screen to answer and howled silently to himself.

No, no, no!

CHAPTER FIFTY-SIX

Trembling from fear and exhaustion, Lily realized that staying alive was sometimes just a matter of timing. In this case, perfect timing.

As soon as Bigboy and Fish pushed her, Sara, and Darrell at gunpoint out of the tower toward a battered black car, Silva appeared out of the dusk. The grizzled, thick-armed, beret-wearing man in combat fatigues wormed his way through the crowd leaving the tower, with several large friends in tow.

"We are agents of the Teutonic Order," Bigboy said right away. "Perhaps you do not realize who you are dealing with—"

"In fact, I do," said Silva. "Two men who might be

dead in"—he checked his watch—"twelve seconds, if I don't tell my friends here not to kill you. And right now, I'm forgetting what language they speak."

"Eh?" said Fish. "All I got from that is twelve seconds."

To make it clearer, Silva's friends surrounded the two agents, who released their captives. Silva peeled the gun out of Bigboy's fat fingers. He took Fish's carving knife, too. Then he hurled them off the side of the nearest wharf into the water.

"Oops," Silva said. "Littering. My bad. Go get those, will you?"

"Eh?" said Fish. "In the water?"

"That's right."

"Galina Krause will not appreciate your treatment of official agents of the Teutonic Order of Ancient Prussia," Bigboy said.

"Would she appreciate digging them up out of the ground?" Silva said.

"She'll come for you," said Fish, and he waved his arm out to sea. "She's got herself a small army of less than fifty—"

"Hush, Emil!" Bigboy snarled. "They will find out soon enough."

Silva looked south across the water. "Thanks for the

tip. Now pinch your noses and dive!"

Lily watched Bigboy and Fish slide off the side of the wharf into the water. "Thank you for the show, Mr. Silva," she said.

"It's just Silva," he said.

Ten minutes later, they were sitting around a crowded table in a market café.

"Silva, you saved our lives, again," Sara said, pressing her hand over his. "You have a pretty perfect sense of timing."

Lily could see a pinprick of blood on Sara's neck where Fish had stuck her.

"My job," he said. "And my pleasure. Seriously, you're so much more polite than my usual bosses." The grazed forearm he had suffered in Casablanca didn't seem to bother him in the slightest. "By the way, that fish-faced goon back there did us a service. My men spotted a mega-yacht about fifty nautical miles off the coast. Now we know it belongs to Galina."

"Her agents stole the Kizil Kule key," said Sara. "They now have two, and maybe both are on that yacht. We assume that Galina doesn't know yet where Triangulum is, or she'd be off to Malta." She whispered the last word.

"I bet she's not even on the yacht," said Darrell. "She

wouldn't have left a key to Ebner or those two jerks from the desert if she had been. She's somewhere else."

"Now that those goons are out of the way, it's only Ebner and the bookseller," Lily added.

"Only Ebner, the bookseller, and the forty others who crew a yacht that size," Silva said.

"She doesn't know about the fourth key, either," said Darrell, "so we have the advantage, which may not be too much of one, but she can't actually get to the relic without us, but on the other hand, if we steal the keys back, we can find the relic without her."

Silva seemed a little annoyed by the time Darrell finished his long sentence, so he just laid his thoughts out in his simple paramilitary way: "We'll launch an assault on the yacht at twenty-three hundred hours."

Which Darrell translated as, "Eleven tonight. Two plus hours from now."

Since the events at Kizil Kule, Lily had pretty much decided to see it to the end. She knew there was nothing else to do, because there was far too much at stake now. They'd go after the keys, steal them, and escape to Malta before the Order knew what hit them. After that? Well, she'd think about that later.

Silva made a few calls, then told them that his associates would meet them at the docks within the hour.

"They'll have your scuba gear with them."

"Wait, *our* scuba gear?" said Sara.

Silva brought out a nautical chart and, moving his coffee mug aside, spread it out on the table. He narrowed his eyes and traced his finger from approximately where they were on the shore to the position of the yacht his men had spotted. "My friends are chartering the fastest motorboat they can lay their hands on, and it'll be a surprise attack, but someone will have to identify the package—the *keys*. My men and I can't do that. We need your eyes on-site."

"Well, I've never scubaed in my life," said Lily.

Silva took a breath. "You're a diver, aren't you?" he asked Darrell.

"Darrell?" Lily couldn't stifle a laugh. "No, he's not."

"As a matter of fact, I am," he said. "My father taught me when I was young. Mom dives, too."

"Whoa. Glub-glub," Lily murmured. "A scuba family. I'm impressed."

"Darrell's not going in the water," Sara said, taking out her phone. "I'll be our eyes on-site. I'm texting the others through Terence's server to meet us in Malta." She paused. It was at the point, Lily thought, that she would have said something about Uncle Roald. She went on. "One way or another, Malta is where all this ends."

"Any word from Terence?" Darrell asked.

Silva shook his head. "Terence and Roald are MIA in Italy somewhere. Paul Ferrere and his team are still on the hunt for them."

MIA. Missing in action. Lily wanted to read any sign of hope in Silva's tone or expression, but the soldier gave up nothing. Sara simply nodded. It was almost too much to watch her go coolly about the task of being a Guardian and a mother while hurting so much inside. Lily knew what that hurt felt like, and though Sara was strong she couldn't shed the hollow stare of separation. Lily knew all about that, too. She'd seen it in the mirror every day since London.

"Two hours, seven minutes," Silva said, ordering a cup of strong coffee. "Until then, we plan."

Two hours and seven minutes, Lily thought. *It's time.* She excused herself and went to find the restroom, if there was one. On the way she turned on her phone.

CHAPTER FIFTY-SEVEN

Two hours later the dark Alanya docks were sleeping. Fishing boats, tourist cruise vessels, coast guard patrols, charter boats, and every other kind of vessel were tied up at the pier for the day.

The air was warm, but Darrell was freezing, shaking at the thought of what the next hour would bring.

An attack. Armed men against other armed men. His mother in the middle. Why he hadn't felt the same in Casablanca at Drangheta's villa, he didn't know. Maybe because he hadn't known about the flood then. Now something dark was moving toward them, like a huge wall of water, and it just plain scared him.

He tried to think of an excuse for his mother not to

go with Silva, but the guy was right. They needed one of them to identify the keys for sure. There was only going to be a single shot at this.

Darrell walked up and down the wharf. Other than Silva and the sketchy man at the harbormaster's hut he spoke to, no one said a word. He paced. They all paced. They watched and waited it out. At seven minutes past eleven, a motorboat putted noisily over to them. It was decked out as a fishing boat, with thick nets draped over it. Darrell remembered Bingo's plane and guessed the nets might be a kind of camouflage. Silva caught a rope tossed to him, pulled the boat, and tied it up to the dock. One of the men jumped up on the boardwalk and handed Silva a cell phone.

Silva studied the screen silently, then turned to them. "Take a look. The first shot is Galina's yacht yesterday morning. The second is now. Notice anything?"

Darrell studied the two photos of the yacht. They were taken at different times of day, so it didn't strike him at first what Silva was hinting at.

When Lily took the phone and swiped back and forth between the two images several times, she saw it.

"The waterline?" she said. "The waterline changed from yesterday to today. The yacht was deeper in the water yesterday, by several feet, but now it's not. So it

431

was heavier when it arrived? It unloaded something?"

Sara turned to Silva. "What do you think it means?"

"I think it means we now have two missions," he said. "Extract the keys, and find out what the Order is unloading in the water between here and Cyprus. Let's move."

Mist rolled over the dark water.

Lily's heart ached as they motored into the eerie blackness. She knew she'd been falling deeper into herself from the moment she and Darrell were crammed into that niche at Kizil Kule. Why? Being smashed up against him didn't mean anything, did it? No, of course not. Then why was she so . . . so . . . *not here*?

Because of "the news" from home.

Two hours ago she'd enabled her phone, tapped in her mother's number—it was early afternoon in Austin—and the wail that greeted her and the torrent of tears and her mother's shaky and near-inaudible whisper crushed her. Then the news.

"Honey, Lily, we decided to try to make this work. Your father and I—put it on speaker, would you?"

Lily heard the phone toggle. "Dad?"

"I'm here, honey," said her father, drawing in a sharp breath. "Okay, so, we decided that the only way to do this, to be a family again, is to start new. Fresh. Completely. With you. The three of us. The way it was at the beginning."

"And it has to be away from here," her mother continued. "From Austin. There are shadows here, but there are better places. And you have to be with us, Lily, honey. That's the way it will work. Will you come home, honey? Now? We want you home—"

"We need you home, honeybunch," said her father.

She'd had no chance to say anything so far, and now didn't know what to say. "Away from Austin? What do you mean?"

"Should I tell her?" her mother said. "I will," her father said. "In Seattle, honey. We found a house."

"You can't go around the world like this," her mother said. "It's crazy and dangerous, and we need you here—"

"No," Lily said.

"—and seriously, Lil, it's the only way this is going to work. You know, we could come to you, pick you up—"

"No," she said. "Didn't you hear me? I can't just up and leave."

"Lily, this is serious," her father said. "Whatever you're doing there is just wrong, some kind of dangerous fantasy. The Moores are crazy worried about Becca, and we are about you. We're coming to get you. Just tell us where you are, and we'll—"

She hung up.

She was going to say that she would call them back, but she hung up. She powered off her phone and stuffed it away.

A family. Fresh start. Seattle. Just wrong.

Now, hours later, she was still dumbstruck. She clasped the boat's side railing with both hands, afraid that if she didn't steady herself, she'd throw up or be sucked into the water or both. *Just be here now*, she thought. *Be here.*

When the boat was within a half mile of the yacht, Silva said, "Good," and the captain cut the engine. They were in position, bobbing on the waves. Her throat tightened. She felt dizzy.

Sara placed her hand on Lily's arm. "Are you all right, honey?"

"Fine," she said. "Let's get those keys."

As they drifted in the darkness, the stone-faced crewmen—silent so far, though most of them didn't speak English anyway—dressed themselves in scuba gear and checked their handguns, which they then wrapped in plastic sheaths. Silva pulled out his infrared riflescope and trained it on the yacht in the misty distance.

"They're still unloading," he whispered. "Look now."

Sara used the scope, then passed it to Darrell, who gave it to Lily. She saw a large crate lowered from the deck, down the side, and into the water. Four scuba-wearing divers took hold of the chains supporting it and descended with it.

"What could it be?" Lily asked. "Are they dumping something?"

"The divers have single tanks," Silva said. "They'll have to surface soon."

"In less than an hour," said Sara. "At the longest."

It wasn't long at all. Not even twenty minutes elapsed before the chains came up dangling and empty. The divers were not there.

"Where did they go?" Darrell asked. "What's down there?"

"Wait, where exactly are we?" Lily asked. Silva told her: halfway between Turkey and Cyprus. She sucked in a sudden breath. "Oh my gosh. The chart. I need to see the chart." Silva gave it to her. She called up the remote server where she stored her data, found what she was looking for, and studied the chart side by side with her phone. Her heart skipped a beat. "Oh man."

"What is it?" asked Sara.

"At the beginning of March we got that coded

435

message from Uncle Henry."

"It's what started all of this," Darrell said. "What about it?"

"Uncle Henry said 'tragedies' would begin all over the world, remember? Well, one of the very first ones we found—I think it was me who found it—was an oil tanker sinking in the Mediterranean. Off the coast of Cyprus. At the time, it was just one of the weird things going on, but last week, when Becca and I were being bored in Florida, I looked up all the tragedies again and marked the coordinates here. I didn't remember it until now, but look."

35°50'35.76"N
31°57'53.68"E

Silva located their boat's coordinates on his phone. "That's here," he said. "The tanker sank right here."

"The wreck of the tanker," said Sara, "the wreck *three months ago*, is part of Galina's plan? What on earth is she doing down there?"

Darrell looked from Lily to his mother, at her face, into her eyes. What he read there shook him. Dr. Sara Kaplan, senior archivist at the Harry Ransom Center at the University of Texas, Austin, had been changing right in front of them. He'd noticed some of what was going on—her leadership, of course—but not all of it. The researcher, teacher, administrator, and mother he loved had—while still being all of those—become a person of action.

A Guardian, sure, but also an operative and a soldier.

Her bronze forearms had muscled over the last months since her abduction to Russia. Her face had taken on a kind of strength since London that he hadn't seen before. And now, she was forcing the mystery of where his stepfather was to take a backseat to stopping Galina and protecting the Legacy.

Then, when Silva offered her a pair of oxygen tanks, saying, "We need to see what's down there before we go for the keys, and we need you with us," his mother slipped on the harness like a pro.

"Ooh, Sara, take the wire," said Lily, tugging the camera and audio contraption out of her bag. "I threw it in here after Monte Carlo. Remember, that nice man Maurice Maurice told us it's waterproof. We'll sync it to watch on Darrell's phone and see what you see. I'd use my phone, but it's nearly out of power."

"Great idea," Darrell said. "We need to keep tabs on you, Mom."

She gave him a flat smile, then hooked it on and tested the connection to their phones. "Keep the boat behind the fog bank," she said to the one man who would remain with them. "We'll be back as soon as we see what's down there."

Darrell tried to give his mother a reassuring smile, but the muscles of his face wouldn't cooperate. As she hugged him he blurted, "Don't die."

"Keep your bubble stream out of sight," Lily said. Sara hugged her, too.

Darrell watched three crewmen slip over the side, then his mother, and finally Silva. They let their belt weights pull them down below the surface. Soon the bubbles cleared enough for Darrell to see on his phone what his mother was seeing. She mingled with the divers, and they were on their way down and toward the yacht.

Lily murmured something so low it might have been praying. Darrell found himself doing the same. The image on his phone was tiny to begin with, but as his mother sank from the surface, the water became murkier, until it was almost black.

"Lily," said Darrell, "what did I do? Sending my mom down in the water like that. Am I crazy? My mom!"

"Darrell, she can do it. She's not as fragile as you

or me, or any of us. She's the one person holding us together here."

Which was both good to know and not so good. He was supposed to step up, wasn't he? Ever since his real father had vacated the scene, it had been Darrell and his mother, and he felt responsible for her. Be the man of the house. Her being close meant that he could be a goofball sometimes, but not when she was risking her life. "Lily, I—"

"Shh. Look."

A sudden stream of white shot through the thick darkness on the screen. His mother's camera jiggled, then steadied and moved in. There it was, tilted under a rocky shelf two hundred feet under the surface. The wreck of a giant oil tanker that had capsized and sunk three months before.

Only it wasn't a wreck anymore.

It was no longer on its side, and it had been shifted under a great rock shelf, hidden from the surface and probably from any kind of satellite surveillance. It was enormous in length and breadth, and it was lit up like a huge underwater factory.

A gigantic secret base.

"So for the last three months," he whispered, though he didn't have to, "ever since the tanker sank, the Order has been building . . . this? What in the world for? Lily, it's enormous. How could the world not know about this?"

She stared at the screen of her phone. "The Order sent in a salvage crew, maybe, or hijacked a real salvage crew and pretended to cut the tanker up, but they built a base instead. Darrell, it's kind of James Bondy."

"Yeah, but we're looking right at it! How could they do this?"

"Because the Order has people everywhere," she said. "Because a whole bunch of corrupt people and agencies were involved. They must have been bribed or somehow forced to cooperate. Galina knows how to force people, that's for sure."

"But why?" he whispered. "What is it for?"

Outside the tanker, and going in and out of a series of loading platforms, were what appeared to be dozens of divers. His mother saw—and so could they—that the upper decks inside the ship were intact, and that there was oxygen, since the personnel visible through portholes did not wear oxygen tanks.

"Sara, if you can hear me," Lily said. "That crate we saw being lowered from the yacht. Can you see it now and find out what it might be?"

Sara must have heard, because she swam lower and

aimed her camera through the porthole at one of the holds that was sealed and had oxygen. The image came back: a crate marked with several characters. Lily took a stab. "Korean? We'll take a screenshot and check it later."

"And there's something Russian," Darrell said, pointing to his screen. "There's a red star and it says K-twenty-seven. We'll look it up to see what that means."

Through his mother's camera, they watched one crate after another move into the tanker's cargo bay. But that wasn't all. Some crates had been unpacked, and there were what appeared to be missiles or rockets on platforms, a rigging of thick cords connecting them, a wall of computer screens, and several giant concrete canisters lined up in tandem. The onetime wrecked tanker was now an extraordinary high-tech laboratory—or war room. It seemed impossible, but there it was.

Silva came into view on the screen and gave the thumbs-up.

"They're returning," Darrell said. "Good. Get my mom out of there. We've seen enough."

They had all seen enough to make their blood run cold.

CHAPTER FIFTY-EIGHT

"The tanker is filled with an array of nuclear devices," Silva said as he climbed over the side of the motorboat and helped Sara in after him. "Some I've seen before, others not. A few of them are not the most modern. If I'm correct, K-twenty-seven is a Soviet submarine that sank in the nineteen eighties. But no matter how old they are, those guys are hooking them up in sequence. There are also eight, maybe ten large concrete-encased miniature nuclear reactors. Bottom line," he said, "the Teutonic Order appears to be building its own nuclear warehouse."

Lily watched the blood drain from Silva's face, as if he had just realized the implications of what he'd just seen. For a soldier of his war experience, it was frightening.

"But what for?" Darrell asked. "Why are they stockpiling nuclear bombs?"

"No, they're not all necessarily bombs," Silva said. "I can't tell you if she's building a giant warhead or something else."

"Something else . . . like what?" asked Sara.

He shrugged. "A large reactor? Maybe it's both that *and* a weapon. All I know is that she's got a lot of firepower down there for something, and it's not good."

Lily shivered. "Copernicus told Becca in London that something like a nuclear event happened when his astrolabe traveled in time. The hole in the sky. Maybe this is all for that? And whatever Galina's doing under the water is part of the same thing? I don't know. What else could it be?"

"The deluge," said Sara. "Lily, it's what the Mother warned you about in Tampa. It's what Becca and Wade discovered in France. Maybe it happens in the future. We don't know. But one thing is sure: Galina has far more power than we dreamed, which makes it essential she doesn't get any more relics. None!"

"Then no more talk," said Silva. "We need to extract those keys."

No one spoke while the crewmen exchanged their tanks for fresh ones. They rechecked their weapons. Then it was time. They entered the water, Sara and Silva first. This time all the men went, leaving Lily and Darrel alone on the boat with strict orders to stay low and stay put.

A short quarter hour later, using the riflescope, Lily spotted them bobbing up outside the hull. They were near the front of the yacht. Silva removed his face mask, slipped his hand inside his armored vest, and pulled out a black object the size and shape of a squashed baseball.

Darrell's phone crackled. "Yes?"

"Is there anyone on the front deck?" Sara asked.

Darrell sighted the deck through the riflescope. "One, two guys. They're moving back toward the main cabin now. No. No one's up front. Why—"

Before Darrell could finish, Silva heaved the black object up over the side of the yacht. It smacked down on the deck and exploded in smoke and shrapnel. The windows of the front cabin crackled and shattered.

"Whoa!" said Lily. The crew of the yacht reacted instantly, shouting, calling for men from below. An alarm began to howl. A dozen or so armed agents raced to the blast site; some ran for fire extinguishers; others scanned over the side.

By that time, however, Sara, Silva, and his men were

gone from the surface, reappearing a few seconds later below the rear of the yacht. A grappling hook shot up the side, hooked on the back railing, and a rope ladder fluttered down the side of the hull.

The team climbed up in a flash. The grenade must have been partly a smoke bomb, because thick gray clouds had billowed up from the impact and now shielded Sara and the others.

"They're on board," said Lily. "I can't believe this. Your crazy mother. Imagine if your dad saw this."

"Both would freak," he said. "My real dad *and* Roald."

They soon lost sight of the extraction team on the deck.

The image on Darrell's phone, already hazy from the smoke, flickered, was grainy, shaky, but as soon as Sara and the others pushed their way down the stairs to the aft cabin, there was the sound of gunfire.

"They've been spotted," Lily said.

"Silva's good. I have to think he'll protect her. But if she gets hurt . . ."

The video blacked out, returned briefly, then died altogether. No audio. Silence from the phone. Gunshots continued below deck. Smoke blew everywhere.

"I knew it!" he snapped. "Lily, I'm not just going to—"

"No kidding! It's your mom!" She studied the dashboard. "How do you . . ." Then she saw a red button and pressed it. The engine roared to life. "Ha!"

Taking the wheel, she pulled the throttle back, and the boat shot off toward the yacht. This was something she'd never done before. It seemed easy enough. You hit the gas, point the boat, and it goes there.

"Cut it back a bit to keep the noise down," Darrell said, his eyes on the yacht.

The smoke from the bomb wafted across the water, stinging their eyes, but it covered their advance. Soon, they were under the rope ladder. Lily cut the engine like she'd seen the captain do. Darrell tied the boat's rope to the ladder and grasped the third rung, caught a foot on the bottom, and pulled himself up. She climbed up after.

Gunfire crackled in the air around them, but when they reached the deck, they realized it was all coming from below. The deck was far larger when you were on it than it seemed through the scope. Darrell looked both ways, then ran toward the stairway into the lower cabins.

"Not that way," she said. "To the front and through the blasted windows. They're all tangled up down those stairs. We should go in the front. Keys first."

"Yeah, but . . . no, you're right. They're the soldiers. We're the key getters."

They crept along the railing around the side of the main cabin. Not only were the windows smashed, but one of the steel doors lay partially twisted on its hinges. There was no one in the front room, so no one heard Darrell kicking the door over and over until there was room to crawl through. Lily was happy she'd guessed right. The fighting really was in the rear of the yacht.

Maybe remembering Casablanca and the episode of the zip cuffs, Darrell hung back to let her take the lead. She pressed ahead as if she knew where to go. The cabins they passed were empty. She kept moving forward, then down to another deck. The rooms were smaller there. Then a sound. Intermittent beeping.

"The communications room?" she whispered.

"Maybe. It's not where the keys would be. Keep going." Darrell trotted down the hallway to the next door, a hatch-like bulkhead with a cross-shaped handle.

Lily glanced in the room.

Banks of computer terminals lined two of the walls. She recognized one of them as a radar station. The green concentric circles, the digital hand sweeping around like a fast clock hand. *They're tracking something,* she thought. But watching the blip for a few seconds, she saw it didn't move. The thing was stationary. She made a mental note of the blip's coordinates.

42.454°N

13.576°E

"You're wasting time!" Darrell hissed, reaching for her hand but ending up not taking it. "Look, the shooting's slowed down. Maybe there's a standoff. Now's our chance." He nodded toward the bulkhead. After he turned the handle, they moved silently through the hatch, then down a set of stairs two at a time.

Suddenly, there was Silva, his finger pressed to his lips. Darrell mouthed, *My mom.* Silva tilted his head behind him, and there was Sara, gripping a pistol—so un-mother-like, so cool. Darrell only half resisted the urge to hug her, which was touching, but the gun battle fired up again behind them. Silva's men were taking on the Order a corridor away.

Silva nodded, and Sara eased past Darrell, then Lily, pressing their shoulders down as she passed them, until they were crouched on the floor. She and Silva were inches from the next bulkhead.

Lily didn't see what the signal was, but Silva spun the handle and kicked the hatch wide. There was a sudden face, the barrel of an automatic, but Silva was on him, thrusting his sharply angled elbow up into the guard's chin, sending the guy to the floor. Sara kicked the automatic away, snatched it up, and slung it over her shoulder. So cool again.

"Is this it?" Silva asked, pointing to a small but apparently heavy wooden box sitting on a shelf in the cargo hold.

Lily and Darrell were on it in a flash. They popped the box open, unwrapped a thick velvet covering, and saw the two keys. Without a word, Lily collected them, gave one to Darrell, and took the other for her bag.

"Security," she said.

"Security," he agreed.

"And we're out," said Silva. "Up the stairs."

They tore up the stairs, Sara behind them. There followed a series of shots from the rear of the yacht. They halted. Ebner von Braun stood quivering next to one of Silva's beefy commandos, who had a gun pressed to Ebner's head. His face was pasty white, his jaw trembling. The yacht's crew surrounded them all, but it was clear they wouldn't risk a move with Ebner in custody. The bookseller stood beside him, his hands up, shaking like a trapped mouse.

"Back," said Silva, pressing his handgun into Ebner's

chest. "Back to the ladder. Something tells me you'd be a pretty good prisoner, but first, von Braun, you're letting us go."

"I hope you have a good imagination," Darrell said breathlessly. "You'll need it when Galina asks why you let us slip through your creepy fingers."

Lily was impressed for the second time in one day.

Ebner looked as if he would explode in rage. Sara reached the ladder and held it. Darrell climbed down, then Lily, then the commandos, and finally Silva with Ebner. Lily hadn't expected that twist, but it was necessary, or the yacht crew would open fire before they could escape.

Poor thin, pale Ebner struggled with every rung of the wobbly ladder.

When they were safe on the motorboat and out of range of the yacht, Ebner turned his beady eyes to Sara. "What are your plans with me?"

"I should take you prisoner," she said, "like you and Galina took me. But we need to move quickly."

"Where to, might I ask?" Ebner said.

"That's it." Silva pulled him to his feet. "Any last words?"

"I have one," said Darrell. He stared Ebner in the face. "You—" he said, and used a word Lily couldn't believe

450

he even knew. His mother gasped, but Darrell had nailed it. Ebner didn't smirk or laugh as he had so often before. He simply gulped in a breath as Silva pushed him off the boat into the water. He flailed around, but Lily guessed that he'd survive. No, they weren't killers. Not like he was.

As soon as their motorboat eased up to the dock, Lily checked her phone. Three voice mails. She entered into her GPS app the coordinates she'd read off the yacht's radar screen.

"Italy. There's a radar blip in central Italy. Sara, I think it's at Gran Sasso. Galina knows where Roald is."

Sara's face was brittle, as if it would collapse in tears if only she let it. "Not knowing about him is . . ." She didn't finish. "Malta. We need to get to Malta."

CHAPTER FIFTY-NINE

Rome, Italy
June 9

It was just after one a.m. when Wade—crammed with Becca and Julian in a taxi speeding to Rome's airport and ready to fly off to Turkey to meet the others—received Darrell's terse message.

In possession of two keys. Meet in Rabat, Malta, ASAP.

"Malta?" he asked. "The island?"

Julian's phone was already out. "A short hop by helicopter. Dad may have a fit, but I'm chartering a chopper for us and a jet for the others."

It seemed barely minutes later that they were buckled into a Eurocopter AS355 twin-turbine helicopter, soaring due south across the Mediterranean, the newly forged key still warm in Becca's go-bag. The confirmation came soon from Sara that their jet from Turkey would arrive in Malta within an hour of the slower helicopter.

Roughly one and a half hours later, the helicopter began to descend, and Wade caught sight of the island of Malta, a dark shape in the darkness of the sea, but sprinkled from end to end with tiny flickering lights.

"It looks pretty peaceful," said Lily.

"Now it does," said Julian. "Pilot, please land just south of Rabat, away from the center of the city. There's open space there."

"I suspect to do so finely," the pilot replied, in a reasonable attempt at English, then followed it up with "yet." He swooped the chopper over the eastern side of the island. "I respect the nightlies, fellows," he said, "but I not can land without personal lightings, not this blackness of. If you have enemies, they will spit us."

"Spot us," said Julian. "And that's fine. Nothing to do about that."

"Okay, everything, nope."

Wade nodded. "We'll get to Rabat and wait for the

others. They should be here in"—he checked the phone Julian had given him in France—"about an hour. Until then, we lay low."

The pilot finally chose a dark and more or less flat area called Ghar Burk, a collection of farmers' fields a little south of the city.

Once on the ground, they hurried into Rabat from the west and quickly established a beachhead in an all-hours music club.

Because Becca had the *ocularia*, but Lily and Darrell had the second and third keys, she had to wait to decipher the next part of the diary until she had the second key in front of her and could examine it for the lens combination.

Waiting was hard.

The lights in the club were low, and Wade felt exhausted. Candle flames moving slowly inside hurricane glasses on the tabletops didn't help, either. Faces wavered in and out of the light, faces in half shadow, ghostly faces, though none of them, Wade suspected, would ever imagine what might be coming. He couldn't keep his thoughts from straying to the final flood. The deluge. It was too frightening to think about, but he couldn't think of anything else. They were all tired. The trip from Budapest to Clos Lucé to Rome to Malta had worn them out. No matter how great Sara was, or Julian, not having his father with them made everything worse.

But the big work, the real work, was yet to come.

If he could, he'd go out there, find the relic, and get off the island. The darkness unnerved him, like a storm was rolling slowly toward them, but they had to stay to meet it. Besides, as Silva had said, a battle waged too soon was a battle lost. So they waited, as the music—coming softly out of speakers on a small bare stage—flowed among the tables and into the black night and Becca tried out one combination after another of the silver lenses, hoping to hit on one to read the silver page's final clues, but not finding it.

"I hate not knowing," she said, blinking six eyes at him through the lenses' latest configuration. "I might just stumble on it. If I keep at it. But I have to keep at it."

If I keep at it.

Maybe it was the darkness, the candles, the odd quiet, the danger, the flood, but Wade's heart tingled then, as if dozens of tiny bells were strung along each of his ribs and Becca had run her fingertip lightly across them, setting them swinging. He felt dizzyingly lightweight, maybe from the helicopter's quick descent, maybe from the exhaustion, maybe from neither of those things.

Darrell would punch his arm playfully if he knew any of that, but let him punch. Becca rubbed her temples and rolled up her sleeves in the heat. He glimpsed the scar from the arrow wound Galina had given her in Guam. He remembered her telling him that she'd taken her last antibiotic in Paris. Even in the dim light he could see the wound was still pink.

If I keep at it.

He now remembered waiting in the desert under Bingo's plane, and that moment when they'd found Vela together in the cave on Guam, and that earlier night on their first quest, when they'd all slept under the stars in Rome.

If I keep at it.

After everything that Becca had been through, the poisoned wound, its scar on her arm, her enduring the blast by Kronos, her blackouts in London, the frightening chase in Casablanca, the shootouts in Monte Carlo and Budapest, to still *keep at it* was beyond cool.

It was heroic. It was strong. It touched him.

And that word *touched*, as it formed in his mind, set the bells chiming again and his chest ringing.

"Answer it."

Wade focused his eyes. Becca was looking at him. "Sorry, what?"

"Someone's texting you."

He blinked, swiped open his phone, read the brief message. "Darrell, Lily, and Sara will be here in ten minutes."

It was the slowest ten minutes of Becca's life. But they allowed her to imagine once more the incredible meeting of three minds. Barbarossa, Nicolaus Copernicus, Leonardo da Vinci. And she and the others were following—*had* followed, for the last week—their footsteps across Europe and Africa all the way to the tiny island of Malta. Being away from her family was tough, often, but this? Despite all her self-doubts and worries and awkwardness, this was what she was about. This was her.

When the crew from Kizil Kule finally entered the club, hurrying through the dark room to their table, there were only a couple of hugs and welcomes before they got to business. No fuss. They were Guardians.

Given what they were facing, it struck Becca that their greetings might just as well be the good-byes of people going into battle. Both Lily and Sara seemed closer to the edge since Budapest. *I'll step up, then. As much as I can.*

"Here." Wade set the newly forged fourth key on the table.

Sara shook herself out of her thoughts. "It's just like them," she said quietly. "Wow. It could have been made by Leonardo himself. The gears and the wires. It looks motorized. It's beautiful."

"Adriana's really good," said Julian. "And fast."

"What about the third key?" said Becca.

As Darrell placed the Budapest key on the table, Lily set down the one from the Kizil Kule tower in Turkey. Becca moved it behind two candles on the table in front of her and slid the mirror glasses on. "Someone scraped this."

"I had to," said Darrell. "In case Ebner and his goons found it. What I scraped off were a couple of Maltese words—"

"Becca, they were 'lahar gar-gar'!" said Lily. "And they mean 'the final flood'! Can you believe it?"

It shook her. "The final flood," Becca repeated. "Holy cow, it all connects. All the way back to the library in Tampa. The quest for Triangulum started there."

"And we hope it ends here," said Sara. "Becca, can you read the code on the key?"

Becca set the *ocularia* back to their previous setting and studied the key. There were tiny numbers on it, this time on the rim of the bow. "Got it. Three-six-five." She clicked the lenses into the proper combination. Tilting the diary into the light, and with the *ocularia* focused directly on the page, she read the last clue. As before, it was an infuriating word riddle, but this time it was written in English.

She read it out.

No rats will see the star feast on bones

"It's not Nicolaus's handwriting," Becca said. "This is from Leonardo."

"I didn't know he knew English," said Sara.

"Maybe he didn't," said Darrell, pushing his chair back from the table. "It doesn't make much sense. This leaves me out."

"Okay," said Becca, "but Leonardo knew about Malta from the beginning, and this is based on his being here. Even if he didn't know where Copernicus and Heyredden later hid the keys, he knew where the silver arm was buried."

Wade moved close over Becca's notebook and stared at the words. "At least the riddle is short. I mean, it's clever, but maybe not insoluble. It doesn't rely on strange wording so much. It's perfectly understandable from that standpoint."

"You're not," said Darrell.

"And it's creepy," Lily said softly.

"It might help to say it in different words," Sara said. "No rats will see the star eating the bones. Anything?"

"Still creepy," said Lily.

"Granted," said Sara. "But *rats* and *star* have the same letters. They're mirror versions of each other. Leonardo was all about mirrors and riddles and backward writing, so what if we reverse those two words. Does it read any differently?" Her phone rang, and she stood to answer it. "Hello?" Listening, she walked away.

"Mom's right," said Darrell. "What if it's actually, 'No star will see the rats feast on bones'?"

"Slightly less creepy," said Lily, "and maybe this is the real riddle. It's like, where do rats feast on bones? Well, a cemetery, right? So we could be looking for a cemetery."

"But if no star will see them do that . . . ," said Wade, trying to be involved, but distracted by Sara's call. *Could it be Dad? Or Paul Ferrere? Sara is listening, not speaking.* "Then maybe it's . . . sorry. I lost my thought."

"Inside a church maybe," said Julian. "Tombs in a church."

"They don't normally have rats inside churches," said Darrell. "Crypts, like in London?"

"Or catacombs?" said Becca.

"Catacombs. I like it," said Wade. His stepmother was looking at her phone now, enlarging an image, maybe. He wanted to go over, but didn't. He felt himself letting the others figure this out. *Is it about Dad?*

"I'm looking up catacombs," said Lily, firing up her tablet for the first time in quite a while. It didn't take her long to find references to a famous series of burial tunnels on Malta called Saint Paul's Catacombs. "Here's a map of the graveyard tunnels.

"It's kind of a maze," Darrell groaned over Lily's shoulder. "And it could go for miles. How are we going to find a tiny relic in all that?"

Becca shot a look at Lily. "Are you thinking what I'm thinking?"

Lily narrowed her eyes. "I'm not thinking anything, so no."

"The grid," said Becca. "The grid we found

all the way back in Nice. Remember?" She turned the pages gently until she located the original clue they'd found all those days ago.

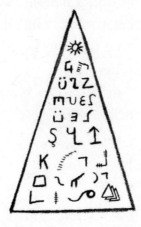

"Wade, you remember what you said?" said Becca. "That maybe these aren't letters, at least not all of them? Well, what if they're actually directions?"

"Directions," said Lily. "Like directions to the maze inside the catacombs?"

"Yes," said Becca. "Look, if you take out the letters spelling *gümüş kol*, we're left with angles and lines. Maybe they lead to the center of the maze."

Wade stood up. Sara was sitting at another table now, still just listening. Julian was on his feet, too.

"I don't know," said Lily.

"Work with me here," said Becca. She spun around Lily's tablet and set the diary next to it. "Look at the first character after the *g* in *gümüş kol* and at the map of the tunnels."

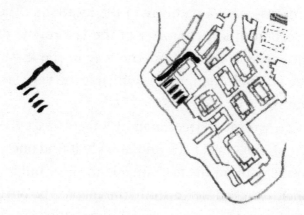

Then she traced her finger over the catacombs map on the screen. "If you look at the extreme left-hand part of the map—*sol*, right?—you can see that the shape of the tunnels is the same shape as the first character on the grid. If you superimpose the shape of the character on the map, it takes you right inside."

"Then what?" said Julian. "The next character gives you the next direction?"

"It could work that way," Darrell said. "I like that. Disguising directions as letters. Typical Leonardo."

The more they studied the pictogram, the more it

seemed that if the end of each character was joined to the beginning of the following character, they actually would describe a route through the catacombs.

"It's brilliant," said Julian. "Leonardo has given the Guardians—us—a pathway to the location of the relic. The second-to-last character of the last row is the end of the maze. It could show the way to the final room, where we find Triangulum, which is the very last symbol on the grid."

"Can we get a street map of Rabat?" asked Darrell. Lily took the tablet back and quickly found one.

Wade, still on his feet, unable to sit or interrupt his mother, watched Becca study the map. "The only problem," she said finally, "is that the entrance that lines up with the grid isn't one of the public entrances. Either that or I'm not reading it right."

"You're reading it right," Wade found himself saying. He shifted the tablet closer and on the street map ran his finger along an arc in the direction of the street. "A neighborhood was built over the place where they entered the catacombs five hundred years ago."

Sara came back to the table and sat. "That was Paul Ferrere. No news. He still can't get in, but he sent a grainy photo. But it may not be your father or Terence or anyone we know. Sorry, boys." She shared the picture with Wade and Julian; it looked like nothing to Wade: shadows, two figures. "Boys, I'm sorry. Paul has two teams scanning the area. Apparently nothing *looks* wrong."

"Except that it is wrong," said Darrell. "Dad's unreachable, and a flood is coming."

"Then let's do what Copernicus told us to do," said Sara. "Find the relic and keep it away from Galina."

Julian nodded, his face hard, trying not to express his worry. "We think we may know where to start looking." He showed Sara the map on the tablet. "The catacombs under the streets."

As Wade listened he thought about his father. What *did* the photo show? Why send it at all? Was there seriously nothing more anyone could say?

"The most obvious entrance to the maze of tunnels," Lily said, enlarging the street map, "is on the east side of Katakombi Street, just north of where it splits like a wishbone."

"I'm going to go out and find some tools. A sledgehammer, maybe. Some flashlights," said Julian. "I'll meet you there. No time to lose. Let's move."

CHAPTER SIXTY

The streets of Rabat were darker than dark, but because there was almost no light in the streets now, the stars were brilliantly visible overhead. Very much as they might have been five hundred years ago.

Becca glanced back at Wade moving behind her. "You okay?"

Shrugging, he double-stepped up to her. "No, but this is all we can do now."

Minutes later, Lily stopped, consulted the map, turned completely around twice, and raised her finger and pointed. "That building. I'm pretty sure. The passages to Triangulum are under it."

Not more than a minute after that, Julian arrived

with a sledgehammer, a walkie-talkie, a large flash-light, and a handful of mini flashlights, which he passed around to each of them. "These things weren't exactly lying around, but I left enough euros that the owner could buy a dozen hammers."

"A whole set of them?" said Darrell.

"In different colors," Julian added. "I thought about digging up a pistol or two, but that's partly what got me thrown out of Morocco."

"No guns is just fine," said Sara.

Luckily, the entrance to the catacombs appeared to be not under a house, but under a shop, which at that time of night was closed and empty. Julian jokingly raised the sledgehammer to the back door, but Sara and Darrell quickly chiseled the door open a crack without destroying the lock.

Darrell squeezed ahead, and they followed him inside. Becca and Sara pushed through three differ-ent rooms of shelving—it was something like a general store—before they found a door to the cellar. That was unlocked. Taking a hint from Julian, Sara left a pile of euros on the counter with a note apologizing for any damage they might cause. They climbed down the stairs. Julian switched on the large flashlight. After all the darkness, the blast of white was intense.

When her eyes had adjusted to the change, Becca saw that the cellar was hewed from rock, unfinished, no more than a storage area. Crates, cartons of stock, sacks, and cans were stacked along the walls on the floor or on metal shelving.

"It reminds me of the warehouse in the medina in Casablanca," said Darrell. "Which, like everything else lately, seems from another lifetime."

Sara aimed her light around the room. The floor was uneven, slanting down away from the stairs. "Look for a blocked-up—"

"There. To your left. *Sol*," said Lily.

The wall included a patch bricked up with stones, but the stones were different from the others in the wall, and the patch was roughly door-shaped.

"That's the west wall," said Becca. "It works with the map."

"They walled off the entrance," Wade said. "I bet some people don't even know they're living with catacombs underneath them."

Darrell helped Becca and Lily clear the area, moving the crates away and setting up the light to shine directly on the wall. Julian took up the hammer and swung it underhand at the patched wall. Stone dust flew back at them, but little else. He overhanded the hammer five or six times before Wade took over. With just a few discrete blows, the stones began to collapse inward, tumbling into the darkness. A breath of dry air fluttered through the opening. Wade shone his flashlight into the hole.

"A passage. I see it. It goes straight, then turns."

A few more blows of the hammer, and the opening was wide enough for them to crawl through. There came a sound of vehicles roaring along the roads above them. They shot looks at one another.

"Galina?" said Becca. "Already?"

"Let's assume it is," Sara said. "We need a first line of defense. Julian, sorry to ask you to do this, but would you stay up here?"

He looked back at the stairs leading up. "Are you sure? You don't know what's down there."

"It'll be more dangerous up here," said Lily.

Julian cracked a grin. "I don't mind that. Here." He handed one of the walkie-talkie units to Sara and the hammer to Darrell. "Galina *will* find us. She finds everything. You hurry. I'll hold the fort."

Nodding somberly, Sara took the lead, aiming the light ahead. Becca eased behind her, consulting the Leonardo grid under her own flashlight. "Straight through," she said. "Then right, another right. Straight ahead. Now left."

They burrowed from one narrow passage to another. In each one, their lights made wavy shadows on the walls. At first, they passed through simple tunnels, but soon the path led downward and began to take on a strange quality of . . . habitation, Becca thought. As if someone was down there, alive and watching them. She remembered the Mother in Tampa, and Leonardo's description.

Twelve women in death-black robes edged with silver, hooded to hide their faces from the light.

Soon they came upon rough-hewn cutouts or niches in the walls. Some of them were empty; others held wooden or ceramic boxes; in still others were piles of loose bones. And yet, nothing about the place was frightening or scary to her. It was more like walking through a church, which they had done so many times since the relic hunt began.

No, Becca thought, the fear would come when the Order discovered them.

"If the silver arm of Barbarossa One is actually buried in these catacombs," Darrell whispered, "it's kind of incredible, isn't it? In the middle of Malta. The Ottomans never conquered it. But buried here is the mechanical hand of an Ottoman pirate."

"These catacombs were known for that," Sara said. "Maybe they never expected Ottomans to be buried here, but I read that Romans and Christians and Jews are all resting in these passages. It's unique about this place. And fitting, don't you think?"

"This whole search has been about that," said Lily. "Different people from different countries than the ones we know."

Borrowing the system of angles penned onto the grid, Wade now threaded under the low ceilings, right, left, straight, and so on, traveling another fifteen or twenty feet below the surface from where they began. Then Wade stopped. He shone his light left, then right.

"Problem?" whispered Sara.

"Yeah, I should lead," said Darrell. "Or Lily should."

"The last squiggly isn't possible," Wade said. "There's one more direction on the grid, but the path ends here. It shouldn't end. Becca—"

"On the floor, look," she said, sliding up next to him. She directed her light down. "The path goes on, but the opening's been sealed over like the first one."

She and Wade both moved their hands along the wall. "This is rough, like stone," he said, "but it's not stone. It's like mortar or something. Leonardo and the guys must have walled it over. Darrell, it's hammer time."

Darrell shooed everyone behind him, then he swung the hammer underhand at the false wall, as Julian had done upstairs. The blow chipped a section out. Another. Another, and there was a hole.

Becca moved up close to him and held her light to the opening, as air rushed out from the chamber beyond.

"Do you see anything?" Darrell asked, close to her.

She felt herself tremble. "The walls inside. There's something on them."

A harsh crackle on Sara's walkie-talkie shattered the moment. It was Julian, rasping the warning they all dreaded. "Heavy vehicles . . . circling the shop. German voices shouting. They know."

Sara barked back at him. "Julian, get out of there before they arrive. We need a free man on the outside." A responding crackle sounded like "Roger that."

The Teutonic Order, and Galina, were coming.

"Mom," said Darrell, "maybe we should wait, hide, or maybe—"

"It's too late to stop now," Sara said. "They'll find us. *She*'ll find us. Even if we hide the keys, Galina will force her way into the tomb. We can't risk her destroying the relic. We're Guardians. Let's hurry it up."

As quickly as they could, Darrell, then Becca, then the others pushed in the remainder of the false wall and climbed over the debris. When they shone their lights around the room, they were stunned. The room was perfectly round.

In the center of the roundness, like the axle point of a wheel, sat a vast stone table that Becca had read was called an *agape* table. It was the stone circle used for meals and ceremonies by the families of the dead, although it was clear that the stone had been altered. The disc had been divided into four concentric rings, and four notches had been incised into the surface— the holes for the four keys—one notch on each of four rings.

They were not aligned, though Becca didn't doubt that when the keys were inserted, something would happen to align them.

But the stone disc was not the strangest thing in the room.

The walls of the round room contained a vast panoramic drawing from the floor up and all the way across the ceiling. It was a mural of a flood, and it was obviously by Leonardo da Vinci.

Becca trembled. "It's the *Deluge*!" she said barely audibly. "And it's huge. Oh my gosh, do you know what this is? Leonardo's doodles? This is an unknown painting by the greatest artist who ever lived. It could even be the last work he ever created!"

The storm, with its scrolling waves and dizzying chaos, whirled and whorled around and across itself and completely around them, and the largeness of it was terrifying, as if the room itself were flooding right then.

"This is what the Mother was telling us," Lily said to Becca, almost whispering. "She knew this picture. She'd seen it. It's what Copernicus told Leo was going to happen—*is* going to happen—if Galina gets the relics. He's telling us that the relics are the only thing protecting the world from this . . . catastrophe."

If the room went suddenly and deeply silent, it also seemed to Becca to grow in sound. It was as though the walls exuded a kind of terrible song, like the atoms of stone joined together in a choir of stony voices, overlapping one another, droning and moving, breathing in and out, a jarring discord that emerged from the silence of the underground and went back into it, only to roll out and sweep over them in heavier, angrier waves. She shivered and shuddered and could barely stand.

"Quickly, the keys," said Sara.

Lily, Darrell, Becca, and Wade each brought out a key. One by one, they moved into place to insert them.

"On my word, enter them in the locks and turn them," said Sara.

But Sara never gave the word. The hush in the room was broken by the sudden thunder of stomping boots. It got louder, louder, until two dozen armed mercenaries poured into the round room, filling it. Their automatic weapons were out and aimed. One man brought a huge lamp. It made the room glow with silver light.

No one in the chamber moved for one minute, two minutes; then Becca heard a single set of footsteps in the final passage outside the room.

CHAPTER SIXTY-ONE

Galina Krause appeared like something from beyond the grave.

Wade almost ached for her, evil or not. The way she looked struck him. She was deeply ill, her face a thing of shadows, her eyes, one blue, one silver-gray, flashing in the darkness, but her skin so sunken as to seem transparent, a thinness stretched over bone.

A death mask.

Whatever Galina was suffering from, it didn't stop her from menacing them. Her gun was drawn, as usual, as she walked slowly around the vast stone circle. In the white of her face, her eyes burned darkly with—what? Rage, need, fever? Maybe all three.

"The clues we must work through to find these relics, no? The technology, the guesswork, the gossamer connections. It's enough to drive one . . . to give up. Finally, it was this." She removed from the pocket of her leather jacket the glittering assembly of diamonds and silver they knew was the Serpens relic. "When all the keys were found, it was Serpens who directed me here. And so we have done it, haven't we, Kaplans? Together we have achieved what no one else could. Enemies, joined in a common goal. My congratulations. And look, all of you are gathered together in a single place. How touching. Ebner, take the relic keys from them."

Ebner von Braun, who before this had not been visible, stepped out from behind his mistress and scuttled across the room. He had three nasty scratch marks on his forehead as if he'd been mauled by a cat. He took the three ancient keys and the newly made one.

"Quite nice," he murmured over the last one. "Clever, you figuring out that the final key needed to be created. Saving us the trouble."

Wade scanned the perimeter of the room. His brain ticked. "What are you doing in the water off Cyprus?" he asked.

Galina shot him a look, but held her gun steady as she moved around them. "All you need to do is pray."

He wanted to do something, knew he had to, but there were at least three guns trained on him and the same or more on each of the others. He felt the search collapsing around them, as if the flood had already started.

Ebner inserted the first key in its place in the circle. *Click.*

"You're building a nuclear arsenal," said Sara. "Why?"

Wade said it under his breath. "The deluge. We know. Copernicus knows."

"Knows? Present tense?" Galina stepped up to Wade, drawing in a long breath. "Did the girl tell you? Becca?" Galina smelled sweet, like flowers that had been freshly cut. Flowers and something else.

Ebner pressed the second key into its place. *Click.*

Darrell shifted his feet to test if the guards reacted. They did, pushing him back. He smirked. "You've collected nuclear devices in the sunken tanker, and you want to use them as leverage."

"Or revenge," said Lily.

"We sent the pictures to people," Wade lied, wishing he'd thought of it. "Lots of people. They identified the devices. They know what you've got there."'

"You know nothing," spat Ebner. "You are bluffing to save yourselves."

Sara stared at Galina. "No, I think we have it just right. You're doing all this to get something. Using those devices would destroy the Mediterranean. Even you couldn't weather that disaster. No, you want something. And you want it in a hurry. That's been obvious from the moment you emerged after two months. Two months of what? You're sick. That's easy to see—"

In two strides Galina was in front of Sara and slapped her face. "You know nothing at all!"

Cursing, Darrell pushed away from one guard, but the two held him back.

"All hail the ineffectual son!" Ebner sneered. *Click.* The third key went in.

"It's your deadline," said Becca. "You have a deadline, and you need something before that happens—"

"Silence!" Galina said as Ebner dropped the final key into its slot on the outermost circle with a resounding click. "Turn them! Turn the keys!"

Taking two himself, and calling over a soldier to take the other two, Ebner turned the keys counterclockwise three complete turns, until they stopped.

All at once, the rumble of stone grinding against stone filled the room. It thundered beneath their feet and over their heads. The four rings of the great disc began to turn. They revolved independently of one another, each in the opposite direction from those next to it.

The inmost circle began to rise up out of the disc to a height of about three feet on a thick post of coiled silver, like a screw reversing itself. It stopped rising but continued to rotate, while a brilliant silver object, an armored arm, rose up out of its center.

Galina's eyes were riveted on it.

It was the arm of Barbarossa One, the *gümüş kol*, a strange and grisly and exquisitely armored device with blades running down the outside seam, and articulated fingers, each coiled tightly as if holding a sword.

Wade saw the cables about which Becca had read to them from the diary. They connected the wheels with the base of the pedestal and down into the bedrock below. If someone *had* attempted to break his or her way into the hidden vault for the silver arm, the cables would have snapped and uncoiled, releasing the ceiling above and crushing not only the hand, but the room and everyone in it.

One by one, the outer rings stopped moving, from the largest ring to the smallest, their stepped levels creating a staircase to the central stone.

When the central disc stopped, the silver arm was fully visible, waiting to be freed from its stone pedestal.

"Ebner, retrieve the arm."

Obedient to his mistress, the scrawny physicist stepped up onto the outer ring. The moment he did, there came another sound: stone sliding along the ground around the perimeter of the room. Shapes moved out of the deep shadows, as dark as the shadows themselves.

"The Mothers!" Becca cried. "The Mothers have come to protect the relic!"

Galina's agents swung around, startled to see tall figures, larger than life almost, cloaked in robes of black and silver, wielding the same curved blades the diary had described. In a split second, everything that had happened over the last week compressed to this single moment.

"*Gharghar!*" the Mothers cried in unison. The flash of their blades was blindingly swift.

"Everyone down!" Sara hissed, pulling Lily to the floor with her.

Galina's men shot wildly. The lamp exploded, plunging the room into darkness. "Mom?" Darrell cried out. Had anyone been hit? Wade couldn't tell. One, two automatic rifles clattered to the floor. Men thumped to the ground, shouting out across the room. The Mothers' blades clashed and clanked. You could hear their swords slide into flesh. The terrible sound of fabric ripping, the sudden moan, the thudding as someone collapsed on the floor.

Where was Galina? The silver arm? He couldn't see.

Wade scrambled across the floor for Becca, something guiding his way in the dark. He crawled with her back to the others, hiding under the lowest disc. Darrell and Lily lay on their stomachs. Sara, too. A new manic burst of gunfire began. He tried to shield Becca lower, when she turned. Her arm was wet, warm. Blood?

"Becca—"

But she was moving away from him. He felt her slide away across the stone rings toward the center. Bullets rang out, blasting silvery stone from the surrounding walls. "Becca!"

At the height of the chaos, Darrell somehow moved with his mother out of the chamber and back into the passages, Lily trailing behind. Wade saw that Sara had one of the knights' automatic weapons. Then a body crashed into Wade, knocking his head to the floor. Silver light flashed behind his eyelids. He rolled over. It was Becca. The silver arm was in her hands. "We can leave now—"

Everything buzzed in his head. His body went electric. All at once, Sara yelled, "Galina!" And opened fire.

He kept in a low crouch with Becca beside him, barely able to move, but the two of them found a way to push forward under Sara's cover. Instantly, the Mothers formed a wall of slashing swords behind them. He didn't know how it was possible, but he and Becca were suddenly in the passage, with Darrell and Lily urging them on. Dust filled his eyes, his mouth. Now they were stumbling in the upper tunnels. Now they were crawling into the cellar of the shop, hands and arms dragging them out into the smoky darkness. They were outside. Becca was clutching the silver arm of Barbarossa, the Ottoman pirate.

Seconds later they were crammed in a stolen Jeep, Julian at the wheel. He tore off like a madman toward the helicopter, while out the back Sara fired round after round at the knights pouring up from the ground.

They had the relic.

CHAPTER SIXTY-TWO

Nice, France
June 10
9:43 a.m.

Morning. Blue, white, warm. Darrell leaned against the railing on the balcony of the Ackroyds' apartment. Distant traffic noise and the warble of voices in different languages mingled with the aroma of baked goods and coffee wafting up from the Place du Palais.

He breathed it all in. Things were good.

Two hours before, his mother and Julian had nearly simultaneously received the same photo of Terence and Roald, smiling broadly together, taken at Gran Sasso that morning. Both accompanying messages had similar though not identical texts, but with the same basic message.

So sorry! No phone service, only text. All's well. Meeting over. Good work done. Here's us, leaving this morning. Meet us, Alitalia Flight 348, Nice, Tuesday, arr. 10:55 a.m.!

Incredulous but overjoyed, everyone cheered and jumped around the apartment, but that didn't stop Sara from jetting off a sharp reply about how terrified they had all been. Roald's reply to that came swiftly.

Totally my fault. Explain all soon! Love you all!

At first, Darrell thought he'd squash himself into the car with everyone else—he just wanted to be there to join in the hoopla—when a second message came from Terence to Julian, sent just before their flight.

Keep relic in home safe when you come. Do not bring with you.

Well, yeah. It was so obvious. Though this text was different enough in tone, more serious than the first one, to cause some concern. Madame Cousteau would of course remain to guard the apartment, and Silva was also coming to stay in the apartment on the floor below.

Still, something told Darrell that the silver arm should not be alone, so he decided to stay at the apartment as a precaution. When he asked who was going, they all said they were, except Lily, which was good, except that the way she said it was weird.

"The Citroën's too small for all of us," she said. "It'll get too huggy in there."

He didn't know if this was Lily's way of saying that the five seconds they'd been mashed up in that niche in the tower in Turkey was ten seconds too long, or if she was specifically staying behind to be with him.

His brain heated up at the thought, so he stopped using it. He simply looked down from the balcony at the colorful bustling square and counted it all good. After all, they'd just located a third relic, and that was beyond awesome.

Score another one for the Guardians.

"Dad's friends in Nice have assured me that the Order has no current footprint in the city," Julian said from the dining room, where the remains of breakfast were spread on the table. "Still, Silva will be moving into a flat on the floor below with a half dozen of his best men. Just until we move the relic."

That was a comfort to everyone. Since they'd brought Triangulum back to Nice, Julian and Wade had worked together and found a way to remove the relic—a dazzlingly bright silver triangle with razor-sharp edges as cold as ice—from the silver arm. Julian had then placed the relic along with the arm in his father's safe in the computer room.

As she gathered her things for the trip to the airport, Darrell's mother said, "If I haven't said it before, thank you for everything, Julian. We couldn't have done any of this without you. Really, you're a prince and a soldier."

"Oh, gosh," he said, popping a fresh fig in his mouth from the fruit bowl. "There are miles to go before this is over. The Morgan in New York has fended off one robbery attempt, but it won't be the last. Galina will keep trying. And then"—Julian cleared his throat—"there are the international papers."

"What?" said Lily, toying with a crust of toast. "Not more tragedies?"

"That's just it," he said. He slid several English editions across the table. "There's nothing. In fact, none of the press—newspapers, television, internet—says a single word about the tanker off Cyprus. The same thing with Malta. What happened there has been completely ignored."

Darrell searched the papers quickly. They all did. There wasn't a single word about any of it.

"Makes me wonder what else the world doesn't know about," said Becca.

"My calls to Dad's pals in British intelligence tell me that London has given a wink to the whole thing, at least publicly," Julian added. "It'll come out soon enough, I think, but right now it's still developing and too important to risk causing panic."

"Too important that the Teutonic Order has become a nuclear nation?" said Becca.

"So we double down," said Wade. "We don't trust anyone. The Order has friends in high places? Well, we have friends all over the world."

That was true enough, but Darrell was stuck on the words *nuclear nation*.

The Order had real power now, a capability beyond imagining. They were a force for evil, and only da Vinci's apocalyptic visions could do justice to the horror that could happen—and maybe *would* happen soon.

The deluge. The horrors. The end of days.

All that power, along with the world's silence, was a deadly combination that he—and Wade, Lily, Becca, and their parents and friends—had to fight.

But not alone. After the last week there were more Guardians than ever.

Julian grabbed his car keys. "The final bit of bad news is from China."

"Not the Scorpion relic?" asked Lily.

Julian nodded. "Our people at the Ackroyd Foundation in Hong Kong report that your old friend Feng Yi was found with two bullet holes in him. Galina Krause now has the Scorpion relic, the real one."

Darrell watched his mother stop and take a breath. "Bad news, yes, but not surprising." He noticed that she was dressed, for the first time in days, not in body armor or scuba gear or desert camouflage, but in a sundress and flip-flops. "Not surprising at all."

Darrell knew that it was a matter of time before all the relics were found, and probability suggested that Galina would find her share of them. But it was disappointing. They were ahead, but only barely. Three relics to two.

Vela was safe in New York. Crux was secured in the basement vaults of the British Museum. And now Triangulum, disengaged from its silver arm, was waiting to be transported to the Vatican Museum, where the Ackroyds had some close friends, including, Julian hinted, the top man there. Before long, Triangulum would help them discover where to look for the *next* relic.

"The silver triangle will give up its clue," Lily said softly but firmly as she stood next to Darrell at the railing. "There will be a way forward."

"The sixth relic, whatever it is, will be ours," he said. "We'll get it. It's going to be ours." He knew every move their little family made, toward a relic, away from a relic, every step they took, no matter where it was, changed them, aged them, made them less like kids and a lot more like warriors, hunters, soldiers. What he didn't know was what they would all become by the time they finished the quest for the relics. What was the endgame of the Frombork Protocol?

Wade stood up. "Just about time to go to the airport," he said.

"See you two soon," Sara said. She smiled at Lily and gave Darrell a peck on his cheek, and that was it. The whole group of them left together in a bunch, leaving Lily and Darrell alone with Madame Cousteau. The silent housekeeper eyed the two of them on the balcony, and stood at grim attention by the door.

It was 10:14. The sun warmed the cast-iron balcony railing. Darrell leaned against it and watched Lily close her eyes and shiver.

* * *

Three hundred or so miles southeast of Nice, Roald Kaplan took a short step away from the narrow cot in his cell and nearly collapsed. His head felt heavy, sloshing with hot water; his balance was way off; his stomach rolled and rolled; he was seasick. Impossible, since he was over five thousand feet beneath a mountain in the middle of Italy, surrounded by bedrock.

It's in my blood, he thought. *Something they gave me.*

The cell—an office, really—was small but not uncomfortable. Both hands pressed against the cinderblock wall to steady himself, he blinked hard, to keep himself focused, to keep himself from being sick. What had happened, after all? They'd taken his phone, Terence's, too. Where was Terence? Where had they taken him? What was Galina planning? The flood? Petrescu was enigmatic, confused, but the crazed woman was clearly behind everything that had happened to Roald and the others imprisoned beneath that mountain for the last . . . how many days? Three? Five? What *was* the flood, anyway? Petrescu had ranted about a flood, but soon enough the director had been taken away, too.

"I called Sara," he said. "I remember that." He took another step toward the door. It clanged open before he got there. A stony face appeared. A soldier, armed with an automatic weapon. Two others stood behind him.

"Come," the man said. English was not his first language. "Is time."

Twenty meters away, Galina Krause walked arm in arm with the blank-faced Marin Petrescu, past one security checkpoint after another.

"The lockdown is complete," she said.

"The world will know of this!" he said.

"But not in time to do anything about it," she said. "The laboratory is closed. A minor incident involving the accidental escape of liquid argon. Internal damages. Better for everyone that the laboratory is temporarily off-limits."

"They will know! They will come!"

She paused in one of the long hallways. "My dear Petrescu, the world has other problems to deal with. Terrorism. Russia. Climate change—"

"This is criminal!" he said, his face a ball of red skin. "This is a crime!"

"I prefer to think of it as science," she said, resuming the march to the laboratory. "All the physicists you summoned have arrived. We have food and supplies for four months. Those men and women will be my team."

Another set of doors whisked aside. She walked him through.

He was silent.

"Come now, Doctor. I am of the belief that when one is ill-treated, the only proper response is revenge. This is my revenge, Dr. Petrescu, my vendetta against an ignorant world. And yet you see, by allowing me access to CERN's laboratories, you have saved the world."

"You will be caught." More subdued this time. The man was beginning to understand the futility.

"No, Dr. Petrescu. This facility is mine."

Galina held her phone up to his face. Swiping the screen, she produced the image of a tanker full of nuclear devices—from raw materials to detonators to warheads to miniature reactors.

"These devices are separately armed and connected in tandem. They can be detonated collectively within sixty seconds of my giving the command," Galina said. "I assure you, I do not want this to happen, but your failure to assist me may force my hand. Will you be the one responsible for such destruction?"

"But why the reactors? Why?"

"You'll discover that very soon."

"The world will rebel against your tyranny, your madness!"

"You forget, Dr. Petrescu, that the world loves not knowing. People want to be ignorant. It's simply too much trouble to know the truth. I have ordered the deaths of hundreds of men and women these last months, but no one has bothered to connect the dots. These deaths don't affect them. People only want to feel safe. And by giving me the key to your laboratory, Doctor, you have made them safe. After you."

Roald stumbled down the same hallways he had days ago, his brain clearing with each step. His guards forced him down a set of concrete stairs to another hall. At the end of it they unlocked an oversize set of steel doors, pushed him through, then locked the doors behind them. He found himself inside the giant laboratory Dr. Petrescu had shown him when he and Terence had first arrived.

Where is Terence? Is he here?

He was not. But the lab was filled with people he knew or recognized: a nuclear-energy specialist from Taiwan; the foremost Brazilian researcher in subatomic particles. There were Monique Sené of GSIEN in France,

Sir Reginald Benton of the University of London, Janet Conrad of MIT. He saw representatives from the Fermi labs in Chicago and Germany, the Los Alamos Neutron Science Center, Brookhaven, and the nuclear-physics group from the University of Kyoto. They stared at him, stunned, silent. They were surrounded by perhaps fifty armed paramilitary troops. Maybe more.

Knights of the Teutonic Order.

On the wall of the laboratory was a large digital clock that hadn't been there before. It must have just been installed. Oddly, the clock ticked backward—from one hundred four days, twenty-two hours, three minutes, seven seconds.

Six seconds.

Five.

Among the scientists was a man he didn't recognize. He was bound to a chair in steel cuffs. His face was gashed, sliced, bandaged, his arms and legs bloodied, blood soaking through his tattered suit. His expression was blank except for the eyes, which showed the fire of pain and rage. Even sitting, it was clear that he was powerfully built, though he needed a hospital badly.

"I'm Roald Kaplan. Who are you? Why are we here?"

"So. Roald Kaplan. We meet at last. My name is Ugo

Drangheta. Why are we here? Me, to be killed. You for some other reason."

"You're not a scientist?"

"No. I was following you. I believed you to be the one who could help me. Then we were attacked."

"We?" Roald looked around the room.

"My lovely Mistral may have been killed by the colonel. I don't know."

The steel doors whooshed open. Galina Krause entered, followed by Dr. Petrescu, who looked haggard and shrunken. They were accompanied by a dozen armed men, who were wheeling in a large platform. The assembled scientists were pushed to the perimeter of the lab, away from the man cuffed to the chair.

"What is all this? What is that junk?" one of Roald's colleagues whispered. "Roald, tell me."

He couldn't speak.

The platform contained a great pile of girders, plates, rods, arc-shaped struts, stacks of levers, loose hinges and joints, gears and pipes, all gleaming with the color of a dark sun. Each item was wrought of the reddest gold he had ever seen.

Roald recognized the fragments from the diary's sketches.

This was the broken skeleton of Copernicus's original

astrolabe. The bits and pieces found at Olsztyn and Kraków and Prague and elsewhere over the last two months.

Galina Krause walked slowly up to it. Her face was drawn, her cheekbones prominent and razor sharp. Her two differently hued eyes burned like torches in the darkness around them. The doors sealed behind her.

"Ladies and gentlemen," she said. "You will use your expertise to assist me in reassembling this device. If you do not . . ."

She produced a handgun, aimed it point-blank at the man called Ugo Drangheta, and pulled the trigger. The scientists screamed. Two fainted dead away. Roald nearly fell, his head pounding with the blast of the gun in that room. He was horrified to see a man become a corpse with less than a second ticking off the clock.

Sliding her pistol inside the flap of her leather jacket, she said, "You see I am serious. Oskar?"

Roald was shocked to see the little bookseller emerge from behind the troops. "People," he began, "you will have access to the Voytsdorf Ledger. This document will be used to aid your assembly of this centuries-old astrolabe."

"And soon," Galina continued, "thanks to the generosity of Dr. Kaplan here, you will be able to consult the private diary of Nicolaus Copernicus himself. As we speak, it is being obtained."

"What?" said Roald. "No. No!"

Galina stepped toward him, smiling coldly. "Oh, yes, Dr. Kaplan. The diary will be here this afternoon. Colonel?"

Choking back anger and confusion, Roald watched a man in a military uniform emerge from behind the ranks of the troops guarding them. As he drew near, Roald felt his stomach convulse. He had seen the man once before, five years ago. He knew the face, although it had changed since then. Turned to stone.

Colonel, she called him?

He hadn't been called *Colonel* five years ago.

Five years ago, his name was Radip Surawaluk.

He was Darrell's father.

At the Nice airport, eight men in black fatigues waited in parking area six. Twelve miles away, another six agents dressed in flowery sport shirts strode across the Place du Palais de Justice toward the Rue de la Préfecture. One of them carried a heavy green duffel bag.

At that moment in London, Ebner von Braun secured the last straps of his bulletproof vest. It pinched. "On my signal," he whispered.

He stared as icily as he could at the twenty-four armed operatives crowding in an abandoned Underground tunnel under Bloomsbury. Ahead of them stood a hatchway leading into a series of passages beneath the British Museum, where the relic named Crux was secured.

His phone buzzed. He opened it. A man in a navy-blue suit had sent him a text. His man inside. At the same moment, several locks on the far side of the hatch clicked in sequence.

Taking a deep breath, his heart palpitating, Ebner whispered, "Now."

The hatchway swung back on its hinges, and the Order poured through.

Back in Nice, Darrell waited on the balcony of the Ackroyd apartment for Becca, Wade, Julian, and Sara to return from the airport with his stepfather and Terence. Lily stood next to him, looking out over the square, her arms folded across her chest. The sun was rising in the sky. It was quiet up there, just the two of them, although Madame Cousteau was still on guard inside.

Darrell decided to say aloud what he'd been thinking for a while.

"Lily, we've escaped death way too often." It was

a dumb way to begin a conversation, but he went on. "Are we blessed? Or just lucky?"

She nodded slowly, didn't answer.

"I mean, I was born blessed," he said comically. "The rest of you guys, I'm not sure of. I'm just saying Galina could have killed us a million times over."

She turned to him. Her eyes were as blue as the Mediterranean. Her hair was going gold in the sunlight. She opened her lips to speak, then didn't.

"But that's not what she's after now," he said. "You see that, right? The Teutonic Order will follow us to the ends of the earth, but not to kill us. That's not the problem. That's not what we have to be afraid of."

She didn't offer anything, but he was on a roll, so he kept going. "We don't have to be afraid of dying, at least not by her hand. It's . . ." He didn't want to say it, but did anyway. "It's everyone else. My mom, my stepdad, Terence, Julian. Even Paul Ferrere and Silva and Carlo. All those people. They're expendable. But we're not, the four of us. Don't ask me why, but Galina needs us. She proved that by not killing us, by letting us keep searching for the relics. We're part of her plan, Lily."

He stopped there, then threw on the last little bit that seemed needing to be said. "Maybe one day she'll realize that maybe she doesn't need us. But right now she does. The question is *for what*? And the answer is what really scares me, you know?"

He didn't know the answer, so he backtracked. "Galina will keep us around until the end. It's what she'll do to everyone and everything we love. That's the problem—"

"Darrell, stop." Lily searched his face with her blue eyes, and it seemed like she would say something or cry or laugh, but he didn't know which. "No more."

"No more," he repeated, then turned from her and watched the people crisscrossing the square below. His tongue felt thick. "Look, I know you don't think I'm the sharpest at some stuff, but I know you're not happy about your parents. You're broken up about it, and—"

"Darrell," she said, stopping him again. "I'm not sure I can keep doing this." She touched his arm. "You know, no. That's not right. I *am* sure. I have to go home. My parents want me to come back. Need me to come home. To be part of a . . . it sounds so stupid . . . a new beginning with them." She blubbered that out, crying through the words. "I hate it, but it's probably right. They're right. No more relics. No more of this stuff. No more Galina."

"Are you kidding me? Lily, no."

"I thought I could ignore it, just be with you."

"Me?"

"You guys, all of you. But this will end anyway. The relic hunt will. Maybe if I go back now, my family won't. Won't end, I mean. Maybe we *can* stay together."

"But what are you going to do in Austin without all this?" he asked her.

"Not Austin. Seattle. My parents and I are moving."

"Seattle? There are no relics in Seattle!"

"You're not listening to me," she said. "Look, I've thought about it a lot over the last week. A lot. And I can't do this stuff anymore. At least for now. I just have to say good-bye to it. I have to be with my mom and dad. I owe them to try. That's all. That's all."

Darrell felt his insides turn to water and his head go empty.

"Lily, you can't. In the tower . . ." He stopped there. Why did he go there? Nothing *happened* in the tower. They were squished together, and it was nothing. Yeah, it was nothing, but he shouted a curse inside his head and blurted it out. "In the tower, it was—I mean, I really like you."

"Darrell, please—"

His phone buzzed. He ignored it. It buzzed again. He looked into her eyes, then at the screen. It was a text. Not from his mother. It was from Paul Ferrere.

Gran Sasso in lockdown. Roald and Terence inside. Need Silva.

"Wait, what?"

There was a sudden dull snapping sound—once, twice. Darrell's neck froze. A door slammed in the apartment behind him. Bolts slid closed.

"No, no . . ."

"What is it?"

He spun around. The housekeeper stumbled in awkwardly from another room, clutching her hand to her side. There was blood soaking down her blouse.

"*Prenez votre relique!*" she gasped. "*Partez maintenant!*" She thrust a small box at Darrell, then fell to the floor. "*Allez!* Go. Elevator. Go, now!"

More gunshots. Silva shouted from the stairs. A stampede of boots pounded outside the door. The door frame shook; the knob flew across the room and clattered against the wall.

Lily took Darrell by the hand. "Run!"

TO BE CONTINUED in *The Copernicus Legacy: Crown of Fire*.

AUTHOR'S NOTE

From the beginning of this Copernican journey, it's been great fun to mix fact with fiction in a particular way. Of the historical characters in this book, probably the most famous other than Copernicus himself is Leonardo da Vinci. While Copernicus is considered the originator (discounting Greek and Arab star watchers) of the heliocentric theory of our planetary system, published in book form in 1543, students of what are known as da Vinci's "notebooks" have often remarked on the Italian artist's much earlier statement, "The sun does not move." I have explained the anachronism of this remark in two ways: first by imagining a conversation between the two men, and then by adding a simple question mark to the end of Leonardo's statement. You're welcome. It's still Copernicus.

Literature about da Vinci fills many libraries besides my own, but I want to single out a couple of wonderful volumes: *Leonardo da Vinci: Flights of the Mind* by Charles Nicholl and *Leonardo: The Artist and the Man* by Serge Bramly. About the Barbarossa brothers I found no full-length books, though entries in BrillOnline's *Encyclopaedia of Islam, Second Edition*, as well as portions of *Empires of the Sea: The Siege of Malta, the Battle of Lepanto, and the Contest for the Center of the World* by Roger Crowley, were extremely helpful. *An Army at Dawn: The War in North Africa, 1942–1943* by Rick Atkinson and the novels *The English Patient* by Michael Ondaatje and *The Sheltering Sky* by Paul Bowles, as well as the latter's *Points in Time: Tales from Morocco*, aided my North Africa research.

ACKNOWLEDGMENTS

First and foremost, I want to thank Jane Abbott, my elder daughter, for her magnificent rendering of one of da Vinci's Deluge drawings. It appears in chapter 53 of this book. Jane may have a career as a forger ahead of her, which, as her father, I will naturally support. I also wish to thank my younger daughter, Lucy, whose fellowship as an English guide at the Château de Chantilly some years ago inspired her namesake at Clos Lucé in this book.

I've been privileged to communicate with a host of Islamic scholars during the writing of the story. I am grateful first of all to Professor Martin Nguyen in the Department of Religious Studies at Fairfield University for his more-than-kind assistance with the niceties of mosque behavior and Arabic language, translation, and spelling. He gave unstintingly of his time, at a time when I most needed it. I am also indebted to J. L. Berggren, professor emeritus in the Department of Mathematics at Simon Fraser University, for directing me to the *Encyclopaedia of Islam* and for his on-point research suggestions regarding the Tunisian portion of the book. Finally, Nidhal Guessoum, Mohammad Odeh of the International Astronomical Center in Abu Dhabi, Nabil Ben Nessib at King Saud University in Saudi Arabia, and his gracious brother, Riadh Ben Nessib at the Cité des Sciences à Tunis, were instrumental with regard to features of al-Zaytuna mosque in Tunis.

Travel to all the settings in which an international thriller unfolds is daunting and, given one's writing schedule, often quite impossible. So I want to thank Christopher Socci for his colorful personal evocations of Morocco; they allowed me to conjure with more confidence a faraway place in word and mood. Naturally, all the errors and stylistic gaffes here are completely my own.

I want to acknowledge my longtime agent, George Nicholson, who passed away during the final stages of revising this book. For over two decades George was my supporter, my reader, a thinker of great wit and compassion, an elegant gentleman, and a friend who I regret not being able to talk to anymore.

To my wife, Dolores, always my first and closest reader, thank you for putting up with me and with this, my longest book to date. I feel as if we've been around the world, too. To all the hard-working people at Katherine Tegen Books—to Katherine, to my editors Claudia Gabel and Melissa Miller, to Alana Whitman, Lauren Flower, Ro Romanello, and Karen Sherman, thank you for flying with me—to the sun and back—on this Copernican sojourn.

FOLLOW THE ADVENTURES OF

Jack McKinley in the mysterious, action-packed series that takes place throughout the Seven Wonders of the Ancient World.

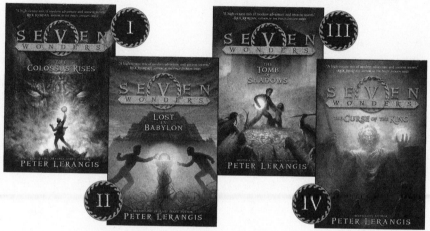

For teaching guides, an interactive map, and videos, visit **www.sevenwondersbooks.com**

DISCOVER THE HISTORY BEHIND THE MYSTERY!

HARPER

An Imprint of HarperCollinsPublishers